"Come, PenDragon." She waved him inside. "Speak your peace, for believe me, I will speak mine."

"In all my days, Sinead, *that* I have never doubted."

"You will not like it."

His hand on the door latch, he arched a brow. "So, we are to do battle, are we?"

A strange excitement suddenly coursed through her blood. "Aye, and you'd best not be wagerin' who will win."

His green eyes sharpened, grew darker. "I have never lost a war, Sinead."

"Then be prepared, PenDragon. You will taste defeat today."

Her challenge laid like a gauntlet, Connal carefully closed the door. From the moment he'd stepped inside, his gaze never left her.

And he'd no desire to cease staring, either.

Because no matter what he must do, needed to do, Sinead O'Donnel of the house of DeClare, Princess of the Nine Gleanns of North Antrim . . . made him remember, with one look, that he was a man.

And witch or nay, she was the most desirable woman in Ireland. . . .

Books by Amy J. Fetzer

Published by Zebra Books

THE IRISH KNIGHT

Amy J. Fetzer

ZEBRA BOOKS
KENSINGTON PUBLISHING CORP.
http://www.kensingtonbooks.com

I type this the day after the terrorist attacks on America in New York, Pennsylvania, and our Nation's capital. So it is, with an aching heart and tremendous sympathy, that I dedicate this work to the memory of the innocent souls lost to us, to the valiant men and woman who perished trying to rescue them, and to the families left behind.

Your country weeps for you.

And to the survivors of New York and D.C. True heroes and heroines . . . you faced unbelievable tragedy, and the world is humbled by your courage.

Chapter One

1193

Connal was tempted to kill the messenger.

Aye, he thought, tear his scrawny neck from his shoulders and kick his skull across the hot sand.

Instead, he tightened his grip on the parchment bearing King Richard's seal and read the declaration again.

Richard's words were precise and final. Return to Ireland and secure the oath of the Irish kings and his earls before Prince John could do more damage. And specifically, unite Richard's strongest allies in Ireland . . . the house of PenDragon and the house of DeClare.

It was enough to make him grind his teeth to powder.

Marry Sinead?

His king could not ask more of him.

His gaze still on the parchment, Connal closed his eyes briefly, tightly, reconciling himself to the task ahead. Duty to the king, he reminded himself. Had he not sworn to Richard that he would do aught to keep him in power? Regardless of how Connal felt about England forcing religion on these people? At that thought, shame swept up to grab him. Connal battered it down.

He'd no time for regrets or conscience. He was honor bound to obey.

He fished in his purse, his gaze still on the parchment. "Aziz," he said to the young Moor who stood to his right. "See this man well tended, with water, food, and a soft bed to spend the evening."

Connal flipped the coins, then spun about, striding down the thinly mapped dirt corridor between a sea of tents. Soldiers and knights stepped back as he passed, peasants scattered, grabbing their children out of his path. He ignored it all and the three men following him as he ducked into his own pavilion. He went immediately to the flagon of wine resting on a small table and drank from the spout, washing away the taste of disappointment thickening his throat.

Three men ducked inside behind him.

"Not pleasant news, Lord PenDragon?" Sir Galeron asked, and Connal recognized the man's goading tone.

Connal cast the knight a thin glance. "I do not recall issuing an invitation." He drank some more.

And only the tall Maniluke, Nahjar, bowed and made to leave.

"I know," Galeron said, waving Nahjar back from the entrance. "Mum says I'm cheeky like that. Nahjar is never ten feet from you, PenDragon, so that means naught. Though I'm at a loss as to Bran's excuse."

"PenDragon's tent is more comfortable." With that

Sir Branor dropped onto the plush divan flocked with pillows and flung his leg over the carved side.

Connal kicked his dangling foot, glaring, and Branor straightened. "You are not fit for proper circles, Sir FitzSimmons."

Bran scoffed. "Are any of us?"

"Speak for yourself," Galeron said, tugging at his surcoat.

Nahjar folded his bare arms over his naked chest, spreading his feet wide. His fierce look dared anyone to deny him access to the pavilion. Connal opened his mouth to order them all out, then snapped it shut. "Bloody hell," he muttered, splashing wine into three goblets, keeping one, then handing the others to the knights, knowing Nahjar never drank. He moved to the basin on a small table, filling the bowl with water, then soaking a cloth. He washed the dirt from his face and throat and when he pushed back his sleeves, he noticed that beneath the eternal sun of this land, his skin had grown as dark as Nahjar's.

I am a far cry from the pale Irish youth they will remember, he thought, memories of what he'd seen and done the past years to others to survive, flooding through his mind like dirty water.

Behind him Branor and Galeron exchanged a concerned glance. Nahjar shook his head, silently telling them not to pursue the matter.

Bran plunged ahead regardless. "Give, old man."

Connal stared into the depths of the basin, his hands braced on the table. "King Leopold has given King Richard over to the Holy Roman Empire till he can raise his ransom."

"Good God, that will cost him," Sir Galeron put in.

Not what his return will cost me, Connal thought.

"Sajin PenDragon," a voice called, and he recognized it as Aziz's. He didn't bother to answer. The lad would find him soon enough, he thought, and took another swallow of wine. "Sajin?" Aziz said from the entrance, out of breath.

"You really must not run in this heat, lad. 'Twill kill you."

"I am accustomed to it, Sajin."

Connal twisted a look over his shoulder at the young man. He'd known Aziz since they'd shared a set of shackles in a Saracen prison three years past. The young man, no more than ten and seven, had grown no taller, with no more meat on his thin bones. But he was loyal, and to Connal that counted for more than strength.

"The messenger is eating in the cook's tent."

Connal nodded, pleased. "I am leaving this place, Aziz; you are released from your service to me."

The young man's disappointment flitted across his features. "I wish to remain with you, Lord PenDragon."

Connal shook his head. "I am returning to Ireland."

"What?" Branor and Galeron said at once.

He looked at the knights and Nahjar. "You three are free to go as you will. Take your treasures and vassals and seek new fortune."

"Not bloody likely," Galeron said.

"Aye," Branor agreed. "Ireland sounds like a nice change."

Nahjar only grunted agreement.

Connal scoffed. "It will be winter by the time we get there, Galeron. Snow. Remember that infernal stuff?" The thought of Ireland, snow and ice and frosty wind, brought little relief from this land's scalding heat.

He dismissed Aziz and the youth sulked out of the tent, his head bowed. Connal couldn't ask him to join him. The dangers were tenfold, and although the voyage would be months long, the lad was not accustomed to the cold of Ireland.

Branor straightened in his seat, leaning forward to brace his arms on his knees. "Why do you not want us to join you?"

"Aye, 'tis rather insulting, PenDragon," Galeron said, and Nahjar sent him a scowl.

"There is little fortune and glory in Ireland."

Nahjar scoffed to himself, eyeing Connal with those dark eyes.

"And you believe 'tis the reason we are your retainers, m'lord? For the glorious riches?" Branor gestured to the lavish pavilion, the bolts of vivid silks shot with gold, the numerous chests of spices and coin, payment for Connal's services to his king and from Saladin himself.

Connal's features sharpened with regret. A skirmish in Cypress had bonded them all forever, and he knew the men felt he'd saved their lives, but in truth, their aid in the battle had saved him. Though Nahjar, on the other hand, had been a Turkish slave from the land near the Black Sea, part of a mercenary order when Connal had come upon him. He was dying then, stabbed and beaten nearly to death. For what, Nahjar would not say. Yet now the mercenary served him. And did it almost too well.

"Nay, I suppose not," Connal finally said. "But know this, once in Ireland, I will not be leaving." Not without the will of King Richard.

Heat-blistered silence passed before Branor asked, "What has Richard asked of you, Connal?"

"I'm to secure oaths of Irish kings and nobles, including his own earls, afore John Lackland can inflict more damage. Simple enough task, aye?" He scoffed into his drink, taking sip before dropping tiredly onto a camel saddle he used for a stool.

"I see the advantage Richard seeks in you," Branor muttered, raking his fingers through his black hair.

" 'Tis your home, PenDragon," Galeron said softly, all teasing gone.

Connal lifted the goblet to the light, turning it at the stem and watching light play magically across the jewels studding the silver. Home? Briefly the word dazzled in his mind. It had been so long since he'd had a true *home.* He'd been no more than a traveling vagabond for years now. "My duty is to Richard first."

" 'Tis another portion of the king's missive you've denied us."

Only Connal's gaze shifted. "I'm to unite the house of PenDragon and DeClare. Permanently."

Galeron whistled. Nahjar looked between them all, a bit confused.

"And to do this you must marry, correct?"

"Apparently."

Nahjar chuckled, and Connal's gaze shot to the former slave.

"Wonderful," Connal groused. " 'Tis *my* troubles that finally bring a smile to your painted face, Nahjar."

Nahjar's lips stretched a bit further, pulling at the thin ribbons of tattoos that arched away from his eyes, nose, and mouth like the feathers of a falcon. "It is chaos, Sajin, only if you choose to see it as such."

Connal did not want to hear the man's philosophies right then, and focused on emptying his goblet.

"Married, eh?" Galeron folded his arms and leaned against the thick center post of the pavilion. "Oh, the ladies will be fainting from the sheer disappointment of it."

Connal snarled in his direction, then set the goblet down with more force than necessary. He stood and called for Aziz. When the boy arrived, he gave him final orders to pack. Connal looked at Branor. "We will hire a ship, or purchase one, if I must. Then find more for the troops." His eyes glittered like bottle glass, and he pinned Branor with a hard stare. "We leave no one behind who does not wish it." He scooped up a leather purse from the chest and tossed it to Galeron, then promptly added two more to the cache. "Supplies, Sir Galeron. Food, water, a few men capable of sailing the damned ships would help, I imagine."

The bit of levity was lost on the men. The knights continued to stare, waiting for Connal to name his betrothed.

He did not. And instead, he stripped off his hauberk and strolled outside in less than perfect garments. His white linen shirt snapped against the hot dry breeze as he adjusted his sword. Branor and Galeron ducked out and stood near, frowning behind his back. Nahjar moved to the right of Connal, where he always positioned himself.

Connal called for their mounts.

"Who is she, Connal?"

"DeClare's eldest."

Galeron grew thoughtful. "Haven't heard about her."

"And you won't. I imagine DeClare has kept her sequestered. My only hope is that the contracts and missives to Raymond and my father have not reached Ireland in time, and she is already married and well-bedded to some chieftain's son."

"Good God, you loathe this woman?"

Connal hesitated, scowling more at himself than the

question. Hate her? Nay. Distrust her? Very much so. "Let me say that I would rather suffer in a Saracen prison, torture of the Turks"—his voice rose only a fraction with his temper—"than deal with this one Irish witch."

Galeron's brows shot up and he glanced at Branor, his look bespeaking his disbelief. "A witch? That could prove interesting."

The squire handed Connal the reins of his war-horse. "It could prove bloody damned hellish," he growled, checking the girth and the care of his animal. His movements jerked with each word he spoke. "I grew to knighthood around the spoiled brat. Whilst her father trained me, she interfered in my life whenever she had the chance, and followed me like a lost puppy for nearly five years." The memory of the little child using her magic on him, the agony of it, surfaced to silently stir the old humiliation in him again. 'Twas past, like most of his memories, dead and buried.

"So . . . you broke her heart."

Connal's gaze shot to Branor.

"How many times?" Galeron asked as he pulled his own mount near.

Enough, Connal thought. Enough that she would be no more pleased about this than he was. He didn't want to imagine the trouble she could bring on the king's plan when her temper was up.

But 'twas his duty. His loyalty to his king tested. Again.

And the reward of land dangled afore him like freedom to a condemned man, he thought, and swung up onto the saddle. The silver-gray stallion, a gift from his king, pranced regally beneath him, its black mane and tail shivering in the sun. "Nahjar, come with me. You two, join me at the harbor." He wheeled around and rode toward the sea. Toward a ship that would sail him back to Ireland.

To an island he'd not set foot on in thirteen years. A land his soul hungered for.

Winter, Northern Ireland
GleannAireamh
Three months later

Connal halted at the top of the wide sweeping glen. Sharp gusts of frosted air steamed from his horse's nostrils as his mount pranced, eager to continue the run. Below, the shore stretched for over a league, as untouched as he remembered it but for the fishing boats tipped on their sides like sleeping turtles waiting for spring to return. GleannAireamh. Nearly forty leagues south of GleannTaise, 'twas the grandest of the gleanns. Ripples of snow covered land folded and creased upon itself, wild moors bracketing the rocky walls gently sloping into the sea. 'Twas untamed but for the crop of cottages dotting here and there. In spring 'twould be alive with green, he thought, and though the weather was no warmer, the terrain was less treacherous than GleannTaise.

On the hill above the sea lay the ruins of an ancient castle.

*Croí an Banríon.*The heart of the queen, its blistering white stone blending with the snow, its reconstruction nearly complete, yet halted now for the weather. Weather he'd missed. A land he'd missed. He hadn't expected to, but the instant the long boat scraped Ireland's shore, Connal had experienced a wave of something close to joy.

Home.

He glanced to the side, at Raymond DeClare of the O'Donnel's astride his mount. Though his hair was liberally salted with gray, he looked no different than when Connal had left Ireland. A belted earl, his garments were rich and well appointed, yet 'twas the O'Donnel tartan slung across his chest and shoulder that spoke of his loyalty and power. An English chieftain, Connal thought, mildly amused.

"I imagine she is down there, somewhere," Raymond said, and Connal frowned at him.

"You know not where she is, my lord. A'tall?"

Raymond smiled, the brogue he'd acquired growing heavier. "It would not matter, Connal. She is her own woman and where I think she is last, she never is."

Raymond watched the man's features tighten with understanding. He did not offer more of his daughter, for if Sinead was to marry this knight, then he would need to discover all that she was on his own. Raymond almost grinned at that, and if the situation had not turned so grave upon Connal's arrival, he'd have found all this rather amusing.

"Then she knows I am here, Your Grace." Anger seethed that she did not have the decency to show herself to him.

"Everyone does, Connal. Your arrival has been heralded from Donegal to south Antrim. And I'm afraid to say, lad, not all joyously."

Connal ignored the sting of that. "I care not, my lord. I have a duty to tend and 'twill be done."

"Shall I remind you what my thoroughness to my duty to the king nearly cost me?"

Memories spat through Connal's mind like the biting

breath of a dragon. "I do not seek to build a fortress on the Sacred Stones and destroy the faith of a race."

"Oh?" Raymond arched a brow. "Then what, pray tell, were you doing on the Crusades?"

Connal's lips flattened and when he made to respond, Raymond waved him off. To defame the king's choices was treason. Nor did DeClare take offense at the jibe. His regrets were long since dead and he had learned from them. But this young man, he thought, had changed greatly. He felt no warmth near Connal, little laughter, and much attention to duty and honor. 'Twas not such an awful thing, but the young knight kept his opinion in silence, something Connal had never done as a lad.

Raymond considered that after the death of King Henry, the knight's loyalty had come under question far too often for any man's liking. With good reason. He'd been Henry's favorite, and when the king's sons warred on him, 'twas Connal who led the counterattacks that defeated them. Yet after the king's death, he'd been ostracized, for neither Richard nor John believed Connal PenDragon's loyalty could be trusted. 'Twas a grave mistake on their part. For in that time and against his father's wishes, Connal had become a mercenary, his skills at warring legendary and gaining him a reputation that, in Raymond's opinion, surpassed his father, Gaelan.

Those battles had hardened him, Raymond knew. They did every soldier. As they had with him. Until Fionna had awakened his heart and touched his very soul. *Dare I give my Sinead over to this man? When I know little of him these past dozen years?*

"Nay, Connal," Raymond said into the silence. "You do not seek to build on the Sacred Stones, yet I think it no worse than that you seek to take my child from me."

Connal sighed, his breath frosting the air. He'd reconciled himself to this on the voyage here. He respected Raymond and Fionna as if they were his own parents. The man had trained him into knighthood, and though he'd seen him but once more since King Henry placed the sword on his shoulder, he'd missed the man's counsel and friendship. And he did not want to destroy it, at any cost.

"My lord . . ." Connal stared out onto the land for a moment, then looked at DeClare, speaking honestly. "I am nay more pleased of this than she will be."

Raymond scowled. "Then I will petition the king. He cannot force her to wed."

"Aye, he can, and you know this. King Henry forced you to take an Irish bride."

"I did so willingly, and the woman of my choice."

Connal scoffed. "Not until 'twas nearly too late, my lord."

Raymond put up a hand for silence. "This is not about me, PenDragon. 'Tis about you wedding and bedding my daughter when she may not wish it. Sinead is more . . ."

"Headstrong than afore?"

His lips quirked. "Aye. She must be." Instantly all humor faded from his features. "Her life has not been simple, Connal. She is no stranger to hurt and I will not have you give her more. Never. No matter how much I imagined you wedding my daughter, if she does not wish this match, I will fight the king for her. Sinead does as she needs, not as she wishes," he said cryptically. "And even Richard cannot stop her."

Connal arched a brow, doubt bright in his clear green eyes.

DeClare studied him, anger blending with faint amusement. He would learn soon enough. "I warn you only once, lad." Edged steel sharpened his tone, the seasoned look in his eyes gone glacial with impatience. "Remember whose daughter you seek to master." With that DeClare called to his knights and spun his stallion about. He rode to where he knew Fionna waited patiently near the high road to the castle, the sound of hooves thundering in the winter quiet.

Connal sighed and pinched the bridge of his nose.

"Good go, Connal," Galeron said from behind him. "Anger the earl, make him not want to give his daughter's hand, and destroy the king's—"

"Enough!" Connal snapped. His gauntleted fingers clenched the ice-stiff reins as he searched for the patience and calm that had kept him alive in the Saracen prison. "We arrived two days afore and she's yet to show herself."

"Mayhaps she does not know," Branor said.

"Oh, she knows." And that proved she was still the spoiled girl, Connal thought, urging his horse forward. His gaze narrowed suddenly as he noticed a figure moving slowly atween the mist of the sea and the silent fall of snow.

The hair was unmistakable. Incredibly long. And red. Like a vivid banner of defiance to test his patience again.

Chapter Two

GleannAireamh

Upon an outcropping of rock on the edge of the shore, Sinead stood, the wind and cold battering her face, snapping at her cloak. To the right of her in the sand, a sword pierced the shore. Near her feet, a tiny fire hovered a breath above the stones.

She lifted her arms toward the sky and tipped her head back, her fur-lined hood pooling on her shoulders, letting loose the heavy mass of hair.

It fanned out behind her, undulating ribbons of deep, vivid red as she gave thanks for the bounty they had now and for the snow and cold that would tenderly hold beneath its white blanket the wild things waiting for spring.

The sea roared, foaming in swirls, and she smiled. Fish

leapt from the dark waters like arching arrows before plunging into the sea.

"Come, come. Ahh, you have not forgotten our need of you, little ones," she whispered, and the flames near her feet rose higher.

From behind her, a crystal flurry of snow raced across the land and funneled around her, enveloping her, glittering in the sun so desperate to reach the earth. It tickled her cheeks and lifted the heavy hem of her cloak. The elements were playful this day, she thought, laughing softly as she lowered her arms.

The sea softened, and a tranquil calm settled over her as the fire died into naught but a whisper of smoke.

"Conjuring, Sinead?"

Sinead tensed, but did not turn. She'd no need. Though his approach hadn't penetrated her concentration moments earlier, his presence in Ireland had. For days now, he'd perched himself in the dreams she tried forcing from her mind every night. The voice was deeper than she'd suspected it would be. And sharper. She could almost feel the anger and distaste he bore her in the past. And his impatience with her now.

So bleeding what?

Connal O'Rourke PenDragon was a royal pain in her Irish behind, and she'd no desire to be near him. He was a mark in her life, nothing more. Once a boy she adored, he was now only the proof of how an innocent heart can rule.

And ruin.

Her right hand shot out and the sword left the sand and came into her palm.

Connal cursed softly.

Sinead knew he'd not come all this way to leave her be, so she turned, the hilt of the sword grasped in both hands. The flare in his eyes, the quick glance up and down, told her that he'd not expected her to look as she did. Thirteen years past was a long and innocent time ago, she thought, managing to smother her shock at the sight of him as well.

Wee faeries, he was a giant. Standing several feet from her on the rocky slope, he gazed back with a stare that held naught but his green eyes. No hint of old friendship, no tenderness, no greeting. The cold of the wind compared little to the ice of Connal PenDragon's glare.

It burned into her soul.

She did not like it much. Nor had she expected more.

Wind stirred the fur-lined mantle draping from his shoulders to the ground, and beneath it, his arms were folded over his chest, metal gauntlets glimmering in the smattering of sun hovering above. Clad in dark brown leather hauberk and silver chain mail, he was without a helm, yet his garments bore the trappings of the English as if they were branded on him. Chilled air caught his sable hair, showing the red still lingering from his childhood, and a long thin scar running straight down a cheek earned as a man. She inspected him further, seeking the boy she knew, the newly knighted lad who'd made her heartbeat skip.

And she found him gone, replaced by a man her soul did not recognize.

"Nay, I am not conjuring, PenDragon. Not that my doings are yours to inspect."

Connal frowned, the bite of her words hitting him in the chest. He never dreamed the girl who'd cast on him, who'd followed him, who'd interfered with his training and too often sent other girls running—was this same woman.

No longer the girl, atall, he thought, but a woman

full grown and breathtakingly exquisite. He could easily admit that, for she'd been a beautiful child, yet he knew better than anyone the foul temper that lay hidden behind those innocent deep blue eyes. And the havoc it could wreak.

Yet . . . those moments past when she was speaking to the elements, 'twas how he would forever remember her. Sparkling in the gloom of winter. Green velvet and snow-white fur. Her hair obeyed the wind, the long locks wrapping across her chest as if shielding her from him. The charms woven in the scatter of thin braids flashing with sunlight and mystery. Her green gown and cloak spoke of nobility, the large gold Celtic knots trimming the hems shouting the princess she was, regardless of what England had decided. And she carried herself as such. Her chin tilted above the wisps of white fur, her eyes teeming with challenge.

"Your doings are my business now, Sinead."

She put up a hand. "Speak no more, PenDragon. I know why you have come. 'Twill not be a marriage atween us."

"And why not?" He'd known she'd deny him, but why was he feeling jilted all of a sudden?

"Because I say 'tis so."

His lips twitched with amusement, but Sinead could see the condescension lying beneath it. "You cannot defy the order of the King of England, Sinead."

She scoffed, almost rudely. "For a king who cannot remain in his own country long enough to keep it?" She lifted the sword and started walking. "Open your eyes closed by the English, PenDragon, and watch me." She marched past him, toward the castle road.

He caught her arm.

He half expected to feel his palm burn.

But he only felt—energy. Pouring from her and directly into him with the force of a blade plunging into his skin. Sharp, almost numbing. His heart thundered and rolled in his chest, threatening his breathing, making him labor for it. As if he'd run the distance from GleannTaise.

Instantly he let her go. "What did you do?" His gaze moved roughly over her painfully beautiful features.

Her lips thinned along with her gaze. "You accuse me of casting on you already?" Her fingers tightened on the sword hilt. "I am no longer a willful child, Pen-Dragon, but I see in that judgment, you have not changed." She looked down briefly at her fingers on the sword. "Yet all else has."

He scowled. "What the bloody hell does that mean?" When she did not respond, he took a step closer and added, "Say what you will, Sinead. Offending me has never stopped you afore."

She looked him over, his English garments, his English sword and manner. It almost broke her heart to see it. "Even your brogue has faded," she whispered, and the grief of it swept her. "I choose my own destiny, knight. I work it, fight to keep it. I will not be told what to do or whom to wed—especially by a king who hasn't the decency to visit a land he rules."

Connal refrained from arguing that she'd no choice but to obey and said, "His brother is prince regent here."

"And know you the mishandling he's done? For the love of Bridget, he rewards Ireland in pieces as if 'twas a puzzle, then takes it away at the whim of a . . . boy! And we suffer. Battles have escalated to bloody wars and Ireland is in more turmoil than England."

"I am here to settle some of that."

A single tapered red brow lifted. "Are you, now? For the good of whom, PenDragon? My Ireland or your England?"

The slap of her words stung and he straightened, glaring down at her. "This is my home, too."

Her gaze raked him unkindly. "If 'tis so, then why has it taken you a dozen years and a king's decree to get you to return?"

The air stilled between them, and Connal felt the sorrow in her voice that he could not ignore. It sounded so much like his mother's when he'd visited Donegal. But he had his own reasons for not returning. For not wanting to relive his last moments here and feel the burning shame of it. And, he vowed as he had that day, to keep them private. He would battle legions to keep it that way.

"I've been . . . occupied," was all he could say.

"Ahh," she said thoughtfully, sage wisdom in the look. "Forcing a faith on the infidels? Slaughtering for the riches of Islam? What will you do to my people, my faith, in the name of the king?"

Her implications scored through him, and his features sharpened to near menacing. He took a step, looming over her like a great beast about to devour. "I am a knight of King Richard, Sinead. 'Tis my duty. My kind are necessary for peace!"

"I am not blind to the art of politics," she snapped back at him, unafraid. " 'Tis not your *kind* that offend me. 'Tis the man who hides behind the shield and sword of another and forgets his own kin that does!"

"Ireland held naught for me, then," he said, trying to keep his temper in check.

" 'Tis selfish thinking, sir knight. You fled to follow the English, yet whilst I have remained and weathered the storms of conflict, you now return to take what is mine?" She leaned closer, her blues eyes ablaze with challenge. *"Never."* She turned away and marched up the hill, using the sword like a walking stick.

"Sinead!"

She kept going, seeming to float over the snow, her cloak dragging several feet behind her.

" 'Tis done, woman," he called. "Antrim belongs to the king."

Her voice carried to him on the cold wind. "And so do you."

Connal scowled blackly as he climbed the rocky slope after her, toward his men positioned on the hillside.

"I see that did not go well either," Galeron muttered, handing over the reins to Connal's horse.

Connal scoffed, then looked to where she was, walking near the trees. " 'Twas more tame than I expected." Yet he knew she would only gain momentum and unleash it on him. She was hiding more of her feelings, much more than she let on. And though he knew 'twould be wiser to leave it unsaid, he could not.

He mounted his horse, and as he adjusted in the saddle, he glanced around. "She is alone? Completely? Where are her retainers? Her guards?" Though she carried a sword, 'twas too heavy for her to wield.

"There was no one, m'lord," Galeron said, frowning between the two as the lady made a path toward the castle road.

" 'Tis just the sort of trouble she'd enjoy," he muttered and rode toward her, calling her name. She did not respond, covering more ground than he thought she could on foot. As he neared, he noticed a small covey of tiny birds fluttering around her, chirping a greeting, one settling on her shoulder. Several brown rabbits emerged from hollows nearly covered in snow and pounced after her like eager puppies.

She paused to cup a straggling baby rabbit in her hand and cuddle it close. She spoke to the creatures, though he would hear no more than the muted murmur of her voice. She set the baby rabbit on the ground, encouraging it to hop on its own, then continued on her way. A smile tugged at the corners of his mouth. The bunnies were like brown bubbles popping up and down in the snow behind her and covering little distance.

A sound, one he recognized instantly, pierced the quiet, and Connal twisted to look behind, then watched in horror as a hail of arrows sailed through the air and pierced the rabbits trailing behind her. The birds scattered.

"Cease fire, cease!" he shouted as her legs failed her, buckling, and for a moment Connal thought she'd taken an arrow. His heart pounding, he leapt from the saddle as she twisted to look at him. Bleak disappointment shone in her eyes. Then an arrow skewered the infant rabbit nearest her.

Blood splashed the snow.

Her low moan sang on the air.

"Sinead!" Connal shouted, yet before he reached her, she rose and lifted her gaze to his.

"You have been here but days and already you have brought death with you."

Her words hit like the arrow tip, deadly and where he thought himself shielded. Memories bled past his barriers, swelling with resentment. "God above, woman, they are warriors, and hunt for food when they can. 'Tis instinct!"

Her eyes flashed with impatient anger. "Not a soul

in Antrim has gone hungry since the end of my mother's banishment! We see that all are well fed and we hunt what is necessary!"

We? "Most of my men will live outside the castle and will not be provided for except by their own hand. And afore you start to make more demands," he interrupted before she could, "I will give no such order to cease hunting."

"Then tell them to hunt the full grown." With the sword, she pointed to the bloodstained snow. "Not the babes!"

They were the most tender, he wanted to remind her, but wisely kept his counsel. " 'Twas accidental. For that I offer my regrets." He glanced at the game at his feet. " 'Twill not be wasted."

She made a rude sound. " 'Tis already a waste! Warn them—" She nodded toward the handful of knights and troops. "If they kill the young not yet able to breed—we will have no food atall." She swept her cloak up across her shoulders and melted into the forest.

Connal blinked and wondered why he was so shocked when she vanished, a wisp of red mist left behind with her footprints. He'd never seen her do that as a girl, and though forewarned, he'd hoped only her mother could weave such magic. What other talents did she possess? And how was he to deal with them? As her husband, he could forbid her to use magic. Instantly, he knew 'twas impossible. The land and people would survive, but Sinead would rebel. He dropped his head forward. And, no doubt, with her usual subtlety.

The wonder and awe in his soldiers' voices penetrated his thoughts, and briefly he glanced back at the crowd of armored men and soldiers. Most looked frightened, except Galeron and Nahjar. Did she have to make such a display before the wary? Obviously she thought herself safe from those who'd easily kill her for merely whispering the word *magic*. Including a few in his own ranks.

You have been here but days and already you have brought death with you.

The thought thrust images into his mind, the guilt to swiftly ride over his spine like claws. He pushed them down deeply, his gaze falling on the dead rabbit at his feet. 'Twas minor, food for his men, but the thought of bringing death and destruction to his homeland sickened him.

He tipped his head back, his gaze roaming the land.

He was finally home, prepared to face the demons clinging to him for thirteen years whilst more cropped up to prick him.

The soft crunch of snow came to him, and he turned as Nahjar approached. A great tower of fur, the Moor looked like the rest, odd, out of place, especially with the tattoos on his face and the neatly wrapped turban on his bald head.

"Should I be protecting your carcass from her as well, Sajin?"

Connal slid him a thin glance. "I have survived a prison of Saladin the First; I can certainly handle one woman."

"When? I saw no sign of it."

Connal growled something under his breath that was not fit for the ears of even a seasoned Moor, then mounted his steed, Ronan, and gave orders to head to the castle.

He rode ahead, determined to do the king's bidding . . . even if it meant tying Sinead to the altar. He'd witnessed oceans of blood and war and would not allow a woman to stop him now. Sinead's defiance, he thought, was simply wasting his time.

Prince John slumped in the chair, his elbow resting on its arm, his finger tapping his lips. He stared toward the window, watching motes of dust powder the air for several moments till the men around him fidgeted.

Then, only his gaze shifted to the spy. "He is in Ireland already, you say?"

"Aye, your highness." The messenger did not look at him, his gaze downcast. "He has been ordered to wed."

John sucked his tongue, then glanced around, his tone rueful. "My brother believes he can lock doors to me still by sending emissaries," he muttered, his chancellor and head of his war counsel agreeing. His gaze flicked to the spy. "Who is this bride?"

"Sinead of the Nine Gleanns."

John eyed the messenger up and down. "You say that with reverence, Irishman."

"The lady is daughter of Fionna O'Donnel and Lord Raymond DeClare, my liege. And a . . ."

The man hesitated.

"What keeps you from speaking up now when you have already betrayed your people?"

The messenger flushed with anger and lifted his gaze. "She is a witch."

"Liar."

"Of course, my lord," the spy dared to say, yet his hands trembled.

John relished the man's fear, then glanced at his counsel. One man, dark haired and standing in the farthest reaches of the throne room, nodded ever so slightly.

John's attention came back to the Irishman. The house of DeClare and PenDragon united. The thought made John sit up a little straighter in his chair. Though he'd never met either earl, he'd heard enough of their reputations to make him ill. He should have taken their holdings afore now, but since peace was well in the north, he did not. And how had he not heard of this unmarried daughter of DeClare's? "Tell me more of this woman." He reached for a bowl of figs and examined the fruit afore he bit into it.

"She is from a very old family. Her lineage ancient, sire. Like her mother, she wields the elements."

And my brother will use her against me, John thought, discarding the stem and wiping his hands on an embroidered cloth. "You believe she can do such things?"

"I have lain witness to it."

"Really? How fortunate for you. A witch casting spells." He spared a jeering glance at his counselors. "Next you'll tell me of potions and bubbling cauldrons."

Soft laughter echoed in the stone chamber.

"Do not underestimate this woman, sire."

John frowned at the man's tone. 'Twas a warning, filled with rage. "There is something you are not saying."

The Irishman boldly lifted his gaze, first looking at the other men, then to the prince. He did not question this act of betrayal. For 'twas vengeance, justice. Two lives for two taken. 'Twas owed him this, and he did not care what the prince wanted; all he desired was letters of marque and coin to gather a squad. 'Twould be him, the Irishman thought, who would deliver the final blows.

"Aye, my liege," the messenger said, pausing to level his gaze at the prince. "The witch is the most powerful. There is none who've come afore her that can match her skill. Even her mother. Now she has PenDragon at her side? Forgive me for saying so, my liege, but he has the king's ear and both have no love for you."

The spy let that brew in the prince's mind.

But all the prince said was, "Hum?" then spat another fig stem into his palm and dropped it into a bowl. He rose and moved off the dais, the messenger coming to a crouch and backing away as he walked to the window. That PenDragon had not bothered to show himself at court spoke of the danger the man could be to gaining the throne. He thought himself untouchable because he carried Richard's seal. And with Richard's ally wedding this fabled woman? Bracing his arm on the sash, he looked back. "What powers," his tone spoke his doubt, "does this woman possess?"

"My liege?"

"I must know all there is about her," he said impatiently.

"She can create out of thin air, melt metal, move atween this world and that of the spirits." At the prince's doubtful look, he hastily added, "She can change her shape to that of a cat, a deer, or a dog."

John's fine brows rose. " 'Tis impossible." But the consequences rolled through his mind and magnified.

The Irishman flinched; although his tone was soft, the bite of it lanced his courage. "I have no reason to lie, sire."

"Find her, bring her to me." John knew he had to have her under his power before she could do aught for Richard. Or to him. John looked at the man, his gaze traveling up and down his poor garments, the dirt and mud he left on the fine carpets. "By law, she should be executed for even speaking of witchcraft. As should you."

"But sire—"

John's gaze narrowed. "Get out afore I change my mind," he said in a low threat.

The messenger paled, backed away, then quickly left.

John looked at his counselors and shrugged. "Keep her, burn her at the stake, I do not care. But Richard will not have her, nor aught that comes with marrying off the woman to PenDragon. But," he said, pausing to be certain they hung on his words, "if she is truly powerful, I want her. *Without* PenDragon to interfere." He eyed the group, making certain his message was clear without speaking the words. He turned his attention to the scene beyond the window again. "Find someone she loves. That should keep her in line when the time comes."

Not a man in the chamber dared contradict him.

He liked that.

He liked that very much.

Chapter Three

Astride her white mare, Sinead rode atween the tall gates into the center of the bailey. Monroe, her personal guard, strode forward. And saving that scowl all day just for her, she suspected.

"My lady, how many times must I remind you to warn me when you leave the castle grounds?" Monroe said, reaching for the reins that were not there, then disgusted that he'd forgotten she used none.

Sinead smiled as she dismounted. He really was making a fuss this time. "A thousand, mayhaps?"

A frustrated sound rumbled from him, yet he did not give voice to it.

"I am fine, Monroe." She patted his arm, and her horse Genevieve found her own way to her stall. Together they walked toward the tall doors. "I was only on the shore; surely you knew that."

Aye, he did know, had seen her mount grazing

patiently on the high road, but that was not the point. One he'd stressed with her daily and was surely going to make him an old man soon. "Lady Sinead," he said tiredly, "with you, I never know what to expect."

She pushed back her hood to look at him. "I am predictable, am I not?"

He scoffed as only the captain of the guard would dare in her presence.

"Do I not rise each morning to see to the order of this castle? Do I not visit the villages each sen'night? That is predictable."

Monroe tried to hide his smile. She sounded defensive. "I can foresee only that you go about unprotected, and you give me sleepless nights of worry."

She paused on the steps as he forced open the heavy doors. "Forgive me, Monroe. I will tell you, then, that I plan to remain inside till the morrow."

He flashed her a speculative glance, doubting that, too. "If you say so, my lady."

She laughed softly, nudging him as they walked inside. The warmth of the castle hit her first, then the sights and smells. She inhaled the aroma of roasting meat and watched the bustle of people as she unfastened her cloak. Women with armloads of linens and platters moved quickly; young pages arranged tables for the coming meal; the children raced between servants and vassals. Yet at the sight of her nearly everyone stilled and looked her way.

And for the first time since she'd become lady of this castle, she saw fear.

PenDragon, she thought, and his warmonger reputation has brought this. She smothered her anger and smiled at her folk. They went back to work, yet continued to glance her way.

"There is talk of what will come, my lady," Monroe said so only she would hear.

"Naught will change, Monroe, I will see to it."

"But the king's orders—"

She flashed him a hard look that stopped his words. "Naught will change for these people. This I vow."

But what will change for her? he wondered, frowning, "I offer my aid anyway I can, my lady."

Sinead's features softened and she felt her eyes burn. Her knights and Irish warriors were more her friends than her vassals. When her father had given her the right to rule, they had come willingly to her side, each accepting her for what she was, and for that her heart belonged to them all. But she was aware of the consequences.

"My gratitude to you, Monroe, but understand this could be an unpleasant time. I've no notion of how to fix this without starting a war."

He nodded and touched her forearm. "I know you, my lady." His lips quirked. "You will find a way."

His confidence overwhelmed and she could only nod, sweeping the cloak from her shoulders. A young girl rushed forward to take it and Sinead smiled her thanks, then bent to accommodate the girl's small size. "Tell Glassa to ready all the chambers. We have guests coming."

"More than the earl?" the girl said, glancing at Sinead's parents sitting by the hearth.

"Aye, lovey, and big ones too."

The girl's eyes widened before she hurried off.

"I have readied quarters for PenDragon's vassals," Monroe said, handing over his fur cloak to a page.

Sinead nodded. "Excellent, but his knights shall bed inside." At his frown she added, "These men have returned from the Crusades and should be welcomed well this night." The matter of Connal and the king's decree had naught to do with treating a person well, and as was due their station. She would never shame her people, her parents, nor herself because she resented Connal's arrival and the meaning of it.

As Monroe went off to see to the matter, she walked briskly across the hall, calling, "Meaghan, Kerry, Brian!" and clapping her hands. With each strike to her palm, the candles puffed with flame, offering a soft glow to the dusky stone walls.

The three servants rushed forward, and she gave instructions for the night's feasting and answered a dozen questions, trying to put them at ease and disliking the fear in their eyes. As they went to work, she moved to her parents, kissing her father's cheek and hugging her mother before she motioned to a servant to refill their mulled wine.

"How went your meeting with Connal?"

Sinead eyed her father, declining the offer of wine for herself. "You should have led the man a merry chase across Ireland, Papa, and back to the sea."

He smiled that innocent smile she usually loved. "I am too accomplished at map reading. And I taught Connal."

"Well, mayhaps 'twas all of your teachings that remain, for he was as I expected." *As I have dreamed,* she added silently, and Connal's face flashed in her mind. Handsome. Goddess above, he was so very handsome. His skin warmed by the sun, his features sharply carved as if honed in granite. She shook her head, clearing the image. "He is demanding, arrogant, and believing he can return when it suits and take this prize without so much as a by your leave."

"Sinead," Raymond said quietly, "the castle and lands are your dowry. And *you* are the prize he seeks."

She scoffed. "He does not seek my hand, Papa. He has been *ordered* to do so. He would not care if I were a fish monger's daughter."

"But you are not." Her father's voice snapped with anger at the situation and not at her, she knew.

Fionna moved forward, touching them both. "Connal and his retinue will arrive soon; mayhaps we should talk in private?"

Sinead did not look to see who might be eaves-dropping and nodded, leading the way to the solar tucked under the staircase. She did not want her folk to bear the troubles she had. 'Twas her duty to see that their lives were simpler. Richer.

Once inside she moved to the far corner, where a bench was fashioned in an alcove of the wall. Tall narrow windows of colored glass flanked her and let in a glori-ous blue-tinted sunlight that was quickly fading to dusk. Bracing her shoulder against the wall, she pulled her legs to the side, her skirts draping over her feet. Her father moved to the hearth, sitting in the padded chair across from her mother.

Their heads together, they whispered among them-selves, yet she paid their conversation no mind. If they had something to say to her, they would. It had always been that way. She could blame them for her outspoken-ness, she thought as she ran her finger down the frosted glass, staring out into the side yard. A mound of snow covered the summer garden, and she was eager for the warmth of Beltane to shower the land green again. Yet for all her powers, she could no more bring summer to her doors than she could keep the king from destroy-ing her life.

Sighing, she tipped her head down, fingering the silver chain wrapping her wrist and worn smooth with age. She thought of the day her mother bound her from wielding magic. For years she'd been unable to cast a single spell, make a flower bloom. She'd first felt trapped and betrayed, then had grown accustomed to it, learning the truth of pure magic and the power she would one day wield. 'Twas a grand gift, she thought. Her mother had been so very right in denying her the power. She'd been young and impulsive, and as the years passed since then, Sinead was ever grateful for her mother's wisdom. And now Sinead was wiser, cautious. Yet she continued to wear the chain to remind her to take care with her magic.

Aye, misjudgments and heartache bred wisdom of their own, she thought, and yet, when the power was returned to her, the force of it nearly tore her in half. And brought back the seeing dreams, the nightly visions that had not tormented her for years. The power, she thought, still pulled her apart. Pulled her away from being ordinary, pushing away those who did not accept or understand the truth of it. And brought her suitors who could not love her honestly, for she was a witch of the craft.

Her throat tightened and Sinead swallowed, sending useless self-pity to the winds. She'd little need of it, and told herself she did not care that those men had wanted her for her power, for themselves.

But 'twas a lie.

For in the back of her heart, in the old spot where she'd held Connal so dearly as a child, where her dreams were harbored and never examined, she did want more. Desperately. And she was glad she was still bound from working magic on him. Not that she would ever be so careless with her gift again, she thought. But once, in anger, she'd turned her power on Connal, onto a boy she'd insisted was her heart mate.

'Twas naught but a childish infatuation, that. In her eyes then, he was Ireland's hero, a prince, and only fours summers old, she'd viewed her tiny world as an adventure, filled with mere "things" to bend to her will. She'd made her mother miserable, Colleen frantic, and had turned Connal into a goat.

Well. Half a goat.

And with it, she'd broken the first rule of the craft: Do as thou will, in it harm none. Shame swept her, and she lowered her legs, staring at naught. It mattered little that she'd been innocent and unskilled. The transformation was incomplete, and excruciatingly painful.

He'd never truly forgiven her. Nor did he trust her.

From that day, he'd done his best to push her away, avoiding her to the point of being cruel. 'Twas not until she was in her eighth or ninth year that she had turned her back on her heart. And given up on finding any peace.

She looked down at the bracelet. Connal would never know she was bound from weaving magic on him still. That was one thing her mother had refused to remove whilst he'd trained in GleannTaise. After he'd left, she'd forgotten about it. And about him. He'd broken her heart a dozen times, and although she could break the binding spell, she would not. 'Twould be betraying her parents. And that she would never do.

"Sinead, you are not listening."

"Aye, Papa," she said, then looked up and smiled. "I am not. There is little need for discussion."

Fionna regarded her daughter with sympathy. "I beg to differ, my lamb, 'tis your future we speak of."

" 'Tis the king's notion of a future, not mine."

Fionna rose and went to Sinead, pulling her toward the fire. With the flick of her hand, Fionna sent the flames to roaring as Sinead settled in the padded chair vacated by her father. The pair stared down at her and when she wanted to stand, her father held her in place.

She looked at them both. "I will not lose all I have struggled for now. Not to Connal." *Not for a marriage decreed by a king and not for love.* Sinead had little time to consider all the options and she felt a trap closing in around her. Her first instinct was to fight it as best she could. "The king wishes to use me to bind our house with Lord Gaelan's and Connal wishes only to do his duty to his king and be done with it."

Over her head, the parents exchanged a smile.

"I will not be a duty, a *chore* to any man. And he has made it clear marriage is a . . . *task*. A bothersome one at that. If 'twere possible, I would marry some old sot ready for the grave rather than spend a life convincing Connal PenDragon that I will not use magic on him."

"Then I shall tell him the truth," Fionna decided and moved to the door.

"Nay!" Sinead stood sharply and her mother frowned, folding her arms and waiting for more. "I would have him speak his true feelings, and not because he believes he is safeguarded."

"Mayhaps he would relax more if he knew," her father said softly from behind her, his gaze straying to his wife. He arched a brow at Fionna, the look generating a little hope for the worried sire.

"Connal would not believe it. He chose to reject my gift and with that rejected me. Though the man has little to be proud of himself."

Raymond eyed his daughter, then looked to his wife.

Fionna sent a silent message to him: *This treads deeper than we think, husband.* DeClare nodded slightly, moving to the large carved desk and lifting the crease-marked parchment. "I can fight the king on this," he said.

Sinead rushed to her father. "And what will that gain you, Papa, beyond the king's wrath?"

"My daughter's happiness."

Sinead smiled tenderly, tipping her head and gazing deep into his warm gray eyes. "Oh, Papa"—she stroked his cheek—"I am who I am, what I am. That will never change. But if I do not obey the king's wishes, will he not simply send another to wed me?"

"Possibly," Raymond said, "but that would not gain him the union he needs. And even a marriage atween Connal's sister and your brother would not grant him the allegiance he desires, for neither are the first born."

Sinead took a step back. "Richard might want an alliance of our families, Papa, but the only reason he bothers with me is for the great armies you, Lord Gaelan, and Connal possess. Legions of vassals to fight and die for his stupid causes." Disgust laced her voice. "I know there are few who've believed in his Crusade." She shook a finger at her father. "You and Gaelan to start."

He caught her hand, clasping her fist to his chest. His heart picked up pace when he thought of the trouble her outspokenness could cause. "Do not speak of that, Sinead. There are allies to the king so strong they would easily kill you for uttering the words."

Her smile was infinitely patient. "And there are just as many who would kill me because I am a witch. 'Tis no new danger."

"Sinead, be sensible."

"I am, Mama," she said, turning to look at Fionna.

"You have taught me well, as did Cathal, and Father has seen that I have not been sheltered."

"As if I could stop you," he said on a short laugh.

She hurriedly pecked a kiss to his cheek.

"Your father and I want the best match for you, Sinead."

" 'Tis not possible."

Fionna's expression fell into sadness and it pierced Sinead's heart.

"Do not worry over me so. I cannot wed Connal for, like the others, he has reasons of his own for wanting the marriage and 'tis naught to do with matters of the heart." Sinead moved away from them, not seeing her father's face crush with guilt as she wrapped her hands in her velvet sleeves to stand near the fire. The blaze jumped and rose and she shushed the flames to a calm flicker.

"He has changed so. He is hard and cold, and I can feel the distance our past has lain atween us." He resented her, for being the one chosen for him, for being a witch, and for every little pain they'd inflicted on each other years past. And she could not begin to consider that he was more English than Irish and that he'd abandoned his people, their ways. That, she thought, hurt her the most.

She looked at her parents, her mother standing near her father and both openly wearing their concern. "What I felt for him as a child is dead and buried."

"But do you care for him?" Raymond sought some shred of tenderness atween the pair. Something that would give them all the chance to be happy about the king's decree, for as much as he wished to fight Richard on the matter, the king was not in England and others would see this match sealed. Then, to compound their troubles, should Prince John learn of it, he could easily kill them both before 'twas done. Without the alliance of two houses and the oaths Connal would gain, Richard's kingdom would slip quickly from his grasp. Raymond's only hope was that if Sinead must marry, 'twould be to a man he trusted and loved, to a man he knew would protect her with his life.

And not allow her natural defiance to stop him from the task.

"I say again, daughter . . ."

"I heard you, Papa." Sinead tipped her head back and stared at the ceiling for a moment, then closed her eyes. *Do I care for him?* 'Twas almost laughable to think on it overlong. Yet she could not ignore the sensations she'd experienced when she'd realized Connal was returning. The hope and joy, the childhood heartache. And upon seeing him again, the desire and need of a woman for a man.

Strong and powerful, Connal PenDragon was burned into her heart, and though she could not tell if 'twas old memories or new possibilities that ruled her, she recognized her desire for him. 'Twas intense, enough that when he had touched her arm, she'd sweltered beneath the cloak and gown amid the swirl of snow and icy wind.

"Sinead?" her mother pressed.

"Aye, of course I care. I have known him most of my life, Mama."

"He is like a brother to you?" her mother asked.

Her head whipped around and she gaped at them both. "Connal? Great Goddess Mother, I have never thought of him as a brother." Her hands on her hips, her gaze shifted between her parents. "What are you trying to say?"

Her parents exchanged a glance.

"Answer this one question, love," Raymond said. "If you were to choose, and all was right, would you choose Connal?"

Her eyes widened. "You mean to ask, if he were not cold and bitter, would I choose him? If he would see me as a wanted bride and not a duty price to his king? If he had not accused me of casting on him in the first moments we'd met again . . . if he'd not broken my heart a half dozen times . . ." She paced, her body radiating heat as her temper rose. "If he nay longer detested the magic I can wield," she scoffed rudely, "or even the woman I am . . . if he were all of the man I once glimpsed, then . . . aye!" She stopped and whirled to face them. "I would choose him."

Her father grinned.

Her mother fought a smile.

Sinead shook her head, her hair cascading over her shoulders. "But he is none of that." Her voice fractured, and briefly she glanced away. What had happened to the boy inside the man? she wondered. "We have naught to begin with. At least you and Father had love."

"Love takes time, Sinead."

She looked at them, her tone clipped. "Well, Connal possesses little time. For me, for Ireland, and for the future this alliance will bring us. He gives it and his heart for his duty to the absent king."

Raymond opened his mouth to argue the point when a knock rattled the door. Before Sinead could stop her, Fionna waved a hand. The wood portal swung wide open.

Connal stood just beyond the threshold, his garments richly appointed in silver over a green so deep 'twas nearly black.

His gaze locked with hers and Sinead experienced a sudden hard yank anchored somewhere near her heart. Her breath skipped and rushed. And she recognized the sensation; 'twas the same feeling she'd had at four, at nine, and had banished from her heart for thirteen years.

A call of the soul.

She almost hated him for bringing it back when there was little she could do to stop it.

Connal stood frozen for a moment, stunned again by the ethereal beauty of this woman. "I wish to speak with you, Sinead." He took a single step inside and bowed to Raymond and Fionna. "My lord, my lady. In private, if you please."

"It does not please me, PenDragon," Sinead said, folding her arms. "We have naught to discuss."

"There again you are wrong, princess," he said, and the husky sound of his voice coated her with warmth.

She did not trust it one bit, fie on the man.

"We have a future, whether you like it or nay."

Raymond inclined his head to Fionna and they moved to the door.

"Papa?"

Raymond regarded her even as Fionna slipped past him and out of the room. "Were you not saying 'twere no new dangers?"

Sinead's spine straightened, and she lifted her chin, giving her father a hot look before they left, then turning it on Connal.

"Come, PenDragon." She waved him inside. "Speak your peace, for believe me, I will speak mine."

"In all my days, Sinead, *that* I have never doubted."

"You will not like it."

His hand on the door latch, he arched a brow. "So, we are to do battle, are we?"

A strange excitement suddenly coursed through her blood. "Aye, and you'd best not be wagerin' who will win."

His green eyes sharpened, grew darker. "I have never lost a war, Sinead."

"Then be prepared, PenDragon. You will taste defeat today."

Her challenge laid like a gauntlet, Connal carefully closed the door. From the moment he'd stepped inside, his gaze never left her.

And he'd no desire to cease staring, either.

Because no matter what he must do, needed to do, Sinead O'Donnel of the house of DeClare, Princess of the Nine Gleanns of North Antrim ... made him remember, with one look, that he was a man.

And witch or nay, she was the most desirable woman in Ireland.

Chapter Four

And this Celtic beauty is yours, a voice whispered in his head.

Or she would be, when he reasoned with her.

If that was possible, he thought, and doubted his capabilities, for he'd not expected to be attracted to her. But then, what man would not want such a female for his wife? A woman of beauty and enchantment; Sir Galeron, in his infinite wit, had reminded him of such since those moments on the south shore.

Connal did not need a reminder. Merely looking at her stirred a man's imagination. Folding his arms over his chest, he studied Sinead, who until a few hours ago had always been a girl in his memory.

She stood in the center of the solar, pure Irish defiance permeating her like a faery's fire. He knew her as a mischievous child, a troublesome, love-struck adolescent, but now, because of the king's edict, he would know her as a woman.

Intimately.

For the rest of his days.

The thought stuck Connal as almost humorous. He no more wanted to marry than she did. He knew his reasons, but hers? She was older than most brides, though he did not wonder overlong as to why she had not married already. She was stubborn, defiant, and willful. Naught a man needed in his life.

Where another woman would offer peace and contentment, Sinead offered endless days of turmoil. And fights. She was itching for one now. He could tell in the way she stood, in her tapping foot. His gaze rose slowly from her slippered toe, lingering over her body, lush and shapely inside the green gown. A leather, silver, and gold girdle draped her hips, bringing focus to the smallness of her waist and the graceful curves flowing beneath the fabric. Circling her throat was a gold and silver torc, the head and tail of a dragon adorning the ends and bringing his attention to her bosom nearly spilling from its fitted confinement.

A fantasy ripe for a man's imagination.

And that she would be his sent a warm twist of desire racing through him.

"Why do you look at me like *that*?"

The distaste in her tone caught his complete attention. "And just how am I looking?"

Her hands on her hips, she cocked her head. "Like I am one of Colleen's sweet comfits and you have the only spoon."

Connal schooled his features and pushed aside the exotic thoughts flying through his mind. 'Twould not do for this woman to know she aroused him. She had enough power over him with her magic alone. "I gaze upon you as my bride, Sinead."

"Then cease, for I will not be so."

He moved toward her. "You cannot stop this marriage."

She stood her ground. "I can do more than you believe, PenDragon. I am mistress of *Croí an Banríon.* Not you."

" 'Tis merely your dowry, Sinead," he said, as if they'd had this conversation a dozen times before. "You only hold it in your father's stead—"

"Do not speak to me like the child I was," she cut in with open disgust. "You know naught of this land, these people. Nor me. And be warned now, knight of Richard, *I* rule the gleanns. I am chieftain."

Connal's gaze narrowed and he folded his arms over his chest. "Till we are wed, mayhaps."

"Nay, now and forever. 'Tis my blood right to protect these people."

'Twas truth; she did have stronger ties to the land, to its Druid beginnings, but Connal planned to reclaim his own, and this little tantrum of power was not going to stop him. "And so it will become mine as well."

"You are a fool if you think I will relinquish to you. We are done."

When she lifted her hand, to no doubt travel elsewhere, he snatched her wrist. Fear flashed in her blues eyes, there and gone so quickly he was not certain he saw it. But he felt her anger, the energy of her, coupled like oil and wine and seeping into him. Two distinct sensations, both powerful, and he fought them. The answering sensation was almost painful. Connal refused to bend to it.

"You will remain in this chamber and speak with me." His patience was gone, and when she opened her mouth he jerked her closer. "Nay! You owe me this much."

Sinead battled silent old fears as the heat of his body penetrated her clothing, his strength slipping into her through his grasp on her wrist. It softened her knees and she ignored the meaning of it, the old spirit of her heart trying desperately to escape its cage. She preferred it locked away, and when her senses fell into the warmth and scent of him, she tore from his grip.

"Whatever debt you believe I need pay has been paid by the cruelty you showed a young girl."

Old shame filled him and his voice softened. " 'Twas years ago."

"Aye, and done atween us. Yet whilst you walked away from Ireland I remained faithful, and we have survived well without the touch of the king or you."

"Be that as it may, the king's touch had returned when he put his seal on that order." He pointed to the parchment he'd given Raymond and that now lay on the carved desk. "You have had your time to play lord—"

She inhaled. "Play!" Goddess above, she never wanted to slap a person so much afore now.

He went on as if she had not spoken. "My duty is to Richard first and I will obey . . . as will you!"

Sinead's eyes flared and the fire in the hearth rose and licked the mantel.

He glanced at the blaze, then to her, saying, "By God, you are just like your mother. Cease that afore you burn us to the ground."

Sinead waved and the fire went out completely. Connal blinked at the curls of smoke, but she cared little. She would not wed a man who saw her only as a step to please his king, to more riches and power. "You cannot have this castle and lands without my consent. And Richard knows this."

His look was infinitely patient. "Hence, the marriage."

Her hands on her hips, she glared. " 'Twill be a wee bit of trouble doing that without a willing bride."

"Willing or nay, you are only a woman; you have no say in the matter."

Sinead growled under her breath, the corners of her eyes lifting like a cat's, and for a moment, Connal thought she had never looked more magnificent. Till she spoke.

"That asinine, pompous statement proves you even *think* like the English! *Your* own mother ruled. As did my grandmother, Egrain, and hers afore. Take no comfort that you can succeed with that argument in this house." She looked him up and down. "I know not who stands afore me and calls himself a son of Ireland."

Her words gouged at his pride and Connal held supreme control over his outrage. "You know naught of me," he ground out between tightly clenched teeth, glowering down at her. "I have not laid eyes on you since you were but nine!"

"And what I see does not please."

"For the love of Saint Bridget, why do you not simply say it all and be done with it!"

"You deny that you are Irish with every word." He frowned.

"You speak in their tongue, dress in their ways," she said in Gaelic. *"You* command an army who has done naught but kill by the order of an English king who can't remain in his own country long enough to keep it. A man who has not set one foot in his kingdom except to take his crown afore hieing his grand self to the east to conquer in the name of his *God.* "She inhaled slowly, forcing her temper and tone down into calm.

"Why would you follow such a man and, Goddess forbid, kill for him?"

Connal held her gaze with his own, the uncertain question in her voice stinging him with the tiny plea to understand. She would not. No one would. For he would never reveal why he fought so hard for Richard. Never reveal to her the truth of his life.

"My reasons are my own and not your concern."

Sinead's brows knitted softly and she wondered at the emotion passing over his features just then, before he closed her out. "Your knighthood has become your badge, but 'tis the only one I see you wear. And it has made you the unwelcomed son in your own land."

He looked away, and a muscle in his throat worked as he swallowed repeatedly. Sinead felt his agony and experienced a bruising to her soul, a shadow she dared not examine. There is darkness in him, she realized. "You hurt more than the people by returning."

He turned his head, scowling defense branding his handsome face. "I have hurt no one." *Except you,* his conscience shouted.

She stepped back, giving him a thorough glance up and down. She had made mistakes in her past, but clearly he was not willing to admit to his own. "The trail is here and you will find it, PenDragon," she said cryptically. "Or it will find you."

His brows furrowed as he gazed down at her. Something was very wrong. The bitterness in her tone was unmistakable. This was not the Sinead he remembered. As a youth, she'd been carefree and wild and cared naught for what tomorrow would bring. 'Twas one thing—likely the only thing he'd admired about her. That she lived for the day and that day alone. Aye, she was a woman full grown now, but what had occurred these past years to banish that enthusiasm for life?

"I will not spend my life with a man who can so easily turn his back on his countrymen."

"Again you speak of falsehoods."

"Do I now?" she asked and stepped back, closed her eyes, and raised her arms.

God above, she was conjuring again. "Sinead," he warned, "do not do this."

"Frightened, warrior?" she goaded yet kept her eyes closed, her hands out, her palms up.

Connal wanted to grab her and shake her, make her stop, his anger brewing stronger as her power hummed on the air. Yet he could not tear his gaze from her as the space between her hands shivered and sparkled. He blinked, curiosity keeping him rooted to the floor. His attention slipped to her face, the serenity in her features, the beautiful fall of her red hair. Something wove over her, through her, when she cast. A peace he could see and a wish he could touch it. Earth, wind, fire, and water bent to her will, but Sinead herself, he realized with stunning clarity, was an element of nature.

How did a man not feel inferior to such a woman?

The air undulated, glittering with a silver light, and Connal blinked, lowering his gaze as a silver sword appeared, lying across her palms.

His eyes flared.

Oh God above.

'Twas the sword King Henry had presented him the day he was knighted. A duplicate of DeClare's, yet while Raymond's hilt was studded with gems, this one bore Celtic knots, the design weaving over the hilt and up the blade a bit. The top third was serrated like Raymond's, yet in the center of the cross guard was a dragon with green jeweled eyes.

He lifted his gaze to hers. "Where did you get that?" he asked softly.

"Exactly where you suspect, PenDragon."

Sorrow colored her tone, and Connal searched his memory. Nay. She hadn't been there when he'd thrown it down at his father's feet. When he and Raymond had tried to convince him not to leave Ireland to become a mercenary after Henry's death. He'd learned more than of the death of his king that day. He'd learned secrets and lies from the people he'd trusted the most. And that a once favored knight of Henry—was meaningless, scorned in the next royal court.

"Nay, Sinead. 'Twas in England. You were not there."

She shrugged as if it did not matter. "Yet I carried it on the beach this day."

He did not wonder why he did not recognize the blade afore. 'Twas *her* he saw on the shore, and naught else.

Sinead lifted the weapon, its sharp edge gleaming in the candlelight.

Connal made no move toward it.

"Tell me now that you have not given your back to your heritage. You have discarded Ireland as easily as you discarded this." She started to bring it to her side and he stopped her.

"Why have you kept it?" The words wrenched from his throat.

"If you do not know, then you do not deserve it." He reached, and Sinead stepped back. " 'Tis mine for the keeping, PenDragon."

"What use is a weapon to you?"

"This belonged to a prince, and I see he is dead."

"Aye, the prince is no more, but the man lives and will be your husband."

"Nay! The man I see afore me is a traitor to his people."

Instantly heat rose through his body, rage pulling at his chest. His fingers curled into tight fists.

His knuckles cracked, one at a time, in the silence.

His look was murderous, and fear danced in pinpricks over her skin.

"Dare you speak to me thusly!" he shouted, advancing a step. "I have killed men for less of a lie!"

"I speak the truth. You war on your own people!"

"I have done no such thing!"

In the face of his rage, she calmly arched a brow and gave him a caustic look. "Did you not serve DeLacy at Roscomon, against King Rory O'Connor?"

Connal felt himself go pale. 'Twas his forty days owed. His first battle.

"You slew your brethren, PenDragon. For King Henry. And now you come here to do his son's bidding and take more of Ireland from Irish hands."

"Ireland is ruled by England, Sinead. Conquered! Accept this and you will live longer!"

"Do not threaten me, PenDragon."

His scowl turned thunderous. "I make no threats to you, only the truth. Richard has spoken and 'twill be done!"

"Not as long as I am mistress of the Nine Gleanns. Go back to your mighty Crusades, back to your king's side, and fight his *holy* wars. You made your choice years ago. Ireland does not need you."

Connal felt as if she'd just sliced into his heart, and he bled inside, refusing to let her see how deep the cut sank. She was a stubborn, righteous female, and he was already weary of this argument. He pushed his fingers through his hair, muttering a curse, seeking calm in a sea of magical turmoil. "By God, Sinead, why do you fight this?"

"I cannot wed a man I do not respect."

Connal's head snapped up, his gaze locking with hers as he lowered his hand.

Her words struck like a fatal blow, and he did not think she could wound him more. Nor did he understand why her words scored his heart so deeply, but they did. And the cut of them spilled in his acrid tone. "I do not want a wild witch for a wife either, but I *will* be your husband," he said with a finality that scared her. "And I do not have to earn your respect."

She tipped her chin, her blue eyes cool and hard. The sight unnerved him.

"Nay, Connal O'Rourke of PenDragon. You do not." Her voice wavered, and Connal's insides shifted with a strange pain. "But if you wish a marriage with me for the sake of your king's word"—she lifted the sword, holding the blade point down, the hilt gripped between her palms and at her breasts—"then you must earn back my heart."

She tipped her head down and vanished.

Connal stared at the empty solar, a wisp of red smoke left behind as he stood there, helpless and seething with outrage. By the gods, in the course of moments she'd delivered more insults and degradation than he'd experienced in the past dozen years.

Slew your brethren. Ireland does not need you. A traitor. To your own people. A man she could not respect, he thought, plowing both hands into his hair and gripping the back of his neck. His heart pounded in his chest, anger pushing against his need to throttle her. He'd killed for less of an insult, and aye, he'd committed actions in his life that gave him no pride. Witnessed more that tore his insides to shreds and still left him to bleed. But he'd suffered the consequences.

Yet he'd suffer more now for a handful of Ireland to call his own.

He lowered his hands, forcing his hostility under control. He was a traitor to no one, but that the words came from Sinead, from a woman who was the very heart and soul of Ireland's magic, burned through him stronger than he'd thought possible. She thought him villainous, without conscience or respect for his past deeds, and in the silence of his mind he admitted that his future bride could have accused him of no greater crime against Ireland.

It gnawed at his belly, his pride. His honor.

'Twas something he could not accept.

Or forgive.

Connal strode to the door and flung it open, his gaze going to where the earl stood with his wife near the hearth. He moved to them.

Fionna looked past him to the solar. "Where is she?"

"Gone."

"Vanished?" At Connal's nod, she asked in a low voice, "What did you say to her?"

"The truth. We are to be wed and naught will change that."

Fionna groaned and looked accusingly at her husband. "Great Goddess, does knighthood *breed* insensitivity and callousness?" As Raymond scrambled for a suitable defense, her gaze shot to Connal. "What else?"

"Forgive me, my lady, but 'tis best kept atween us."

"Then you should keep your voices down," Galeron said from somewhere behind him. Connal glanced over his shoulder, his gaze sharpening on the man before he turned back to the earl.

"My lord," Connal began, trying to keep his voice pleasant, "why give a woman the robe of authority?"

Raymond arched a brow at being questioned.

"Why not a man?"

Fionna stiffened, her gaze sharpening on Connal. "Why, indeed? Women," she said tightly, "are less apt to go warring. There has been peace here since Sinead was handed the reins."

"With magic, I am not surprised."

Fionna's eyes widened. "Then be surprised again, PenDragon. For magic had little to do with peace. Free will is not an element to manipulate!"

Connal realized his error and bowed slightly to Her Grace, thankful the noise of the hall and preparation for the evening meal drowned out their conversation. "Forgive me, my lady, I did not mean to offend."

Her nod spoke her forgiveness. "You hold old hurts close when there are new ones folding over them, Connal."

Connal sighed and rubbed his forehead. Splendid, he thought. Infuriate another witch, and the earl, and Sinead, he thought, wondering how he lost control. Then he knew—Sinead and her insults and slurs. And when he'd sworn not to let her affect him, he realized 'twas impossible. The woman plucked at his nerves as if they were strings of a harp. He was already sore from the music.

"I need to speak with her, now."

Fionna caught his elbow before he could take a step. "Why do you want to?"

"We must resolve this. You know as you did when

Raymond was ordered to take an Irish bride. I must, *we* must obey."

"Aye, I understand that, but feel you aught for her?"

He chuckled, and the sound surprised him. "Naught that I would call tender."

Fionna's features sharpened, her gaze suspicious. Raymond folded his arms over his chest and regarded him.

"I would never harm her, you must know that. We have begun badly." 'Twas a mild assessment of their new beginning, he thought, looking around the great hall. *We ended badly too,* he thought, and an old image came to him; a young Sinead shouting encouragement down at him whilst he'd trained. She'd made it harder for him to concentrate, harder for him to keep his friends with the teasing he garnered because of her attention. He could recall each and every fistfight she'd caused. He'd been forced to work thrice times harder as any squire to prove he'd not gained favoritism.

He'd *had* to push her away. She was a girl and he was trying to be a man, to earn the right of knighthood he'd coveted since he was a lad. He'd been cruel and heartless, he knew, but he could not live the life he wanted with a child at his heels. He did not regret it then and would not start now, he told himself, and yet the day he'd put an end to her pestering was the last time she'd spoken to him.

DeClare leaned close and murmured, "In whatever you decide, be careful of my daughter's heart, Connal. She is strong and willful, but she is as vulnerable as any woman. Probably more so."

Connal doubted that, for aught could penetrate that thick skull of hers, least of all reason and logic. "She is also more powerful than any other woman, my lord."

Raymond nodded sagely "As the king had ordered

me to take an Irish bride, I chose the woman of my heart." Briefly, he smiled down at Fionna. "I have given this same power to Sinead." Connal's shock slapped across his face. "With good reason. For when I—"

"Raymond, nay," Fionna interrupted, gripping his arm.

He looked at his wife and leaned near to press a kiss to her temple. "I trust him," he whispered. "And only because the king has ordered this marriage contract does he have the right to know."

Connal frowned between the couple, a sense of dread rising up his spine. Guilt was firmly painted across Fionna's features. A guilt that bore deep hurt and regret.

Fionna shook her head, her voice breaking a little. " 'Tis private, love, do not."

Raymond nodded and looked at Connal for a long moment before he said, "When I chose for her, I chose badly."

Connal's features tightened. She'd been betrothed? To whom? Did she love this man? And why was she not wed now? 'Twas clear by Fionna's closed expression that she was not pleased Raymond had said this much, and whilst curious of the circumstances that ended the betrothal, he recognized that something close to jealousy was working beneath his skin.

Raymond inched forward and said, "I say this only that you understand that if she chooses not to marry you, then I will send her away to safety and face the king's consequences myself."

She would not allow it. Connal knew without asking, without discussion. As she'd done many times before, she would stand her ground and suffer the end result herself. He could not let that happen. 'Twould mean the king would not have his alliance, 'twould mean her death for defying him—or her father's for allowing it. And 'twould mean the worst failure to Connal.

Suddenly Galeron appeared at his side, begging their pardon for interrupting, and Connal twisted. The man gestured, and before he looked, he noticed his knights staring upward in complete rapture.

Connal's gaze swept to the curved staircase, then he turned fully.

His heart took a sharp dip, with awe and pride. And his breath left in a sharp gust.

"In all your days, with all we have seen these past years," Galeron whispered close to his ear, "have you ever witnessed the like such as that?"

Connal could only shake his head as Sinead descended, a regal beauty in poise and grace. 'Twas hard to believe this was the same fiery creature hurling insults at him earlier. She exuded power and confidence. Her body clad in a gown of a deep rich blue, she looked every bit the chieftain. For slung across her body from shoulder to opposite hip was not only the stripe of her O'Donnel tartan, but those of nearly a dozen more clans.

Her loyalty spread across her body in blues, greens, yellows, and red plaids.

Richard, he thought, *look what you have sent me to fight.* For winning her would be harder than winning earls and Irish kings.

Then across the expanse of the hall her gaze locked with his. She hesitated on the last steps, and a tender look passed over her beautiful features.

'Twas a surprise, full of infinite pleasure, and enough to send a bolt straight into his heart.

And Connal knew, without a doubt, he would fight this woman. Fight to possess her. Fight for the piece of Ireland she would bring him. But never, he thought, give up his heart to her.

Chapter Five

Sinead's breath caught for an endless moment.

Connal stared with such utter possession she felt stripped and bared to him. As if he could see beneath her gown and know she was flushed with the heat of desire. Trapped in his gaze, she could not move. Unaware of the others staring between them, or the exchange between her parents. She only saw this man.

This Irish knight who'd come to lay his claim to her.

Nay, came through her mind with saddening clarity. To claim her lands and people. Not her. 'Twas never about wanting her. 'Twas the armies the king wanted, the joining of two houses, and Connal was ready to sacrifice himself to do it. And she was the altar.

But oh, Great Mother, 'twas not fair he be so handsome. Hardheaded. Arrogant. She looked upon him not as a lad newly knighted but as a man, scarred and seasoned with battle, and in the lines of his face saw how he'd aged. In ways she could not begin to fathom, and silently she insisted she did not want to learn of the death he'd seen and wrought.

The thought of Connal battling for duty and not for purpose broke her heart.

She took the last step, yet as Connal moved toward her, his approach was cut off by his knights crowding about her. She smiled as they introduced themselves. A few were quite pleasant, yet just as many held themselves back and spared her the briefest courtesy. So, she thought, a line had been drawn atween Connal's men in this.

He will blame me for that, she thought as her gaze caught on the oddest-looking man standing off to the right. His face was startling, and when he saw her crowded by knights, the turbaned man pushed between the mass and stepped close. The others parted slowly, and she wondered if 'twas his size or fear that allowed it. He was an impressive sight. Tall and massive across the chest and arms, he wore his clothing for decoration and not warmth. His shirt was bright yellow silk shot with embroidery at the neck and cuffs, and about his legs were yards of black fabric, draped and tucked beneath a wide belt strewn with weapons. Though none carried a sword inside the hall, he did, a long curving thing fashioned inside a sling on his back. Sinead craned her neck to meet his gaze, high up as it was. His stare was black as midnight and intense. And the way he looked her over, she half expected him to open her mouth and inspect her teeth.

"She is a beauty of untold words, Sajin."

Sinead glanced to find Connal strolling near, sipping from a goblet. He was more devastating to her senses up close, fie on the man.

His lips quirked, his gaze sweeping over Sinead, and she felt possessed again. "Aye. Sinead, this is Nahjar."

She tested his name. "Nah-jar. You were a slave of the Turks, aye? But also a Moor?" He nodded and she reached, running her fingers over the black markings on his face. "Why did you do this?"

"Am I not fearsome?"

She tilted her head, considering that. "You look like a peregrine, a falcon." She ran her fingertip down to his cheek. " 'Tis beautiful."

Nahjar's expression filled with shock and contrition. "You do not fear me?"

"Have I reason to?"

He thought for a moment. "Nay, you are Sajin's woman. I will protect you with my life, as I do him."

She glanced at Connal and their gazes clashed. Connal had proven well he needed no one and naught but his fealty to Richard. She looked back at Nahjar. "Protect him? Well, 'tis good then. You have to get him back to his king in one piece or all this oath signing will be for naught, aye?"

Nahjar smiled, the look almost evil. Sinead returned it, then glanced at the table being prepared before bringing her gaze back to Connal. He was staring at her oddly, curiously. "You have aught to say to me, PenDragon?"

Connal just noticed she'd yet to call him by name. "Aye." Alone, he would ask her about her failed betrothal and the why of it. Then he leaned closer, his tall presence and broad shoulders smothering out anyone nearby as he said, "With you, there is always more to say."

Nahjar discreetly backed away.

"Should you not be about gathering these noble oaths

for Richard? On the morrow mayhaps?'' She smiled with false innocence.

Such sass, he thought. "Ready to toss me out on my ear, are you?''

Her gaze drew an imaginary path from head to foot and back. " 'Tis doubting I am, that you could be tossed anywhere.''

"Not even with magic?'' he could not help goad.

She shook her head. "Have you been gone so long you have forgotten the rules, PenDragon?''

"I am aware of them, yet that did not stop you once, did it?''

"You harp on a prank a child played years ago?''

"I have long since forgiven your attempt to turn me into a . . . goat.''

His skin reddened a bit and she did not enjoy it. "I was wrong then, and I know the change hurt you. Mother took my magic from me that very day.''

His brows rose with his shock.

She fingered the chain of silver on her wrist. "I regained it only five years ago.''

He eyed her. "But all those times when you were trailing me?''

A humiliated look passed over her features and sharpened her tone. "Think back," she said, her voice low as she glanced about to see if anyone was listening. "Did I conjure when you shouted at me afore the entire castle? When you pushed me out of the stable and said I was just a spoiled whelp, that I meant naught to you and never would, did I cast on you?''

Her old hurt spun like sharp ice, slicing him. "I was a boy, Sinead.''

"A man, ten and six summers, about to be knighted.''

He nodded at the truth. "I cannot take them back but . . . forgive the words of a thoughtless lad."

Her shoulders went back and she waved it off. "Think no more on it. Long ago I accepted I was naught more than a thorn in your side." *As I have now,* she thought. "But I have made misjudgments afore and imagine I will again."

Her exhausted tone, the deadness of it caught him in the chest, and Connal wondered at his part in it. Sinead moved away. He blocked her path. "We have settled our past, Sinead, yet I will not leave until the present is made right."

"You cannot make it so. So I suggest you depart for more important matters."

"When I do, I expect you to wait for me."

He's grown arrogant as well as simpleminded, she thought wryly. "I am not leaving Ireland; I belong here. 'Tis my people here, PenDragon, nor would I be idle when they need my help." She scanned the crowd, knowing each person by name and family. 'Twas her destiny to see her clans never wanted, that they never feared for their homes. She looked at him with brittle eyes. "And if I were inclined to wed, which I am not, I would marry for the speakings of my heart and not for your king's alliances."

"A love match has little to do with marriage."

The muscles in her chest squeezed down on her heart, smothering her. *He has no hope of love,* she thought and realized more than in his manner and his fealty to a faraway king had changed. What had darkened his heart so deeply that he would want this marriage only to please his king? Such loyalty was twisted afoul, and the loss infuriated her. For there was no need of it.

" 'Tis everything to me, knight."

Her obstinance clawed at Connal, threatening to unearth his anger again. She wanted love and ballads; he needed only the signed document for his king. Yet at his silence, her expression fell into such misery, Connal again wondered if this man she'd given her hand to still possessed her heart. "You love another?" The words moved past his lips afore he could stop them.

He held his breath, not knowing why or what he would do if she said aye.

The question surprised her. Love another? Did he think 'twas so easy to give away her heart? That there were hundreds to choose from? She was the strongest of her kind, and with that came consequences. Loneliness, scorn, to be hunted only for the power of her magic. Hated for it. And a broken heart when she trusted it to the wrong man's care, she thought, then flinched at the memory. She kept it close as a reminder, for she'd a greater responsibility than to herself. Magic, her every power, existed within perfect love and perfect trust. 'Twas the very soul of who she was. And within the only realm she could wield. Or she would die.

"Nay," she finally said, releasing a soft sigh, then looked at him. "There is no one."

But there had been, Connal thought, for the sharp agony in her eyes spoke of deep wounds. And he felt them, not knowing from whence they came, yet he *had* felt the cuts to her soul that had not healed. The sensation of it surprised him and he looked away, uncomfortable. To care too deeply, he'd learned, made him vulnerable. He could not afford such a luxury. Death usually followed.

"Good," he said, looking out over the castle folk, his voice brisk. "I did not want to have to fight another man for you."

"Goddess forbid."

Only his gaze shifted to hers, pinning her. "Make no mistake, Sinead, I will."

Unexpected tenderness welled inside her, only to crash as he said, "You are mine."

Her shoulders went back. "I am no man's possession."

"Many wish to possess you, or kill you for what you are."

"I am what I am for them." She gestured to the people. "For the land. I've little use for magic to better my life, yet 'tis part of me, my heart, my blood, my soul." She stared up at him, wishing he could understand and wondering where the boy who once did had gone to die. "And *men* wish to possess my gifts, but not the woman. I am well versed in the dangers, PenDragon."

"Use my name, for God's sake."

"Connal was a boy I once loved. PenDragon is a man I do not care to know."

He flinched as if she'd slapped him yet kept his gaze even. "You *will* know me, Sinead. Well." He inched close enough that his leg brushed hers. "As a wife knows her husband."

'Twas his expression, almost predatory, that sent prickles of heat spiraling down her arms. "We are not destined, knight. In our youth, we shared hurt and anger; now 'tis replaced with a fresh divide you have brought us with your English thinking. I see no benefit from this to Ireland. Or to me."

She moved around him and went to see to the preparations.

The scent of roses and spice left in her wake, Connal watched her, thoughts and feelings colliding upon one another. His curiosity rode him so hard that he wanted to drag her into privacy right now and demand she tell him about this man she was to wed. Willingly. And yet a whispered voice told him Sinead would offer naught. Naught but insults, he reminded, his anger over her accusations rising above all else.

He gripped the goblet, his gaze following her as she instructed her clansmen. And it struck him briefly that even in her elegance, she did not look out of place with the servants, that she teased them, praised them, yet was not above lending a hand. As she was now, crouched on the floor to release a table leg caught in the stone. God above, she was a walking contradiction of womanhood.

Nahjar approached. "You are a most fortunate man, Sajin."

Connal let out a long-suffering sigh, wondering over the fortunes of being the only man in King Richard's service who would marry a witch for his liege.

"She has fire and heart."

"Of that I have no doubt." Connal finished off his wine and briefly wondered if she'd bring that excitement to their bed.

"Do not let your anger color your judgment, Sajin."

Lowering the goblet, Connal looked at Nahjar. He'd always taken Nahjar's intuitions to heart, for rarely had he been wrong. "I am not."

Nahjar folded his arms over his chest and scoffed. The not-so-subtle sound told Connal he was fooling no one. Not even himself. For when he looked at Sinead, much more than anger clouded his opinion.

Sir Galeron was captivated. Completely. By the castle, the beauty of the land, and the woman who ruled them.

Accepting that Lady Sinead was lord here was easy for Galeron. His grandmother was a Scot, and she'd ruled her clan till her death, with an iron fist and a heavy dose of humor. And he found a great deal humorous about the present situation. Especially in the way Connal kept staring at Lady Sinead, though he did not want to be caught looking. And what man here could take his eyes off her? She was exquisite, the light dusting of freckles across her nose intriguing him, and if she were not entangled with the king's order, he would have sought her hand the instant he clapped eyes on her.

'Twould have been a false hope, that, for Connal possessed her attention. And she did not like it, he could tell. She'd look at the man, then shake her head over the fact that she had bothered. Yet after hearing a bit of the conversation the two had in the solar, Galeron decided there was more atween these two than either suspected. And he was enjoying the bloody hell out of Connal's discomfort.

'Twas as if he was seeking flaws in her where there were none to be found. Even in the celebration of his return, she'd left no pleasure unanswered. By God, in the embrace of an Irish winter they had dined this night like kings. Mutton, venison, seasoned quail eggs, cream-filled comfits, and a splendid array of exotic dried fruits from the east from Connal's stores had graced the castle table. The platters were heaping, wine flowed, and amid the peal of laughter, music breezed over the festivities like a gentle cloud. It had been a long time since any of them had been treated so well, yet it did little to lighten Connal's entangled mood.

But then, PenDragon had a reputation for not giving an inch of battleground. And the cause of his suffering was perched on the edge of a chair, hanging on his every word. Galeron let the monopoly of her go on longer than he should have, he knew, but 'twas simply too amusing to see Connal lose his control to a woman. Especially when months of torture had not done so.

He glanced at his comrade and shrugged, then turned his attention to the Lady Sinead.

"Connal," Branor whispered close to his left. " 'Tis bad enough that Nahjar strikes fear in these folk, but if you continue to glare at her, I seriously believe the earl will take offense."

Connal schooled his features and wished he could hear. She was ignoring him, blatantly. Her head tipped close as Galeron murmured into her ear to be heard above the carousing in the hall. As her hand caught her hair back, he watched her expression grow from anticipation to a slow smile as Galeron spoke. Then she laughed delicately, as if she had not shredded his honor in the solar that afternoon, as if she had not called him traitor and told him to leave his homeland. It ground down on his pride and could not help the heat of impotent anger seething through him.

Branor cleared his throat as another reminder, and Connal sought a needed distraction. He took a step back, leaning his shoulder on the mantel and watching her people celebrate with his. Beneath the glow of a hundred candles, the castle walls were alive with color, warmed with tapestries and banners of cloth draping the ceilings. Children lounged on a rug left of the hearth as two older boys played a game of chess. A few inches from Connal, a black cat lay perched on the mantel, its tail swinging slowly, its green eyes shifting. The elegant creature turned its head, its disdainful stare pinning him. Connal shook his head, looking at the crowd.

Croí an Banríon was a gem tucked in the mists. With

its west wall to the sea and its position on the hill, the castle was impenetrable. From the parapet he could walk the entire perimeter and see for a hundred leagues. Straight-walled, with three levels aboveground, the ancient stones were the heart of its construction, the rock base aged and weathered. The masons had rebuilt it in nearly the same fashion as it was five hundred years before, with corridors and stairs leading up and down from the main level and four towers facing the four elements. The hearth was fire, faced to the south, the north to the land, the earth, west to the water, the sea, and east to the moors, where the icy wind skated across the rocky earth and slammed into the tallest wall.

'Twas a castle built on magical lands, for a sorceress of the greatest power.

"PenDragon?"

Connal looked up and met her gaze. He loathed that she smiled so sweetly.

"Galeron tells me you were wounded?"

"More than once," the knight said, and Connal shot him a quelling look.

"Aye."

"When and how?"

Connal frowned. Her concern seemed more like eager curiosity. "I was in battle." He shrugged. "Wounds are the risk."

"But where did you take the wound?" Her gaze slid over him, and Connal experienced a sudden hard rush in his veins.

"In my leg," he said, and her features dropped briefly with disappointment. "Would you rather it be my heart?"

"Be it you who would ask such a thing," she scoffed. " 'Twas mere curiosity."

There is more to this, he thought. "Soon, lass, I will show you each one," he said softly, and his voice caressed the distance between them.

Sinead flushed with embarrassment at his meaning. "I'd prefer that you did not, my lord. You wear them well enough on the outside."

He scowled at that.

"My lady," Branor jumped in, "do you not fear attack here? You are far from GleannTaise and without an army."

She was taken aback. "I beg to differ, Sir Branor. Though not as strong in numbers as PenDragon's, 'tis sizable and well trained."

"Who leads? You?"

She shook her head, giving him a patient smile. "Monroe." She gestured, and the tall dark-haired man moved to her side. "This is the captain of the guard, PenDragon. Words of combat are his familiar talk."

Monroe looked down at her, the corner of his mouth jerking shortly. "My lady's safety is my duty now."

"And I know I make it difficult, Monroe." She rose and touched his arm. "You have been a rather good sport about it all."

Connal's gaze flicked between the pair. Monroe was an Irishman, with massive shoulders, and though his hair needed shearing, 'twas easy to see the friendship Sinead bore him.

"You have made me a patient man."

"Tolerant, would you not add?"

He grinned.

Connal frowned.

"War is an inevitability, my lady," Branor said.

She looked at the black-haired knight, and in a voice strong and clear and filled with conviction, she said,

"Not in the gleanns. Not if I can stop it." Her gaze fell on Connal, and she said, "I will leave you to your tankards."

Connal nodded, saying naught as his men begged her to remain a little longer.

"Nay, nay, enjoy the comforts here," she said as she moved away, tossing over her shoulder, "I have other duties, you know. The Fey Sidhe to tend, brownies to root out. Stars to make," she said, waving elegantly toward the sky

"Sinead," Connal said in warning, and could not help but smile at his men, Branor especially, gaping in confusion, not knowing if she was teasing or nay.

She paused and twisted, her blue gown wrapping her body as she looked back over her shoulder. Her gaze went immediately to Connal's. Her expression made no excuse, but 'twas her smile, he thought, that came from the depths of her.

And the impact of it nearly knocked him to the rushes.

His attention remained riveted to her as she took the stairs, till she disappeared around the curve of the wall. Connal knew she slept in the uppermost tower, close to the stars, and the image of her in her bed would keep him awake half the night.

Sinead watched like a helpless child as the sword pierced his side and drove deep. Blood seeped from the wound as he pulled the sword out, tossing it aside before he fell to his knees, then to the ground. Where was his armor? Where were his men? His hand clasped over the gaping wound, blood flowed swiftly over his fingers and soaked the ground. His moan of agony cut her in two, bitten off by pride. He reached for someone, tried to rise, and she heard her name whispered on his lips. Then he fell back, his final breath rattling his chest till 'twas empty and hollow.

Sinead sat upright in her bed, the last of her scream echoing in the stone chamber. *Connal!*

She covered her face with her hands and took slow, deep breaths. Nay. Not again. She trembled down to her toes and swallowed, catching her breath and the heart that was lodged in her throat. She sniffled and swiped at the tears on her cheeks, angrily shoving her hair back over her shoulders.

Perspiration glistened on her skin and she tossed back the blankets and furs. 'Twas little relief and she left the bed. Her hand trembled as she reached for her robe. Tying the sash, she grabbed a velvet blanket, throwing it over her shoulders. She paced.

For all her power she could not stop the dreams. The day her magic returned to her, they had begun again and the blissful years of innocence were long gone. Dreams of peril woke her often, dreams of happy events and coming storms. She never ignored them. They always came true.

"My lady?"

Sinead tipped her head and looked around the drape hanging from the bedpost. "Come closer, Kiarae. I am fine."

The faery fluttered a tiny bit around the heavy cloth and peered. "You screamed."

Sinead's eyes widened. "Did I wake anyone below?"

Kiarae shook her head, then came to settle on the coverlet. "You should tell."

"Nay, do not ask that. 'Tis toying with fate and destiny to know what is to come." She shook her head. The dreams ruled her when they came, and she had learned that she could only offer warnings, for the trouble she saw was never clear and precise.

But this time 'twas Connal. And he'd died. Somehow she felt 'twas her fault, her doing. Great Goddess, she was only thankful she did not see him in her dreams whilst he battled in the east. She'd have never slept for the past years. But she'd known he was coming here the instant he stepped on Irish soil. For this one vision had begun in earnest, and the goddess was telling her to be careful. To mayhaps do something to stop this prophecy.

He would never believe her. None but her parents had known of the dreams. She'd experienced few before her magic was bound and was too young to grasp what they meant. She could hardly recall them now. Yet after her mother took her magic, one final vision came, faint and disjointed. She had not understood any of it then. But her father had, and it had saved Sinead's life.

What could she do for Connal? He would take the warnings in bitterness, she thought, and discard them. As he had his armor.

The dream flashed in her mind, his features still with death, blood pooling on the ground. Suddenly she wrapped the velvet blanket tightly about her shoulders and moved to the door.

"My lady? There are many men in the castle this night."

"They will not see me," she said and left the chamber, chanting a concealing spell as she quickly took the staircase to the parapet, her bare feet slapping the frozen stone. But the sensation of helplessness beat at her soul, overwhelmed her, and she burst through the door, rushing to the wall and gripping the stone ledge. She inhaled deeply, the icy wind bruising her face and making her eyes sting. It did naught to banish the dream.

It came again and again, with horrifying clarity, as if demanding she see what was not there. Tears choked her throat and she bowed her head, fighting back a scream and trying to empty her mind to the call.

The wind whipped her hair free, snapping it like cloth.

Nay. *Nay.* He cannot die. He cannot, she pleaded.

"Sinead?"

She whipped around, gripping the blanket. From the darkness, Connal emerged like a dragon from its blackened cave. He stopped, his gaze raking over her.

"By God, woman, you think to freeze to death to avoid marriage to me."

She shook her head, unable to push words past her throat.

His gaze fell to her bare feet. In a stride he was inches from her, sweeping his cloak from his shoulders and onto hers.

Then he lifted her in his arms and headed toward the stairs.

Chapter Six

"Nay! I do not want to go below."

He did not break stride. "You will."

"Put me down," she said, and the fracture in her voice made him stop. She tipped her head back and moonlight shone down upon her tearstained face. His scowl softened and he moved to the far wall and crouched, setting her on the stone.

Hurriedly he wrapped her bare feet in his cloak. "Minutes, Sinead, that is all I will allow of this."

"You are not my keeper, PenDragon."

"Well then, you need one, woman. God, this is absurd."

At least the corridor of stone flanked them, breaking the pounding of the wind. Guards were a few yards away, warming themselves at the pot fires, and paid them no mind as he rested his back against the wall, his elbows braced on bent knees.

She shivered and snuggled into the velvet, wondering why her concealing spell had failed. Obviously, she decided a moment later, she'd not been concentrating enough.

"This is ludicrous."

"You were up here," she accused, staring at the spot near her toes.

"Only to inspect the fortifications."

She made a disgruntled sound. "Oh, aye, do not trust that we have not been breached in centuries, eh?"

" 'Twas a precaution, not an affront to you."

"You not only distrust me but those loyal to me."

"I have not been here long enough to pass judgment."

Her gaze snapped to his. "They would die for me, PenDragon, as I would for them."

"Well, you shall accomplish that out here for naught but stubbornness." He chaffed his arms, and she realized he'd been in the East so long he was unaccustomed to the cold. She extended her arm, rotating her hand in a quick curl over the stone near him. Fire appeared.

Connal flinched and cursed, drawing his feet back.

As if scooting a bowl across a table, she pushed the blaze a bit farther his way. Connal gaped at the tongue of fire hovering over the rock for a long moment, then looked at her.

"You have gifts I did not know existed."

"And you hide yours."

"Do not speak of that."

She'd suspected he'd suppressed his ability to sense emotion with animals, and his answer only confirmed it. "Certainly. Shall I add it to the lists of subjects you refuse to discuss?"

"If you like."

She shook her head. "We will gain naught like this, you know."

"I know." Sadness crept into his voice just then. "Why did you come up here at this hour?"

She shrugged.

"For the first time you have naught to say, no insults to fling at me?"

"I have spoken only the truth."

"I am not a traitor," he growled.

She lifted her head and gave him a serene look. "You warred against your own; what does that make you?"

His gaze thinned, looking like glowing green coals in the dark. "A man who followed his duty owed to service."

"You can justify betrayal in the name of duty? I cannot."

Connal raked his cold fingers through his hair, thinking she spoke her feelings loudly and too often; her words came like knife pricks to his skin. "I swear I'd like to tie you to a chair and gag your mouth."

A short laugh escaped her and his gaze jerked to her. "My father has said that often."

"Did he ever do it?"

"He forbade me to speak for a se'night once. I managed one afternoon." She turned her head slowly. "I cannot change who I am."

"Regardless, we must come to an agreement."

"I agree you should be gone and leave me be."

"To what? To be unwed and alone?"

She'd resigned herself to that long ago. " 'Tis preferable to a marriage that is no more than papers signed."

" 'Twould be more than that," he said, his voice husky and taking the chill from night. "And I think you know that already."

She did, Goddess help her. And she did not like it much, either. 'Twas base, this attraction for him, instinctive, and she tried portioning it with old feelings she'd borne him, but 'twas naught like she'd felt for him with a girl's heart. Aye, she thought, this was primal. Almost a savage need. And she knew where that feeling had taken her before.

Slowly she turned her head and looked at him, inspected him, and Connal watched as her gaze swept his shoulders, his arms, then dropped to his hands. She stared for a moment longer, and he wondered what played through her quick mind. Suddenly she stood, a snap of her fingers putting out the fire before she headed to the stairs.

Connal climbed to his feet, watching her move away in a flowing robe of fabric and fur, and warred with the benefits and disadvantages of pursuing this at the late hour. He strode after her and caught her arm. She yanked wildly. "Sinead, listen to me."

"Leave off!" she shouted and he released her, coming away with his fur cloak as she ran to the stairs. He followed. "Stay away!"

She overtook the stairs, torches snapping to flame as she passed.

She entered a chamber and flung the door closed. Connal shoved it open. She turned, her eyes wide.

With terror, he realized, and he stepped no farther. "Sinead."

She shook her head, her hair wild, her expression crazed. By God, he thought, what had gotten into her? She was choking for air. "Let me help you."

Turning her face away, she shook her head and put up her hand, palm out. He waited, his fingers curling into fists as she took several deep breaths.

Then suddenly she looked at him, the tension gone as if whispered away. "Forgive me. I am fine."

He frowned. "You are not. Tell me what ails you so."

" 'Tis unimportant." Her tone refused any prodding, and she moved to the window, throwing it open. The hard gust of air from the moors bolted through the chamber, stirring the drapes on her bed, the tapestries warming the walls.

"Close the window, for God's sake."

She inhaled. " 'Twill be a while afore you are accustomed to the cold," she said.

"But not the smell of fire."

Sinead turned sharply and frowned. He was gone, and she looked out the window but saw and smelled naught but the tang of the sea. She rushed after him, taking the stairs to the parapet again and turning right. She ran toward the north tower.

Gripping the edge of the stone wall, she searched the black horizon.

"Fire." He pointed "There."

The glow flickered against the evergreen trees. Distant, and red. "Oh Goddess above." She grasped his arm. " 'Tis near the English fort."

Instantly he turned back into the staircase. Sinead tipped her head down and vanished, appearing in her chamber. Immediately she threw off the velvet and reached for her clothes.

His cloak clenched in his fist, Connal strode through the castle, banging on doors, not knowing where his men slept and not caring whom he woke. He reached the chamber where he was to have slept and found Galeron dressing. He tossed Connal his sword and armaments.

"And here you thought 'twould be naught but gaining a few signatures, aye, Connal?"

"Wear your armor," came from behind.

He spun and found Sinead fastening her cloak. "You are not joining this," he said.

She slung a leather satchel onto her shoulder as she brushed past him. "You forget, knight, I am chieftain of the gleanns. 'Tis you who must join me." She clapped, torches spitting to life, her voice carrying through the castle, yet she did not shout. Her father appeared in the corridor, pulling on his tunic. "I need you here to see to the safety of the castle, Papa. Monroe will come with me."

Raymond nodded, Fionna at his side and belting her robe. His quick agreement made Connal's step hesitate. *He trusts her,* he thought. The earl's acceptance of his daughter's role chaffed at Connal's duty. She was a woman, and a small one at that.

In the bailey Sinead swung up onto her white mare and ordered the gates opened. Monroe was at her side; nearly twenty vassals assembled behind her whilst squires still hustled horses and arms out of the barns.

"Sinead!"

Connal grabbed his horse by the mane and mounted. As the gate parted, she bolted, leading the way.

The ride was black and treacherous, the darkness and crusted snow making progress slow. Connal rode alongside Sinead and Monroe, yet none spoke. The glow of fire groped through the trees and she looked at Monroe.

" 'Tis east Armagh," she said, and her gaze pinned

Connal. "The village, not the fort," she said. "Remain back. We will approach."

He looked to argue.

"We waste time now, and if English troops did this, you will only frighten them more." She raced ahead.

Monroe looked at Connal, nodded once, then rode after her. Her men followed.

"Damn woman thinks she's invincible," he muttered and followed.

Sinead slid from the mare's back, rushing to the burning house. People were trying to douse the flames with blankets and crack the ice on the frozen well in the hope of water. With the wind, the flames only flared. Sinead threw her arms high, palms up. She called on the elements, her voice loud and demanding, and as she lowered her hands toward the ground, the flames smothered to naught but heavy curls of smoke.

The villagers groaned with relief, some sitting on the ground where they'd stood to catch their breath. She looked at her captain. "We have not had trouble for three years now. I do not understand."

He shook his head, agreeing as he helped a man to his feet. "I will see to the livestock and search for tracks, my lady."

She nodded and walked toward the well.

"Oh, Lady Sinead, thank God." A woman dropped a smoldering blanket, staggering.

"Katherine, sweet stars!" Sinead rushed to the older woman, helping her to the stone bench in the square and blotting blood from her forehead. She checked her for more wounds, then swept off her cloak and wrapped it around the woman. People converged on her, stumbling out of homes and hiding places. Sinead swept a sobbing child into her arms and soothed the lad as she inspected and questioned each for wounds. Then her gaze scanned the people for the mayor. Her heart pounded.

"Dougal! Show yourself!" Please, she prayed.

Her mother's old friend walked forward from the dark, tossing aside the spade, and she hurried to clasp him. He patted her back, coughing up smoke.

"I am unharmed, lass."

"Thanks be to the Goddess," she whispered, then leaned back. "Is anyone badly hurt?"

He glanced around to be certain before saying, "A few bruises and cuts. No one died, thank God." He looked at the smoking cottages and stone houses. "My thanks, my lady. We could not stop it afore it spread."

Sinead only nodded. "What brought this?"

Dougal sighed, looking far older than he should at his age. "The English troops from yon fort." At her frown, he shrugged and said, "They needed food. And we gave it. But 'twas not enough to their liking." His gaze shifted past her and widened. Sinead turned, handing the child over to him.

Connal and his knights stood poised on the rise.

Gradually people grew quiet and still, the men handling their swords or dirks. Children moved behind her and their parents. "Fear not, my friends," Sinead said to ease the terror building around them again.

Connal did not take his gaze off Sinead as he spoke to Branor. "Place the torches about and light this land. Then surround this village, and send Nahjar and Sir Peter to search for the path they took." He glanced at the sky. Dawn would not come for another three hours, he surmised, and they'd accomplish little till then.

He walked his horse slowly closer, gesturing for the others to remain back.

"Who is he?" Dougal asked her, his gaze moving between the knights and the vassals. "They do not wear the tartan like DeClare's knights do." He looked directly at Sinead. "What has happened that you travel with strangers, my lady?"

The distaste in his voice was not lost on her. "Be calm, Dougal. 'Tis Connal PenDragon."

Dougal inhaled sharply. "Well I'll be diggered."

"I could not have said it better."

Dougal eyed her, then the man. "Did I not learn you were to wed him?"

Her spine stiffened. "You were misinformed."

"Aye, my lady."

She looked at Dougal, a man her parents trusted over the years and had made the leader of this town for his loyalty to them. "Not a word, Dougal."

"I would not dream of it, lass."

Connal dismounted, and Dougal pushed his way around his folk. "I never thought to see you again, boy."

Connal smiled and shook his hand. "Dougal, you look well."

"You look like you walked from the gates of hell."

Connal ran his fingers down the side of his face and offered a small smile.

"And brown as bread, too."

"The sun of Cypress and Syria."

"So the stories were true; you warred for Richard."

His brow furrowed. Dougal folded his arms over his chest and stared. Connal's gaze flicked to Sinead. The old man shrugged. "I do not need my lady to speak the words. News travels slowly but well in the gleanns."

"So I have gathered."

They talked softly for a moment, and Connal was aware of the hundred pairs of eyes examining him like a swine at a county fair. A boy moved past, glaring at Connal and the other knights. Connal met the lad's gaze, frowning and wondering what he'd done to earn that hatred. Then the lad spat in his direction before scampering off to join two others his age.

Dougal cursed softly.

Connal's bland expression remained fixed on his face as he focused on Dougal.

"They remember you, my lord," Dougal said. "To them, you became English. Now, now," he said when Connal looked ready to explode, "not that 'tis a bad thing to be. Lord Antrim is a fine one, but he has no excuse for being English. He was born that way." His gaze rode over the breastplate, vambraces, and metal gauntlets. "You were not."

"Am I to be chastised for my garments or my duty?" he said dryly. He did not get a response, nor had he expected one.

Sinead came forward, pulling on her cloak, giving Connal an I-told-you-to-stay-back look before calling to Monroe. The man strode to her side. "Give what stores the men have to these people. And leave five troops here to help repair the damage in the morn. Another five to guard the village." She looked at Dougal and he nodded agreement, thanking her before turning away to his folk.

Sinead watched Dougal rally the people to repair the damage in the morning, then looked at Connal.

" 'Twas the troops from the fort," she said. "For food." He nodded, and she was glad he did not dispute her.

"I will go speak to the marshal." He turned to do just that.

She caught his arm. "This is not your concern."

Connal was not going to argue again that they would be wed and this land would become his responsibility soon. Yet his reasons went deeper. He'd fought the Crusades for strangers. How could he turn his back on these Irishmen and women? "You will not even accept my help?"

"What will you do? Punish them for being hungry?"

"For stealing and ravishing this village, aye."

"Aye, they should be punished, but what will they do to this village if we exact it? Nay. This village and the next provide well for the English soldiers. Myself, I brought a wagonload of food from the castle's winter stores to them only last month. Yet like land mongers, the greedy come and take more!"

She moved toward her horse with angry steps, bent to lift something off the ground, then flung herself onto its back with a practiced agility. *She rides without saddle or reins,* he realized. Monroe mounted, and when she bolted onto the road, he called out to her, then sighed and looked tiredly at PenDragon.

"Marry her, my lord. Quickly."

Connal's brows shot up.

"A man has only so many hairs to turn gray. And I'd prefer them to be yours."

Connal's lips quirked and he raised his fist. Troops and knights gathered behind him and he bolted to the chase.

Within the next half hour, the English troops were assembled like children about to be scolded. 'Twas not

Sinead's doing, but Connal's. Her calls to the guards went unheeded until he'd ridden past her up to the gates, heedless of her warning to mind his own business, of course, and summoned the marshal. The careless "Who the bloody hell do you think you are?" was tossed down at him from the guard tower.

Connal only stated his name.

Quietly, calmly, when she knew he was seething with anger.

Within seconds the door opened, troops filed in a haphazard line, and the marshal, in his nightclothes and a cloak, hurried from the small English fort.

The brigade stood now on the frozen ground. Connal said naught, remaining in the saddle and looking down upon them like bugs needing a good squashing.

Sinead prayed he would not do anything foolish that would come back on her people. Yet she had to admit, he presented a splendid vision of power and strength. In the darkness, lit by tall torches, his breastplate gleamed with the coat of arms of King Richard. Without a helm, he shielded naught from the English troops and made eye contact with each one. His mount pranced, rearing once, its hooves clapping hard on the stone before the steed settled. The marshal flinched and took a step back.

Sinead rode up beside him, Monroe at her side. The marshal's gaze hopped between her and Connal. Pen-Dragon looked at her, inclining his head ever so slightly toward the marshal.

"Marshal Westberry," she said. "Your troops attacked one of the villages and set fire to homes."

"They did no such thing."

Connal shot him a quelling glare. "Do not speak till a question has been put you, Westberry."

Sinead dismounted and walked up to the man, certain to get his attention on her and not on PenDragon. "They did, sir. The people have no reason to lie. The evidence left speaks enough." She thrust an English helmet at him, forcing him to take it. "The trail leads to your door."

The marshal held her gaze, his lips tight. "I did not sanction this!" He tossed the helmet on the ground behind him.

"So you have no control over your troops, then? They can leave the fort and go prey wherever they please? Leaving you undermanned?"

His face turned molten with suppressed anger, and Sinead surmised that he did not unleash it because of the man astride the stallion behind her.

"I thought as much. Now would you tell me why you broke a treaty that has been in effect and untarnished for three years?"

"We had no food."

"You were given supplies by the very villagers you burned."

" 'Twas not enough."

"You should have come to me, then."

"There was little time. My troops are freezing their arses off and hungry now."

"Really?" she said, her gaze dropping meaningfully to the marshal's round belly.

Westberry flushed and tucked his cloak about him, his face pinched and angry.

"And this is the excuse you offer for burning the homes of innocents who have fed you? To rape the village of their winter stores when in three years' time you have done little to provide food for yourselves beyond hunting on my lands!"

"The deer are too sparse to hunt," he said.

'Twas untrue, she thought. They were just lazy. "And yet, have I not provided for your men regardless? What happened to the wagon of goods I brought? 'Twas enough to feed all of you well."

The marshal glanced between her and PenDragon. "They will not eat the food touched by a witch."

Sinead stepped back as if he'd slapped her, and when Connal thought she'd grow angry, she simply nodded.

"Fine. I will not bring it again." The marshal stammered and she put up her hand, silencing him. "But when there is no more, I shall gladly lock you in chains afore allowing your men the opportunity to harm people who have been most generous."

The marshal paled.

"I will not see people die of hunger, no matter how daft your reasons. My other recourse is that you will gain your winter stores in the next county, beyond Armagh. I will send a messenger to the chieftain and ask if he will provide. If not, you have little choice but to accept my hospitality. Because if you raid," she said, and her voice turned deadly, her blue eyes glittering as she took a step closer, "I will see you spared naught but the full measure of the law. English law. *And Brehon.*" She arched a tapered brow. "Do we understand each other, Lord Marshal?"

He stared into her eyes and swallowed his tongue. "Aye, Lady Sinead, we do."

He looked up at PenDragon, but Connal said naught, admiring Sinead's calm and wisdom.

"You will send a squadron of men to the village and repair the damage, at your costs. Dougal will report to me the results. They will make full restitution, Lord

Marshal, and since you condoned the raid, I will hold you personally responsible for their conduct."

"As will I," Connal said from behind her.

Her shoulders stiffened.

Westberry nodded, shivering violently.

"Get you inside out of the cold, man," she said and turned away and mounted her horse. The troops rushed inside the gates, yet as Sinead rode back toward the castle, Connal sidled his horse close and cut off Westberry's retreat.

The marshal looked up at him. "Why are you here, PenDragon? With her?" He glared at Sinead's back.

"My affairs are not privy to you, Westberry. But yours are to me. King Richard has sent me here for just this reason." The marshal paled. "And the lady was too generous. . . ." Connal leaned down till they were nearly face-to-face. "I would have simply gutted you."

The marshal teetered where he stood, his knees faltering. Then suddenly his back stiffened and he sent the knight an affronted glare. "You cannot speak to me like that! 'Tis an open threat to a subject of the crown."

"Is it now? And are not these villagers subjects of the crown?"

Westberry looked to debate, his gaze jerking briefly past him to where Sinead had ridden. "Aye, but you are no more than an Irish prig with royal favor."

Connal moved the mount closer, his voice still as ice. "Your greed sent you here, Westberry, to the outpost of the uncivilized. And this Irish *prig* knows exactly why."

The marshal fell back against the doors of the fort, and whether he trembled from cold or fear, Connal did not know or care.

Yet the marshal's gaze was filled with a feral hatred Connal had seen often. And heeded.

"He forgave."

Connal scoffed rudely as he gave the marshal some breathing room. "He simply forgot about you. I, on the other hand, will not."

He wheeled about, bolting hard after Sinead

Westberry watched him till he was no longer there. Then he smiled, certain he'd done as requested and come away unscathed.

Sinead remained in the village, in Dougal's house, whilst she tended the wounds of her people. As she wrapped a man's burned hand in a thin cloth, she wondered where they'd find the thatch to repair the burned roofs, and the wood for walls. With winter biting the trees, there was little to spare. Finished, she nodded to the fellow and he smiled, thanking her, and left.

Yawning hugely, she corked her bottles, folded cloths, and, after a fashion, simply dropped into the chair and closed her eyes. The fire crackled and popped comfortingly in the hearth, the wind outside barely penetrating the thick stone walls. Dougal snoozed in a padded chair near the blaze, his wife and children warm in their beds. And safe.

Sinead's mind drifted into sleep, the moon sinking as Father Sun rose to greet a new day. And in the straightbacked chair, She slept without dreams, without visions. A loud crack jolted her awake and she sat up, grappling for the tottering bottles and looking at Dougal.

Rubbing his face, he stood, frowning toward the door, then moving to open it. Morning sun spilled into the warm house and Sinead leaned out to see, then left her chair and stepped out the door.

PenDragon knights and troops hauled wood and

stones. She walked the path to the road, searching the lane. She spotted Connal leading his war horse toward the home across the way, the animal struggling to drag the pallet harnessed behind him. 'Twas laden with stone and pieces of wood.

"PenDragon," she called.

He did not look up as he stopped the animal and gave it a pat. " 'Tis too cold to waste a moment, Sinead."

She watched in awe as he lifted a large rock off the pallet and walked—upright, she was not too stunned to notice—to the burned corner of the house. He positioned the stone in the absent wall, then strode back for another, fitting it in neatly. He yanked away the charred wood and filled it with mud and grass, then forced in more stones.

Bareheaded and without his cloak, he'd discarded the armor and gauntlets. His hands were caked with wet earth as he dipped into the bucket for more. He'd torn down the entire two walls and had only a small portion left to replace. Farther down the lane near the well, at the first home they'd found burning, his soldiers worked tirelessly to repair the roof with what little they had. Someone had placed an oiled cloth across the damage, and men were now securing it with pegs and nails, then laying saplings and winter grasses over it. The owners were helping, and talk was congenial.

She looked back at Connal, then walked across the avenue and stopped at his side. "Why?"

He was about to slap more mud into the crevices, yet paused, not looking at her. "These are my people, too, Sinead. And aside from the cold, I do not believe Westberry's men would have done a decent job."

She simply nodded, her throat so tight she had difficulty swallowing. Shame filled her. Who was she to question the depth of his compassion? She'd thought only the worst of him. And to even ask why was an affront to the knighthood he prized so well. He was sworn to protect the weak and downtrodden, and though her folk were neither, this day they needed. She might not accept his part in her life, but he already did.

He pushed mud in, watching his moves. "Nary a comment from you, lady?"

"Forgive me for questioning you," she said, and hoped he did not notice the fault in her voice. "And you have my gratitude, PenDragon."

He shook his head, cramming more in the cracks. "By God, I wish you would cease calling me that."

"Do you not like your name?"

He made a strange sound on a snicker of breath. "It sounds like an insult from your lips."

" 'Tis not meant to be."

He lashed his hand out to the side, throwing off the mud, and stood, facing her. Taking a rag from his belt, he cleaned off his hands, gazing down at her. Though her head was bowed, he could see a smudge of soot on her chin and the breeze tore at her single braided rope of hair. Beneath her leather cloak, she wore an aged gown, its deep rust hue faded to a dull clay. It had made her look like any other maid and less the guardian of the elements. He saw her again facing Westberry. With dignity and grace, and aye, wisdom. Connal would have done much worse. She had the power of magic at her fingertips and could have, without harming, scared the life from the marshal. He understood her control, especially when he'd felt the true pitch of her anger.

She wanted peace and would sacrifice justice to see it done.

"Calling me PenDragon is formal, and distant. We

cannot go beyond, lass, if we keep so much animosity clearly there."

She did not look at him, yet he heard her breath catch when he touched her chin, smoothing the soot. Then he tipped up her face.

Her eyes were closed, and when her lashes swept upward, Connal suddenly had trouble drawing air into his lung. "Sinead?" The anguish in her eyes slayed him, blistering his heart.

"To say your name makes us familiar." It sounded foolish to even her ears. But 'twas so. "And I will admit 'tis difficult when I cannot trust your intentions."

"They are honorable, this I vow."

"But they are not of your heart." Sinead stared up at him, her soul suddenly breaking free to plead for more than duty. "They honor the king's wishes. Not yours, nor mine, and we will be the ones to suffer the consequences."

Connal could not argue but to say, "I know this. But 'tis the way it must be."

"Nay," she said, stepping back, and the gloss of her blue eyes beckoned that she say more. " 'Tis the way it can *not* be."

She turned away, whistling for her horse, and in the center of the street mounted the mare and rode away. Connal's gaze was riveted to her back as she paused by Monroe and spoke. Clearly the warrior did not care for her decision, whatever it was, and Connal tossed down the rag and started for her.

But he heard the sharp command of, "You have my orders," afore she rode toward the path to the castle. Alone.

Monroe looked at him, his gaze accusing him of an unspoken crime before he went to finish the work. Leaving Connal to wonder why she continued to fight this marriage and why hearing his name from Sinead's tart mouth had suddenly become a quest that rivaled that of the Holy Grail.

Chapter Seven

Marshal Easton Westberry listened intently as the soldier gave his report.

"You remained hidden?" The frost on the man's helm spoke of exactly how long he'd spied on the village. "Of course you did." He laughed congenially. "Or Pen-Dragon would have slit you from arse to chin strap." His grin was wide and slow as the soldier's expression went slack, his complexion paling.

"They left five warriors behind to guard the village, lord marshal."

"Relay to all to stay away from that village. Leave them be."

The soldier nodded, eyeing the tankard of wine on the rough table. Westberry cleared his throat then, and the soldier's gaze snapped back to his. He did not offer his personal stores to the troop and both knew he never would.

"We have enough food to last till the bad feelings are soothed. Lady Sinead will make good her promise to provide more, regardless." Aye. She was so willing to assure there was no more trouble rather than seek recompense right now. But she would. He did not doubt that for a moment. She'd adhere to the letter of the law because she was fair and female. But PenDragon, he was another matter altogether.

His law was his sword, and his right as a knight of the realms.

He could do all he'd threatened. Mete out justice as he saw fit in the name of the king.

Richard the Lion Hearted trusted him. With more than anyone thought possible, he knew. 'Twas the reason for the attack. He smirked to himself at that, but the pleased look did not last long. The Irish whelp was not a man to disregard. Though PenDragon had seen to the damage himself, that proved him to be not far from his base upbringing, but also of a gentle heart for the people. And it would be his downfall.

Easton was to do nay more for the time. Delay them in GleannAireamh, and delay the marriage of Lady Sinead and the Irish knight. 'Twas all Prince John wanted. Easton did not care why, really. Stripped of his lands and title, he'd been sent here in punishment, he thought, with a disgusted look at his meager surroundings. And he'd do anything to escape exile for another Irish winter. Even throw himself in with Prince John. Richard deserved to be dethroned for the way he'd treated him. And for what? 'Twas not as if he'd killed anyone. 'Twas just a little thing, keeping that girl in his cellar.

Easton dismissed the soldier. The wind was howling through the open door, and he barked at the man, "Close it and be quick about it!" He leaned toward the

fire, warming his pudgy hands, then inched his toes out
from under his robes and furs toward the blaze.

Godforsaken place, Ireland. Filled with naught but
godless heathens and snow. Suddenly more than cold
prickled his skin, a feeling as if someone laughed behind
him. Slowly, Easton looked back over his shoulder, his
gaze scanning the empty chamber.

Aye, he thought, pulling a knife close. Godless heathens and red-haired witches.

Something had changed between them, Raymond
thought as he secured his bags to the saddle, then moved
to check his wife's mount. Around them, his knights
champed to be off, squires moving quickly to load the
wagon.

"You see this?" Raymond's gaze moved meaningfully
to Connal as he yanked on the straps of his saddlebags.

" 'Tis hard not to notice. And we are not the only
ones," Fionna said, her gaze shifting between the pair.
Sir Galeron and Branor stood behind Connal with the
tall Moor. The foursome had been ever watchful over
the safety of the castle since their return from the village,
though Sinead's vassals were, without question, strong
and vigilant. Yet 'twas the way Connal kept looking at
their daughter that gave her pause. 'Twas not a bad
stare, she thought, but nor was it pleasant either. Regret-
ful? Or was that hope?

Fionna moved closer to her husband. "You think 'tis
wise to leave them like this?"

"They are not children, love, and I trust Sinead and
Connal to find a solution to this atween them."

"You believe, still, that she will accept him?"

Raymond sighed hard, checking tack that did not

need his attention. He touched the pouch containing the unsigned marriage agreement. "I cannot force her, Fionna." He looked at her. "How can we?"

Guilt spirited over her beautiful features, sharp and pricking his heart. Raymond gripped her arms, gazing deep into her eyes. "Listen to me again, love, 'twas not your fault."

"I keep telling myself that, that we could not have known . . . but my memory is good and I cannot banish the sight of her—"

"She is protected," he cut in, not wanting to relive the detail in his mind or in the words. "By her magic." He chanced a look at Connal. "And I trust him to keep her safe as well. If aught, Connal knows his duty." And, he silently added, Connal would not allow his daughter's independence to stop him.

Fionna sighed against him, laying her head to his chest and listening to the reassuring beat of his heart. But the situation was grave and Sinead's refusal would put them between the king and his orders. 'Twas treason, and although she'd hoped Sinead's innocent heart of old would see Connal as the man she'd once loved, Fionna knew 'twas not possible. And 'twas selfish. Sinead had the right to marry for love. 'Twas necessary for her soul, as it was for her magic. Joining with a man she did not love would be her doom.

When she drew back, she found her husband frowning. She waited patiently for him to speak his thoughts.

"She is a noblewoman of marriageable age, and Richard has found a way to use it." His look was rueful. "He has sent Connal to marshal power on his behalf and that includes Sinead." *And what will I do when Richard learns my other daughters are magical as well?* " 'Tis not Richard I worry over, but his brother."

"You do not think either know of her gifts?"

Raymond shook his head, stepping back. "Only that she is ours, Fionna, and beneficial. Yet whilst Richard contents himself with moving the chess pieces of his kingdom from afar, and right now, finding his ransom, should John learn of Sinead's power, he will try to use it as well. This I am certain."

Fionna nodded, trepidation swimming through her veins. *The battle of brothers will touch my children,* she thought, looking briefly at her daughter. Already King Richard had their eldest son in his army. And tithe paid to the king was feeding a war that neither Fionna nor her husband believed in. How long would it be afore Richard developed a new plan for their family?

"I simply wish Sinead would tell us what she wants."

Fionna shrugged, pulling on her gloves. "Mayhaps 'tis only to be loved for other than her magic."

"At least Connal has not run from her because of it."

She looked up, glancing once at her daughter. "He does not trust her not to wield it on him. And she refuses to enlighten the man. You are right, this is her problem to deal with now, Raymond."

"But she is my daughter and heir and I will see her happy, dammit."

Fionna looked at her husband. His expression was fierce, protective. Her heart burst again with love for him. Sinead had been his legal daughter since she was four summers old and he adored her, doing everything in his power to see that she was happy and never felt that she was anything less than his flesh and blood. Though she was not. He trusted Sinead, and that meant everything to him, to her and to their people. The king would never understand the wisdom and patience of magic. But, thankfully, Raymond had.

"Aye, love, and you want to carry her burdens for her. You cannot. Just as I could not allow her to suffer mine when she was young." She kissed him too quickly for his liking and whispered, "Let us be off so they can mend what ails without our watchful eyes."

Fionna turned away and called to Sinead, meeting her halfway and taking the basket of food wrapped in cloth before hugging her tightly.

Raymond watched them, his gaze darting to Connal as he moved forward to say good-bye. He hugged Fionna as well and, when done, stepped back and stood close to Sinead. She glanced up at him, a weak smile tugging at her lips. He returned it, uncertainty spoken without saying a word.

Raymond would not force his daughter to wed a man she did not want, even if he considered Connal the best and only choice of a husband. For the truth was, he'd chosen poorly once afore and distrusted his judgment. But the truth of the matter was, King Richard had the reins of their lives. And even his absence had not stopped him from wielding his power.

Raymond kissed his daughter, spoke his good-byes, then mounted his stallion. He rode out of the gates, his wife at his side, his men filing behind them, unaware that soon he would feel the bite of his monarch's word, where it would hurt him the deepest.

"Westberry deserves punishment," Monroe said. "By Brehon law at least."

Sinead looked up from the meal she was not tasting. Monroe was to her right, Connal to her left, above the salt; Nahjar as usual was to Connal's left and, farther down, Galeron and Branor across from him. The table stretched afore her, her own vassals eating happily, enjoying the wine and ignoring their conversation.

"Hunger can make a person crazed." She recalled years ago the crimes committed for something as simple as food.

"Sinead," Connal said patiently, "you saw yourself that the marshal was well fed, as were his men. Not a reedy one amongst them." Connal shook his head. " 'Twas at great risk that he waged the attack."

"Aye, a treaty could have been severely torn," Sinead murmured, leaning back in her chair and sipping wine.

"If not for your generosity," Connal said, and Sinead offered a smile at his acknowledgment.

Branor arched a brow at Galeron. Galeron quickly whispered the story Connal had told him.

" 'Twas not generous really." She almost laughed to herself. "The MacGuinness will not be pleased I have offered his stores, and I doubt any attack on his village would go without swift and complete retribution. I did not want a war."

"Neither do I, but why even do this? First, they have food. His troops attack a village, which he knows will bring you to his door. And though he knows he deserves punishment, he seemed confident you would smooth the trouble, even whilst you have the law on your side." Connal shook his head. "The risk was to his fort, his supplies, and his men. He had everything to lose. Westberry has not been near England for some time; I doubt he could be following orders."

"A message to England takes mayhap three or four days by sea," Sinead said softly, then lifted her gaze to his. "And if you know where to deliver it." She let that color the air for a bit, then added, "What if those orders have come within the shores of Ireland?"

"From whom those order were issued is a very long list, my lady," Galeron put in. "He knows he will incur the king's wrath, and the justiciars's, Pipard and William La Petit, if he starts a war."

"They are Prince John's appointments," Connal said, looking at Sinead for agreement. "Westberry is not. King Richard personally sent orders of instruction. I lay witness to it, years past." And the king's rage, he added silently. "Yet, if the marshal is following orders, then Sinead is right, 'tis from inside Ireland that they have come. I believe that Westberry is certain Prince John will show him favor."

"Will he?" Monroe asked, glancing between Sinead and Connal.

Connal shrugged. "The law can be skirted only so far afore even a prince is called into question. 'Tis why Richard wished to gain DeCourcy and William DeLacy's oaths on parchment."

"DeCourcy has been given ten cantreds in Connaught," Sinead said quietly.

Connal's brows shot up. "Athlone Covderg has allowed this peaceably?"

Her mouth curled in a small smile. "As much as would allow without war, aye. They recognize him as King of Connacht."

Connal sat back and mulled this over. It put DeCourcy in great power and in the favor of an Irish king and his armies. If Prince John wanted to crush it, he'd have to take the throne first. He wondered how informed the earls here were of John's intentions.

"Prince John will not be pleased that DeCourcy has so many land titles." Galeron voiced Connal's very thoughts. "Nor that he's in allegiance with an Irish king."

"DeCourcy has more than that, now," Sinead said. "He has the favor of the Irish for his fairness. Aye, he has warred on the Irish." Her gaze flashed to Connal's. For at least one battle, he'd been in that army. "But he has not been one to destroy people, only castles. Pipard shows no favor when he is in a battling mood."

Connal wished he knew more of what had transpired here in the last years and decided that he and Sinead would have to talk more.

"My father signed the oath, as did yours," Sinead said. "I suggest you get the remaining documents completed. 'Twill be a strength John would not dare ignore."

And one, he thought, that put all their lives in danger. "We must leave soon then," Connal said, not mentioning that their marriage was conditional on those oaths.

Sinead nodded and looked down, a sensation of dread suddenly peeling through her blood, her heart. It made her breath catch and abruptly she stood. The knights jumped to their feet, waiting. She waved them back into their seats and excused herself, moving away.

Connal moved toward her, whispering her name.

"I will see to the stores, that you have enough food to last you to the next castle."

"Sinead, look at me." She did, and the worry in her eyes was unmistakable. "I can delay a bit longer."

Her chin lifted a telling notch. "I do not need you to remain, PenDragon. I have been here alone for some time, and will be again."

She shuts the door still, he thought. "By damn, you are too independent."

Her brow lifted smoothly. "For a woman, but not a man?"

His gaze moved over her, leaving a heated trail that swept her breathless. "You are definitely not a man."

Her features sharpened, her beautiful eyes cool. "I must be."

She turned to the staircase and Connal followed, stopping her. On the step above him, she looked him in the eye, frowning. His green eyes were dark and sparkling with heat, with the emotions she'd only glimpsed.

"You do not have to play the role of man any longer, Sinead."

Ah, a male has arrived, all is well, she thought bitterly. Did he think because he wore chauses instead of a gown that that made a difference? He still thinks English. " 'Tis no role, PenDragon, but my duty, and I am quite comfortable with it." Her brows knitted softly. "You desire only the body, and you let it cloud your thinking."

He reared back a bit.

"You think I am blind to it? I do not fear it or you, but neither do I want your attention. For 'tis base."

He was not insulted, for 'twas a truth he could not deny. "And 'tis natural. You are—"

"I know what I am!" she snapped and instantly wondered why she had. " 'Tis in *you* I have my gravest of doubts."

"I beg your pardon?"

"You are an Irishman, a prince"—his lips tightened at that—"but you see a woman and think, 'She belongs to me because the king has spoken,' that she is weaker and cannot possibly know how to rule because Englishwomen do not." She arched a brow, waiting for him to deny it. He remained silent. "My duty is the same as yours and stronger for the disparagement of my gender.''

"I will give you that clearly. But I've the king's orders to follow. And I am here to help, Sinead. *Help.*"

He was here for King Richard and if not for the order, would never have returned. She would not be blinded by her attraction, disrupting as it was.

"Consider this," she sighed tiredly, glancing off at nothing, "when meeting those you grew up with on the field of battle, those who'd once vowed to follow you as their leader." She met his gaze. "Whose sword will you hold?"

"That is unfair."

"Really? Then do not question my motives. Ireland has my protection and my heart, PenDragon. Yours is cut in two. Choose.''

"I cannot!" he growled softly.

"Then do not tell me I should bow to your direction. I know not where your loyalties lay.''

With that she turned and ascended the stairs to her chamber.

Connal rubbed his hands over his face, then kicked at the basket sitting near the staircase. Servants scattered; conversation between knights ceased.

"Connal?" Galeron said.

"What!"

"Your conversations with the lady haven't improved, I noticed.''

"She's stubborn and determined not to take my help.''

"Why should she?''

Connal's gaze snapped to the Englishman's. Galeron shrugged. "She has been a success without you. Why should she change that? And do not say because the king has ordered a marriage, for that means little.''

Connal straightened and folded his arm over his chest, waiting for Galeron to finish. The man was never short for words or advice.

"King Richard does not care who rules as long as there is peace. But what do you offer, aside from more knights and vassals?''

Connal's features tightened. 'Twas the reason he was here, to gain a piece of Ireland for himself. "I am not a poor man, Galeron. If only I can help with that. But we are to wed and she will have to concede." Eventually.

"To you?" Galeron shook his head. "What experience, my lord, do you have in ruling several clans and leagues of land?''

Connal's gaze thinned. Galeron simply stared back, sans the smile this time.

"My father came to Scotland to wed the chieftain's daughter," Galeron said. "Unknowing that *she* was the chieftain and her clan was not willing to give the power to an Englishman, no matter who ordered. So he compromised. She was laird; he was her second.''

Connal scoffed and rubbed the back of his neck. "I bet that was interesting to witness.''

"I wasn't born, so you see my handicap in that, but my uncles tell a grand story of the arguments my parents had, and solving them was usually in the laird's chamber." Galeron wiggled his brows playfully, and a smile twitched at Connal's lips. "Life changed for both of them.''

"Sinead is not willing to compromise atall, Galeron. Her answer is always nay." Nay, Ireland does not need you nor I, nor anyone. She spoke the hated words with every fiber she possessed, as if she was keeping a wolf from the door, and to give an inch would destroy her.

Then Galeron tipped from the waist to lean close and say, "Mayhaps, my lord, you are not asking the right questions," and Connal realized he wasn't. He'd seen only duty. Only his plan. And while that sounded amiable whilst he was traveling here, after meeting Sinead again, after hearing her insults and slurs and feeling the constant wall she mortared between them, Connal understood there was more to the root of her discontent with him than his attire and his duties as a knight. Unfortunately there was little time to resolve it, for they would leave in the morning.

Sinead woke in the center of the night, when the castle was still and only the occasional footsteps of a guard, the groan of a weary maid, or the jangle of a vigilant knight's spur penetrated the silence.

Yet in her chamber she gasped for her next breath, the scream, thankfully, dying before she woke the castle folk. She rolled to her side, squeezing her pillow to her breasts and sinking her face into the down.

Goddess, release me from these dreams.

Again, Connal had bled and died. And once more there was something just out of her reach, hidden within the mystery of the dream. It was too real, too poignant a bruise to her soul to ignore. She could smell his blood, almost taste it. Since Connal had set foot in Ireland, it became clearer, almost pungent, and each morning she tried to counsel herself out of her fears. But they'd laid to rest in her heart and there was no escaping them.

She flopped back on the bedding, kicking off the coverlet. After a moment she left the bed, reaching for her robe. Her decision was firm and necessary. If she wanted to find peace, she had to protect Connal. Even if he did not want it.

Truly, she reasoned, she had no choice.

Connal did not want to leave. He feared for Sinead's safety and those of this castle. The villages. Westberry, and whoever he aligned himself with, was not to be trusted. His conscience needled him to remain; his duty bade him leave now and get the matter done. The sooner he did the king's bidding, the sooner he could solve the problems between himself and Sinead.

Dawn fought the night and her victory spread deep purple light over the bailey. In the saddle he yanked on his gloves, frowning when a young squire pulled Sinead's horse from the stall. The animal's back was laden with leather satchels and a blanket. She had reins this time, he realized, then scowled.

He was about to order the lad to take the mount back into the stable when Sinead walked out of the castle proper, fitted for the journey, her cloak swirling about her feet.

"Nay, Sinead. Go back inside. You are not joining me."

She spared him a glance as she mounted her mare. "I do not need your permission, and truly PenDragon, you must stop being so tyrannical, 'tis growing tiresome."

He sputtered with outrage, Galeron choked on his own laughter, and she waited patiently till he was done, then said, "You seek the clan laird's alliance, the MacGuinness? The O'Toole?"

"Aye."

"Then you need me."

"I can manage fine."

She gave him a patient look laced with the undercurrent of barely checked civility. "Aye, that I've no doubt; however, think on it, PenDragon. I am trusted. You are not. You seek to travel on my lands, without papers or introduction. You seek to tend all the way to King Rory's side, when you warred on him years afore and killed his brothers, his clansmen. Memories are long when it comes to remembering the dead. Who do you think will be most welcome?"

"She does have you there, Connal."

Connal ignored Galeron. His grin was a little too wide. "What do you think I will do? Ride in and slaughter first, speak of alliance later?"

"What I think matters little. What is and will be is the concern. I am coming along. However, for the sake of your dealings, I will be silent."

His bark of laughter cut through the early dawn.

Her lips tightened as she waited till he was done laughing, then said, "When you are speaking terms to the Irish lairds I will neither agree nor disagree. Until you solicit my opinion."

He eyed her. This was a blessing in deep disguise, he thought, his distrust wallowing with his need to have it. "You swear?"

She waved her hand, the motion sparkling the air with a faint banner of blue before she laid her hand over her heart. "So I say, so mote it be." Her fingers wiggled where they were over her breast, and he knew she could not break the oath.

He let out a long-suffering breath and nodded.

Galeron inched his mount closer and said, "That did not leave a mark, did it, my lord?"

Galeron's goading glanced off his back.

As Sinead whispered to her horse, the creature bobbed its head as if answering, yet something else caught Connal's attention. He rode forward and reached to grip the mare's big head. "Oh, for pity's sake, Sinead." His gaze shot to hers. "This beast is blind!"

"Aye. What of it?"

"Great Gods, woman." He inched closer. " 'Tis dangerous to ride a blind horse!"

She tipped her chin. "Genevieve can sense what needs to be seen, and sees a sight better than you, I'd wager. I will not waylay the trip."

"See that you don't."

Arrogant pisspot, Sinead thought.

Moments later, Monroe and a dozen retainers rode up beside her. Their packs were laden with stores, and one man pulled a half wagon of more.

Connal merely arched a brow at the captain.

"Don' want anyone thinkin' you've got her against her will, do we now, m'lord?"

"That, Monroe, is not possible."

Sinead exchanged a glance with Monroe, the captain's regard for her intense with a look Connal did not understand. Sinead lowered her gaze suddenly, and something close to shame swept across her features. His gaze jerked to the captain, but as he'd experienced in the past days, Sinead had more than his loyalty, she had his love, too. They rode.

Chapter Eight

Connal felt her riding closer before he realized she was alongside him. Her presence in the contingent of knights and vassals was like a bright light, a red-haired sparkle amid weapons and armor. She hadn't spoken to him since they'd left the castle, and though he unwillingly admitted he welcomed the conversation, being at the point was dangerous to her. "Get behind me, Sinead."

She scoffed. "I am not the one who needs protection, knight. 'Tis still my land we travel upon."

He sighed tiredly. "Must you argue with me at every turn?"

"When you refuse to see reason, aye."

Behind him Galeron cleared his throat to hide his laughter. "Me thinks the lady enjoys it, m'lord."

Connal glanced at Galeron. The man had spent the better part of the past two days flirting with her, and

Connal admitted that her response to the other man was irritating. She laughed with the English knight, smiled at the man when all she bestowed on Connal was a penetrating look. As if she was seeking something that was not there. Or another opportunity to call him traitor, he decided, his ire pricked. He wished Raymond had signed the marriage contracts, for it would at least give him some power over the woman when he felt annoyingly helpless.

"The lady enjoys my misery."

She looked insulted at that. "I do not."

"Then go home."

She smiled slyly. "I am home, PenDragon. 'Tis you who are not—"

He put up a hand. "Spare me the cuts, Sinead."

" 'Tis the truth."

"In your eyes."

"You wish to marry *me*, PenDragon; whose eyes should see you worthy but mine?" she snapped, and turned her mount back into the contingent, settling herself at Monroe's side.

"Good God, man, stuck your foot into that again," Galeron said as he moved closer to Connal.

Nahjar glanced at the sky in avoidance.

"What, no sage wisdom, Nahjar? You were full of advice in the castle."

"Which you chose to ignore. And I have seen you make no effort to woo the lady, Sajin. What is the difference with this woman? For I have seen females defy their fathers for you."

The words, though casually spoken, unearthed a buried agony in Connal's heart. His expression sharpened with pain, and he looked ahead. The silence was prickled with the clop of hooves, the jangle of bridles.

"Forgive me, Sajin," Nahjar said softly, bowing in the saddle.

Connal waved it off yet could not banish the images filling his mind. The heartless death, the blame laid at his feet. It reminded him that he brought destruction when he gave his heart and would not relinquish even a portion of it again. But with Sinead, the fates were toying with him, taunting him with each nuance of her, drawing him with more than the lust and want of a man too long without a woman. But if he gave, she would be destroyed, as his love had killed before.

"She is the one I must take to wife. Love and sweet words have little to do with it. She is mine regardless." He heeled his mount and lurched a few yards ahead.

Galeron scowled at his back, then glanced at Sinead. She'd heard. He could see it on her face, in her eyes gone dark with hurt. Galeron rode to catch up with his friend.

Sinead watched Connal ride the point, then looked to the trees, seeking anything to keep her mind from her troubles. Why should she be hurt? Had she not just told him that he did not belong here anymore? She should not expect a concession from him at all. But the feelings in her heart defied her brain. She was here to protect him, to keep him safe and alive when she knew he would die. The long-dead emotions she'd had as a child, the sensation of matching souls when she'd first laid eyes on him, were simply the fantasies of a girl. She'd managed all these years not to think of him, not to want what was not meant to be. But being near him was growing increasingly harder and she dreaded the night when the dreams would come and the heart she shielded so diligently would break.

Suddenly she stiffened in the saddle, looking to the

trees. Ahead Connal did the same, his hand closing over his sword. Sinead rode to the head of the line and up beside Connal.

"We are watched," she said to him, yet her gaze was on the thicket of gnarled trees.

He didn't look at her. "I know."

Suddenly the forest was alive, figures emerging, their clothing white and deep brown, making them nearly invisible until they moved away from the cover of trees. Hoods shielded their faces but not their intentions.

Pulling his sword free, Connal swung his mount around to face the attack as men raced from the barren forest, the snow doing little to hinder them. His back to Sinead, he said with deadly calm, "Let them come to you," his expression carved with determination. "Sinead, stay behind me," he commanded.

The enemy hesitated at the sight of the knights, then with a wild war cry, sent a barrage of rocks and stones hurling through the air. Javelins arched like staves of wheat, wobbling before they plunged toward their targets. They missed flesh and struck soil and glanced off rocks.

Crowded by Nahjar and Branor's mounts, Sinead jolted, leaning to see around Connal. Something was amiss. And as a PenDragon soldier raced toward the enemy, she instantly recognized the truth. Pushing her mount between the knights' horses, she shouted, "Nay, PenDragon. Cease!"

A rock struck Connal's temple. He did not flinch and bolted forward, prepared to strike. The sight of him made his attacker freeze where he stood and raise his arms to protect his neck and head. Connal froze, his sword high.

Sinead screamed out, "Nay, they are children!"

Connal whipped around, glaring at her, then looked at the men fighting around him. They had no daggers, no swords. Children?

One young man, armed with only a thick branch, fought a sword-wielding soldier, but his anger was strong, sending the vassal back. The English soldier stumbled and fell on his rear. The Irishman lifted the branch to smash his skull.

Sinead pointed to him. "Nay!" A brittle tree limb hanging over the pair grew instantly viney, and like a scolding mother, elongated to reach down and snatch the thick log from the Irishman's hands and entangle his arms in the vines.

The young Irishman, trapped, stared in horror at his unearthly shackles as his foe scooted back on his rump to safety. She turned toward the others. The troops fought the unmounted Irishmen. Connal's command to cease did not reach all ears.

Sinead rode into the center of it, panicked that more would die if she could not stop this killing lust. She tipped her head back, raised her arms, and said, "Spirits of wind and water, show me your power!"

The breeze turned violent, so strong it forced men to struggle to remain standing. A quick hard rain fell in all directions, drenching them to the bone in seconds. Snow melted on the slope, instantly turning to ice and making those standing there slip and slide downward. Or be trapped harmlessly in it, futilely struggling to pull their feet free of the frozen ground.

The wind whipped her hair nearly straight up, and Connal gripped his saddle horn, bowed his head into the gale, and rode to her.

"You can stop this now, Sinead," he said rather calmly. "Afore we are all naught but frozen statues."

Sinead met his gaze and the rain ceased; the sun appeared as the wind settled. A rainbow curved against the sky overhead. No one moved, staring at the sky, then her. Connal glanced about. Wonderful, he thought; even his soldiers who'd done battle with the Turks looked terrified.

"You've just alerted them *all* to your gifts, you realize."

She brushed damp hair from her cheek and said, "To cease the fighting on boys, I would suffer more."

He sighed. "I know they are children."

She blinked.

He took offense to her shocked look. "I do not war on babies, Sinead, nor do I attack men without weapons." He grabbed a poorly made javelin stuck in the ground and snapped the dry stick in half. He tossed the pieces aside and gave her a hard look.

"My lord, do we give chase?"

He looked at Galeron, then to where he pointed. The boys who had attacked them now scrambled up the icy slope toward freedom. "Nay, let them go."

Galeron frowned. Connal did not respond as he angled away and rode to the one injured soldier. The man staggered to his feet, and Connal helped his squire up behind him. "Ansel, are you fit to ride?"

"Aye, my lord, let us kill some Irishmen."

Connal twisted in his saddle and frowned. "We are not here to war on anyone, Ansel—least of all boys, and . . . I am Irish. Do you wish my death for that?"

"Nay, milord." The squire's pale skin flushed, even with blood oozing from his arm. "But yer one of us, sir."

Although the young man had only served as his squire since his return from the east, Connal wasn't going to take the time to explain further, especially when he didn't know what to say to that. Scowling, he rode to a mounted troop and helped Ansel on the back of another man's horse. Dismounting and moving away, he looked at Sinead, inclining his head to the lad she'd trapped in the vines.

Frantically, the lad fought his bindings. Sinead waved and released him; the youth tumbled back onto his behind. 'Twas justice for starting such a hopeless fight, she thought, riding close and staring down at him.

With a flick of her wrist, the poorly made hood jerked off. "Andrew!"

His eyes widened as she pushed back her own head covering. "Oh, mother of God . . . my lady!" he gasped, his face red with shame. He jumped to his feet, looking at the knight across the clearing, then to his lady.

His eagerness to run showed on his whiskerless face, and her anger simmered on the surface, flushing her cheeks. "Why did you do this, boy?"

"They attacked the village."

She frowned. "You are wrong. They have been with me for days now."

" 'Twas last night."

"Not these men," she said with finality, refusing to explain to an angry boy that Connal's men were traveling then and not this far south yet. "Is anyone hurt in the village?"

"A few bruises, naught serious, my princess."

"Your uncle did not sanction this, did he?"

The lad's shoulders straightened and he gazed straight ahead. "Nay, my princess."

"This is not the behavior of a future leader, Andrew." If the boy could have reddened further, he did. "You've attacked English and Irish without evidence."

Frowning, she looked over at Connal. His troops were gathering the attackers that had not fled into the forest. As he helped a man to his feet, he lifted his gaze to her. His frown immovable, he walked to her side. She offered what the youth had told her. Connal did not argue the matter.

"The MacGuinness will not be pleased with this," she said.

Splendid, Connal thought. A man he needed as an ally now had more reason to distrust.

"Then I suppose we are headed there."

"Nay," Sinead said, and Connal looked to throttle her. "The troops will only raise alarm, and we come for his oath, not his sword in battle."

"Hot-tempered, is he?"

"Do you not remember Duncan?"

Connal's brows furrowed as he drew on childhood memories. "He was not the eldest."

"Afore the English came my father was. Now Duncan leads," Andrew said, and Sinead wished she could calm the fear in the lad's eyes. He had not taken his gaze off Connal, nor could she tell if 'twas awe she saw there or anger.

Connal's stare nearly leveled the boy where he stood, and Andrew took a step back. Yet the boy did not give more; even surrounded by English soldiers and knights, he stood his ground proudly. Connal admired that, and saw himself in this lad. As a boy he'd done all he could to push an English conqueror out of their lives. 'Twas a pitiful resistance, using his slingshot on the man he now called father, Gaelan PenDragon. He'd hated Gaelan then, for his presence marked an end to Ireland's kings, to his own birthright to rule Donegal and the strong threads of the clans. The rage in him then had escalated when he understood that his mother cared deeply for the English lord. And during their marriage ceremony, he'd vowed to kill him.

'Twas his aunt who'd convinced him that his mother had no choice and if not Gaelan, then another would come in his place. 'Twas a sacrifice she made for them all. And 'twas Gaelan who'd offered his strength to Donegal and a hand out to the fatherless boy. He'd brought him into manhood, against his mother's protests, and earned his love. He'd been fortunate to have Gaelan guide him. But this lad had lost his father, his clan leader, and could not see there was no stopping the English invasion after all these years. God above, he was just like Sinead in that.

Just as he had been. Once. And now he was the man to force a boy into battle and rage.

"Who are you?" the boy suddenly blurted out, studying him hard. "You sound like an Irishman."

Connal folded his arms. "Mayhaps because I am."

"This is PenDragon, Andrew," Sinead said. "He is—"

The boy's eyes flared, then narrowed sharply. "I know full well who he is, my lady," Andrew sneered. "But yer English now, eh?"

"Many Irishmen serve King Richard."

"But not all lead the battle on their kin, do they, Prince?" He gave Connal a thorough look, then spat at his feet. "Traitor!"

Connal lowered his arms and went still as glass as the boy darted into the winter-worn forest. The lad's thrashing echoed and still he remained as he was, his fists clenched at his sides. His features offered naught, carved with indifference, yet Sinead could see his anger like an open wound in his eyes. Sympathy swam through her, yet she remained silent. He had to see she was not the only one who thought he'd turned his back on them.

Suddenly he turned and strode to Nahjar, questioning him. Luckily there were few injuries, and all minor. The Irish lads had fled too quickly to be questioned. Connal looked at the ground, dabbed two fingers on the cut on his temple, and stared at the blood. 'Twas a skirmish not worth pursuing, yet he had to see something done about the village.

"Branor, take three men and find this village but do not enter." He looked up at the somber knight. "You will frighten them," he explained. "Find a trail, no more."

"I will see it done, my lord." Branor nodded, pointed to two mounted men and, with them, rode into the forest.

Connal turned back to his mount and swung up onto Ronan's back. He rode to Sinead, stopping short when he noticed her clothing was dry and her hair was curling about her.

"My thanks for sending Branor," she said softly, her smile melting something inside him.

"You think me the worst of my kind." It bothered him more than he preferred.

"Not the worst."

His lips quirked at that evasive response. "You must not conjure like that, Sinead. There are other ways to stop a fight."

"Aye, with the dead."

He went on as if she had not spoken. "I cannot keep you safe if you continually put yourself in danger."

"I am not the threat here, PenDragon. And I can take care of myself."

"Mayhaps, but you are under my protection now."

She thought to argue again, then clamped her lips shut. If Connal wanted to think he was doing her a grand favor, then so be it. Men needed to roar once in a while. She inched her horse closer and with a cloth from her satchel blotted the blood on Connal's temple, thinking she was not about to ask his permission to use her magic when he'd no right to make such a demand.

Connal stared at her as she ministered to him. Her blues eyes sparkled, her scent, of wild roses and spice, climbing through his senses and clawing him from the inside out. The sudden grip of desire was tight and hard, the unearthly power of it coupled with the need to taste her. By God, how could she drive him mad with anger and frustration one minute and delirious with passion the next?

"I know a spot where we may camp for the night in safety," she said softly, examining the wound. "This needs a stitch or two."

He shook his head, his gaze never leaving her lush mouth. "Add it to the hundreds of other scars."

"There are many?" she asked with a glance down his body as she opened a small tin of salve.

"Aye. One day you will see them all."

Amid applying a dab of salve to his cut, Sinead's gaze flashed to his, his meaning clear. Naked, in his bed. The thought made a spot low in her belly clench and flex. Longing stretched through her like a lazy cat, begging for his touch, his laugh, and for him to smile at her. Then his head tipped closer, his breath dusting her lips. Anticipation of another storm within his arms flowed like heavy wine through her blood. She met his gaze, the softness she saw in his eyes swallowing her like the tide. *Oh Goddess, 'tis unfair this weapon he wields,* she thought, for once tasted, he'd be more of a danger to her heart than his armies had been to the walls of Jerusalem.

She dabbed the cut, effectively pushing him back and saving her from another bout of weakness.

Connal shifted uncomfortably in the saddle, his groin full and aching without so much as her touch.

"You should not bring all these men with you to see the MacGuinness."

He chuckled at her avoidance and suddenly craved the day she'd speak his name again.

"Then you will come with me."

She blinked in surprise.

"You would have insisted regardless," he said magnanimously. She was his to protect, he reasoned, and he needed time with her, without so many about clinging to their every word. He wasn't going to woo her, but a little consideration would likely smooth the path to the marriage he needed.

For Richard, or for you? a voice niggled. God above, that was going to be a trial. Galeron was right: He and Sinead had a tidy war waging between them.

"Aye, I would." She smiled. "However, I will keep my word and be silent."

"Praise be."

She made a face. "But . . ."

He chuckled softly, shaking his head and knowing even before that she would not allow him the last word.

"This little fight speaks for the turmoil unsolved." She gestured to the torn, snow-covered ground. "The English conquer and, once done, continue to beat our people down. My parents have seen GleannTaise returned to its glory and the people are well and happy. Yet Mother's touch does not stretch so far. Mine does." Her chin lifted. "The Gleanns are mine to rule. Oh, do not look so affronted, you big ox. You are not my husband, nor would that matter. I will not abandon them to you."

"You would side with the MacGuinness against me?"

That dilemma hit her like a slap. "I will do what is best for my people."

"So will I! And deny that I am without morals or fairness, Sinead," his voice rising with his anger, "and I will . . ."

"What?"

"Gag you!"

She looked affronted and amused. "Oh, now that is truly fair, for certain, knight."

"You are magical," he groused, feeling again the helplessness of his trials with her. "There are few rules I can make with you."

He looked so much like a sullen boy just then, she tried not to laugh and failed. From beneath a shock of dark brown hair, he glared harder, yet there was no anger in the look.

"I make no promises I cannot keep."

"I suppose keeping your mouth shut is too much to ask?"

"In Duncan's presence, aye."

He groaned, shoving his fingers through his hair, and Sinead took mercy on him. "If we hurry we can make it by nightfall," she said gently.

He nodded and went to relay their plans to Galeron as Sinead shifted her mount around his, riding across the clearing to Nahjar. Regardless of the momentary truce, the turmoil he'd thought was gone from Ireland existed, and he was learning how deep the wounds still festered.

He studied her as she spoke to Nahjar and on instinct

knew she was concerned over the wounded. The men would refuse her, especially after that display of wind and rain. For all his warnings, it amazed him each time she worked the elements, and he wondered at the true depth of her power. He'd rather she not have it but long ago had accepted her for what she was. Yet after only a day with her, he realized she was naught like the troublesome female he once knew, and again contemplated why she was so opposed to marriage, and not just to him.

His gaze swept her, her hair trailing over the back of her blind horse—he chuckled to himself over that—to her dainty feet in old leather boots peeking out from beneath the gown and cloak. Her profile in his sight, he admitted that she not only took his breath away, but deep inside he wanted her trust.

And her love? a voice chanted in his mind. *Can you count yourself worthy enough for this woman's heart?* A denial that he needed her love shot through him. He noticed the men staring at her; Galeron, the skilled flirt, said something that made her laugh. The sound floated across the distance like tinkling glass, warming him, and he rode closer as Sinead handed Nahjar the tin of salve. He rode near, curious, as he gave orders to move on.

"See that they clean the wounds and dress it with this," she said. "Wrap the injuries in clean cloths, too, Nahjar. The lads have likely poisoned the javelin tips."

He accepted the tin and went to do her bidding. None would refuse Nahjar, Sinead suspected, then looked at Galeron. The poor man was shivering and trying to hide it.

Sinead could not conjure on anyone without permission so she asked, "You wish to be warm?" knowing Connal was displeased with her.

"Aye. Of course." He eyed her, as did most of the shivering men.

She leaned out, her hand slightly cupped and near his knees. "For the chill and rain I gave, I banish with warmth and comfort," she whispered, lifting her hands slowly.

Galeron's heart skipped a beat as a gentle breeze ruffled beneath his garments, a heavy warmth rolling over his skin, fluttering his clothes to his throat.

"Better?"

He plucked at the knees of his chausses, and realized his garments were dry. "My thanks, my lady." Instantly images of what she could do with those powerful hands collided in his brain, and he considered Connal was damned lucky and too pigheaded to realize it.

"Forgive me for drenching you."

" 'Twas naught to be forgiven, my lady."

"Me, too, my lady," her own vassals shouted, and she repeated the chant, repairing the damage she'd done. Even a few English bravely insisted on her aid.

"Dammit, Sinead, must you cast . . . so often?" Connal said from behind, and she twisted.

"Why have the power if not to use it for the benefit of others? And since you hate it so much, then *you* can remain cold and wet." Not that she could cast on him anyway, she thought, and wondered when he'd learn that truth. She rode to Monroe, ignoring his protests when she told him their plans.

"But your reputation . . ."

"Monroe," she said patiently, " 'tis little to worry over that when wars are waging."

Monroe wasn't pacified and sent Connal a warning look.

Connal recognized it and would have taken offense if he did not know how loyal the man was to his lady.

"Have a caution, my lady; those who'd stop Pen-Dragon from doing the king's wishes will not think hard on taking lives."

The coppery scent of blood suddenly filled her senses, as if freshly spilled in a warning. An instant later, her mind clouded with Connal's tortured face. Her heart clenched painfully, and though she knew Connal was quite capable of gaining his oaths, she could not risk leaving his side.

She angled her mount close to his as she banished thoughts of him dying in her arms. It would not be so, she thought firmly, and wished she had the power to veil him in protection. But she was forbidden, and feared it would be his ruin.

"Sinead?" he said, his gaze shifting over her features. "Are you afraid?"

She shook her head. "Come, PenDragon, let us meet the MacGuinness and get your oath signed."

He frowned at her for a second more, then nodded and took the lead. Yet as they headed west together, one thought scared Sinead, eluded her.

What was that speck of the vision the goddess refused to show her?

And when she could cast the spell of change, bend the elements, why could she not see the hand, the face of the villain who would kill her prince?

Chapter Nine

'Twas a mistake to take the woman along with him, Connal thought as he called to the tower guards and announced himself. Surrounded by the guards who'd been posted along the forest trail, the warriors escorted them to the castle doors. Connal had expected it, as had Sinead, yet the damning looks the men sent him warned of trouble. Sinead, on the other hand, knew a few of the men, and chatted amiably about their families and children, and Connal realized how deeply familiar she was with the lives of her people.

And that he was still the outsider.

The wood and iron doors swung open and Connal saw a tall broad-chested man striding purposely toward them. Sinead pushed back her hood and the man paused and grinned, then rushed to pull her from the saddle.

"Duncan, you crush me! Put me down." She hammered his shoulders, laughing.

"Is that a proper greeting for your dearest, oldest friend?"

"Oldest mayhaps, but dearest? You threw rocks at me."

Holding her off the ground in a burly hug, Duncan MacGuinness spun her about and kissed her hard on the mouth.

Connal leaped from the saddle and was instantly surrounded by armed clansmen. He spoke in Gaelic, warning them back. The clansmen's shock was plain, their weapons lowered cautiously. As the MacGuinness set her on her feet, Connal moved close to her side.

Duncan eyed him, his clansmen, then her.

"He's English," a soldier said, raising his weapon.

"Nay." Sinead put herself between the pair, then looked at Duncan. "This is the King's emissary, Connal O'Rourke PenDragon."

Duncan's eyes narrowed sharply. "My lord," he said stiffly. "Welcome to FairGleann." He bowed slightly and knew no good would come from this. Yet Duncan took heart that with Sinead traveling with PenDragon, he'd not be forced, like the other lairds, to surrender all he'd held dear to yet another English monarch.

Connal smiled slightly, removing his gauntlet and holding out his hand. "A pleasure, Laird MacGuinness."

Duncan shook it, studying Connal closely. "I know your father. And remember you as a boy." His gaze flicked over the tunic emblazoned with King Richard's banner. "A lot, I see, has changed."

"Well, little has here, Duncan," Sinead said, tsking

softly, at the cluttered yard and hoping to defuse the tension. " 'Tis nay FairGleann but Fair Pig's Sty."

Duncan winked at her. "If I'd known I'd have company, lass, I would have cleaned a bit."

She scoffed. "As if you know how."

"I try. But I am merely a man."

Sinead rolled her eyes.

"Laird MacGuinness, we're here on behalf of King Richard."

Duncan's gaze snapped to Connal. "I suspected as much. You've been hailed long afore you stepped on Ireland again, and after all this time I suspected it was for more purpose than a visit."

Connal's features tightened, the telling look he flashed to Sinead speaking more than he wanted to.

"Andrew just returned," Duncan said, then looked at Sinead. "I've your magic to thank for keeping those fools alive, I hear."

" 'Twas PenDragon who noticed they were but poorly armed children just as I did." The ruthlessness of Pen-Dragon's troops and their need to kill more Irishmen still worried her.

Duncan arched a brow in surprise, yet not a shred of emotion passed over his features. "Come then, let us dine and settle what e'er 'tis that you've come to say."

Duncan turned toward the castle, his arm around Sinead's waist, but she stopped after a few steps, pulling away from Duncan and holding her hand out to Connal. Duncan took a step back, surprised and frowning. Sinead grasped Connal's hand, the burning hum of something grand throbbing though her at first contact, and she jerked back, then let him lace her arm through his. She smiled tightly at him, then looked ahead as they walked.

"Does this mean you are softening toward me?" he teased in a whisper.

"Don't be gettin' an imagination, now. I do this so the clansmen at the wall will not take it upon themselves to put a javelin into your back because of that herald on your chest."

"I know." His smile was brittle with regret.

She met his gaze briefly. "Just be fair to them. 'Tis all I ask and all I will say."

Connal tipped his head to look down at her and saw fear. For her people or him, he couldn't be certain. Yet her gaze darted to every corner of the hall as they stepped inside.

What phantom was she seeking? he wondered, and rubbed his fingers over the back of her hand, the motion more soothing to him than her. Touching Sinead gave him a peace he'd never dreamed he wanted.

True to her word, she said naught as Connal laid out the king's request. He almost felt bad about accepting her oath of silence, then recalled what would have happenned if she'd not sworn and was thankful. He studied Duncan, his carved features offering no indication of his thoughts as he read the documents. Rubbing a hand across his mouth, the rasp of a day's beard sounded in the silence. Connal suddenly loathed the position he was in, and memories of the way his mother had fought swearing oath to the English King Henry peppered his thoughts. Would Duncan fight as she had to hold on to the last vestiges of control? Would Connal be forced to summon his army to take this castle and land from Duncan because he refused the king's demands?

The thought made his stomach churn, and when Duncan lifted his gaze to his only a portion of his doubts eased. He did not want to fight his countrymen. Never again.

Duncan knew he'd sign the oath before he finished reading it. 'Twould assure peace and the livelihood of his clan, and that came before his own feelings. But before he would, he asked about the English that attacked his lower crofts.

"I believe 'twas Westberry's doings, Laird MacGuinness, or a braggart under his control," Connal said. "For his troops did the same in a village north, in GleannArmagh."

Duncan sat back in his chair, his glaze flicking between the two as Connal explained further. He looked at Sinead. "You volunteer my stores for Westberry's troops, yet have little to say, Princess?"

"I have given my word," she whispered softly.

Duncan straightened, alarm in his eyes.

Connal remained stoically calm. "She is not here against her will. Tell him, Sinead."

Duncan looked patiently from one to the other.

She lifted her gaze to Laird MacGuinness. "I am here for you, Duncan. Of my free will. PenDragon would not dare force me."

Duncan barked a short laugh. "Not if he knows what's good for him, aye."

She looked affronted. "I would not harm him, Duncan, and you know it! Now your clansmen's treatment of . . ."

"Sinead, you swore," Connal said, and she clamped her lips together.

"You were saying about my clansmen?" Duncan goaded.

Sinead's eyes were cool and hard, yet she remained silent.

Duncan was amused and looked at Connal. "By God, tell me how you managed to get her to shut that acrid mouth."

She made an indignant sound. She wasn't acrid

"When you are mad, aye, you are."

"He is right," Connal said.

"Burns the ears. Even when she was a child."

She stood abruptly. "I said I would not offer an opinion on these oaths, I did not say I would not comment on your behavior as gentlemen!"

"And that is?" Connal said.

"Hideously lacking!" With a sharp snap of her fingers, she vanished.

"Oops," Duncan said. "Look for a hailstorm soon. In your chamber."

Connal laughed softly, sinking into the chair. "You are the one who teased her."

"Aye, but did you see her eyes? By the Gods, she could spit ice with those beauties." Connal had to agree and waved at the bit of red mist she left behind as Duncan rose and went to an elegant table, the piece out of place in the rough stone castle. From a fine glass decanter he poured wine into goblets that he brought to his desk. He offered one to Connal.

"I served with DeCourcy, too, PenDragon. I was his legion commander for a while."

Connal stared.

"I know Sinead holds this against you. I'd heard her speak of it once years back."

Connal's chest tightened. How was he to fight anger that old?

"I'd little prospects like this," he gestured to the castle as a whole, "and mercenary work was my only choice. You'd do well to tell her of me and see the rift settled."

Duncan's intuition over the problems he and Sinead faced made Connal wonder where he'd learned it, or were they simply too plain in their feelings? "Then she will hate you as well."

Duncan shook his head. "She's not capable of such hatred." At Connal's sour look, he added, "Tell her and she will see that some of us do as we must to survive." Duncan propped his hip on the edge of the desk. "She is the soul of the land, my lord. She feels 'tis her duty to keep it pure."

"She cannot and she knows it." Connal drank. "And I will not start a war for the feelings in a woman's heart."

"Wars have started for less. The king lays his law in your hands, PenDragon, yet has she refused to abide it?"

"Nay," he said, conceding that she hadn't fought him on the oaths at all. "The king orders our marriage and she refuses to even consider it." *She thinks me a traitor, more English than Irish,* he thought. Lord above, if she knew the truth, would she accept him or loathe him more? Connal gulped another swallow. "She wants only love, and I cannot give it."

"Love is all that really matters," Duncan said solemnly, watching him carefully.

Connal scoffed, not believing love changed a bloody thing in his life. "I would not have thought you so soft, Laird MacGuinness."

"Duncan please, and aye, soft for a woman, soft for an easier life." Duncan shook his head. "I had a different future planned. Be a mercenary, retire young, marry and raise fat babies." He shook his head sagely and moved to stare out the window. He finished off his drink before he said, "I was not to be laird. But the English slew my family and I was the only one who survived. I will rule till Andrew is ready. But if he continues going about attacking travelers, he will not live so long. For certain I will tan his hide till he drops for the attack."

"Punish him like a man and he will learn. Punish like a boy and he will hate." 'Twas what Connal learned from Gaelan.

Duncan cocked a look at the knight, then nodded. "Aye. I've raised the boy, and not very well."

"He acted bravely, Duncan."

"Yet you did naught when he spat at you? I thank you for not killing the impudent whelp." Duncan poured and drank.

"I expected anger from my kin. Some still see Ireland as it was, and my role with the English breeds hatred. And the Crusades taught me patience."

"I almost envy your adventures."

A shadow passed over Connal's features. "Do not. I would trade them for peace and a home."

Duncan sighed, draining his glass and refilling it again. "Now," he said taking the document and settling back into his chair to sign, "let us get this done."

Connal peered over the rim of his glass as he read it again, then penned his signature. He impressed his seal, laid the paper aside, then lifted his glass in a toast. "To Richard, may he return home in time to squash his brother like a bug."

"Please God, aye." Duncan smirked and tossed back the warm drink.

"Now, Connal, tell me about you and Sinead. Last I recall she insisted to everyone who would listen that you two were mates of the soul. And she was but six at the time."

Connal's throat tightened. "Our match is by order of the king and naught more." *It cannot be more*, he thought. For her sake and his own.

"Oh-ho, prince of Erin, you have been away far too long, and surrounded by too many foreign women."

"And you think to teach me about Irish lasses, old man?"

Duncan snickered drunkenly. "I'm sure you do not need lessons when half my female household lurks beyond yon door, wondering which wench will be in your bed tonight. But I will tell you, her vile temper aside, when Sinead loves, 'tis a force to be reckoned with."

Connal shifted in the chair, scowling. "How the hell would you know?"

Duncan frowned curiously. "She has not told you of the O'Brien? Markus?"

The betrothal.

"Her parents mentioned 'twas a poor choice."

Duncan scoffed rudely, then drained his cup. "Have a caution, laddie. I adore Sinead, but the man who hurts her pays dearly."

"Explain yourself, man," Connal demanded.

"Her father killed him." Duncan promptly slipped back into the chair and passed out.

Connal blinked, stunned, and when he stood and shook the clan leader, the man only muttered incoherently and wiggled his fingers. Connal set the glass aside and left the chamber, working his way around women and asking after Sinead. A young man led him abovestairs to the chamber vacated for him. Sinead, he was told, was farther down the corridor.

He hesitated before his door, thoughtful, glancing

once toward her chamber before striding quickly inside and to the bed.

He brushed back the drape and lost his breath.

God above, even in repose the woman devastated his senses, and a sharp spike of longing shot through him. Her hair webbed her shoulders like a cloak and with her arm thrown back over her head, she looked delicate. Fragile. She stirred, lazily rolling to her side, and the sheet slipped, baring her side and naked back to his hungry gaze.

Then he saw the scar, thin and silvery running from her shoulder blade to curl under her arm and over her ribs.

My God. He bent closer, peeling the fabric, and saw its end was deep.

Connal had witnessed many wounds in his lifetime and knew without doubt that this was caused from the single strike of a whip. He squeezed his eyes shut, wanting to repay whoever had done this to her and wondering after their identity. Had she been beaten like her mother? He could not fathom Raymond or Fionna doing such a thing, ever, and the thoughts racing through his mind ended with a man. This beast to whom she'd given her love.

His fingertips grazed the mark and she woke instantly, her hand flying up. Connal felt the punch of something hitting his chest, firm but not enough to push him back. Sinead rolled quickly to her back, staring up at him with wide-eyed fear. Then she scrambled back against the headboard.

"Stay back, PenDragon, or I will bring this chamber down upon you!" Sinead put up her hand, sending energy toward him, yet naught happened, leaving her helpless.

Connal frowned, standing his ground. "I will not harm you, lass. I swear it."

"I believe little of oaths from men."

Her words spat with full venom and a dark bitterness he'd never imagined to hear from her. "I am not the O'Brien."

She inhaled sharply. "Duncan speaks too much."

"Why did you not tell me of him?"

" 'Twas nay your affair."

"How can you say that? Look at you. You cower from me. Think you I would beat a woman?"

"Nay," she said bravely, and he loathed her doubt.

Connal moved closer, sitting carefully on the edge of the bed. It creaked beneath his weight and that she struggled for more distance fractured his heart. Compassion flooded through him. She trembled delicately, yet valiantly tried to hide it from him. And he took comfort that with the snap of her fingers or the wave of her hand, she could leave, yet remained. Defiant to her fears.

Her gaze searched his face, then lowered to his hands, and he remembered the moments at her castle, how she flinched when he'd reached for her, and on the parapet when she'd run from him.

"Tell me."

"Nay."

"I have the right to know."

"You do not!"

"Sinead," he said patiently, "if I do not know the whole of it, how can we be wed?"

She made a sour face. "We won't."

He ignored that. "He beat you. Why? Or should I be surprised 'twas not for your sass."

Tears glassed her eyes and he felt instantly contrite for his teasing.

"I did naught to deserve it! I was but six and ten and I fell in love with him!" spilled from her. Instantly she wished she'd not spoken at all.

The lines bracketing his mouth tightened. "I'd suspected as much," he encouraged softly and knowing it sent a wild stab of pain through his chest as he imagined Sinead, younger, innocent, and trusting. "Tell me, lass."

She hesitated, her gaze riveted to his, and the compassion she saw there broke the dam of silence. "Markus swore his love for me and was all I'd hoped for, until he learned I had no magic."

"No magic? I do not understand."

"I told you," she said impatiently, wishing she hadn't opened this door. "My mother took it from me. From the day I cast on you, she bound me, and when Markus courted me, he was unaware. Only my parents knew, and though the people understood I was gifted, they thought me . . . tamed."

His lips quirked with tender humor.

"When he wanted me to cast for riches, I refused. For his love I would have given him the world, but I'd no power." She sank into the bedding, the motions drawing her a little closer, and Connal took comfort in it. "I'd been sent to him and his mother afore the wedding. I was alone but for Monroe as my escort. Days afore we were to be wed, he learned the truth but did not believe me. Markus's mother, like his people, obeyed him without question, and when he put me in the tower, 'twas to force me to cast. She did naught to stop him." A single tear slid down her cheek and she dashed it away. "Monroe asked after me, and when all refused to reveal where I was, he challenged Markus's captain. My mother sensed the trouble and she and Father were already on their way to the keep. Markus had just done this when they'd arrived." She gestured to her side. "He'd done far worse to my face already."

Pity and anger kipped across Connal's features and Sinead lifted her chin, not wanting any of it.

"My father's men stormed the castle, for by then Mother knew what Markus had done and had come by magic to free me. But my father was not satisfied with that and took the O'Brien's head." She looked down at her hands. "They have not forgiven themselves for giving me to Markus. Mother returned my gifts that very moment. And Monroe has dedicated his life to protecting me." She looked up, her smile feeble. "Even from myself."

Connal swallowed heavily, imagining those last moments, Fionna's and Raymond's guilt, for if she'd had her gifts, she would have been able to protect herself. Connal felt somehow responsible.

" 'Tis not your fault," she said suddenly, recognizing the look on his face, the feelings rippling between them. She scooted closer, clutching the sheet.

"If I had been more compassionate mayhaps, and let your innocent claims of love die a mature heart's death, then mayhaps your magic would not have been bound against you."

"Nay. I was a spoiled brat who saw the world as her playground then."

"You loved so deeply as a child. How could this man not see the gift of that?"

A leap of joy crested through her heart, for hearing those words from him had been an innocent dream. Yet the truth of it made her scoff, then fold her legs beneath her, as if they were in a garden and not in her chamber. Or on her bed.

"I've been courted well, and by many. They wish for the riches and power magic can bring. They do not understand the rules and want the power I possess." She shrugged as if it did not matter.

"But never the love."

Her gaze locked with his. "Nay, never that."

Connal looked away, harboring his own doubts in himself behind a mask of indifference. Yet the unanswered questions lingered. And he could almost hear her say, *is it possible for us?* And he'd no answer for it.

"Oh, they claim such feelings, but if 'twere true and right, they'd have no need of riches, for love would be the greatest magic."

Connal felt the dangerous slice of her words cut through him. Love was no longer in him to give, he wanted to tell her, but she'd ask why, demand it. And he could not speak the words. It would kill him to admit his crimes.

When he said naught, Sinead could no longer look him in the eye and called herself a coward for sliding down into the bedding and wrapping herself in furs. "You may return to your own chamber."

"I do not think so."

She twisted a look back over her shoulder. He was stripping off his clothing, his sword already propped against the stone wall.

"Do not think to share this bed with me, PenDragon! Sleep on the floor if you must remain."

Her panic unfolded like the wind through the trees, rustling through him. He kept his voice calm and even. "Nay, I am tired as well. You are safe with me, Sinead. For unlike the O'Brien, I have honor."

Sinead did not doubt that, but watching him bare his scarred chest, then lay on the bed, eased little of her fears. He was a mountain of flesh and muscle, his warmth calling to her now. She dared not move closer or find herself on her back and beneath him, yet she considered that this was actually good fortune, lest someone take it upon themselves to avenge England's wrongs on him during the night. Though her dream had him in battle, in the forest, Sinead did not trust that as truth. Riddles were oftimes the root of her premonitions.

"Go to sleep, Sinead. You are protected."

She made a rude sound and, sitting up, lifted one hand to the ceiling. "Veil of the Goddess, drape this chamber. Veil of the God, bind it tight. Protect us in your blanket of love and seal it till the morning light."

Connal rose as she'd chanted and now stared in awe as, when she lowered her hand, a blanket of tiny stars, like light on water, trickled gently down upon them.

"Now we are protected," she said, and dropped onto the bed, her back to him.

Connal settled slowly back down, struck again at how perfectly magical Sinead was. And how deeply unworthy he felt when she did that. Did she not think him at all capable of protecting her? 'Twas damned emasculating, he thought, and tried to sleep.

During the night Sinead stirred and did not wake from a tortured dream, but from a soothing peace she'd sought for a fortnight past. She shifted carefully, opening her eyes. Her gaze moved over his bare chest, torn from war and chiseled with strength. Odd that she felt no fear at the sight of those big hands; yet in a temper, would he hurt her? Markus had not shown his true plan till she'd refused to give him her magic. Yet Connal wanted naught of her gift, nor his own.

Markus's angry words spewed vilely through her mind
. . . *freakish, unnatural. Inhuman.* Still now, they made
her feel unworthy, an outsider to the love her heart
cried to embrace. *Is it my doom to need unquestionable love
to survive, or my doom to never know it?* And if the king
would force her, what was to become of her people, her
land, when she mated with a man who wanted only to
be Richard's first knight, to honor his duty, even with
her as the sacrifice?

She did not know which was worse, to be wanted for
only her magic or needed for the sake of an alliance.
'Twas the way of the English kings, she thought, yet
could not resign herself so easily.

Her gaze lit on the scars painting his sun-dark skin,
each mark of battle beckoning her touch. As a child
and an innocent girl she'd loved this man, and she
recognized now that his dismissal only buried those
feelings deep within her. The longer she was near him,
the harder it was to hide and not drag them out and
question them daily. Was it old feelings she experienced
or new? Was it past wounds that kept her guarded from
him or the knowledge that if he knew her heart stirred
for him, he'd use it against her? He'd discarded her
love once afore.

'Twas a weapon she could not give. Not when his
heart was sealed against her and Ireland. Ah, but what
woman would not want this man in her bed? she
thought, letting her gaze travel the length of him again.
He was braw and handsome and strong . . . the spin of
desire swept through her suddenly, making her shiver,
and when her gaze returned to his face, she found him
staring at her.

He did not move.

"Is there aught you wish to say to me?"

"Nay."

Connal's gaze made a slow prowl over her body wrapped in the sheet. She looked flush and ripe and 'twas all he could do not to reach for her and kiss her endlessly. "Scared?"

She scoffed.

"Good. Go to sleep; our journey on the morrow will be long and fast." He rolled to his side, squeezing his eyes shut and calling on the patience he'd learned in prison.

Sinead slid to the far edge of the bed, burrowed deep under the furs. She slept, safe in the knowledge that he was near, safe in the knowledge that he would not die this night.

In the early morning, Connal awoke sharply, his body tight for pleasure and aching for satisfaction. An instant later, he understood why. Sinead was tucked close to his back, her warm naked breasts teasing him with her breathing, her arm around his waist. Yet 'twas her hand splayed low on his belly that threatened his control. His blood pulsed hard through his veins like a racing horse. His erection flexed and thickened. *Damn me*, he thought, and wanted naught more than to roll over and take her beneath him, fill her, pleasure her and himself.

Yet to waken her any other way would frighten her. For he did not doubt that beating Sinead was not the only act inflicted upon her by Markus O'Brien. The thought of her helpless sickened him all over again, and Connal vowed he would tread carefully. Slowly he slid to the edge of the bed, nearly falling to the floor in his efforts not to wake her. He glanced over at her. She gripped his pillow tightly and slept on.

'Twas almost insulting to be so easily discarded, and he moved to the pitcher and basin, praying for ice cold water and a way to relieve his agony. Yet he knew, the longer he was near Sinead, naught would satisfy him.

Except the woman herself.

Chapter Ten

Wrapped in an oilcloth, a solitary man huddled in the bow of the ship, his gaze on the shoreline ahead. The ship bobbed as it fought the current and icy winds to northern Ireland's shore, and the heavy spray soaked through his already damp garment. Tucked in his hand was a dagger, his only protection against those who'd stop him. And he knew they would try. The wound in his side and the loss of his sword spoke of their last attempt.

He glanced back at the crewmen working the sail lines, the captain eyeing the shore, then him. Moments counted and he feared he'd not reach Ireland in time to sound the warning. The lives of his kin hung in the balance, their value no more than a coin played in a game, a final pawn to be expended in the battle atween brothers.

*   *   *

It had been a while since Sínead felt this wonderful.
A night without dreams, she thought, was as pleasant
as the morn. The sun reigned supreme over the clouds
this day as they rode, the shine of light glittering off
fresh fallen snow. Though Connal was a length ahead
of her, their trek was slow, and a sweet joy filled Sinead
as she looked around. Icicles hung from evergreen trees
like spiral gems, each twinkling back at her as they
passed. She inhaled the cold, crisp air and, losing the
reins, stretched her arms wide. She called to the wild
things.

"Come the wild and free," she whispered. "Come
and show me the life in the barren land of ice and snow.
Nurture my spirit. Nurture the lands. Come forth and
be seen!"

Lowering her arms, she smiled when a few rabbits
poked their faces from the burrows. Birds flew down to
sit upon her shoulder and head. Then a deer trotted
from the edge of the tree line, studying Connal a few
yards ahead of her, then Sinead. The fawn ventured
quickly closer, and Genevieve remained calm as the
young deer walked alongside her mount. Sinead slowed,
leaning down to pet the animal, then looked around
for its mother. A proud doe showed herself, and Sinead
pushed the child toward her parent. But she would not
go.

"Sinead, just what are you doing?"

The amusement in his voice pleased her. "Visiting a
wee bit."

"Really." Connal smiled, riding back to her. She was
covered with birds, some finding a nest in her hair and
peeping with contentment whilst others made a fine

marching line down her mount's fetlocks. She laughed
lightly as they pecked at her hair, and Connal thought
it the sweetest sound. For a moment he simply watched
her, the smile he rarely saw, the comfort she took in
the animals. Then one bird jumped from her to his
thigh, inching its way up, and Connal let it perch on
his hand. It sang prettily for a moment, then preened
for him. He grinned and, with his teeth, pulled off his
gauntlet to stroke the bird's tiny head.

Sinead smiled. The bird was no bigger than a nut
compared to him, like a great beast touching a delicate
flower. The birds chirped noisily, all at once, and
Sinead's brow knit.

"Well, have they any news?"

"Learn that yourself."

His expression went sharp and unruly. "I think not."
The bird flew away and Connal turned his mount ahead.

Sinead said good-bye to the animals, and they scam-
pered and alighted for the trees, plucking a few strands
of her hair before she rode alongside him. "Why do
you deny the gift our family has?"

"I do not deny it exists, Sinead. I choose not to take
advantage of it."

" 'Twould not be a gift then, but a curse."

"Exactly."

"Fool."

His gaze snapped to hers. Her eyes were glossed with
unshed tears. As if his denial wounded her.

" 'Twas given to you for a reason, knight. As was mine.
Not for your advantage, but for others."

He scoffed rudely, and she wondered exactly how
much he loathed her power. He could not accept the
woman she was and her gift of change till he recaptured
his own. 'Twas part of his birthright as a descendant of

the *Tuatha De Dannon*, part of who he was, and hiding it beneath that learned English calm was hurting him. And it pained her to see him fight it.

"Do you not think that mayhaps 'tis harder to fight than accept?"

"Do *you* not understand, Sinead? I do not want this ... gift." He glared at the woodlands, sensations he hadn't known since he was a boy reeling through him. The fright of the animals, wary for the human who hunted for food. "I cannot have it."

He urged his mount forward and, the path wide enough for the horses, she fell in pace aside him.

"Why? Tell me why so I might understand."

His gaze snapped to hers. "I have struggled to gain Richard's trust and being a *creature* would not keep it."

She felt that like a stinging slap. But she was accustomed to such names. "So you smothered it." To avoid scaring anyone, to avoid being marked as she was.

"Aye, and till I returned to Ireland, I lived bloody damned fine without it."

Instead of anger, she smiled with patient understanding. "It comes from the land."

He scoffed. "It comes because of you."

"Me? I have no such gift, nor could I give it. Why would you say such a thing?"

"Because I feel too much near you, and I cannot think clearly with it crowding me." He would not admit that he was in a constant state of turmoil around her, that it took every ounce of his will to keep his thoughts under control. And his focus on his duty and not having Sinead, in his bed, in every way possible.

" 'Tis but lust."

His eyes smoldered, his body remembering the imprint of hers against his spine, her hand low and teasing on his belly. He was still hard from it. "Mayhaps. But I know what *you* feel."

Was her blush as telling as what lay in her heart? "I speak my mind, knight, and anymore, I will conjure against that," she said lightly. "Few women want a man to be privy to their thoughts."

"Not thoughts, but . . ." He struggled to explain, unaware that he was opening himself up to more when he did so. "Heartbeats."

When she gazed at him, patient for more, he felt the gentle pull of his soul. *Damn me*, he thought, reaching out to grasp her hand. Her eyes flared beautifully.

"Like now, I feel your heart's pace hastening. A warmth pouring through you." Her heartbeat tripled and his smile grew full of male arrogance. "And last night I felt your torment as if I wore it 'neath my skin."

"Do you not see the truth, then? As a lad you sensed animals, but age has given you more." Her joy was solitary and short-lived.

He pulled back, knowing she spoke the truth and hating losing the control he'd taken years to forge. "Do you not understand that I will lose all I have if anyone learns of this?" His voice was harsh and deep with self-anger. "What will happen to me and Ireland if Richard denies the rights and favor I have?"

Aye, she understood. Connal had enough of the king's friendship to do his duty as he pleased, at his leisure. It could be easily lost, for Richard was bent on forcing religion on an entire race; the pair of them would matter little. And without that trust, someone else would come in Connal's place and be unwilling to bear the brunt of England's wrongs on Ireland as he had. She admired him for that. But the risk to his life should anyone learn of it was as great a hazard as her power was to her. She could bend the elements, but he was helpless but for his sword and his word of honor. As strong as he was, they held little strength against a council of unenlightened witch hunters. Was this the reason he died in those nightmares, for his gift? The thought reaffirmed her vows to stop the prophecy of her dreams. He'd no one but her to protect him.

"Then I suggest you keep your mouth shut about it."

He eyed her, wondering why she looked scared all of a sudden.

"Be careful with it, PenDragon. 'Tis a gift not to be abused," she said cryptically and left him frowning as he moved ahead on the narrow path.

She glanced covertly behind them, shooing at the animals that had been hopping, fluttering, and strolling the tree line behind them from the first. She kept her face impassive as they traveled and looked back to wave at a troop of rabbits lodged in the snow like rocks, as if bidding them good journey.

Deny in your heart, Connal PenDragon, she thought, *but the world of magic has embraced you.*

Darkness had descended quickly, cloaking them in the small clearing. Around them branches cracked beneath the weight of snow and ice, yet cocked them with their gnarled limbs. Connal sat on one side of the fire and bit into the roasted rabbit, not looking forward to another night alone with Sinead. But 'twas too dangerous to travel in the dark. If all went well, they'd meet Galeron a few miles north of King Rory's fortress by late morning.

He picked at the crisply cooked meat, watching his moves and listening for intruders. Yet anyone could come upon them for all the attention he mustered. His senses felt as brisk as the cold air, overflowing with the fragrances and warmth of the woman a few feet from him.

Only his gaze shifted.

On her knees, she fed dry branches into the fire, her fur cloak thrown back over her shoulders with her hair. His gaze rode unheeded over her body. Her bosom was full and flush in its snug confines, and longing speared through him. She was a small, delicate thing, he thought, her beauty unquestionable, yet Connal did not see that so much when he looked at her, but saw the cloud in her bright blue eyes, the torture she'd suffered for love. And how poor he'd treated her as a boy; then, when she was over her heartache, how the next man nearly killed her for the power he'd abhorred. 'Twas no wonder she distrusted him and his intentions. She'd lost her faith in him years past and he'd done little to regain it since returning. And what had she done except protect what was hers? Relinquishing her hold, even when the king had ordered it, would hurt her.

Yet 'twould be her death to defy Richard's orders.

'Twas to keep Prince John at bay, though Connal had his doubts as to whether it would cause a stir for the ambitious prince. As he tossed the bones into the fire, Sinead offered him a damp cloth. Lying on his side, he wiped his hands and mouth. They'd traveled for days now and she looked no worse for wear, fresh and bright in the darkness.

She stood and he came upright.

"Where do you think to go?"

She held a bundle close to her chest. "For privacy."

He stood.

"I'll have little privacy with you near, PenDragon."

She moved into the forest. She vanished so quickly he called to her.

I am here, came to him without words. *Be patient.*

A shiver passed over his spine to know she could speak to him like that. Squatting near the fire, Connal tore off a chunk of brown bread, his gaze straying to the woods. For the thicket and snow, he could see naught but darkness. She'd been gone for some time, longer than necessary to take care of her needs. Connal stuffed the last of the bread into his mouth and stood, walking into the forest.

He called her name softly, not wanting to scare her or alert anyone who might be about. His sword aready, he moved between the branches and winter-dead vines. A dull light beckoned him, yet he knew she'd not taken a torch. Then he heard the rush of water. By God, in winter?

He stepped farther and the light brightened, and as he moved around a cluster of trees, he stilled. His heart slammed to his stomach, then beat hard and steady.

Surrounded by snow-capped rocks and moss, Sinead stood in the center of a still pool of water. Naked. Her back to him, her red hair spilled down her back and floated on the surface. Steam rose from its depths, frosting the air, enveloping her in a fine mist and sparkling brightly against the darkness. As if the moonlight spilled down on her alone. Beyond and above her, the waterfall was frozen, locked in its graceful pour.

And there were faeries, a half dozen at least, fluttering around her, attending their lady like maidens of the forest.

He stilled, his sword point in the ground, his hands on the hilt as the faeries used cupped leaves full of water to rinse her hair. He'd never seen a real one before, thought them only legends to tell small children.

The sight was shattering. There was a purity in her power, and his gaze moved down over her naked spine and lower. Water slid off her and into the shallow pool as the faeries helped bathe her. She whispered to them, but he could not hear the words. She turned slightly, offering a view of her breast, the swelling curve of her hips, yet 'twas the pleased smile on her face that lit something dead and dying in his chest.

He wanted her, wanted naught more than to take her into his arms. To have her smiling and breathless with pleasure beneath him.

To feel her take him inside her and make him whole again.

His body reacted with the wild thoughts, and carefully, Connal backed up and slipped quietly away. His heart thundered at the thought of touching her skin, of tasting her, and whilst he waited, he crushed the need bludgeoning him and thought of his meeting with King Rory, then with DeCourcy. His duty.

Then she appeared before him, like a flash of light in the darkness. Dressed in a fresh gown of deep red wool, her hair was dry and curling. She sat, braiding the mass into a single plait and not meeting his gaze.

He lay on his side, stripping the dead bark from a twig.

She prepared her bed.

"Nay, come here," he said when she started to lie down opposite him. He patted the space between him and the blaze. " 'Twill be warmer."

Sinead eyed him and he held out his hand in silent challenge. She came to him and Connal shifted behind her, blocking the wind and pulling her close.

She struggled for a moment.

"Shhh," he whispered. "Be still."

"You are like leaning upon a rock."

He snickered to himself. "Keep squirming," he whispered in her ear, "and I'll grow harder."

She inhaled and twisted to look at him. Her gaze searched his. "You saw me in the pool."

He smiled and glanced toward the woods. "Will your friends return?"

" 'Twas improper not to make yourself known."

"And spoil such a delightful view?"

"PenDragon!"

"Connal," he reminded as he reached, stroking a finger down her temple and pushing back freshly washed hair. "You are a beautiful woman." A pause and then, "Especially naked."

She reddened. "You are a . . . scoundrel."

"For wanting what is mine?"

She sent him an indignant look. "Wanting what is *mine*. 'Tis not news you offer, knight."

His gaze moved over her features, landing on her mouth.

"Nay, I will vanish," she warned.

"Nay, you will not," he commanded as his face neared.

Sinead tried to conjure, to move, and yet she felt imprisoned by those words, her heart begging her to stay and taste this man. Learn if she could trust him not to hurt her as Markus had.

"Lust is empty."

He heard the plea in her voice. " 'Tis more than filling."

Hope sprang through her. His mouth neared, his big

hands slowly palming the contours of her waist, her hip, and the experience came without fear, without threat.

The wind stirred around them; the blaze flared briefly.

Neither noticed.

Connal sketched her features, searching for a spark of fear left by Markus, yet found her blue eyes clear and bright and beckoning. "I feel your body pulse, Sinead. Your heart races with mine. I know your breath, your skin, without touching it." He marveled at the sensations pelting him, heat and fire, a cool calm, and the cushion of the earth beneath them molding to their bodies. He trembled with the force of it and leaned a fraction closer, his lips brushing hers, deeper.

Snow fell, circling them in a ribbon of white.

The softness of his lips was like warm wine, a taste, and her body sang with energy, stole her breath. Her fingertips dug into his arm, into the thick muscle of the man she'd once loved. She swallowed, worrying his mouth, and was powerless, suspended between the new feelings in her heart and the doom a loveless joining would bring her. Bring the land.

Pressure increased, and his heat poured into her with a welcoming power. The quickening of it awakened her, her innocence grasping and greedy for him. A powerful shudder wracked her to her bones, a warning of the dangers and rewards to come, and Sinead struggled not to fall as she had before. So willing, so blindly.

A tortured moan escaped her as his tongue slid across her lips, and Sinead inhaled, sinking.

"Could you take my body now and not speak of love?"

His gaze locked with hers. "There is no love left in me," he confessed. "Do not look for it. This is all I have." Instantly, he cursed his honesty when she closed her eyes, her fresh tears hidden from him.

"Then you must not touch me so again."

Her tone quivered, the hopelessness in her words shattering the moment and sending him rolling to his back. He stared up at the night sky, shoving his fingers through his hair. His body throbbed with the agony of unanswered want, his blood humming, and he struggled to breathe evenly. He could have lied, given her pretty stories, but when he looked into her eyes the words would not come. And the truth wounded her, left him wanting to give her what she desired. Not so they would come together, which surprised him, but to banish the hurt her words carried.

Connal did not understand a wit of it and glanced at her back. Unwillingly his fingers slipped over the braid of hair, lightly, for a breath of a moment, before he jerked back and rubbed his face. *She's enchanted me,* he thought. To want with every fiber and be denied. Resigned to a painful night, he shifted to his side. She was curled away from him, nearer to the fire. He rose on his elbow to look down upon her, and she twisted and met his gaze.

He reached behind himself and drew his fur mantle over him. "Come," he encouraged softly, holding up the fur. "Move close and at least this night, take my warmth."

Her brows knitted with doubt.

"My word, Sinead. To . . . behave." Though it was killing him not to kiss her sorrow away right this minute. After a breath, she scooted into the curve of his body. Though the mere touch ignited the desire he'd crushed, he held her snugly, her head pillowed on his arm. He continued to watch her as she drifted into the arms of sleep and brushed a strand of red silk from her cheek.

A single tear gathered at the corner of her closed eyes, then fell. Her breath shuddered softly, and Connal felt a wild stab of regret pierce his heart. He felt it bleed and, lying down, wrapped her snugly in his arms.

Serenity washed through him, and like a sudden wave, muscle and bone relaxed. A tingling skipped over his skin, pulling him into the dream world. He could not remember a time when he felt this content with simply holding a woman.

Pinar had not given me this was his last thought before sleep took him. And she'd been murdered for the want of a single moment of pleasure.

Connal had realized two things last night and this morn when they met again with their entourage.

His mood was foul.

And the cause of it was riding behind him.

Well, three things, he amended. The skin of wine he and Branor were passing atween them offered little in the way of improving his disposition. He glanced back over his shoulder at Sinead. She stopped her conversation with Galeron to look at him, arching that infernal red brow. He faced front.

Once again he could not have the woman he wanted. Once because of deadly custom, and Sinead because he could not love her as she desired. It left him feeling hollow, as if he'd had a great gift and lost it. Twice.

The woman's going to be the bane of my existence, he thought, and the fact that Sinead had not agreed to wed him added to his troubles. 'Twas a formal decree issued by the king and the delay would surely anger their sovereign.

Branor nudged him, offering a skin of wine, and Connal loosed the reins to drink deeply, wishing he could drink away his thought. Scowling over that, he sensed rather than saw her ride up alongside him.

"Will you excuse us a moment, Sir Branor?" she said, leaning forward to look at the knight.

Branor took the wine skin, glanced once at Connal, then nodded, slowing his mount.

"A problem, my lady?"

"None till you tell me why we are headed westerly rather than farther south?"

His shoulders bunched and his gaze flicked to hers, briefly. He'd wondered when she'd realize that.

She eyed him, thoughtful. "The abbey. You go to see your Aunt Rhiannon."

"I thought to pay my respects."

Sinead nodded, agreeing.

But those intentions were a lie. He'd meet with Rhiannon for one reason: to confront her. To know why she'd abandoned him as a babe. Why he let his entire life be a damned lie. Anger seeped into his blood and he fought to mask it in his expression. From infancy to the moment his stepfather, Gaelan PenDragon, spoke the hated words, Connal had thought Siobhan was his mother, and King Tigheran his natural sire. Tigheran had died afore he was born, slain by Gaelan in a single combat for Tigheran's crimes against King Henry. That knowledge had nearly destroyed his mother's budding love for Gaelan. A year after his knighting, Connal learned the truth—that he was the product of a coupling between an Irish warrior and the woman he'd known as Aunt Rhiannon. And that when Connal was a child, Rhiannon let people be slaughtered rather than reveal her lover's identity to Gaelan and Siobhan.

'Twas the reason Connal had left Ireland and become a mercenary.

The reason he'd no right to a title as lofty as Prince of Erin.

He was the son of a murderous traitor. A man weak enough to kill his own kin by the order of Lachlan O'Neil. The son of a woman who gladly passed her child off to the clan as heir to the O'Rourkes rather than care for him herself. The deception was for the good of the clan, Siobhan had claimed. They'd needed a male leader, and though she had ruled, 'twas in his stead.

Connal had spent years keeping the secret, for if anyone knew he was the son of such a spineless man, all he had earned would be lost. Along with the king's trust he valued so well. 'Twas not the taint of his birth that bothered him; there were no bastards in Ireland. But in England, a different story could be told.

"PenDragon?"

His gaze shot to hers. He should grow accustomed to her calling him that, but since last night he'd grown more impatient to cross the line separating them.

"I see great pain on your face."

It was her tone, filled with naught but tender curiosity, that sank into his soul and stirred it.

"Many thoughts to think," he said evasively, and her expression grew more lined with concern.

"Rhiannon will be pleased to see you. She's not admitted visitors for some time now."

"I know." She'd banished herself there and spoken to no one since. She'd refused him when he'd first learned who she was.

"Why do you not go see her and let the rest of us go south? You could catch up easily alone."

Connal admitted he'd considered that and wondered if she suspected the reason why. "I will not leave you or my command for personal . . . gain."

She sighed hard. "It must be awfully tedious to think of naught but what another expects of you, PenDragon, and not what you expect from yourself."

He looked affronted. "You know naught of me."

"Then tell me, so I may."

His brows drew down. He considered that, and a thousand memories of the past years rolled forward to crush his need to release them. The way he'd scorned his father when Gaelan handed a burden to a newly knighted lad of no more than ten and seven; the moment when he charged across Irish soil to slay his countrymen. And how he'd retched in his boots for weeks over it. Then there was Syria, Cypress, the Holy Land. And the slaughter of war and the taking of innocents in a custom so horrific, he could barely think on it without feeling vile and laden with guilt. He closed his eyes tightly and shook his head.

Her hand folded over his where he gripped a dry stick stolen from a passing tree, and his head jerked up, his gaze clashing with hers. The twig snapped. Rage filled his green eyes, and she lurched back in the saddle, frightened by it and the memories it brought.

Then his expression softened, again calm, and the strength it took to master the rage made her relax a fraction.

"When did Ireland lose you?"

Connal rubbed his face. "I do not know."

Together they rode ahead of the group a few yards for privacy.

"What is it that you desire," she whispered, "not what the king wishes, but . . . you?"

He met her gaze, then searched her features, passing like a butterfly over her beauty. "You."

She did not scoff or make a face, yet only the corners of her mouth curved gently. "That is for the king and your lust. So it does not count."

"I—I know your feelings on this marriage—ah, do not speak yet, let me finish, woman."

She clamped her lips shut and nodded.

"I was not pleased either, but I will do my duty." When her expression grew mutinous, he eyed her. "Will you hear me out or sear my ears with your insults?"

"I said naught!"

"But you were thinking of smacking me for referring to our marriage as duty."

She smiled. He was right. "Forgive me; go on."

"I want no harm to anyone, Sinead, especially you. I have much to do here, for the king, for Ireland—nay," he warned, putting up a finger, "you promised to be quiet. The oaths will protect Ireland, and our people. Without the alliances, Prince John can order any and all to raise arms for more wars. With the oaths, they will shield our people from those who would rather see us ousted from our homeland to extinction. By Richard's command, uniting our families will be another mark of his promise of peace. And the oaths take back his control from John."

Sinead was silent, thoughtful, her gaze moving over his features. "I understand, PenDragon, and can see the benefit of oaths and marriages. When you ask, I will help you if I can, but you still have not told me what *you* desire."

He fell into her gaze, like diving into a crystal pool

of blue to slake his thirst; he drank her in, his heart shifting in his chest. "Peace. And to be welcome in my homeland." *And by you,* slid slyly through his mind.

"I wish that, too, but Ireland will be hard pressed to do that, for you *think* English and serve Richard so well. Nay, I do not ask for treason and nor will I commit it, for I know the English rule, but must we come like an army threatening war?" She gestured to the vassals behind them, the armored knights and carts of weapons.

"A threat lives with us, and I believe I can defend us well."

She gave him a light shove. "I do not doubt that either, you ox."

He grinned, then said quietly, " 'Twas Richard's request that I come armed, Sinead. He believes the show of force will warn back John's lackeys."

"Or anger them more."

The moment the words left her lips, the whisper of an arrow sang over their heads and found its target in the thigh of Connal's squire riding behind them.

The lad howled.

"The trees!" someone shouted, and knights formed a circle as Connal withdrew his sword.

"Sinead, stay behind me!" he ordered, reaching for his shield.

Sinead obeyed, the knights smothering her with their protection. The first clash came quickly, Connal's soldiers rushing forward. But the attackers were no match for PenDragon's troops. Larger in size, and with years of experience in the Crusades behind them, they'd hardly gained a few yards before leaving a wake of bodies behind them. Arrows arched through the cold air, piercing tender flesh; blades cut deep and fatal, the resounding screams permeating her skin.

She felt each cry, each blow, and nearest her a Pen-Dragon soldier went down, blood splattering the already drenched snow. Connal lurched forward, wanting to go to him, yet remained with her. "Defend yourselves," she said. "I will leave."

Instantly Connal knew what she meant. "Nay," he said; then to his men, "Surround her." But Monroe was there, blocking her with his body.

Sinead did not have time to disagree and bowed her head, chanting a spell to protect these brave men. To protect Connal. Only she could see the ropes of stars enveloping the soldiers, shielding their bodies from the harshest blows. Yet the ribbon of protection would move no closer to the knights surrounding her. She commanded again, but the death and battle jolted her from the saddle, tumbling her to the ground.

Sinead curled into a ball to avoid the hooves, then waved her hand, the motion pushing the mounts back so she could stand. She raced from the battleground, standing on the edge of a small snow-covered field. Connal had not noticed and she dared not call out, lest she distract him and watch him die. Her gaze fastened on him, the only knight without a helm. He lifted the sword high and swung hard, slicing through bone and flesh. When his assailant tried to stab his horse, he kicked the man in the throat, then beheaded him as he tried to scream. Sinead's stomach rolled, yet she could not take her gaze from him, terrified this would be the moment her dreams would become real.

In the center of the battle, Connal dispatched his attackers quickly, his stallion's hooves crushing any chance of escape. Behind him, Galeron defended his back. When the last man fled into the trees, Connal sent troops after them, then turned toward Sinead.

Only her blind mount remained in the protection of his knights.

His heart slammed to his stomach and he scanned the area.

He saw naught but a bush in the field, its greenery and red flowers stark against the snow. A man headed toward it, then fled into the woods. Branor bolted after the brigand, clipping him on the side of the head with the flat of his sword. Connal's gaze frantically searched the area as he called her name.

His eyes flared as the bush grew, widened. Sinead, he thought as she turned slowly, spreading her arms. The green shrubbery melted into the folds of her mantle, a thousand red butterflies clinging to her hair and cloak. The tiny creatures climbed into the air, circling above her head and painting the gray sky before vanishing.

He met her gaze. "I did not disappear," she said in her defense.

Connal smiled, too relieved that she was alive and unharmed to be upset over a bit of magic. He strode closer, wanting to hold her so badly and yet frowning softly when her gaze suddenly shifted past him. Connal turned in that direction just as a black bolt came spearing out from the trees right at him.

Commanding the wind, Sinead slapped the air and sent it downward. It sped past Connal and he whipped around in time to see the bolt find its target.

In Sinead's heart.

Chapter Eleven

GleannTaise Castle

In the cookhouse Fionna dropped the spoon, then gripped the stone wall as a sudden sharp pain ripped through her. It left her stunned, her breathing coming in short pants, her eyes burning with tears. *My stars,* she thought.

Behind her Colleen chatted away, but when she realized Fionna was not responding, she turned. "M'lady?" She wiped her hand on her apron and stepped closer.

Fionna could only nod, the pain making her legs tremble.

Colleen snapped her fingers at a servant. "Get his lordship." The child raced from the hot confines as Colleen crossed to her. Fionna's hand shot out to grip Colleen's as she faced her.

"Raymond," she whispered, and Colleen looked down, her eyes widening.

"My lord!" she shouted and helped Fionna nearer to the worktables.

Raymond rushed inside, moving quickly to his wife. She turned toward him, her eyes bleak.

"Great Scots, what happened?" he uttered when he saw the blood staining her gown near her shoulder.

Fionna gripped his arms, staring at him with pain-glazed eyes. " 'Tis not my wound but Sinead. Oh, love, she's dying."

"Nay! Nay!" he demanded sharply, as if the word would stop the truth, and he swept her into his arms, carrying her from the hot kitchen and into the hall. He demanded the table cleared, but she would not have it.

"The tower," she managed as blood flowed from her. "She is too weak to fight this. She needs help." Raymond moved to the staircase and prayed for strength to mount the steps.

The hall doors burst open, wind and mist rolling into the hall with the figure of a man. "Raymond!" the man shouted.

Colleen shrieked and rushed to her husband. Garrick held her tightly, kissed her briefly with the vigor of a man half his age, then moved to his leader.

Raymond was already beyond the first five steps.

"My lord, wait."

"I cannot."

"Sire, you must. He's sent someone to kill her."

Raymond froze, and both he and Fionna looked down at Sir Garrick standing at the first steps.

"I was in London. I learned . . ." Garrick struggled to say the words. "Prince John has sent an assassin. After Lady Sinead."

Raymond looked down at his wife, the blood blossoming from a wound that did not exist. "You are too late, my friend." Tears burned his eyes. "He has succeeded."

"Kill the bastard!" Galeron commanded as Connal rushed to Sinead, catching her as she folded.

"Oh, sweet Jesu, Sinead."

"I thought I could send it into the ground." Above their heads, a hail of arrows launched into the trees.

"Well, you did not, dammit."

"Do not swear at me, PenDragon."

Connal's hand shook as he tried to look beneath her cloak. The bolt was imbedded above her breast and she winced and shuddered in his arms when he moved the fur and fabric.

He looked at her gravely. "I have to snap off the shaft, Sinead."

She nodded, her lips gone white as the snow beneath them. "Go on, then." She had no choice, for even her own magic could not help her right now. She opened her eyes, laying her trust in him and, as Galeron held her shoulders, he broke off the thick wooden shaft.

The blood fountained and Connal reached under his armor, tearing at his tunic and stuffing it against the wound. He wasted no time and swept her up, carrying her to his horse. Nahjar waited beside it, taking her, his expression tense as Connal mounted.

"I can ride, I think."

"Do not think to argue with me now!" Nahjar handed her up to him. Her breathing came harder, the slight movement making the wound pulse with the flow of blood. Connal could feel it. Like spilling wine, her life was leaving her.

"You should have let it go," he said, kneeing the horse forward.

Her fingers dug into the fabric beneath his chest plate. "Then it would have hit you."

He looked down sharply, the muscles in his chest like steel around his heart. "I know. But I can survive a bolt, Sinead. I have, many times. I swear, woman . . ."

"I will not live, Connal." She said it softly, sadly.

His heart slammed to a stop. "Aye, you will!" Yet he could feel her death coming, her blood pumping out of her fragile body, her heartbeat slowing. The backs of his eyes burned hot and he cradled her in his arms, riding like a madman toward King Rory's castle.

She will not die in my arms, he chanted. *She will not.*

But the single thought plagued him; the last woman he'd cared about had done just that.

When the surgeon hung over her, about to bleed her, Connal grabbed the man by the back of his tunic before he could cut her and tossed him across the stone floor. "Dare that again and I will cut *you* to ribbons!" he growled, and the surgeon scooted back on his behind, knocking over a chair. "She's bled enough already, you fool!"

Connal ignored the man's fear and strode to the door, bellowing for Nahjar, uncaring that this was Rory's castle, that he had command of it. He paced while he waited, glancing once at Sinead and refusing to look at King Rory, who had not spoken or moved since Connal's latest outburst.

Nahjar appeared, a leather bundle tucked under his

arms. "Do what you can," Connal said, then glared at the others littering the chamber till the room emptied. Only Rory remained.

Nahjar moved to the bed where she lay bare beneath the sheet, pale and frail. Her rattled breathing was the only sound in the chamber. Nahjar examined the wound, then looked at Connal, and he knew they had two choices: pull the arrow out or push it clean through to the other side of her shoulder.

"It is too near bone and her heart," Nahjar said, "If I push it through, it will surely kill her." The sickening feeling Connal had held at bay since she'd taken the bolt swelled. 'Twas always more dangerous to pull it out, and if the tip was winged . . . it would rip her body to shreds.

"Hold her down Sajin, for even like this, she will struggle."

Connal, stripped of his armor and hauberk, moved to the opposite side of the bed, careful as he crawled onto the bedding beside her. His each and every heartbeat was long and aching and he fought his fears and held her down.

She moaned quietly, her eyes fluttering open. Her gaze moved drearily from the tattooed Moor to Connal. He did not have to explain and she nodded.

Nahjar widened the already red and severed skin, and when she whimpered in pain, Connal whispered to her, "Look at me, Sinead."

Her eyes opened slowly.

"Keep looking at me."

Nahjar worked with painstaking tenderness to free the thick bolt. Her blood flowed like aged wine, and though Connal had seen more horrific wounds, he could not watch her delicate skin be so torn.

"You will be fine," he encouraged, his expression harsh.

"Liar."

"Listen to me, woman," he said angrily. "You have caused more trouble than ten Saracens, so do not think I will be denied my justice."

"Idle threats," she whispered faintly, then sucked in a lungful of air with her pain.

Connal glared at Nahjar. "Be gentle!"

"Yes, Sajin." Regardless, the man kept working as he had been.

Connal shifted carefully, bending low to meet her gaze. "Stay with me, Sinead." Usually, in the past, Connal had preferred to be unconscious when Nahjar worked on him, but something inside him warned that if he let her go, he would never see her bright eyes again.

Weakly, Sinead lifted her hand to touch his thigh.

"Can you use your magic?" he asked.

She shook her head ever so slightly. "Mother . . . mayhaps . . ."

Her mother was leagues away in GleannTaise, a useless wish, and Connal knew he'd no power to keep her in the land of the living.

Nahjar jerked the bolt free and she arched in the bed, not making a sound. Not shedding a tear. Then she was lost, her eyes closing, and Connal feared, for the last time. He called her name over and over, willing her to respond, as Nahjar quickly stanched the bleeding, applying a pressure that would leave her bruised. He took Connal's hand and placed it over the wound, then went about preparing to clean and stitch her. Nahjar examined the bolt tip, sniffing it, then looked at Connal.

"Speak, man."

"I fear it is poisoned."

Connal cursed. Then cursed again.

"It smells foul, Sajin. And will fester. The wound will not kill her, but the poison . . . I cannot stop it."

Connal felt as if a black blanket fell over his world, darkening it with no way out. He swallowed thickly and bowed over her, his head on the pillow beside hers. "Do not die, Sinead. I forbid it."

Ahh, PenDragon, he heard in his mind. *In this you cannot order me. I shall find you in the next life.*

Nay! Dammit, do not toy with me like this! Stay alive.

A soft laughter filled his mind. It was effortless and free, in a place that offered no pain, no blood.

"Sinead! Stay here!" he pleaded, his voice fracturing.

Nahjar poured powders into the wound, then made to stitch it.

"Do not close that stench inside her!" a voice said from behind.

Connal looked up, blinked to focus. A tall, barrel-chested man stood in the center of the chamber, and Connal's frown deepened. He was unfamiliar, yet something about him struck a memory too deep to pull to the surface. Glossy black hair heavy with silver fell to his shoulders, braided in the old way, barely shielding bright blue eyes. *Fenian Erin,* was his first thought. Furs wrapped his chest and legs, several weapons filling the belt circling his waist.

King Rory went pale at the sight of him, and Connal didn't consider how the man had gained entry. Without permission the stranger moved to the side of the bed, pushing Nahjar back and glaring at Connal.

"You should know better, O'Rourke."

"Who the hell are you?"

Connal glanced back at Rory, who stood motionless near the hearth.

"He is Quinn," Rory said. "Queen Egrain's first-born."

Fionna's brother. Sinead's uncle. Connal's gaze snapped to the man, and he saw the familiar features of Fionna in his weathered face.

"Help her."

" 'Tis why I've been summoned."

"By who?" But Connal was already moving back to give the man room.

"Her mother, laddie. She bleeds with her daughter as Egrain bled for hers."

"Well, she bleeds, too!"

"Quiet!" Quinn laid his weapons aside, then leaned over Sinead and whispered, "Givin' up are you, little spirit?"

A tiny sound escaped her, and even that gave Connal hope.

"I never thought you'd let such a wee wound stop you," he challenged, and on the bed her fingers closed into a fist.

Quinn asked for a bowl of fresh rainwater and Connal gave it, then made to leave. "Nay, Connal, stay. The rest of you, leave us."

Without argument, Rory moved to the door, Nahjar in his wake, and when they were alone, Quinn looked at Connal. "Put your hand on her wound."

Connal hesitated, aware he could hurt her more.

"She needs strength and I am too old to give more."

From a pouch at his waist, Quinn sprinkled powder into the bowl of fresh water, stirring it three times in the shape of a star, and saying, "Power of the One, ancient and strong, elements of life come to me." He

Take 4 FREE Books!

We created our convenient Home Subscription Service so you'll be sure to have the hottest new romances delivered each month right to your doorstep — usually before they are available in book stores. Just to show you how convenient Zebra Home Subscription Service is, we would like to send you 4 Kensington Choice Historical Romances as a FREE gift. You receive a gift worth up to $23.96 — absolutely FREE. There's no extra charge for shipping and handling. There's no obligation to buy anything - ever!

Save Up To 30% On Home Delivery!

Accept your FREE gift and each month we'll deliver 4 brand new titles as soon as they are published. They'll be yours to examine FREE for 10 days. Then if you decide to keep the books, you'll pay the preferred subscriber's price. That's all 4 books for a savings of up to 30% off the cover price! Just add the cost of shipping and handling. Remember, you are under no obligation to buy any of these books at any time! If you are not delighted with them, simply return them and owe nothing. But if you enjoy Kensington Choice Historical Romances as much as we think you will, pay the special preferred subscriber rate and save over $7.00 off the bookstore price!

We have 4 FREE BOOKS for you as your introduction to KENSINGTON CHOICE!

To get your FREE BOOKS,
worth up to $23.96, mail the card below
or call TOLL-FREE 1-800-770-1963
Visit our website at www.kensingtonbooks.com.

Take 4 Kensington Choice Historical Romances FREE!

♡ *YES!* Please send me my 4 FREE KENSINGTON CHOICE HISTORICAL ROMANCES (without obligation to purchase other books). Unless you hear from me after I receive my 4 FREE BOOKS, you may send me 4 new novels - as soon as they are published - to preview each month FREE for 10 days. If I am not satisfied, I may return them and owe nothing. Otherwise, I will pay the money-saving preferred subscriber's price plus shipping and handling. That's a savings of over $7.00 each month. I may return any shipment within 10 days and owe nothing, and I may cancel any time I wish. In any case the 4 FREE books will be mine to keep.

KN052A

Name _____

Address _____ Apt No _____

City _____ State _____ Zip _____

Telephone ( ) _____ Signature _____

(If under 18, parent or guardian must sign)

Terms, offer, and prices subject to change. Orders subject to acceptance by Kensington Choice Book Club. Offer valid in the U.S. only.

tipped it to her lips. "Drink of pure light, taste of its power. Wash the poison, cleanse her this hour." Quinn poured the remainder of the water over Connal's hand and into her wounds. "Draw from this warrior now, bind his strength sharp and clean. Of the land, of the gleanns, purify our elfin queen." Quinn pressed Connal's hand deeply and Sinead moaned in pain, yet Quinn refused to set him free. Connal could not move; his hand beneath Quinn's felt as if it were sinking into her, giving her more pain, but he could not take his gaze from Quinn's as the man said, "Lady of the sky, of earth and light, Lady of water and fire bright. Gather now and do my bidding. Blood within her blood. Heart within your heart." Quinn's eyes sparkled with a strange light, growing smoky before he said, "So I say, so mote it be."

Connal flinched. A slicing sensation drove up his arm, as if he'd struck his sword against stone, vibrating through him with a painless agony that left him breathless. He choked for air, looking down at Sinead, a tugging yanking through his blood. His skin felt like glass, fragile and hard, his heartbeat slowing with his breathing. He could feel inside her just then, her lungs struggling, her blood moving in her veins.

Then her heartbeat tripled and his fear rose.

Just as quickly it slowed, the sensations fading from him, and he didn't know how long he sat there, his hand on her, her body so lifeless.

Slowly, he met Quinn's gaze. The man was already on his feet and backing away.

"You would dare leave her like this?"

"I have done all I can, my prince." A grim smile curled his lips. "The rest is in your hands."

Connal pulled his hand free of Sinead, his palm sticky

with her blood. Her breathing had not changed, yet the bleeding had stopped. He looked from his palm to her, then to Quinn. And he found himself alone in the chamber.

"Witches," he grumbled, carefully leaving the bed. He stood and the room tilted, and he sank back down, and, after a few moments, rinsed his hand in the basin beside the bed. As the water darkened, Connal frowned at the crescent-shaped cut he did not remember feeling.

It must have happened during the attack, he thought, yet he'd felt no pain. Pitching the water, he refilled the basin and moved to the bed, sitting on the edge beside her. Soaking a fresh cloth, he washed the blood from Sinead's shoulder.

Beneath the crusted blood he found her wound angry and deep.

And shaped like the crescent moon.

King Rory O'Connor stood just inside the chamber, a bevy of servants moving past him with fresh water, cloths, and food. Although they padded quietly, Connal had yet to stir from his position beside the bed, where he'd been for the last two days. He did not bother to look up, entranced by the rise and fall of Lady Sinead's breathing.

Rory closed the door, blocking out the noise. His castle was in an uproar over their arrival. Not because of the army of English soldiers and knights, but for the lady dying in the bed. The thought of what would come if she perished sickened him.

"My lord?" he called softly, stepping close.

Connal scoffed to himself, then looked up at the Irish

king. "I believe, your highness, that I am the one to address you as such."

"I am king by power; you are one by right."

Inside Connal groaned and shook his head. Not this again.

Rory looked down at Sinead. "I remember the child, wild and hungry for life; I remember the girl, about to wed O'Brien."

Connal's features creased deeper. The man's emotions, his concern came to him louder than his voice. 'Twas subtle, he realized, like a whisper barely heard, and tried to ignore it.

"Her plight then rallied a dozen clans to take her back, yet all it took was her father's determination."

Duncan, Rory, and who else had gone after the man who'd hurt Sinead? Then knew if he'd been there he'd have joined the fight.

"I understand, for I've three daughters. All redheads."

Connal chuckled to himself, but the sound fell short of laughter.

Rory coaxed him away from the bedside and to the table offering food and drink. Connal washed, then slumped in a chair, bone tired as he nibbled, his appetite as faint as his hope. Sinead had not moved in hours, her breathing so shallow he had to press his hand to her chest to be certain she still lived.

"We could rally the same for you, O'Rourke."

Only Connal's gaze shifted. "Nay." There is hope as well as anger in this man, Connal thought, then shut out the feelings to concentrate.

"I've a dozen clan leaders ready to take arms against the English. But we are scattered and unruled. You could change that."

" 'Tis sedition to speak of it."

"Give me a reason then, and it best be a good one," Rory said, scowling.

"England rules, and I am a knight of Richard." Connal gestured to his tabard bearing the king's banner and slung across a chest. "My duty is to him."

"But not Ireland."

"Christ on the cross, you sound like Sinead." He rubbed his face. "Does anyone not see that I come to *ensure* peace? And 'twould be treason to seize his vassals for war."

"The cause is just—"

"The cause is empty!" he snapped, then remembered to whom he was speaking and why he'd come in the first place. "We have lost much. Would you have us lose it all, and lives?"

"Lives lost are the price for peace."

"You do not seek peace, O'Connor," he said gruffly. "You seek to drag out what is inevitable. But if you align yourself with Richard, you keep your castles and lands, you rule as you have been. Tradition remains. The Irish way remains. And life in Ireland moves peaceably."

"England gives and takes and likes to take more. But they give to England what is not theirs." Rory gestured to the south, to Dublin.

"I am here to see that we keep what we still have, in the stead of Richard, for if John is put to power, Rory, you know we will lose all. All of it!"

Connal stood, raking his fingers through his hair and gripping the back of his neck.

"Like the Holy Lands," came from the Irish king.

"The people of Jerusalem fought and died as we did. They at least understood the compassion of victory and defeat."

"But you served to crush a race and religion."

Connal spun around. "Aye, I did as I was ordered. I had sworn my oath and never thought to demand conditions to it. 'Twas my bond and all I had. I killed for the king, aye. I killed Irishmen for DeCourcy when he fought you! But I will not do it again!"

"Not even for the chance to rule it as the *Tuatha De Dannon* meant for you to rule?"

Connal did not speak for several moments. "I was not meant for more than I am," he said with a strange calm. "And why should old legend predict my life? Mayhaps this is the motion of my life; I choose for it to remain in this path." His voice dropped an octave. "I am honor bound to stay this journey."

Rory scowled, disgusted.

He would not understand, and Connal considered telling him the truth, yet when his gaze shot briefly to Sinead, he knew he could not. 'Twas his own burden, a private humiliation to be the son of a murderous traitor, and he dared not lose what he'd gained. For more than himself would suffer. Without Richard's trust in his capabilities, without his loyalty left unquestioned, they would all lose. And his dream of a piece of Ireland of his own would be lost.

Rory stared at him for a long moment before he said, "It would not matter to the men belowstairs, Connal. For all eyes, you are the prince of Ireland."

"I am a knight of Richard!" He slammed his fist down onto the table, his anger returning threefold. "And I will warn you now, Rory, you are accepted as king of this *tuath* because Richard allows it, for it benefits all, not just Ireland. He knows you are a better ally than enemy. His liegemen have tasted it in battle; I have witnessed it. But if John is in power he will take it all and press Ireland under his thumb till we squeal for mercy. Do you want that for us?''

"Nay! Yet you want me to pledge my faith to Richard?''

"King Richard asks that of you.''

Rory's look was bitter. "And what do I do for abandoning my people?''

Connal shoved the rolled document across the table. "Read the dammed proclamation,'' he said, exhausted, worried, afraid for Sinead. "He is more than fair, he is generous. He only wishes the oath that if he must fight his brother, you will join his ranks.''

Frowning, Rory tipped the paper toward the fire to catch the light and read.

Yet Connal kept his gaze on Sinead. Then suddenly he rushed near, his hand on her chest, and when he knew she breathed, he knelt beside the framing.

His gaze moved over her face, the bandage covering her breast and shoulder. Tenderly, he swept her hair off her damp brow, his thumb brushing over her skin.

Where are you, little witch? Where have you gone?

A fever warmed her body, yet she was still as loch waters.

He closed his eyes, pressing his forehead to the bedding, his hand sweeping down her arm to grasp her hand.

Her fingers were lifeless in his.

He squeezed them gently. "Come back, Sinead. I beg you.''

"I will sign your oath, PenDragon.''

Connal twisted to meet Rory's gaze, then straightened. The Irish king held the document. He dipped the quill and scribbled.

"I am old, Connal, and I'd held a last hope for us.''

"Peace is much surer than hope, my lord. And we are and always will be Ireland."

Connal's throat tightened, something crushing his heart as from a candle Rory spilled wax onto the parchment near his signature, then with his ring impressed his seal.

Connal could not speak words that would soothe for they would be false, and the impact of his duty and the cost of it to others hit him again. "My lord."

Rory nodded, let out a long breath, then said, "Now, young PenDragon, would you like to speak with the man who did this to your lady?"

Connal blinked.

"Your men dragged him here after you arrived with your burden. I felt it best"—he gestured to Sinead—"to keep him alive. He bleeds yet he lives still."

"Not for long," Connal growled, striding to the door.

Chapter Twelve

Connal left Nahjar by her side and headed with Rory down into the bowels of the castle. 'Twas dark, the air undulating with the odor of must and age and death. A fit place for the bastard, he thought, seepage coating his boots as he moved down the corridor. Torches sputtered as he passed.

"Now, Connal," Galeron said when he saw his face. "The shot was not meant for her."

" 'Twas meant for me. When all was done, and men were dead or fleeing, this man remained hidden to shoot only at me." He stopped before a small cell and waited impatiently for one of Rory's retainers to open the lock. "I want to know by whose orders." He did not look at Galeron and knew where the coiling rage seething inside him came from.

Sinead was innocent. She'd redirected the arrow to

save him. It should be him abovestairs wasting away, not her.

As soon as the door swung open, Connal pushed inside, prepared to rip the man's limbs from his torso one at a time. The prisoner was slumped in the corner and, upon further inspection, dead as a log.

Connal cursed and kicked the arrow-riddled body before quitting the cell.

"He was alive a moment ago."

Connal frowned at the guard. "Was anyone in this cell aside you? Who has the key?" he demanded.

"What are you saying, Connal?" Galeron asked

"His wounds are not that severe, naught near vital organs. Bleed to death, aye, but death? I have lived for days with worse."

"There are other prisoners," Rory said, and a sadistic light shone in Connal's green eyes.

Rory backstepped.

"Show me."

A retainer motioned, then got out of the way. Connal wrenched open the door, grabbed the first man he found by the throat, and slammed him against the wall. "I have known the torture of the Turks and remember its instruction well."

The man stared through wide eyes yet could not form a word of speech. Connal demanded a brazier of coals and a knife.

The prisoner whimpered, his gaze shooting to the others in the cell, then to Galeron and Branor, standing behind Connal. Neither knight spoke.

Yet the king did. "You cannot do this."

"I can. I will. An innocent dies above us, Rory, and this man knows why they attacked the king's brigade. Who sent you!"

"I don' know."

Connal released him, then turned to the brazier and shoved the blade into the coals. "Who sent you?"

He picked up the knife and walked to the man, ripping his tunic from neck to waist. He asked again and again, then lashed the hot knife across his chest. The man howled, gasping for a fresh breath.

"Connal . . ."

"Get thee gone if you've no stomach for it, Branor."

He shoved the blade into the fire and then asked his question again. Each time the man refused, and the hot knife sliced through his skin and cauterized the wound instantly. The odor of seared flesh filled the cell and Connal remembered the Turks, cutting him, working their way up to his face. He lifted the glowing blade.

" 'Twas a man, from the north!" the prisoner stuttered.

Connal did not respond. Sinead was dying and he'd be damned if he'd let the loss be a waste. He ordered the others removed from the cell, and when they were alone, he said, "Describe him."

The description, slender and dark-haired, offered naught, only that the man was not in amongst the attackers. Connal's scowl deepened. There had been no papers on these men, none on the bodies. Branor had chased down at least three, including this one, and brought them back. Perhaps none could read, he considered, but that mattered little. "Why would you follow these orders? Why attack a contingent of King Richard?"

"We did not know it was . . ."

Connal did not believe that. "Why?"

"For you!"

"I know that, you fool." He lifted the blade.

"I . . . I . . ." The man sighed heavily, his lungs working against the pain. Connal cared less, bitter anger racing through his blood. "To stop you, PenDragon. To stop you from sealing a bond with the witch." The man licked his lips and Connal ladled water from a bucket and offered it to him. "They warned not to hurt her."

"They?"

"Englishmen. Two, gentry, educated."

Connal's features sharpened. Prince John's men? Connal demanded a detailed description, and unfortunately, naught of their description sounded familiar. Except the scar on one man's throat.

Scowling, Connal searched his memory as he tossed the blade into the brazier and called for Branor.

"God forgive me," the prisoner said, his breathing labored for the pain crisscrossing his chest.

Just as Branor stepped into the cell, an Irishman came rushing into the narrow corridor, splashing water as he did. "Lord PenDragon—the tattooed man says come, come now!"

Without a backwards glance Connal left the cell, muttering, "If they do not confess, you have the king's right to kill them all."

Branor paled and looked at Galeron, then the Irish king standing in the corridor.

"He is the power of King Richard in this land. Pray they talk." He looked at the prisoner. "His woman lies near death, man. He will show no mercy."

She was in a place with no pain, no sound.

Sinead walked slowly toward the hedge, the doorway in the center like a great wooden hawk. Beneath her feet the ground was warm and loamy with moss, and a gently spinning mist curled at her calves.

I am not of this earth, she thought, and as she moved, the mist cleared, giving her a brief glimpse of her surroundings. Faery sisters and elfin lads peered from the lush shrubbery and trees. A warm yellow glow showered down upon her, the waning mist suddenly sparkling with a phosphorous light.

It shimmered through her and she tipped her face toward the sky and felt its energy seep into her body, sing through her skin. And she knew she'd been in this place a long time.

She glanced the way she'd come, the way she'd thought she'd come, and pulled on her memory that faded by the moment. She was needed, she thought. And yet took a step closer to the gate.

Sinead, come back. I beg you.

Her brow knitted softly and she turned. But she heard no more and faced the gate again. Her hand lifted toward the latch and she was suddenly surrounded by slim willowy figures, their garments gossamer and ruffling in the breeze she could not feel.

Who are you? she thought and never spoke. She was not afraid, and when she turned to the figure, the yellow light dimmed.

And she saw the face.

Cathal, her grandfather. And beside him a woman who looked much like herself.

Egrain.

The choice is yours, little one. Pass with us and know a life held in time till the next comes for you.

Sinead again felt the pull, felt a hand clasping hers, but when she looked down, there was nothing.

Come back, Sinead.

Connal.

She looked at her grandparents, and beyond them stood uncles and cousins and aunts she'd never met, never knew. Yet in one sudden crush she felt their love.

The touch on her hand grew stronger. Words whispered through her mind.

I need you, lass. Do not leave me alone, for I have learned . . . that without you, I am isolated.

Sinead smiled at her family, looked up as faery sisters and brothers shot around her in a specter of light and color. Then she moved away, turning toward the voice, toward Connal.

Then she ran.

Connal clutched his skull and wondered how he could tell her father he'd failed. She was dying before his eyes. He could feel her slipping away, and for the first time in over a decade he wished he possessed the power of magic. Quinn had done all he could, stopping the poison, but Connal felt as if he needed to will her back to him. The wound was no longer angry and festering. The fever had left her last eve, yet still she did not stir. For another day she had lain still as glass and pale as light.

Then he heard her breath rattle and his head jerked up, his hands falling as her chest rose and she turned her head slightly. He shifted to the side of the bed, grasping her hand, touching her forehead and cheeks, and calling her name.

A sweet, poignant joy swept through him when her eyes fluttered open.

His throat was tight and he choked on the knot lodged there. "Welcome back, Princess."

Eyes the shade of summer grass and glossy with emotion gazed back at her, and what she never suspected
lay in his expression, in the lines of his face. Sweeping
her hair back and holding it, he leaned down close.

"You scared the life from me, woman."

The fierceness of his words touched the embers long
ago buried. "Forgive me," came in no more than a
rasp. He offered her a goblet of water, holding it to her
lips. She sipped, her gaze sweeping up to greet his before
she settled back. There was a current between them
that had not been there before, a soft snap of energy,
like distant lightning.

And he recognized it, smiled wanly, and Sinead felt
her heart shoot around her chest.

"You almost left me."

Me, she thought. " 'Twas tempting."

He paled. "God, do not say that, even in jest." The
past days of torment slaughtered him, hourly cut him
to ribbons he had to gather on his own. He did not like
it much and cared not for it to happen again.

She shrugged, then winced. "Death is not so easy to
resist."

"But you did."

"Because I heard you."

His features tightened.

" 'Tis true then, what you said?" Her gaze skipped
over his face.

His guard went up. She could see it in his eyes. "What
did you hear?"

Her heart sank like a stone in a dark pool. "If you
do not recall then 'twas naught to matter, is it now?"
She lowered her gaze to her folded hands on her lap.

"Sinead, look at me."

She did, and Connal knew he could not so easily

dismiss the feelings tearing through him. Not this time. "I *am* alone without you."

"Nay," she said, sitting up carefully, her face close to his, one hand clutching the sheet to her chest. She grabbed his arm for balance when her world tilted for a moment. "You were alone because of that closed heart beating in your chest."

He shook his head. "I am because I choose to be, for to let another so close . . . hurts too many."

She pushed his hair off his brow. "Oh, Connal," she said softly, and he shattered inside at hearing his name from her lips. " 'Tis punishment you do not deserve."

His brow knitted, memories intruding. " 'Tis truth, look at the destruction I have caused you."

She smiled. "I did that. But I am here and your words brought me home."

He touched her cheek, sinking his fingers into her hair and tilting her face upward. His gaze scored each feature into his memory. He thought of the desolation he'd felt, the rage he could not express enough, and the guilt that battered him down. And the eruption came without barriers, without thought.

"God above, I wanted to die for you."

Sinead blinked and capped feelings opened, spread. "I used magic so you would not die."

"But to sacrifice yourself—"

"Shh," she said, cupping his cheek. " 'Twas an accident. I should have been wiser." She relished in the touching and he drank her in like a bird takes in nectar. *He feels it,* she thought and cautioned her heart. "We are both a wee bit wiser now, aye?"

Connal felt himself falling again into her blues eyes, again into the lure of her enchantment, into the place where he'd felt only want and need and hunger. "Aye," he said against her mouth, and her fingers dug into his arm. The flutter of anticipation blossomed through her, hard and pressing inside her, fighting its way out.

"Connal," she moaned.

And then he was devouring her. Like a shattered dam the flood of desire came in a thick eating kiss. Untamed hunger clawed to the surface, torturing him with its strength, crawling around him, through him like a beast unearthed, and quickly willowing around her. He could feel the match of hearts, the pulse of her blood.

The hearth fire crackled loudly. A soft wind stirred around them, sifting through her hair. Over his skin. He pressed deeper into her mouth, and like a wild thing scavenging for more, he hunted the prey, pushing her slowly back into the bed.

Braced over her, he took, his arm trembling, his heart choking him with its frantic beat. And hers answered, growing stronger and stronger by the moment. It throbbed inside him. Fueled him. And his hunger would not be abated, not yet, and she offered him a bountiful feast of her mouth, to take and keep taking. God above, he wanted to take it all.

And when she arched in the bed, her hands finding their way under his tunic, Connal knew he was lost. Her fingers touched his skin and he scooped his arms beneath her, his hands clasping cool, flawless flesh as he pulled her close, mindful of her wound, mindful of the danger this moment carried.

Only a sheet lay between them, a thin layer to be ripped away and the prize shown. He could not taste enough of her and yet remembered she was as weak as a kitten. That she was dying only this very morn.

Yet her response denied it with a ferociousness that drew him tightly into a lush world of her passion. 'Twas unequaled, naught spared from him, and in the back of his mind he heard the sound of the wind, felt its caress, the rushing of the sea.

Sinead drew on his strength, feeling its power lace through her blood as he kissed her and kissed her. The energy pulsed between them, the scent of earth came alive and came to her, a cool mist playing over her skin as she sank her fingers into his hair and feasted on his mouth. Years she had waited for this moment. Years of denying her heart. Of telling herself this could never be, and he would never want her.

The perfect joy of it sang in her ears, and when she wanted more music, he drew back.

A whimper caught in her throat and she kissed him again.

"Sinead, ah, lass, nay, do not taunt me." He tried to slow his breathing and ease her onto the bedding. "This does little for your recovery."

"It does more."

He groaned weakly for her and, catching her wayward hands, pressed them down, calling himself stupid to deny himself and noble for doing just that. "You need to rest."

She scoffed. "My wound bothers me not, Connal."

God above, hearing his name was a sweet victory he would savor.

His gaze drifted around the bed and he frowned at the faint scent of moss and earth, and where had the breeze come from? he wondered, then cast it off to drafty castles. He looked at her and groaned. Settled into the mound of pillow, her lips were swollen from his kiss, her color high, which was good, but she rushed to catch her breath.

As did he.

Then she touched him, a simple thing, the whisper of the back of her hand across his scarred jaw. He wanted to turn his face into it, to nibble his way down to her arms, her breasts. And lower.

"I am well. Your blood is in me," she whispered. " 'Twas your strength you gave that healed me."

He was humbled. And yet he wasn't going to question what Quinn had done. Nor the matching cuts they both bore. He simply accepted it for the gift that it was: her life.

"I did very little," he said for lack of better words.

"Modest, are you now? When you've been preening like a cock on mid-summer's day since you returned home."

He scowled. "I do not preen."

"Not in those garments. By the goddess, have you been in those clothes since I took the arrow?"

"Aye." He looked down at his bloodstained clothes and the moments when he'd earned them came flooding back. She'd bled so much. He met her gaze and knew he must be honest with her. She deserved it.

He rose, refilling the goblet they'd let fall to the floor. Connal frowned at the softness of the stone and tapped it with his toe. It hardened under his touch.

Sinead only smiled, noticing the mist still lingered, even if he did not. "Speak your mind, PenDragon."

He handed her the goblet, then crossed to the table and returned with a half loaf of bread, breaking off a piece for her. She made a face at it.

"You have not eaten in four days and lost some flesh. Slowly," he said when she ate too fast.

Sinead felt the air between them shift with change. "You avoid me now when in my arms you took me into yourself. Why?"

"I cannot speak of the love you desire." *You deserve.*

He expected hurt, expected anger, not the sympathy in her blue eyes.

"Tell me of her."

He looked shocked.

" 'Tis a woman who has left your heart so barren, am I right?" She knew she was.

"Aye." *Mostly.*

He sat on the bed, gripping the post and forcing himself to put distance between them. He should tell her. Mayhaps she'd understand him. He rubbed his face. "This was not the conversation I wanted with you when you woke."

" 'Tis time, then."

"I have seen much, Sinead, done much that I am not proud of."

"Nahjar told me of the prison."

"Talkative, was he now?"

She smiled at the lilt in his voice that had been missing for so long. "He spoke of the torture you'd suffered."

"That was the least of it."

"Tell me of this woman you loved." She tried to keep the jealousy out of her voice. But for a moment, inside, she was the small girl he'd scolded, told that he would never love and she meant naught to him.

He stared off at the tapestry-covered walls, then forced himself to look at her. "I see none of Pinar in you." His lips curved tenderly. "She was dark—her hair, her skin—and bound by strict customs. She spoke mayhaps a handful of words to me and always whispered quickly." His features lined with pain. "She should never have even looked at me. But she did more. She left her father's home to come to me one night. A woman alone on the street of Syria is fair prey to be killed or taken as a whore.''

Sinead frowned.

"She is unclean to them and is blamed for it. Even if she is still pure. She must at all times be with a man of her family till she is wed. And then always with him in public"

"You married her?"

"Nay." Was that jealousy in her eyes just then? "Before that moment, she had no more than smiled at me passing in the market with her family. Her father was the vizier and hated us all, with good reason. We'd taken his power and his city. Whilst I slept, she crawled into my bed." He stood, and when she expected him to pace, he remained rigid, his fists clenched at his sides. "He hunted her down with dogs, and her brothers, and when they found her with me, she was crying, for I was sending her back. Nahjar heard us and came, pleading with the father. I did not speak the language well enough and did not understand the gravity of what she'd done by coming to me. Nahjar told me to let her go. I couldn't and tried to protect her. By God she was terrified, begging me to claim her. So I did." Connal dropped to the bed again, pushing his fingers through his hair. "Her father said naught, spitting on her. Then her brothers grabbed me, held me prisoner. They made me watch as her father . . . cut off her head."

"Great Mother, nay!"

"Aye." He blinked, trying to clear the image. But it still haunted him. "I'd seen battle that was as ugly, but never a simple young girl cleaved for no reason other than for smiling at me behind her veil."

Sinead shifted, dragging the sheet around her and sitting next to him

"You should lie down."

"Shh," she said and slipped her hand in his and leaned against his shoulder. "You blame yourself for this; why?"

"I encouraged her."

"You've a nice smile, Connal, but naught so bright I'd say a lass would fall all over herself to see it."

He smirked and said dryly, "I am agog over your flattery."

She nudged him. "She knew the customs of her people and 'twas forbidden to leave her father's house." She looked up at him. "Did you know the customs?"

"Some, aye."

"Would her father allow you to visit with her?"

"Nay, never."

"Then her death was her own making."

" 'Twas a dammed execution!"

She held him down when he would have stood. "She knew the rules, Connal. She chose to risk her life for a man she did not know. How can you blame yourself?"

"I must take some of it."

"For being under the command of Richard and in that place in that moment in time, aye. Take that and live with it. But not for that single death. I know you have taken lives for the king. But this one—" She shook her head. " 'Twas a burden she gave unjustly." She rubbed circles on the back of his palm, and Connal felt himself relax. "Pinar has already found another life to live, reborn again."

Connal turned his head and pressed his lips to the top of hers. She made it so simple. "You truly believe that?"

"Of course, 'tis the circle within the tree of life. In each death, life is reborn. From the dying flower comes the seed for more. From the last stag, left behind is the young doe to breed anew. Mother earth gives back as she takes. Winter hides the life that is reborn in the warmth of spring." She reared back slightly and frowned. "Did your mother not teach you this as a boy?"

He smiled, feeling old burdens slip away. "She was too busy ruling Donegal in my stead and trying to keep the clans from killing each other." Connal frowned, thinking of the rights that were hers and no longer his.

"The gleanns are fortunate not to have that trouble."

"Except with Westberry."

"Aye. Yet I had not a wee bit till you arrived, you know this."

He sighed. "You tell me often enough."

" 'Tis so neither of us forgets that what we do affects more than ourselves."

"Me thinks you have other reasons."

"Aye, but being a woman I shall keep them secret."

"Tell me a secret of yours, Sinead."

The words came tenderly, with sweet patience, and she tipped her head to look at him. "I . . ."

Connal waited, almost breathless to hear a mystery revealed.

Then she said with all seriousness, "I . . . am hungry and you stink of the dungeon."

He laughed, and with it came a freedom he'd not known he wanted.

And like Sinead, once tasted, he wanted more.

A single figure leaned against the stone wall and watched the festivities. They were not easy to find, the swath PenDragon's soldiers cut through Ireland like swiping a hand in the dirt. He'd been only a day or two behind them till the attack and easily learned of the witch taking a bolt meant for PenDragon. Heroic little pagan, he thought, and was pleased that he'd not been denied his justice on the king's personal mongrel.

Prince John still coveted the woman and someone to use against her. He feared 'twas the Irish knight, and anger stewed in him like boiled beef. *Take her father, take one of her sisters,* he thought, *but PenDragon . . . his death belongs to me.*

He'd no second thoughts of his betrayal, of the damage it would do to his name, to his family. For most of his kin were dead because of PenDragon, for his need to drag others in his fight for the English king. He would die for his vengeance. Besides, Prince John had already rewarded him with a taste for killing. He'd taken Westberry to hell for his failure. The Englishman had begged like a girl and died just as quickly.

The man's gaze flicked to the staircase as PenDragon descended, his smile bloody dammed pleased. His knights rushed forward, the one called Monroe leading them. Whatever he said made them sigh with relief.

So. The witch lived.

The weakling prince would be pleased.

Yet when it came time to kill her, the Irishman wanted to wield the blade. That and to bring back the prize of PenDragon's head.

Chapter Thirteen

"What do you mean, you still will not marry me?"

Sinead kept her gaze forward as she gathered the length of her gown and walked to the staircase. "I think I've been clear, Connal."

Beside her, he descended the stairs into the great hall. "But the other night—"

So like a man, she thought. "Did you not hear your own words?" She waited till he remembered. *I cannot give you the love you want.* "I see you have. And 'twill take more than a kiss to sway me to marry you. Besides, I do not need a husband, and—ah!" she said, putting up a hand to stop the grand decrees of the king she knew were coming. "And then there is the matter of your torture of those prisoners."

He should have known she'd learn of that. Damn. "That has naught to do with a marriage."

A thin red brow lifted as she paused on the steps and regarded him. "Respect for human life does."

That was like a slice to his pride. "I gained important information the only way I could." He stopped her at the landing, waving back the men coming toward them to greet her. "Divide and conquer."

"You could have done that without cutting them to ribbons," she hissed.

His features yanked taut and he pulled her into a nearby hall. "You were dying! I had your blood on my hands, Sinead. Blood they spilled! I will not put that image aside for some time."

"Do not blame me for your savagery! You could have learned that information without inflicting such pain. Can you not see the ease your gift of magic would bring if you would simply put it to use?"

He hushed her, drawing her farther from the impatient crowd and catching a glare from Monroe, who obviously wanted to see for himself that Sinead was well and Connal had not kept her prisoner in the tower.

"I warned you not to speak of that. 'Twill destroy the trust I have, and then where would we all be?" His glance shot to the right to the Irishmen gathered and staring at him. He'd felt their hatred when he had arrived, and he'd pushed it aside to focus on her. Yet now that she was healing, rather quickly, 'twas harder to ignore. And if he did try, if he did open himself to it, what proof would he have other than caution? This dammed gift of the senses was more of a burden and he loathed that it had grown stronger once he was near her again. For he could feel her turmoil, sharp and on the surface, and that it was coupled with hopelessness bit into his skin.

She did not trust him to keep Ireland in his thoughts.

She was resigned to it. And he suspected naught shy of abandoning his knighthood and starting a war would change that. No matter how good her kisses felt.

"You secure the king's oath, you do the king's work, and I know 'tis duty, I understand you cannot break such a promise."

"Good."

"But what of yours to Ireland?"

"Oh, so I am no longer a traitor and unwanted brother of Erin?"

She waved that off with an impatient sound. "Before all eyes, you represent the king. We were attacked because of who you are."

So they could take you, he wanted to tell her but refrained. Connal was terrified at what Prince John, a dangerous man of such power, could do to her if he did take her. "What would you like me to do, Sinead? Hide till Richard has what he needs, leave so you can go back to ruling peaceably while the rest of Ireland suffers?"

Her gaze narrowed with barely checked anger. "You tread upon weak ground with that, PenDragon."

He took a slow, deep breath to ease his temper. "I am not Ireland's enemy; how often must I speak this? I want what is best for peace, but in finding that we are both in danger now. There are men with power playing games around us and we are their targets."

"Why? I am no threat."

He laughed unkindly. "You are because you wield the elements and they cannot. Because your mother does, and because of our families, Sinead. The armies have always been a threat to Prince John's throne," he said with disgust. "My trust with Richard is a threat he cannot overcome, even if he kills me, for Galeron is sworn to step forward to complete my duty. But 'tis *you* he wants. *That* is what I learned last night.''

These men obviously did not know the extent of her powers. "They said this?''

He nodded. "They do not want us to marry.''

Her lips twisted wryly. "Then so would it not behoove us *not* to marry?''

"That will matter little; wed or nay, they will try more than arrows before I secure the oaths and put them in Richard's hands.''

Sinead winced suddenly, pain tripping over the back of her skull with the image of Connal on the battlefield, a sword piercing his side. "Then it makes no difference.'' Not to him, she thought sadly. She was still a duty, a mission to perform for his king before going on to the next obligation. Sinead tried not to feel the sting of it; but then, she'd known this for so long. And her heart once again ruled and left her bleeding.

"Must I tell you again—''

Her temper flared and the hot scent of spice suddenly filled the area. "Spare me the proclamations of the king against those of your heart!''

She drew her arm high, the sleeve blocking her face. Then she was gone.

"Damn.'' He glanced around and found red flowers at his feet. He picked up a handful, inhaling her scent. "Sinead,'' he said, looking to the ceiling. "We are not done.''

"Lose her again, did you, lad?'' Galeron smiled as Connal walked from the corridor.

"Find her.''

Galeron nodded and, motioning to Nahjar to follow, went to search.

As Connal moved to look elsewhere himself, Monroe approached. "Where is she?"

"Off throwing something, I imagine, and wishing 'twas at my head."

Monroe's gaze narrowed. Connal waved it off tiredly, then noticed a guard rush from the steps that curved toward the back of the castle and into the dungeon.

"Christ on a cross, Monroe, go below and see if she is there." Connal knew he'd throttle her if he saw her now.

"Why would she be?"

"Trying to save my eternal soul, I suspect." At the man's frown, he added, "I believe she's attempting to heal the prisoners."

"So they can be executed?"

"I doubt that thought ever occurred to her."

"Then tell her."

"And have her defend her attackers to me?"

"She would not."

"Monroe, your lady covets life in all things, be it her enemy or nay. 'Tis her nature. Bloody hell, she is nature."

Monroe folded his arms over his chest, listening patiently. "You wish to reveal something I do not know, my lord?"

Connal scowled. "She thinks magic can protect her always, and the past days have proven to me that weakened, Sinead is as helpless as any woman."

Monroe stared for a moment. "I agree."

"Then you can understand my troubles when she refuses to obey me. Even if to protect her from herself, her magical ways."

"My lord, 'tis been my duty since—"

"Since the O'Brien hurt her."

Monroe let out a long-suffering sigh, as if he shed a great burden. "Thank God she told you."

"Why?"

Monroe met his gaze. "Because, my lord, the O'Briens are a mean lot. And Markus had brothers." With that Monroe rushed toward the stairs leading below.

Brothers. Connal stopped cold, his gaze ripping over the faces littering the great hall. He examined each one, mentally marking off his own men and the Irish king's guards. King Rory was suddenly at his side.

"You are going to send my folk running with that look, PenDragon."

Connal merely glanced his way, searching for the unfamiliar still.

"What do you seek in my home?" Rory asked quietly.

"An assassin. More than one, I'm afraid."

Rory's gaze moved slowly over the crowd. "There are so many, but I will tell you each is familiar, down to the last babe."

"Be sure, your highness, I beg you."

God above, trouble came to him threefold this day, Connal thought. And for a brief moment he felt something . . . anger? Bitterness? He could not be certain, but 'twas as if it reached out to swipe a claw down his back. He turned, saw Branor, then called to him and two other knights. With them came his squire.

"Spread out and find Lady Sinead. Discreetly." He did not want to alert anyone.

The men moved off, and Connal gave quiet orders to the squire to prepare to leave. He warned him of discretion. Then he faced Rory. "My thanks for your hospitality, sire, but we depart."

"When?"

"As soon as I find my lady."

* * *

Sinead fastened the leather and fur cloak at her throat. "I will meet you outside the castle walls."

"You will come with me now."

Her gaze snapped to his. Hooded and heavily cloaked, his face was barely visible. "You wish this to be clandestine. Then leave the army and put a squire in my cloak." She tossed the velvet mantle at him and he snatched it from the air. He handed it to Nahjar.

"That was the plan." The troops would leave at dawn, and with them, someone wearing Sinead's cloak and his banner. It would give them enough time to get to DeCourcy's without mishap. He knew he could protect her if she would just obey him. Once, he thought. All he asked was one time to have her compliance. The woman was going to turn him gray and old, and he suddenly had great admiration for Monroe.

"I can move between the worlds, Connal. But I cannot do it for anyone else without a strong spell. And you have insisted we have no time for that."

"I do not want you from my sight. Now come with me." He held out his hand, his mantle sliding back.

She tipped her chin and faded out of existence.

Connal ground his teeth and left the chamber, leaving Nahjar behind to give the impression of it being occupied, and to be alert should anyone try to enter with plans to take Sinead's life. Without armor or spurs, he moved soundlessly through the castle, the stone fortress silent but for the groans of a few finding a comfortable spot to rest. He left the hall through the cook house, moving across the yard to the west portal. Glancing for onlookers, Connal fell into the shadows and slipped out, remembering once when he'd done this as a boy, leaving GleannTaise Castle, angry with Raymond for refusing to train him, only to discover that Sinead had followed him. 'Twas the moment she'd confessed her heart to him, a child of no more than four or five. And moments later she'd been kidnapped. He recalled the beating he'd taken trying to help her, and the feeling of failure he'd lived with when he had to tell her mother he'd failed. He would not do so again, he thought, his heart pounding with the memory and the sudden fear that she would not be where they agreed.

But she was. And he let out a breath as she stepped from beneath the tree. He tossed his mantle back over his shoulders and secured the leather bag his squire had prepared. He glanced at her, frowning at the odd look on her face.

Sinead stared at his garments, something akin to pleasure working through her. Gone was the chain mail, the leather tunic he often wore, the chausses and hauberk that spoke of England and studded with pewter. In its place was a deer-hide tunic, finely stitched and tanned dark gold with black and linen trims. Simple, elegant. Irish. His sword belted the garment and his legs were encased in braided leather the color of autumn so snug she could scarcely tell where the fur-lined boots began.

He noticed her inspection. "King Rory lent them."

"They suit you well," she said softly.

The catch in her voice brought him up short. "Do not get ideas, Sinead; they are only clothes."

"They are Irish clothes, Connal. And you wear them well."

Ah, the power of that smile is unequaled, he thought, returning it as he realized 'twas the simple things that pleased Sinead more than gifts of gold. "Come, we must make haste," he said, grabbing hold of the saddle to mount.

"Are we to find Genevieve along the way?"

He glanced. "The blind beast is in the stable. Too many saw it and know she is yours to make this work. She must leave with the rest. My horse is there, too, and Galeron will ride it and wear my banner."

Sinead nodded. " 'Tis gallant of him."

Connal rolled his eyes and mounted, then reached for her, depositing her before him.

"Would it not be best if I rode behind? Should we be attacked, how can you fight?"

"Should we be attacked, I want you to do that disappearing thing and hide." He adjusted the reins and headed south, slowly. "Promise me."

She tipped her head to meet his gaze and saw the grave concern in his eyes. "Aye, I promise."

He shook his head. "Your oath that you will not try to help me as you did with the bolt."

She looked at him as if he'd grown antlers. "I cannot swear that."

"By God, must you be so dammed stubborn?" he said between clenched teeth. "And who said the other night we'd grown wiser?"

There was a pause before she said softly, "If I swear with restrictions I've bound myself, and I will not do that again."

In the dark, his expression flinched with sympathy. "Forgive me, Sinead. I forget oftimes that there are rules to magic."

In the moonlight Sinead saw the concern he showed and the fear he held from her. It touched her and the words tumbled out. "I swear to you, should the need arise, I will use my magic to protect myself." *And you,* she added silently. "So I say, so mote it be." She touched her heart, and Connal sighed when the night air glittered softly.

"Good enough." Without pause, he kissed her, a quick play of lips and tongue that left them breathless and burning.

Her eyes drifted open slowly, her senses stirred and drained in the same instance. In the moonlight he held her gaze trapped with his own. She did not have to see his eyes to know. They had the power of touch. How long could she defy her heart for her pride? she thought. And would he always see her as more duty than woman? More goal for his king than need for himself?

"Rest," he murmured in a tight voice, and she settled back against him as he directed the horse southward. As the animal picked its way through the darkness, Connal shifted her on his lap, a bit shocked and pleased when she slipped her arms around his waist and laid her head on his chest.

Her sigh was audible in the dark, like a ripple against his body. "I am safe only here, Connal."

His throat tightened and he kissed the top of her head tucked beneath his chin. The words were a gift, a rite of passage. A piece of her trust. And he realized he would rather die than lose it.

John DeCourcy stood at the window of his private chambers, his hands behind his back, his gaze on the activity beyond the thick stone walls. The courtyard was populated with lords and ladies, some waiting for an audience with him, some there to pick up a bit of gossip or a new lover. He loathed that his beloved castle had turned into such a ground for intrigue. But such it was.

With Pipard and La Petit's appointment and the loss of his power as justiciar, DeCourcy sought other means to keep King Richard in power. The ten cantreds in Connacht was bargained more for his old age than for power, but the alliance with Covderg gave him a foothold until Richard returned from the Crusades and settled his little brother's interfering. Prince John ruled Ireland, aye, but when Richard learned how he was using it, the situation would change.

The wind kicked at the drifts of snow and he smiled to himself. Ireland was a land he'd easily loved, despite having fought against most of her kings and lairds for Richard's father, Henry. He almost missed his battles with Hugh DeLacy and was glad his son was of better temperament and less ambitious.

A knock shook the door, and DeCourcy smiled to himself.

"Come in, Walter."

The door swung open and the man strode in, chain mail shaking, armor chinking.

"How the bloody hell do you always know 'tis I?"

DeCourcy smiled patiently. Walter was the image of Hugh, big and robust, and he was not going to reveal that he was the only one who shook the hinges with a single knock. It proved to DeCourcy that the man had confidence.

"What brings you here?"

Walter tucked his helm beneath his arm and stepped near the fire roaring in the wide hearth. "I've news from the port."

DeCourcy pulled the velvet robe close, chilled, then sat in a carved chair near the fire.

"You should divest yourself of that armor, Walt, afore you cook inside it."

"I am accustomed," the younger man said, settling easily and leaning toward the blaze to warm his hands. "I heard that someone readies a ship. Aye, I know it's a port, and that is what it is for," Walter said with affection, knowing DeCourcy would point that out. "But Richard's banner was spotted."

"I'm to understand 'twas not intentional?"

Walter shrugged. "I was riding the street near the wharf and a chest fell off a cart. I'd thought little of it till I saw a coat of arms. 'Twas Richard's."

If Walter thought such news would shock DeCourcy, he was mistaken. The man, whose calm helped him through many a battle, only looked mildly interested. If Walter was not used to it, it might have irritated.

"The owner of the cart confessed?"

"I admit that it did not dawn on me till I was some distance away." He blushed a bit at that. "When I returned there was no sign of cart, man, or the others surrounding him. But 'twere English, that I can say. These men were commonly dressed but did not carry themselves so."

DeCourcy frowned. Prince John's men, mayhap. In disguise? Or had they plans to use Richard's banner as a ruse? "Pipard and La Petit could be behind this. Gathering an army? But for what? They're the justiciar here now."

"Mayhaps to take to England? Or the Crusades?"

It was possible, DeCourcy thought, but word was, Richard was returning. Since then, DeCourcy knew little more that. He trusted few at Prince John's court to tell him the truth.

Without knocking, DeCourcy's wife pushed into the room, directing servants with trays. Affreca glanced at her husband, smiled gently, then quietly supervised the meal being laid out. "Join us, Walter?" she said without looking at him as she let the servants out.

"My thanks, my lady, but nay, I've duties." Walter stood and John's wife, an Irishwoman, daughter of the King of Man, moved close to her husband, fussing with the velvet blankets. 'Twas a good match for one made for alliance, he thought.

"Learn what you can of Prince John's doing. Go to Pipard and make yourself a nuisance if you must. Or send a trusted man to do it."

Walter nodded, picking his helm off the floor.

"A woman would find out more," Lady DeCourcy said softly.

The men exchanged a smile.

He was nearly to the door when John asked, "How did they carry themselves?"

Walter turned smartly to face him and found DeCourcy with his arm around his wife's waist, as if caught in the act of pulling her onto his lap. It made him smile.

"Like soldiers. Well trained, efficient."

"And?"

"That makes them deadly, my lord."

Chapter Fourteen

They were well beyond the boundaries of the gleanns by late the following day, and Connal was thankful for his Irish garments as they passed through yet another village. Wearing Richard's coat of arms had not been helpful thus far, and though he could ride through without notice, Sinead was recognizable and drew a crowd of folk if they stopped to rest near homes. He'd watched her play with children, offer herb cures for the sick and, much to his irritation, made a dry well flow with water for the village folk. He'd warned her about using her gift for all to see, but she ignored him. *Damn me, but I should not be surprised.*

Say left and she will go right, he thought, and yet whilst he purchased some food and wine for them, Connal kept his gaze on Sinead as she stepped into the trees and vanished. It gave him pause, the sight of her moving through a doorway that did not exist, and after all they'd been through on this journey, he was not comfortable with her being alone. Even to relieve herself. Though she'd balked at his close proximity the entire trip. Hurriedly paying the proprietor, he slung the sack over his shoulder and headed into the woods. Apprehension slithered over his spine when he did not find her, and between his worry, he swore he would tie the woman to his saddle to keep her safe. He trudged on, calling her name. They were farther south, the air a wee bit warmer, the snow only in patches and melting. His boots sank into the soggy earth, his voice echoing through the barren trees. He was nearly running when he smelled smoke.

He stopped short when he spied several men huddled around a small fire, the land close to them surprisingly void of snow. A niggling feeling crept up his spine as Connal moved closer. Gypsies, he thought after a better look. He searched the band for their leader, and deduced the fellow on bended knee was in command. There was an air about him that could not be mistaken. His hair overlong and shaggy, he fed damp wood into the flames, speaking and gesturing to someone, yet his broad shoulders blocked a view. Then he sat back on his haunches, and Connal's heart slammed to his stomach.

Sinead. Damn her hide! He'd been worried that she'd been hurt or stolen, and here she was, sitting comfortably around a gypsy's fire, laughing. With a stranger. The leader leaned forward and, their heads together, she smiled at the man. A tender smile she'd yet to bestow on Connal this day. His gaze riveted to her face, something akin to jealousy speared through his blood. She was his woman, his by order of the king. And after her injury, she'd no right to scare him like this.

Forcing himself to remain calm, he stepped into the

clearing and called, "Sinead," when all he wanted to do was snatch her up and cart her from the forest.

She looked up, her features pulling tight with guilt.

His hand on the hilt of his sword, his grip tightened when the man grasped her arm, as if holding her down. Connal took a step closer. Quickly, she removed the man's hand and came to him, putting herself between him and the gypsies.

"I should do as I thought and tie you to the horse," he said between gritted teeth. "What the bloody hell possessed you to wander off?"

"I did not wander," she snapped. "I knew you would follow. And they are harmless."

"To who, Sinead? Ireland?" Connal made a rude sound. "They thieve on the less fortunate."

"Nay, they only survive." Though his gaze was directed beyond her, to the gypsies, Sinead sensed his anger. Their discord had no place here, and yet 'twould be her fault if he unleashed it on the innocent.

"When will you cease thinking the worst of me?"

She blinked.

"I can feel it, the unsurety in you, the doubt you hold for me," he said.

Though his expression was fierce, his voice colored with hurt, her smile was slow and light.

"Do not look so pleased with that, woman; I am angry with you for vanishing like that."

"You found me easily. So what is the harm? Is it mayhaps that you found me with another man?" She was goading him, opening herself for hurt, she knew, but Sinead could not help it. She wanted more from Connal, more than duty, more than simple friendship, for in her dreams she not only saw his death. She saw the hint of future, murky at best, but there. 'Twas that she clung to.

"Any man is a threat to you."

She inclined her head to the gypsies. "I have naught that they want."

He scowled. *But you do,* she was not saying aloud. Her land, her right of rule. A piece of Ireland for himself. Aye, he wanted more from her, and Connal was beginning to question his right to it. What had he done to earn it? "Come with me now. We must leave to meet the contingent afore reaching DeCourcy's."

Sinead nodded, took a few steps away, and yet when she opened her mouth to speak, the tallest of the group moved to stand in front of her.

"What say you here? And what business you have with the lady?"

Behind the gypsy's back Sinead rolled her eyes. *This is why women should rule,* she thought, and moved around him. "If you think 'tis flattering, you are sadly mistaken."

" 'Tis none of your concern." Connal spoke to the gypsy as if she had not.

The man's sword came up, the point positioned near Connal's heart. "I am making it mine."

Connal loosed his weapon from its scabbard. " 'Tis unfortunate for you then, for she is my woman."

The leader scowled, glancing for confirmation from her.

Connal arched a brow, waiting.

Sinead ignored the tiny thrill Connal's words gave her and looked at each man as if they had turned into toadstools, with just as much brains. "Well. Go on, then." She waved to get the battle done. "Off with his head! Cut each other to ribbons, since you seem ever intent on doing so. Without cause."

Connal's lips pulled in a flat line, his skin flushing a bit.

She looked at the gypsy. "Challenging him will gain you what, sir? Gold? He carries none. A horse? 'Tis yonder"—she flicked a hand toward the village—"and the beast is exhausted from carrying us both."

Her gaze snapped to Connal. *Neither my honor nor my life is at risk,* she thought, and Connal sheathed the sword.

"I only thought—" the gypsy began.

"Nay, you did not bother to use your brain, or the two of you would not be so ready to battle like hounds over a bone that does not exist," she said, leveling an irritated look between both men. "You growl and roar when simple patience will solve. If I thought womankind would be better, I'd think of a way to make you all mute!"

"I am well chastised, Lady Sinead." The man looked sheepish as he sheathed his sword. "You may stop berating me now."

Connal fought a smile. "Me thinks she enjoys it so."

She looked at them both, her jaw dropping. "Oh, fine." She threw her hands up and walked toward a frail woman huddled on the ground.

"The lass has a fine temper." The gypsy gestured to the ground, the melted snow, and the burst of red flowers.

Connal glanced and smirked to himself. "Aye." And she looked magnificent when that temper was up, he thought, watching her with the other woman. Connal felt a sudden rush of shame from the gypsy woman, a dark despair and fear of him. Nay, he thought, of all men save the one standing beside him. He shifted his gaze to the tall bearded gypsy. His garments threadbare, his hair overlong and shaggy, did not quite hide the bearing in him that came only from education and breeding. Nor did it shadow Connal's memory. " 'Tis good to see you, Dillon."

The man's features sharpened, and he scratched at his beard. "She thinks you do not recognize me and saves me the shame."

" 'Tis no shame to keep your family together," Connal said, his gaze traveling over the people. "What happened? Why are you not in Connacht?"

"As was with your mother and your kin, O'Rourke, the English came."

Connal felt the full brunt of his words like a blow to his middle. Dillon was a chieftain, ally to Maguire and lord over West Connacht. And now he was forced to steal and feed off the winter's land. In King Henry's time, the clan leader would have been given the rights back after swearing oath, as Ian Maguire had to his father, Gaelan. "Did you not swear fealty to Richard? 'Twould have gained you the right to rule and mayhaps the castle and lands."

"The English attacked without warning; we had no choice but to defend. We never stood a chance. They sacked the castle, killed my father, and did God knows what to my sister." His gaze flicked to the hunched woman Sinead spoke with. "She's not uttered a word since. I thought naught could be worse than when they killed my wife." Dillon's voice fractured. "But I was wrong."

A hard stab of rage hit Connal in the chest. "By God, tell me who did this! I will find the bastards and bring them to trial."

"Really?" Dillon scoffed. "For 'twas under Prince John's banner they came."

Connal muttered a foul curse. England's grasp on his homeland was harsher than he thought. And it enraged him. He admitted that this was what Sinead had been trying to make him see these weeks past. And he'd been blinded by duty.

"Do not step into this trap, man," Dillon warned. "Not for us." His gaze lowered briefly to the English sword bearing the king's heraldry on the fist cuff.

Connal noticed.

"If you do, you will have to choose."

Dillon gauged that fierce look and decided he was fortunate to still be standing.

"I will do what I can, Dillon. The O'Malley belongs with his clan and they belong in Connacht. Not wandering the lands like—"

"Beggars?"

"Forgive me. I did not mean to imply—"

Dillon put up a hand. "I know what we have become. I only hope that King Richard will correct his brother's mess when he returns."

"He is returning. I suspect he's managed to gather his ransom by now."

"Gather ransom? Why does he not simply send word to his brother for it?"

Connal made a face and told Dillon what he knew, knowing he could trust Dillon and, in doing so, offered assurances that this horrible plight could change. And by heaven, it would. Connal would see to it.

"Then you best be off, aye?"

"Aye, if Sinead would obey me and come along."

Dillon barked a laugh. "Obey? Sinead? She always was impetuous."

" 'Tis too gentle a description," Connal said, folding his arms over his chest, his gaze on her. "You know, my mother raised me to have a tender spot for women. I'd like to think she had a reason for reminding me of it constantly. Me thinks this is it."

Dillon laughed, a wealth of turmoil released in the deep sound.

Sinead lifted her head and, across the clearing, met Connal's gaze. She gave the young woman one last touch and hurried to the men. Her gaze flicked between the men as they tired to contain their chuckles.

"Somehow I think I've become a source of entertainment."

Wisely, neither man acknowledged that.

"Go on, Sinead," Dillon said and kissed her hand, recognizing her concern for his plight. "Leave your worry here. There is naught you can do to change this." He inclined his head to PenDragon. "And it appears you have more of a challenge than I."

The sight of the man touching her so intimately sent Connal's imagination racing like a rutting stag. He smothered it and thrust out his hand for Dillon. They shook, and Connal said, "I will help, Dillon, because this is not what King Richard intended for Ireland."

Dillon nodded, his expression resigned of hope, and it made Connal more determined to find a solution. It also meant he had to do all he could to maintain Richard's trust.

Sinead waved to Dillon. "Good journey to you, my friend," she said, then stepped into the snow-covered trees. Connal cast one last glance back, then followed Sinead.

Dillon looked down at the sack left at his feet. Picking it up, he opened it, then with a whispered thanks turned to offer the food and drink to his people. He'd lost much these last years and Connal PenDragon, he realized, had left him with his pride still intact.

And hope. For the first time since he held his dying wife, he had hope.

When they were deep in the forest, Sinead stopped, and before he could drag her along, she dipped her hand beneath the fluff of snow, coming back with a bit of grass and flowers, nearly transparent for the chill. Then she sank to her knees in the ice and snow, spreading out her cloak around her.

Instantly Connal knew what she was about. "Do not do it, Sinead."

She sent him a hot look back over her shoulder. "Oh, for the love of Bridget, man. I cannot leave them so destitute. What friend would I be when I have the power to help?"

"You cannot conjure on them."

Her blue eyes snapped with impatience. "Oftimes, Connal, you are too arrogant for words. I do so *for* them, not *to* them."

With a dismissing look, she lifted her arms, palms out to the sky. The grass and frozen flowers glowed in her hand. The air around her brightened with gentle radiance, and Connal stared, his heart skipping a beat as she tipped her face to the heavens. The hood fell back, her red hair spilling to the ground in a soft fall of autumn's breath.

"Lord of the sun, Lady of the moon, come to me, fill me with your blessings, grant me the power of change."

Tiny sparkles of light surrounded her, becoming part of her skin, singing in ribbons from her fingertips and into the sky. The breeze of light surrounded the band of gypsies, high above them, to serpentine within the trees.

"Lord and Lady of the sun and moon, I invoke thee. I ask thee to grant me the power of change for these kind people. A gift they gave me, a gift I return to them threefold. Let Dillon see the stag that he may feed his clansmen. Bring the liquid of life near and plentiful to ease a thirst for more. Bestow the creatures of the forest to offer warmth for garments and in boots to shield against the wrath of the Lady's winter till the Lord of the sun grants us Ostara." Her breathing came faster, the radiance intensifying. "So I say, so mote it be!"

The ribbons of light fell, showering the gypsies, and Sinead lowered her arms and slumped forward.

Connal rushed to her, gathering her in his arms. She tipped her head back. A sweet contented smile graced her lips. He swept her hair from her face and brushed the back of his knuckles across her cheek. Her skin was incredibly soft and cool. "Are you ill, lass? Does the wound pain you?"

"Nay, but I fear I am a wee bit weak still."

Unsatisfied with that, Connal flipped back her cloak and in the chilled night pushed the shoulder of her gown aside to see the wound. 'Twas closed and healing faster than he thought possible.

She saw his shock, then took his hand and turned it over, showing that his cut had sealed and left behind only a thin white scar. She pressed his palm to her shoulder, the warmth of his touch pushing into her wound. Connal flinched as energy shot up his arm and quickened through his body.

"Know that this has always been in you, Connal," she

said softly. "I can not give it, nor take it from you. Only you can see the secrets that embrace you."

"Sinead, I do not want—"

"Do you think that when a hundred men vied for my hand and not my heart that I did not wish I was ordinary? That when I had no friends who did not want me to grant them wealth that I did not deny this power?"

His gaze raked her features, his mind imagining the lonely life she must have led surrounded by people who wanted more from her than they gave.

"But 'twas impossible to deny. As this is in you." Her grip over his palm tightened, and he felt the surge again. "You have accepted my gifts, why not your own?"

He struggled to put thought to words and failed.

"You reject a blood right, Connal."

" 'Tis not my right at all."

Sinead's brow worked a bit. There was much anger in those few words, and she wondered at the root of it. What other secrets did he keep from her? "Know me well, PenDragon, this." She pulled his palm from her shoulder. "Would not be so if that were true."

Sinead shifted upright, her face inches from his.

"And you already know this or you would not have found me in the forest."

She kissed him briefly, quickly, and when she sensed he wanted more, she stood, waiting for him to do the same.

Connal closed his hand in a fist. Bloody hell, he thought, he hated when she was right.

"DeCourcy awaits, as does your Aunt Rhiannon."

Connal stood, staring down at her.

"When you are ready, Connal. You will tell me what troubles you."

Never, he thought. For he could not put voice to his

shame. His blood sire had been a traitor and, like his true mother, both had let their own kin die rather than give up each other to save a single innocent soul.

Armor gleamed silver in the morning light. Hooves pounded the hard cold earth as trumpets sounded a herald to the guards of the castle. Nestled in sharp cliffs with the sea at her west, the fortress was iced with snow melting in the unseasonably warm sun.

Ostara comes early, Sinead thought, riding alongside Connal. She smiled. For whilst his knights wore armor, Connal did not, choosing to wear yet another set of garments lent by the Irish king. The gesture spoke to her, more than he knew, she thought. 'Twas a pride radiating from him. It sang to her heart.

"You've been smiling at me all the day," he said without a side glance.

"Mayhaps because this is the last oath and we are done."

"Then 'tis to England we head."

"Good journey then, for I shall remain here."

"Nay, you will join me." He kept his gaze ahead.

"Whatever for?"

God above, he could feel her rebellion churning in his blood and smiled to himself. "You are my betrothed and Richard will want to meet you."

Sinead looked away. She'd no desire to meet a king who moved lives around like chess pieces on a board. And she was honest enough to admit she could not keep from telling him just that. She'd little time to think on the matter when the gates opened wide to allow the retinue inside the bailey of CrackFergess Castle.

A soldier had been sent ahead, and Sinead watched

as DeCourcy came forward, his swagger strong for a man his age. His hair peppered with more gray than black, he greeted Connal with a smile and a strong hug.

He looked up at her. Sinead bowed her head slightly. "My lord, good day to you."

He did not speak at first, then found his voice. "Ah, PenDragon, you are more fortunate than I thought."

"I shall not debate that, my lord," Connal said, then moved near Sinead, helping her from her mount. Her hands smoothed his shoulders, touching the fur and fabric of his garments, and he smiled down at her. 'Twas such a little thing, the clothes, and yet they pleased her so well. He knew it; without asking, he knew. Sweeping an arm around her waist, and as DeCourcy's captain of the guard shouted orders, he followed the lord of the castle inside.

The instant they entered, heads turned. Servants froze as the din dropped to the shuffle of feet, the clearing of throats.

Sinead's gaze swept the interior, then came back to him. She frowned. His gaze was intense, moving rapidly over the household. "Connal?"

"Remain close to me, lass." Still he stared, studied.

"You feel something?"

He nodded. Connal did not know what to think of it, but the moment he crossed the threshold, rage hit him like a hot blast of summer. His skin was suddenly damp beneath his clothes, his muscles bunching. He could no longer ignore this gift and recognized what Sinead had been saying all along. 'Twas an advantage he could keep hidden and use wisely.

Sinead inched closer to him, laying her hand on the fur of his cloak as she tipped her face up. Her smile was false with worry. "What is it?"

"Anger, a great deal of it. And, I think, 'tis directed at you."

Her smile fell slightly. "I am accustomed to animosity, Connal."

"I am not. Do not show them your power, nor leave my protection."

"This I swear."

His gaze jerked to her. "Impossible. I've never gained your compliance so easily."

"Wanting to give it and demanding you get it are two very different things, knight." The slyness of her smile, the look in her eyes sent his heartbeat escalating. Then she kissed him, a soft touch of the lips that drove heat down to his toes. His grip on her tightened, her body lying against his, and when he was want for more, and privacy for it, a voice interrupted.

"Ah, begging your pardon, PenDragon. If you can drag your attention free, lad," DeCourcy was saying, and he looked at him. "My wife."

Sinead left the protection of Connal's side and came to the woman. "Affreca, you look radiant," she said, hugging the slender woman.

Affreca closed her eyes, rocking her like a child in her arms. "Ah, little one, you have grown into a beauty."

DeCourcy scowled at his wife. "Affreca, my love. You did not say you knew Lady Sinead."

"You did not ask, husband. And she was a child when I saw her last." She kept her gaze on the younger woman, pushing her hair back, and as Sinead loosened the cloak, Affreca handed it to a servant. She pulled her toward the fire. "Come, gossip with me. 'Tis been years since I heard aught from the north. You must share."

Sinead glanced over her shoulder at Connal. He took

a step closer, but DeCourcy stayed him with a hand. "She will be fine."

"Forgive me, my lord, but she is mine to protect." Connal gestured to Nahjar, and the tall tattooed Moor took up residence behind Sinead.

DeCourcy's eyes widened at the sight of the man, and without pause, Branor stood to his right. Connal nodded, pleased, then faced DeCourcy.

"Let us find a place of privacy, my lord. For Richard needs your help."

DeCourcy led them to his private chambers off the great hall, and whilst servants laid out food for the knights and carried more out to the soldiers, Connal stepped into the chamber with DeCourcy.

Before DeCourcy closed the door, Connal stole a glimpse of Sinead with Affreca, their expressions animated and her body glowing with her smiles. His heart lifted, yet the sense of doom he felt inside these walls had not changed. From a whiskerless boy to an aging crab of a man, they had their attention on Sinead. And Connal recognized that he was indisputably jealous.

"Connal," DeCourcy said, and he faced the man. His gaze snapped to the other man already inside.

The man rose quickly, meeting his gaze, and Connal recognized him as one of *Croi an Banrion*'s knights. "Sir Phillip, what brings you here?"

Phillip glanced at DeCourcy. "My liege has sent me."

Connal frowned. "There is trouble?"

"Nay, sir. I know only that I am entrusted to give you this." He held out a thick packet.

"He's been here for a day, PenDragon, waiting. I thought it best that he remain unseen."

Connal took the packet and excused himself, moving to the far end of the chamber near a window. He sat on a padded bench fashioned into the depth of the wall and broke the wax seal. Opening the packet, he scanned the contents briefly before his gaze shot to the other man's.

"You know what you have brought?"

"Nay. The O'Donnel . . . ah, Lord DeClare said that 'twas for you alone. Would you like me to leave, sir?"

Connal shook his head and opened the smaller of the two folded papers and read. In DeClare's own script, the note spoke of knowing Sinead had been hurt. And his gratitude for his help. Connal could debate that, but the tone of the letter was grave. DeClare was aware of assassins sent from England. And though the man would never dare inscribe a treasonous word, he hinted that he was positive 'twas by the order of Prince John, and to be warned, there could be a traitor in his own contingent. His own men? Or the men brought from *Croi an Banrion?*

Connal paused, rubbing his fingers over his lips, then gestured for the man to sit and enjoy the wine DeCourcy poured for them. The earl felt the enclosed document would either ensure no more attacks or that they would worsen. But 'twas his only choice.

I fear for you both, son. And I am still unsure if I will lose my child for this act. She is fair stubborn as her mother and would ignore her heart if she thought it best for others concerned.

Connal believed that she was the target, as the prisoner had said. For killing Sinead would do little politically but bring the mourning of half of Ireland. Connal, on the other hand, knew his place in court and with Richard. And John's hatred of anyone aligned with his brother. He was, as he saw it, one step closer to a peace that John did not want. For if the prince could incite enough against England, he could rally men to his cause against his brother's throne.

Connal kept reading.

She is our greatest gift and I give her to you.

You will know when the time is right to tell her.

Frowning, Connal folded the note and broke the second seal.

He did not know whether to be filled with relief or trepidation.

For inside was the marriage contract between the house of PenDragon and the house of DeClare. Signed and affixed with the seals.

In the eyes of the king and church, he and Sinead were legally married.

God above, he thought, his troubles were just starting.

Chapter Fifteen

In the dark of night, Sinead flinched, her body arching like a well-strung bow in her sleep. In her mind, the images were clear with the taste and smell of battle. With the blade singing deep into Connal's flesh. Invading. Tearing. She tried to see who'd done this and mayhaps prevent it, but her mind's eye focused on Connal as he yanked out the sword, swallowing a moan of agony as he threw the weapon aside and fell to his knees. Then to the ground. Blood flowed black, then red, from beneath his tunic and onto the snow and mud. He clutched his side, calling her name, struggling for volume when he'd no power to give it. Clutching his side, blood rivered over his fingers. He reached out toward her, tried to rise, then dropped like a stone, her name the last whisper on his lips as life left his body.

"Connal!"

At her cry, Connal rushed into the chamber, half

dressed and waving Galeron back as he ran to the bed. For a heartbeat he froze at the sight of her, twisted in the sheets and whimpering like a child. He sat on the edge of the bed, grasping her shoulders. "Sinead!"

She clawed at him, calling his name. Tortured sobs wrenched from her, choking off air. God, she wasn't breathing. Pulling her upright, he shook her. She snapped awake, dragging in a hard lungful of air, her stare blank.

"You are safe, lass."

"Connal?" She blinked, sniffled; then she threw her arms around his neck and clung with a fierceness that knifed through him. She trembled violently. Her fingers dug into his back, one palm skimming his side. Then she hugged harder.

"Ah, God, Sinead." Her shudders vibrated into him and he rubbed her back. "All is well, love, all is well," he crooned.

She only buried her face deeper into the bend of his throat, nearly climbing onto his lap to get closer to him. "Oh, Connal," she sobbed.

"Your scream was . . . horrifying."

"Did I wake anyone?" she asked almost desperately.

"Only enough to alert Galeron. He stood guard at your door."

She moaned with embarrassment and, frowning, Connal pushed her back to look at her, smoothing her hair from her face. Her eyes were bleak, and he brushed a kiss to her forehead. " 'Twas only a nightmare."

She tipped her head, then suddenly kissed him, her fear boiling over, without control.

Instantly he sank into her mouth, pulling her onto his lap with a pleasured groan. She curled her body around him, dragging him back onto the bed with her.

Thoughts fled as tightly wrapped desire spun free, her heartbeat thrumming through her and into him.

'Twill always be like this, he realized, his hand scraping down her side to her thigh.

The fire flared, scorching the mantle.

Mist-laden air whispered with a sweeping hand, buffeting where skin met and blended to one. Above them vines pushed through the stone walls, nature seeking to shield them in a cocoon of desire.

And still they kissed.

A little desperate sound came from her, drove into him, and Connal knew he would never feel anything like this with another woman. She was the only one he wanted. Desired. Needed.

Not for lands and castle. Not for the king. But for his soul. For the saving of it. And when her hands slid from his neck, splaying across his chest, he did not think of all he kept from her but thought only of her, her mouth on him, her touch—combed with hunger and smothered in fear. "You dreamed of me, I can feel it," he said against her mouth

Dare she tell him? she thought. Would he cast her warning off? Would the simple telling make his death happen? She risked all and admitted, "Aye, aye."

Her voice fractured with the admission and she rained kisses over his face, then captured his mouth again, in command of his senses, and he would willingly give her their rule. But 'twas alarm and the need to obliterate it that drove her. He knew from experience, and as much as he wanted—and by God, with her so warm and eager, he wanted naught more—Connal knew it would only stay the fear for a moment.

He wanted it gone, for her. And when Sinead came to him like this, he wanted her heart unfettered.

The thought shook him to his core, ripped away his doubts, and when the sheet between them slipped and her soft, sleep-warm bosom pressed to his bare chest, Connal groaned in frustration and forced himself to ease back. His weakness for her showed itself when she reached for him, her mouth seeking his, and he took. For another long glorious moment, he took. He was helpless with her—no power, no strength. For Sinead filled him with more than desire. She filled him with hope. And a love he'd dismissed and discarded for duty and honor.

He tore his mouth from hers and stared into her blue eyes.

Aye, he thought, almost sadly. He'd gone and fallen in love with her. And he was lying through his bloody teeth about more than that.

She whispered his name, touching the band of his chausses. "God, woman, cease." He caught her wrist. "I am not strong enough." He indulged in a thorough look at her breasts, exposed and awaiting his attention, till he saw the tears in her eyes and knew he was right. He ground his teeth and called himself noble when he covered her. " 'Tis your panic speaking, lass."

" 'Tis more than that." 'Twas her love, the threat of it, and her inability to control anything, she thought as she touched his face, her fingertip tracing the scar at his jawline. "Aye, I am frightened for you."

Terror lingered, the unknown haunting her. "You saw my death, aye?"

Her eyes widened a bit.

"I've come so close too often not to see it happen in my nightmares." His smile tried to tease. "And you called out my name." Her eyes teared and he groaned with sympathy. "I will be ever cautious. Does that please you?"

Not nearly enough, she thought, nodding. The fear she felt now was incomparable to what she'd first experienced with the dreams. 'Twas stronger, deeper. And it bruised her heart. She'd spent years suppressing the emotions ruling her to protect herself, and even if he never loved her, she knew she could not survive without Connal.

She gazed into his green eyes, soft with compassion. "You must be more than cautious, Connal."

His brows furrowed. "What else do you know?"

The moment strung between them like a thin thread, his expression earnest. She said naught.

"Sinead, I feel your worry, your terror." He could taste it, he thought, and caught her face in his palms. "I must know to protect you, and . . . ah, do not tell me you do not need it," he chided when she opened her mouth to speak. "We have already seen what can happen even when I am near, magic or nay." His hand stroked over her wound, faded to a crescent of red. The terror he'd felt when she was dying, when she was so lost and unreachable to him only days ago, ripped through his heart. He'd nearly lost her forever, and the profound sorrow of it had left a mark on his heart. A telling cut that seemed to dash away the clouds of his mind. Sinead was more than his woman, more than his bride chosen by the king and duty. She was the second beat of his heart. And it left him troubled, for to have her completely was to reveal himself to her, and he was not ready to lose so much.

"Do you not know that I will accept what you say with value?"

Sinead searched his face, her soul begging for freedom, to share with him parts of herself no other knew. She swallowed and said, "Since I was a child I have had dreams of things to come."

His expression did not change.

"When Mother took my magic, the dreams eventually ceased and I found peace for a time." She gathered the sheet tighter to her breast. "Only once have I ever wished for them back."

"To know Markus would hurt you." Connal wanted to resurrect O'Brien so he could kill the bastard himself.

She nodded. "I have dreamed since you stepped on Ireland. 'Tis the same." She looked away, wondering if she put his life in greater danger. But if he knew, would he not distrust a bit more, and see what is not clearly there? She forced herself to look him in the eye. "And in each vision, you die."

Her voice broke, the sound cutting into his skin.

" 'Tis not unlikely," he said gently. "Given the powerful men we must deal with. And what I felt when we arrived here."

"If someone wants me, Connal, they are willing to kill you to do it!"

"You cannot blame yourself for aught that has yet to be."

"And if warning you brings this to come?"

"Do you not see?" he asked patiently. "It can only help."

"You take a sword in the side"—she touched the very spot—"and die."

'Twas why she was so interested in the location of his wounds when they were still in GleannAireamh, he realized.

"And I could do naught for you!"

His gaze snapped to her face. Silent tears slid down

her cheeks, and she tried to stop them. He reached for her, pulling her onto his lap, and she came willingly.

"I could not help you," she sobbed and tipped her face to meet his gaze. "I am bound from doing magic on you." She lifted her wrist to show him the thin chain of silver. "Mother bound me from ever touching you with it."

His brow furrowed. "Forever?"

"Aye. To break the oath that I've kept so long would be defying my ancestors."

And likely steal her power, he thought.

"But now I cannot cast to protect you. I cannot use my gifts to shield you, and if I thought breaking this vow would aid us, then I would."

It touched him deeply that she would risk her very being to love him, to protect him. But that she could not cast on him made little difference afore and now. "There is more, though; tell me," he said softly, running his hand over her bare arm, the feel of her skin beneath his palm at once soothing and heightening his desire.

"The sword. 'Tis not familiar, but I only see it pushing into you." She swallowed the ugliness of that fabricating in her mind again. "I cannot see who wields it—he is out of my sight, or I do not remember—but there is something I *must* see."

"Any sword is dangerous and I will be wary of them all."

She shoved him. "You make fun of me!"

She tried to leave his lap and the bed, but his body trapped the sheet beneath him and kept her there. "Nay. But this changes naught, for we already know someone wishes to stop us, and we have finished what we came to do."

"We leave for England, then?"

"Aye."

That brought no comfort, for she felt the danger would follow them more closely. "You do not go to see Rhiannon as you wished?"

His body tensed beneath her, around her. His lips thinned to a flat line and she could feel him pushing her away. She touched the side of his face, turning it toward hers. "You ask me to share with you and yet do not with me."

Abruptly he put her aside and stood, his back to her.

"She does not concern you."

"Blessed be, you are a stubborn man."

"You talk of stubborn?" he said, rounding on her. "You are—" He found her just pulling a robe onto her shoulders.

She looked up and stilled. His gaze moved heatedly from her face and the pale flesh she slowly covered. His body, already taut for her, hardened. He was thankful for the shield, yet the image of her full lush form was imprinted in his mind. *I will surely go mad,* he thought.

"Aye, PenDragon. Stubborn." She jerked on the sash. "Too thickheaded to see I do not wish to hurt you. To see that we must begin with trust."

"Have you entrusted yourself to me?"

She looked at him as if he'd grown horns. "I have this very night and afore. And do not think you can avoid this."

His expression sharpened.

"How can you deny what could be atween us in the same breath you have asked me to trust you?"

"Lives are not threatened with my business with Rhiannon!"

She shushed him. "You'll wake the entire castle."

"As if your scream already did not."

She arched a brow. "And if someone finds us, here like this?" She gestured to his half-naked body, her robe, and the fact that they already looked as if they'd tussled in her bed.

He had the nerve to grin. "Then you will be duly compromised and my wife the morrow."

She made a sour sound and walked around the bed to the sitting area: a pair of chairs near the hearth and a long narrow eating table set back from the blaze. She snapped her fingers and the branch of candles on the table burst with tiny flames. "That is not the way I wished to find . . ." Love, she wanted to say, but let the sentence fade to, "Myself wed." Grabbing a pitcher of wine, she sloshed some into a wooden cup and drank, then flicked a hand toward the fire. It burst to life, curling around the wood.

"Careful. You will set this place ablaze." He frowned at the charred edge of the wood mantel.

"Go to your chamber, Connal."

He moved to the table, running his fingers over the surface. "You are angry with me." How furious would she be when she learned her father had signed her freedom to him, to protect her?

"I am vexed with your constant need to hide bits and pieces from me." She eyed him over the rim of the cup.

"I have done things you do not need to know." And he did not need to remember.

"I care for the man afore me, not the youth who left Ireland over a decade ago."

His shoulders moved restlessly, and he took a step closer. "That youth is gone."

"But still as foolish."

He felt her soften toward him, setting the cup down as he approached. "Do you care so well, Sinead?"

He stopped close, the heat of his body like a force pushing past the velvet garment shrouding her. "We would have shared not even one kiss if I did not, Connal." *If I did not love you so.*

"I want to share more. Is there a mark I must pass?"

She lashed a hand toward the bed. "Me thinks you have hurdled one such mark, PenDragon." Aye, she thought, swept it aside with one look. The one he wore now. "You do this to distract me, I know," she warned, holding her anger tight. "I want your confidence and you want to . . . play."

He laid his hand on her waist, then tugged her closer, gazing down into her crystal blue eyes. "I want more than to play with you upon yon bed, Sinead. I want to feed on your passion. Drink your cries"—he leaned and whispered in her ear—"and taste you beneath my mouth."

Her breath snagged in her throat. Images blossomed in her mind and sent her heartbeat racing.

"All of you."

He was near, his breath dusting her temple, his lips moving over her hair, her jaw. She'd but to turn her head and unleash the storm. And she would be lost. And she would die. "Bedding me is in exchange for your trust, then?"

He scowled, anger surging through him. "Nay. Good God, woman, you think me so cold as to—"

She braced her hands on his chest. "I think you are afraid of what your darkest secrets will do to what we build now, Connal," she said, sketching his features. He'd been alone so long and it had scarred him deeply, leaving him like a wounded beast batting away any tenderness for fear of more pain. "Know you now that you have tossed my love back at me countless times. . . ."

He started to speak and she silenced him with a finger to his lips. "And I shall still risk handing my heart to you."

Her declaration struck him full force. He offered naught and she gave. He gained whilst she sacrificed. Trust was not so little a price, he thought, and as he thought back, she'd given hers from the moment she'd sworn her oath in the bailey of *Croí an Banríon*. She deserved better and he wanted desperately to speak the words that lay deep in his soul, words only she could hear. "You are right, I am afraid." He let out a breath and curled his arms around her. "We have come far, love, and again you will look upon me with a jaundiced eye. I cannot bear that."

"Have more faith in me," she said, then laid her head on his chest. "For I have thus in you." She squeezed her eyes shut, tightening her hold on him.

"I've been a foolish man."

Her smile was slow. "Did I not mention that afore?"

He chuckled lightly. "Aye, and I am certain you will again . . . oh, good God."

She frowned and he nudged her, then gestured behind them. She twisted to look toward the far end of the room near the window.

The darkness was bright with soft green and blue balls of light darting to and fro. An instant later, like the pop of a fire, faeries appeared.

Sinead smiled. "Galwyn! Kiarae!"

Hovering in the air, the faery prince glared between the two, ending on Connal. "So my lord PenDragon, what think you to do with my princess on this dark night?" Dressed in a tunic of green leaves, his stance was defiant, his hand on the hilt of his tiny sword.

"None of your bloody damn business," he growled.

Sinead swung a look at Connal. "Do not be rude."

"They are naught but trouble." Connal had not seen a faery since he was a boy and had thought them only legends and the thing of dreams.

"They are my friends; now behave."

Connal looked at her, astonished.

"I had few playmates as a child," she explained and did not see his sympathetic smile as she gestured Galwyn closer. His mate, Kiarae, fluttered ahead, tisking softly as she pulled the robe higher over Sinead's bosom, then sent Connal a scolding glare.

Connal winked at the female.

Sinead sat in a chair near the fire and the faery prince perched himself on her kneecap. "Are Mother and Father fairing well? My sisters?"

"Aye, but will not be when your father learns of this." Galwyn gestured to the mussed bed.

"Sinead . . ." Connal said, his gaze locked on the faery. He knew from stories that they were a mischievous bunch and could only wonder at the tales they'd take back. "Tell this creature we are betrothed."

She opened her mouth, but Galwyn spoke up. "There has been a ceremony?"

"Nay."

"A contract signed."

"Nay," Sinead said, and Connal flinched inside. Obviously DeClare had not confided that in the faeries.

"Then I beg to differ, PenDragon; till at least signatures are affixed, there is naught atween you—" Galwyn looked at the bed—"but lust."

"Shh!" Sinead said and brushed the faery back. He went tumbling to the floor.

Connal choked a laugh. The gall of the little speck, he thought.

Galwyn did not think it so funny and flew up to point his tiny sword at Connal's face.

Connal, his hand braced on his hips, snapped his jaws at the sprite.

Before he could bite his wing, Kiarae grabbed Galwyn's arm and yanked him back, whispering heatedly. All they heard was, "He started it."

Sinead hid her smile and said, "Kiarae, can you not control his temper?"

"Nay more than Connal can do yours, I suppose," she snipped over her shoulder as she soothed Galwyn.

Connal grinned. "Impossible, is it not, lassie?"

"Quite so, my lord," Kiarae said with a deliciously sly look in his direction, her skin glowing to show a blush.

Galwyn rolled his eyes and still glared between the two humans. "We've been sent to see if you are well and fit."

"And rather annoyed at the chore, I see."

"We were at the winter festi—"

Kiarae pinched Galwyn. "Nay, nay, Princess. Of course not."

Galwyn glared, Kiarae snubbed him, and Sinead hid a smile neither faery would appreciate.

" 'Tis dangerous here." Kiarae's wings fluttered and crystal ash dusted the air. Her blue-white skin glowed to nearly translucent, her snow white gown making her almost invisible in the firelight.

"Connal is always near."

"Aye," Galwyn said with feeling. " 'Tis the danger we speak of." He tossed his head, blond hair sparkling the darkness. "Why *is* he here at this late hour, half clothed?"

"Less than half," Kiarae said with an admiring glance at Connal. For a moment Galwyn looked jealous.

"I had a nightmare."

Kiarae moaned in sympathy.

"Connal came to me."

"Well, 'tis over; send him away."

She looked at Connal. He stood like a great oak, his arms folded, his expression saying he would not be budged. "You may try if you wish."

Neither made the effort.

Sinead grinned as the faery fluttered down to settle on a peak of a log. Kiarae, who was centuries older than her, looked no more than sixteen summers old. Even with the unattractive scowl. The faery folded her arms and tapped her foot and the motion felt oddly familiar to Sinead. Galwyn flew down to stand beside the girl faery, his hand ever ready on the hilt of his tiny sword. Sinead's gaze shifted from one faery to the other.

"You have seen me, now go home."

"We are to remain with you," Galwyn groused as if 'twere a hated chore.

"I have nay needed a nursemaid for some years now."

Galwyn looked at Kiarae. "I told you she would be like this."

"Aye, love." She sighed tiredly. "That you did."

"Then *do* something," Galwyn said, frustration in his tone.

Kiarae leveled him a tight, you-are-a-stupid-male look Sinead had seen before, then grabbed his hand, pulling the prince of the forest back so she could not hear. Kiarae was only a bit less fierce than her lover, but Sinead had known since she was a babe, the pair were overprotective and meddlesome. But harmless.

She did not need any meddling right now.

Connal continued to stare, amusement on his face.

"Should you not be keeping the yearling trees green,

Galwyn?'' He peered over the edge of Kiarae's wing, then pushed it down. ''And why are you not seeing the sleeping flowers do not die?'' she said to Kiarae. ''And where are your sisters?''

''They gather for the feast of Imbolc,'' Kiarae said.

Sinead frowned. '' 'Tis not for a month.''

Kiarae shrugged, and silver-blue dust scattered to the floor. ''We are little. It takes time.''

Sinead laughed lightly, and out of the corner of her eye she saw Connal rub his mouth to hide his humor.

Kiarae left Galwyn's side and fluttered in the air afore Sinead. ''You have told him of the dreams? All of it?''

Sinead exchanged a glance with Connal. ''Aye.''

Kiarae sighed, obviously pleased. But Galwyn was still cranky. ''Well, I do not like that he is here, like that, in the dark. And . . . and—'' Galwyn struggled for more reasons, and Connal suspected there was a bit of jealousy growing here.

''You impeach her honor, and mine, with those words.'' Connal reached for the back of his tunic and plucked the male from the log, holding him up for inspection. ''What is atween us is private. Sinead is wise enough to know what is best for her, and that, my little friend, is me.''

Kiarae flew to Galwyn's defense. ''Unhand him!''

''Connal,'' Sinead said. '' 'Tis not wise to anger . . .''

''I am speaking man-to-man. Am I not?'' he said, dangling the faery, and the tiny sprite looked suddenly honored. ''Galwyn does not trust me. With good reason,'' he added with a sly wink at the faery lad.

''*I* trust him,'' Sinead said, leaving the chair and coming to Connal's side.

Connal's smile wavered with that, and he released Galwyn. The faery huffed and adjusted his tunic.

Sinead stood with her back to Connal. "Tell Mother and Father we are well."

"And that *I* sent you on your way," Connal added, pulling Sinead back against him.

The faeries looked at each other, then at the humans, and grinned. "Adieu," they said and blinked out of sight.

Connal laughed quietly. "Those were the playmates of a witch?"

"My guardians." Sinead tipped her head back to look at him. "Aye, and if I know them, and I do, they are not so far away."

He frowned. "They would not—"

"Aye, they would."

Connal sighed hard, then kissed her forehead, not trusting himself to do more. "I shall find my bed," he groused and with a lingering touch, walked to the door. He paused his hand on the latch and frowned back at her. "You were alone a lot as a child?"

She nodded.

"That has ended, Sinead; you will never be alone."

He stepped out and closed the door.

"Neither will you," she whispered. "If you will only learn to trust, my love. Neither will you."

Chapter Sixteen

Connal was rarely farther than two strides from her, yet his mind was elsewhere. The look on his face, mapped with concern, spoke more loudly than words. Sinead studied him where he stood with his comrades, Lord DeCourcy and a crowd of knights. He held a goblet but did not drink. He listened to conversation yet did not contribute.

'Twas his manner since they'd returned from a ride upon DeCourcy's lands. Connal's request to see the township and villages had come as a shock, as had his insistence that she come with him.

"They are as much my kin as your tenants, my lord," he'd said to Lord DeCourcy. "I would see their wellness fair and right as much for myself as to report such to the king." DeCourcy had taken mild offense but had complied.

Connal's words were simple and telling. And with

them, he took another piece of her heart. And gave back uncertainty. What was to become of them, their lives, once they reached England and stood before the king? How long could she continue to defy a monarch and, likely, shame Connal?

He lifted his gaze and met hers across the great hall.

She felt it climb over her, sweep across her body and face with the mastery of touch. Her skin warmed beneath her borrowed green gown, tingling with energy and begging her to recall his arms around her, the exquisite kisses they'd shared last night. Like the one in the Irish king's chamber.

'Twas a dark haunted kiss of deep possession, carving an imprint in her that would tear through if she allowed it. A moment of reckoning. A cry from her heart she feared would never be answered.

She loved him. Her soul had known it since childhood. Her woman's heart had refused till now. The very realization left her breathless, her soul opening to fill with the love she was destined to offer him. Her gaze trapped in his, she thought . . . would he ever be able to accept it? Without conditions? Even the mention of it closed him like a slamming door and left her again, alone.

His brows furrowed softly. Could he sense her now? She prayed she was deft enough to conceal her feelings, for ever since she'd taken the crossbow bolt, he'd let himself experience what he'd kept trapped inside for years. *'Tis a grand fine mess you've made,* she told herself. Since his return to Ireland, she'd wished him to accept and trust the sixth sense in himself, and now that he was, the disadvantage was to her own heart. He was still so unwilling to concede much of himself to her and she wondered what still kept him tucked away in the English facade that serving King Richard had fashioned around him.

"He devours you with his eyes," Affreca said from her seat beside her.

Sinead laughed to herself, for they'd been chatting about her family, and clans. " 'Tis good then, for oftimes he bludgeons me with them."

DeCourcy's wife touched her hand, and Sinead looked at her. "My John tells me the king has betrothed you to him."

"The king has spoken. I have not agreed."

Affreca frowned.

"I have the right to choose." *And I choose him if only he would love me back,* she thought.

Affreca smiled patiently. "I did, too, from a select group of men."

"I had no such selection." And she had made them all unsuitable, she knew, and agreeing to wed Markus had been a poor excuse to abolish Connal from her heart.

"He is not fit enough for you? Not handsome and virile enough?"

Sinead flushed a bit and looked at Connal. "Aye."

"Honorable, trustworthy?"

Sinead did not hesitate. "Aye, he is that."

"And you love him."

Her gaze snapped to Affreca's.

"He is simply too unsure to see it."

"Connal is unsure of naught, my lady."

Aye, Sinead thought. He was certain his past made him unworthy of a loving heart. He was certain of his duty to the king. And he was certain she would wed him because the king had so ordered.

Hooey, she thought.

He spoke of duty and dictates, and yet she truly was only a bargain. Only without her lands and castle, without her magic, would she know if she held a place in his heart. But as that was not possible, she'd never know the truth.

" 'Tis your perception of him that is at fault, Sinead."

She frowned, confused.

"You are, some say . . . a legend. Ah! That is not a pretty face you make." Sinead smiled, contrite. " 'Tis clear to all who watch that he cares deeply for you and yet, mayhaps, he hesitates to say more, for he wonders if he will ever measure up as a man."

Sinead blinked, wide-eyed. "Look at him, Affreca." She gestured toward Connal. "Are you not seeing the same man as I? The rest of the world should measure so well against him."

Affreca took a stitch in the embroidery laying across her lap. "But magic is not a thing one can best in a joust, you know."

Sinead was aghast. " 'Tis ridiculous. One has naught to do with the other."

"To you, mayhaps. But men, they are strange creatures."

Sinead looked back to Connal. Aye, he'd resented her gift afore, and yet now he'd accepted it. He'd asked her only not to use it afore anyone here. And of course, last eve, not to burn the castle down around them. Yet she understood why he'd suppressed his gift of the senses for so long. She was an oddity to all because of hers and yet had years to grow accustomed to the knowledge of change. She realized what trouble it could cause him, what she had caused him. Especially now with an assassin at their heels. None would wish to be near him if they knew. Yet the benefits were his alone.

And mayhaps the king's. But Connal was not willing to trust the secret with anyone but her.

That alone won the battle inside her.

"Go to him," Affreca whispered, and Sinead did not spare her a glance, rising and moving through the throngs of people toward him. He tore his gaze from Monroe and watched her approach.

'Twas exhilarating, the way he looked at her, the feeling of belonging sweeping through her in potent waves. His arm swept around her waist, the gesture at once possessive and comforting. *As it was, so it is again*, she thought, trying to contain the hurried pounding in her heart.

Connal reined back sharply and did not bother to turn around. "Sinead, I know you are there, dammit."

"If you know, PenDragon, then do not swear at me."

PenDragon. A telling mark that she was angry. He dropped his head forward, thinking he should have known he would not get so far from her without her knowing. But he had to do this alone.

He wheeled his mount around and found her standing in the road, her hands on her hips, her foot tapping. Angry, aye, he thought, but damn delectable. Last night sprang through his mind with amazing clarity. Her taste. The feel of her body wrapped around his as they kissed, and—suddenly angry she'd risked her life, he rode toward her, taking small pleasure in her wide-eyed expression as he bent and snatched her from the ground. He rode for a few more yards, depositing her on his lap before he yanked back on the reins.

"You little fool! After all the trouble we've had, why

did you leave the encampment and the protection of the guards?"

"To find you! You slip out in the dark and do not tell me? Think you I will not worry?"

"I can care for myself."

"I do not deny that," she snapped, "But did my telling the dream not mean a thing to you?"

"Did my warning not to leave your guards mean naught to you?" he snapped back.

"*You* are my protector, PenDragon. You have claimed such often enough. Now you abandon me?" Sinead knew 'twas unfair, but if he trusted her he would have at least told her he was leaving the camp.

"I would have returned by morning, lass. And your dream served its purpose, a warning."

She gripped his arms. "It happened out of doors, Connal."

It was her expression that snagged him. Her earnest eyes, the fear.

He groaned and pressed his forehead to hers. "Forgive me for scaring you."

"Do not do that again."

"Now will you return to Nahjar's care?"

"Nay. I'm going with you."

"I think not."

Her look was impatient. "Do not get all swelled up and red with fury, Connal. I can go alone, ahead of you, if I wish."

She lifted her arms out, palms cupped to the sky, something she did and needed for her most powerful magic, and Connal pushed them down. "Nay, you will not, and how do you know where I go?" Even as he asked the question he knew 'twas ridiculous.

"We are but a few miles from Saint Catherine's Abbey."

He stiffened, looking away, and when the horse jostled beneath them, Connal realized how unwise it was for them to be standing in the open road. He glanced about for a suitable place to camp and talk her out of joining him. This, he needed to do alone. He had to convince her to return to the camp by her choice or she'd simply conjure and reappear again, and likely in more danger.

Abruptly he set her to the ground, then dismounted, grabbed her hand, and pulled her and his horse into the thicket of trees. He went about checking the area, and after a moment decided they were hidden well enough and could see anyone coming down the road.

He whipped around when he heard, "Goddess of the Moon, God of the Sun"—she lifted her arms high, palms out—"hear me. Veil us in your protective light, from arrow and sword, from harm and sight." A gold light radiated from her, a thin barrier between her and the world. "So I say, so mote it be!"

He heard a creaking sound and reached for his sword, glancing about. The trees curled, trunks bending back to cup the small clearing. Overhead branches elongated, stretching to meet each other like the weave of threads and envelop them in a dome of rowan trees.

She lowered her arms and met his gaze.

"Good God, Sinead. If you can do that, can you do something to protect yourself from harm?"

Moving closer, she gathered dead branches and leaves, dropping item into a pile. "Aye, but I have the power to control the elements to safeguard myself, Connal, not the power to control free will."

Connal added a few sticks and, rolling her wrist, she brought fire into her palm. She spilled it on the wood.

"That is good to know at least."

"Why?" Then she smiled and said, "Think I put a spell on you?"

Too late, his look said he'd thought about it.

She shook her head. She decided it did not matter. "Emotions are free will. And whilst some people do not show them, inside they cannot be changed." She stepped within a foot of him. "This sight of the heart you have, I do not."

"Good. No man wishes a woman to have more power than he," he said without thinking. He flashed her a sheepish smile. "I have wondered often these past weeks, how was I to be equal to you when you can command the elements with the flick of your hand?" He knelt to feed cracked logs into the fire. "Since I was a boy, I'd resented the bloody hell out of it. You had magnificent tools to alter lives and yet you played with it."

"I was a child then, and knew no better."

"I could not shake loose of that. Till now."

She frowned, edging closer to him. "What changed your mind?"

"That you do not toy with it. That you use it to better lives and property when all hope is lost."

"Ah," she said. "To see with thine eyes has made it so. But not me speaking such did."

He opened his mouth and after a false start burst with, "Aye, I did not trust you."

" 'Twas rather mutual."

On one knee, he fed the flames, refusing to look at her and see the unanswered question in her eyes. *Can you trust me now?*

254 Amy J. Fetzer

She did not ask it, and when he stood, she was inches from him. She laid her hand on his chest, as if to keep him there. Connal felt the burn of her touch swell beneath his clothes and focused on her, his senses sharpening with a razor's edge. Emotions came with images, crowding upon one another. Within her was a locked door eager to be opened, yet she refused, butting against it to keep it closed. So much so, he felt her heartbeat quicken, and the connection that simmered between them—intensified.

Her gaze searched his. "Speak to me, Connal."

His expression hardened, shaped with exclusion.

"You keep a part of you from me like a hound held at bay by its master," Sinead said. "You left Ireland in a rage, I know this. You'd cast your sword at your father's feet and swore never to return, yet you spoke as if a life had ended."

He took a step back. "It had."

"Whose, then?"

Her confusion pummeled him, and he did not look at her, his gaze on the fire. She deserved an answer, he told himself. She was his wife, and though she was unaware of the binding, the burden would eventually reflect on her. He released a long slow breath, his head bowed. He'd never shared this with anyone. Anyone. How would she react? Would he lose what tenderness they'd gained? He wanted badly for her to understand, to know what drove him from Ireland those years back.

But it would cost him his pride.

"Connal?" Tension radiated from him like the fire's warmth, bunching his muscles. In the quiet, his knuckles cracked. The turmoil staggered her.

Orange light christened his hair with fire and Sinead reached out yet did not touch him. "I swear by the

Goddess I will not judge you. I only need to know what wounds you so deeply."

Her voice was soft, lingering in his mind for a moment, soothing with a lilt of the homeland he'd missed so much. His throat tightened and when the words came, they were harsh and low. "I was seven and ten that day, newly knighted and waiting to wield that magnificent sword in righteous service," he scoffed. "But I'd yet to kill a man for my king." He rubbed his face, pushing his fingers through his hair and gripping the back of his skull with one hand. "I said what I thought they wanted to hear. That I was eager to fight for righteousness. When inside I was afraid that in the first taste of battle, I'd piss on myself and rust the armor."

He laughed without humor and did not look at her.

"Gaelan thought I should wait. I did not. I wanted to earn my spurs. King Henry himself had knighted me. His finest knights had trained me. Educated well beyond my friends. And I was bigger than most my age."

He tipped his head back and the wistfullness in his expression sliced open her heart.

"I was still clumsy, and late at night I would walk a thin log carrying pails of water because I heard Gaelan say it had taught him to be agile. Over and over I practiced, then filled the buckets with stones, then iron. I was determined not to fall on my arse when I first put on that armor for battle. I would have done aught to be a knight like Gaelan." His expression darkened as he looked at her. "I'd lost my right to rule as Prince of Donegal when he married Siobhan and had accepted it then. Gaelan was the only father I knew and I loved him. I respected him and what he'd made of himself."

"And you wanted that?"

"Aye. I did." He rolled around, his shoulders braced against a tree. "I thought I would return when he needed, take his place as his heir. He'd declared it so, for I had the blood of a king in me." He scoffed meanly, pushing off and taking a few steps. He met her gaze. "I heard Gaelan arguing with my . . . mother. She was insisting something be kept from me. Gaelan thought 'twas best I knew the truth, for if someone should learn of it, I'd be accused of a falsehood and my knighthood stricken from me. I needed to be prepared."

Oh, my stars, she thought. "Rhiannon," she whispered and did not know how she knew.

His features yanked taut, sharp in the firelight. "Aye. She is my mother."

"I don't understand."

" 'Tis all rather clear, is it not?" came bitterly. "She birthed me in the abbey and gave me to Siobhan to raise. So you see, I haven't a drop of King Tigheran's blood in me. Nor his wife's. I've no right to *ever* be called prince."

"Gaelan knew the truth and still named you his heir," Sinead said, confused, and taking several steps closer. His look stopped her. "You left for the lie they told?"

He shook his head. "Nay. That I could forgive, for I loved Siobhàn and Gaelan and knew well they loved me. But I was young and angry for the secret of years. Yet 'twas my sire that broke the bond."

Connal plucked his dagger from its sheath at his hip, turning it in the firelight, testing the sharpness with his thumb. Blood blossomed and dripped. He watched it splash on the ground.

She rushed forward, taking his hand; then, using her sleeve, she blotted it. She swiped at the blood on her own hands.

He suddenly gripped them. "You have the blood of a traitor on you," he said with a deadly calm.

"Nay, I do not."

"You said it yourself, Sinead. I killed my own kin."

"War breeds strange loyalties; England is here and will not leave," she said, hovering needlessly over the tiny cut. "And your knighthood is a sworn duty." She met his gaze. "I said that to wound you. Out of anger over your absence for so long. To hurt you as you had done to me."

He pushed her hair off her face. "I am no better than what you claimed. I turned my back on Ireland and traded my family for a mercenary's life."

"Aye, you did. I can no longer judge your reasons, and these past days you have weathered the cost well. Your past and parents meant little." He looked doubtful, and she said, "Did not Rory wish you to raise arms? Was he not ready to stand behind you and fight?"

He blinked. "How did you know?" She was near death then.

She shrugged, accepting that she did. "Rory has always been a bit of a rebel. And Rhiannon—who was her lover?"

"Patrick. He loved Rhiannon so much he came to her when our people were being slaughtered and still she did not tell her sister, or Gaelan. She hid him. He murdered his own brothers for Lachlan O'Neil, and she knew. Both of them let hundreds die and still Rhiannon said naught!"

"That is her burden, hers and Patrick's. Not yours."

He stepped back from her, his cold gaze falling on her like a hammer. "Patrick is dead. Ian Maguire told me he perished taking a sword meant for Gaelan."

"His sacrifice was to save what was left of his honor."

He sneered and tossed the dagger. It pierced the ground at his feet. "It does not matter."

"It does if you think this is a shame you must carry alone." She rushed to him, cupping his face when he would turn away, turn inside. "Nay, look at me, you big ox, and listen well to these words. You are naught like this man who fathered you. He did not touch your life but in death. You are the son of Siobhàn and Gaelan." She released him, yet stood close. "And he was wise to tell you, for you must not only be prepared for others to know the truth, but for you to see that you are the man you are, not for the blood in your veins but for the truth of your heart."

His gaze searched hers heatedly.

"Patrick was honorless. I know the tale. I know Lachlan threatened his family with death. What would you do if someone held your sisters' lives and ordered you to kill all those who stand inside *Croi an Banrion* now to save them? Think of Patrick and how difficult the choice was to him. His love for his family forced him to do it. Rhiannon's love for Patrick forced her to keep it secret or the kin of the man she loved would die."

Connal tried to put himself in that position as he'd done so many nights in a Saracen prison. And if Siobhan, Gaelan, or any of his sisters were held? And if it were Sinead he must kill to save them? He swallowed thickly, the thought twisting through his gut, tearing at his soul. "He could have come to Gaelan. He could have betrayed the betrayer and come to Gaelan."

"Aye, but he did not trust an Englishman. And 'tis done, Connal. *Done.*"

Connal rubbed his face with both hands. "Aye, aye, I know, but God above, these years have not lessened my shame."

"Then make peace with yourself."

His head snapped up, his hands lowering.

"The blood in your veins matters little." She moved close, taking his hand in hers. "It spills red." She laughed shortly. " 'Tis more Irish than mine, actually."

"Jealous?"

She shook her head and laid her palm over his heart. Her eyes were soft and smoky as she said, "This is who you are. Here"—she patted his chest—"beneath this flesh and muscle, all that matters is why this heart beats strongly, why it hurts and loves and needs." He covered her hand, gripping her fingers. "We cannot control the heart, Connal. But the soul is eternal. Be at peace with yourself and forgive Rhiannon."

His gaze thinned.

"She waits for you."

"She does not know I am near."

"In yon abbey she abides a score of years for your forgiveness."

His hands slid downward, the back of them grazing her breasts, and he heard her breath catch before he framed her waist. "You wish that?"

She shook her head. "Only you can grant it."

Connal sighed, a terrible weight sliding off his shoulders with the telling. "I cannot promise it."

She ducked to look under his bowed head. "You will consider it?"

His lips curved. "Pestering me already?"

"I will not attempt to sway you, Connal, but I will stand beside you if you need."

Connal's gaze searched hers, wanting now what he'd denied himself, what he swore he could live without. "Why?"

Because I love you, she thought, yet said, "If we cannot share the burdens as well as the joys, we have naught."

"Even without this night, we have had much more atween us."

Her shoulders moved uselessly. "You want a marriage for land and castles, but in truth, it will be made by us alone."

Connal instantly thought of the contracts tucked away, secreted from anyone, especially her. Tell her, he thought. *Get it done and start anew.* But he could not. It had been her only leverage and now she'd feel the weight of the king's word harder than anyone. Harder than he did now.

He spoke only from his heart. "Aye, I did want that, and I cared less about who I hurt to get it. Forgive me, love, for I regret those words. I needed a piece of Ireland of my own. A home. For I had lost the right. But 'tis not the land that makes me want now, Sinead, but you."

Her heart skipped to her throat, making her words hoarse. "Bodies joined is trivial—"

She was still so full of doubt, he thought, and could not blame her. "You are smarter than that. If all I wanted was your body beneath me I could have seduced you last night." She looked adorably indignant and he tipped her chin up and brushed his mouth over hers. Instantly she worried his lips and shifted closer, thigh to thigh. "Nor would I have put up with your insults and slurs, your distrust and—"

She covered his mouth with her hand. "Forgive me that."

He peeled her hand aside. "I have. And I do desire you," he growled softly. "Madly. But when you lay dying, I saw the inconsequence of it." She went suddenly still and his voice softened as the words poured from his heart. "I did not see a castle and lands, alliances and the king's bonds. I saw my life without you, and I could not bear to live it alone."

"Connal," she said in barely a whisper, feeling his torment.

"I need you," he said fiercely, shoving his hand into her hair and locking his gaze on hers. "God above, I cannot breathe with you this near, and I do not breathe when you are far from me." He swallowed thickly on his pride and said, "We *are* destined, Sinead."

Her blue eyes filled with tears.

She swallowed a sob, the folds of her heart spreading wide. "Aye, your soul is mine, Connal; even when I denied it, your soul was part of mine."

His breathing rushed, the gift of her words spiraling through his blood, clawing with heat and wonder and salvation. He laid her hand over his heart. "Then tell it to rest, for I have found its mate."

With trembling hands she touched his face, his throat, his chest, and then smoothed his hair back. "Do not say the words if you do not have them in your heart, Connal, please."

"I have denied them long enough to the one I should have spoken them." He pressed his forehead to hers and drew a shaky breath. "I love you, Sinead."

Her lip quivered and she tried to smile as her heart took flight on gossamer wings. "You are the only man I can love, Connal." She pressed her mouth to his and moaned, "And, oh, how I have always loved you."

He kissed her, and as they fell willingly into each other, the forest bloomed around them, celebrating the love born centuries before and the mating of long-lost souls.

Chapter Seventeen

The door inside her heart unlocked and with it a flood of emotion and sensations washed over him, through him, making his body tremble. Energy poured through his blood, given from her, taken into him, and Connal moaned with the pleasure of her, with the knowledge of her love, with the acceptance of his.

She loved him, and the glory of it surpassed all reason and thought. He knew only the purest joy. His kiss deepened, his arms tightened, as if to pull her inside himself and clean away the rubble still left there. The air around them warmed and sweetened, and Connal felt burdens lift and tranquillity seep into his soul.

The power of it sent them to their knees, clinging, mouths melting and molding with urgency and heat.

"Ah, Sinead, Sinead," he murmured, his voice rough with the emotions flooding his heart.

"We are one, Connal, can you not feel it?"

He did. His blood rushed and matched hers. His heart thundered and hers mated with the tempo. He gazed into her eyes, and for the breath of a moment he was in her world. In her soul. The light of her magic filled him and he trembled.

With the flare of his eyes, Sinead knew he understood and felt as she did. As she had for so long. "I have loved you since I took my first breath."

"And I till my last."

Her eyes teared. "Come to me, Connal. Claim me now."

Tenderly, he stroked her hair back. "I'd dreamed of making love to you elsewhere."

She smiled with tender humor. "Ah, my knight, it matters not where"—she touched the shape of his lips, her eyes intense—"only that the love within is true."

"Oh, love," he choked, " 'tis so." He pressed his mouth to hers again. " 'Tis truly so." It stunned him, the feelings he could have when he allowed them freedom. She'd defied him and he adored it. She'd fought with him and he felt more alive with each word. No matter how viperous, no matter how cutting, she breathed life into him again, and the chance to love her surpassed all his wants.

Save one.

Joining with her.

Making her truly his.

Erotic images filled his mind, driving need down to his boot heels as he swept her tightly to him and kissed her, a wild play of lips and tongue. Connal knew he would die for his want of her, of loving her. Need, sharpened with hunger and new-born love splintered through them.

Cloaks fell. Her hair tumbled to the ground like autumn's red fire.

His tongue outlined her lips, laving at the taste of her, and she responded wildly, eating at his mouth, clawing at his chest as if to tear into him.

"I want to touch you; take this off," she commanded, and he hurriedly uncoupled his sword belt, tossing it aside. No sooner done, her hands slid under the layers of his tunic, fingers meeting flesh, and his muscles contracted beneath her touch as she pushed the fabric off over his head. He did not feel the cold, only her, only her small hands riding over his bare skin and leaving a scorching path.

Sinead felt his power under her fingertips and marveled again at the great size of him, the dozens of slashing scars marking his skin and telling a story of war and battle. Skin taut over muscle and bone, brown from the Arab sun. He watched her intently as she feathered her fingers over calluses left from his armor, then inhaled as she bent and slicked a moist circle over his flat coin nipple. A chest full of air hissed out between his clenched teeth; his fingers tightened on her waist and she kept tasting, each stroke deeper, more certain, more determined to exact pleasure, and when her mouth met his, Connal drank in her very breath, hooking his thumbs in the neck of her gown and pulling it down. Her breasts spilled from the confines, grazing his chest. He enfolded the rounded flesh, thumbs teasing circles around her nipple until she arched into him and enjoyed. He bent his mouth to her and wrapped his lips around the little nub and drew on her, her soft cries filling his mind, nuturing his soul. She touched his chin and he looked at her as she rose to slide her gown off her hips. His breath hung in the balance as the fabric slipped downward with erotic slowness, revealing the gentle swell of her belly, then the deep red juncture of her thighs, before dropping to the ground.

Connal stared, absorbing each curve and valley before meeting her gaze. She stepped closer, and from her delicate ankles he rode his hands up to the backs of her thighs. She touched his hair, and he buried his face in her taut stomach, his fingertips digging into her buttocks, and felt himself shudder with want and pleasure. And love.

"I love you," he whispered and dragged his tongue over her smooth flesh. Over the thin whip scar forever marring her flesh. For a fraction of time, he glanced up. She watched, her lungs laboring for every breath, her hands running greedily over his arms, his face. Eager, hungry, lovingly. She smiled, feline wild.

They were like statues, trapped in a sliver of time. Gazes locked. Their only movement was their breathing.

Then he peeled her open and tasted her.

The throaty sound she made spilled over him like hot wine, echoing in the woods. He drove deeply, tasting her in hot lavish strokes and feeling her tremble for him. She rocked, and he felt her blood pulse. He sampled sweetness, and her hips undulated luxuriously, and he gave her more, feeding on her passion.

Her pleasure became his. He felt it sing through her body, spilling into his. Pulling her thigh over his shoulder, he gripped her harder, thrusting two fingers deep inside her. Her cry was bright and filled with honest delight. Free and abandoned to him, and he thickened with hot need to be inside her.

He felt her muscles convulse, her throb of satisfaction race to the peak.

"Connal, oh my stars, Connal!"

Then she came apart, her body flexing, pawing with her sweet explosion. He devoured her pleasure.

Sinead sank her fingers into his hair and felt bathed in fire, the blaze sluicing within her body as it flexed for his command. And she let him have it, wonderfully helpless and shuddering without control. Exquisite. Yet before her fulfillment could recede she slid bonelessly down onto his lap. He held her, kissing her face, her hair, then pushed her legs around his waist and laid her on the ground.

"My stars, I never knew such . . . ecstasy."

"We will know more," he growled and kissed her.

Sinead craved his power, the rock hard thickness of him pressed to her, to break the barrier and fill her deeply, but he would not, his lips wrapping around her nipple and drawing it into the hot suck of his mouth. She curled to him, toeing off his chausses, wanting to feel his weight upon her, but he would have none of it, capturing her hands and pushing them above her head.

His stare scorched her as he said, "I have waited long for this night, Sinead. I will have my fill of you."

She smiled, laughed a little, and obeyed as Connal shaped her breasts, enfolding them, sucking first one taut berry nipple, then the other till she was writhing with untamed indulgence, till her skin was damp from his attention. She twisted beneath him, his erection pressing incitingly to her thigh, and she cradled him between, urging him to come to her. He refused, grinning darkly, and Sinead felt the sweet liquid of his touch down to her bones.

Then she reached between them and grasped him.

He stiffened. Sucked in a lungful of air and met her gaze. "You do not obey well," he murmured softly.

"Aye." She'd no regret in her eyes, only love, and Sinead touched him, boldly learning his shape, running her fingers over his hard length, sweeping the moist tip. He was still as glass. His jaw clenched, his muscles locked, and as she played him with sweet torture, he loved that she was not shy and timid. But then, he'd never expected her to be. Sinead was a creature of nature, wild in her heart, and when she stroked the tip of him against her softness the urge to slam into her nearly snapped his control.

"You will unman me."

"Never."

Neither saw their cloaks spread and river to soft green moss, the trees brighten with leaves. He only knew her taste, how her soft cries and pants fueled him. He fell back onto his haunches, her thighs spread over his, and held her gaze as he pushed himself down. The tip of him touched the bed of her sex and she bowed like a blade of grass in the wind. Brazen and open, she reached for him, guiding him. The moist tip of him throbbed against her, and Connal watched her eyes flare. A near violent shudder wracked him and pulsed into her. His throat worked and he gripped her hips, pulling her closer, and in nearly painful increments he slowly filled her.

He met the barrier of her maidenhead and stopped. But Sinead would have none of it, pulling him down, burying him inside her.

Connal was still, swallowing his breath and failing. He had never felt so exposed, so barren, and smoothing her hair back off her face, he saw the same vulnerability in her dark eyes.

"I hurt you."

"I love you," she said softly, and he knew no other moment would equal this.

He flexed inside her.

"Oh, Connal," came in reward, a soft lush moan that coated him. He moved, withdrawing and pushing slowly into her. Sinead stretched like a lionness beneath him, and braced above her, he thrust.

They danced like the ancients, bodies speaking without a word. Clawing, gripping. She watched him fill her and leave, heightening her pleasure with each measured stroke.

"Look at me, my witch." Her gaze flashed to his and locked.

Her hips rose to greet his, her hair a river of wine undulating with them, her feminine flesh pulling him into tender darkness. He wanted her closer, to feel more of her, and as he sat back on his haunches, he took her with him. The impact drove him farther inside her, and she kissed him wildly, her hip tucking to greet his. Muscles contracted, contours yielding to fit the other as his thickness stroked her body, and Sinead could not get enough, the urgency inside her wanting more, and she met his gaze, her shudders spilling into his mouth.

"Do not hold back for me, Connal," she whispered, moving faster. "Give me your power, all of it, and see where true magic lives."

His body flexed to the crush of her sensuality. Connal gripped her hips, feeling their motion, and she dug her fingers into his shoulders.

Savage desire throbbed, and he tasted it. A pulse of energy that defied the world. She trembled, her eyes tearing, darkening, her fingers tracing his mouth, his brow.

"I can feel all of you, in my blood."

"Aye," he moaned. "Aye, love."

Energy sang though his skin, defining every nerve, every cell in his body. He laid her back, sliding his arm under her hips and holding her off the ground, hovering on the brink of a climax. His features were tight with desire, his body taut against hers as he surged in extravagant rhythm. She answered.

Wet and raw. Primal.

The earth gently cushioned their passion.

Wind poured through their chamber of rowan trees, coating them in mist.

A ring of blue fire erupted, surrounding them in protection, in power.

He shoved and drove her across the mossy loam, and they strained against each other. She curved off the earth's floor, exposing her throat, her breasts to the touch of moonlight. The queen of the witches unmasked in the throes of carnal rhapsody. And he was at her mercy, under her enchantment.

Delicate muscles clawed his, squeezed, and she met his gaze as erotic sensations slammed into him, demanding and hard. Fracturing. The eruption shattered through her, and a deep growl came from the back of her throat, of exhilaration and abandonment.

Flowers of blood red pierced the earth and spread their petals.

He left her completely, then drove deep, once and hard, his climax grinding through him mercilessly and unleashing into her.

He growled out her name.

A chant of love called.

A spell cast for eternity.

The magic of souls reborn and joined.

The ring of fire flared high, yet he only saw Sinead.

Only her exquisite beauty, heard her shudders breaking through her body and into his. In the time of a single breath, Connal knew her heartbeat, her secrets of magic, her fears, and her pleasures. Her love for him was as boundless as the universe and he felt it swallow him, and sank happily into bliss.

They remained so, falling over the edge, watching it in each other's eyes and whispering words of love, of their hearts.

Sinead pulled him down onto her, holding him as the last luxurious tremors of desire careened into sated warmth and contentment. Her hands lingered over his spine, drove into his hair and, as he lifted his head, she kissed him. He felt tears against his cheek and jerked back to look at her.

"Worry not," she whispered, smoothing his hair back. "They are tears of happiness."

He whispered her name, his gaze searching hers, and she swiped at the moisture on his own face and said, "Knight of Richard, knight of Ireland. This"—she lifted her hand toward the sky—"is where true magic is born."

He looked above and beyond her. Fire, as blue as the sea, encircled them, the flames dying slowly, and yet the air was a mass of butterflies, the trees stretched their branches skyward and welcomed the moonlight to drench them. His arms wrapped tightly about her, Connal tipped his face to the heavens and sighed, absorbing it.

She laughed and he smiled, then looked down, touched her face, then kissed her reverently. "You are mine, forever," he said, his claim to her heart as well as her body.

"Aye. That I am, love."

Her expression softened, her fingertips touching his

jaw, her gaze searching his eyes. His heart was open, she thought, accepting. "I love you," she whispered.

"Ahh, sweet words from such a peppered mouth," he teased and kissed her, then rolled to his back.

Connal ran his hand down her spine, her weight on him as precious as the love he had for her.

St. Catherine's Abbey

Behind Sinead, Connal ducked into the darkness of the abbey, his hand at the small of her back. Wind howled in after him and quickly he turned, nodded to the abbess, then closed the door.

Sinead faced him, adjusting his cloak, pushing his hair off his brow, and he gazed down at her, adoring her fussing and wondering where his anger had gone. On the ride here, it left him with each trod of Ronan's hooves, in Sinead's gentle ramblings, but then he saw the woman and a full measure of animosity came flooding back.

Rhiannon. His birth mother. She'd delivered him into the hands of her sister and watched him grow without speaking a word of her past to anyone. The pact of sisters, he thought, was stronger than he could have managed.

Rhiannon sat perfectly still, her body shrouded in a heavy dark habit that flowed over the chair. The whiteness of her coronet showed off her age, and the paleness of her skin. She was of an age with Siobhan, yet the years had been unkind and cruel to her beauty. He stared at her for a long moment and did not know he'd clenched his fists till Sinead took his hand. He looked down at her.

"Ask your questions, Connal. She has waited years to answer them." She released him and moved to the woman. Instantly Sinead sensed death as she bent to tuck the blanket over the woman's feet and lap.

Rhiannon lifted her gaze, her lips curving in a tired smile. "Fionna's child," she said in a weary voice.

Sinead nodded and rubbed Rhiannon's thin-boned hand, the skin papery beneath her touch.

Rhiannon's gaze lifted to the young woman, then shifted behind her.

Connal heard her indrawn breath. Tears formed in her eyes, and her lips trembled. He moved closer and remained standing, even when she gestured to the seat opposite her. Connal glanced to the side and caught a glimpse of Sinead as she whispered into mist and left him alone.

"You have grown into a fine, strong man."

"With no help from you."

She flinched as if he'd struck her. "Did I not teach you to read? Who was it that played games with you, Connal, when your mother tended castle duties?"

"And yet, *you* were my mother."

"Aye."

"Why did you do it?"

Rhiannon turned her face toward the fire, her voice frail as she spoke.

"I was to marry an old king, a man thrice my age, but he had died when I arrived at his manor. For the trip there he'd sent an escort, and Patrick was among them. The captain of his guards. I fell in love with him, and when he took me to his bed, I went most willingly."

Connal clenched his fists, standing near the fire, watching her for a lie. Her eyes were hollow, and though she was shrouded, her frail bones pushed against the pale layer of skin. He heard every labored breath she took.

"On the return to Donegal, he was summoned back. I learned I carried you and remained at the abbey. I sent a message to Siobhan. She remained with me for those months, and when we learned of Tigheran's death, we knew the clans would fall apart and war would come. The clans needed Tigheran's heir. I was without a husband or *coibche* to show my worth and yours." Her breathing wheezed and she paused to draw in more. "The night you were born, Siobhan and I made a promise to each other. And to the clans. And when we returned to Donegal she claimed you as her own."

"Why? Why did you discard me?"

"I did not. I was there with you."

"My aunt. My playmate!"

"I could be no more. Donegal was falling in on itself. Tigheran had disgraced us by trying to kill King Henry, and after his death, we knew the English would come to put their lords in his place. 'Twas a long while afore they did. Gaelan was awarded the castle and Tigheran's bride because he is the man who stopped Tigheran from killing the king. Stupid fool," she said with disgust. "Gaelan killed him in single combat as the King's champion." His look said he was aware of that. "Fine, fine, you know more than I suspected, but not the fear. For after Tigheran's death, the clans wished for another man to rule, and they fought for the right. And that included hurting me and Siobhan. But the heir apparent brought it to a stop. From then, Siobhan had ruled for five years in your stead and she did so well. She was a great chieftain, and without you, without the hope that the line would continue, we would have lost all she'd done in Tigheran's absence, and the wars would have continued."

"You do not know that."

"Aye, we did."

He was not going to argue, for there was no point to it.

"When Patrick returned, 'twas far too late." A sea of regret swept her voice then. "Gaelan and Siobhan were wed and happy. Patrick saw you and knew you were his son."

Connal did not give a damn about Patrick and a useless moment of recognition. "That does not excuse that you let so many die for him, Rhiannon." He could not call her mother. She was never his mother. Siobhan and Gaelan were the ones who'd raised him, who'd showered him with love and stood by him even when he made the wrong decisions.

"I was foolish. I had never thought to see him again. Because he paid no price to me for the birth of our child, he could not come to Donegal. He would have been killed under *Brehon* law for ignoring the honor."

"He *was* killed."

"Aye, and in it, he repented."

"Too late."

"Do you not think I know that!" She struggled for breath, desperately dragging air into her diseased lungs.

Connal watched her fail before his eyes, and sympathy flooded him. He knelt before her, offering her a goblet to drink.

Ignoring the drink, she grasped his hand and energy passed into him. "I am dying Connal. Nay, do not argue."

He couldn't, he thought, for she had accepted it in her heart.

"I've been a fool once. I have paid the price for my heart, for not taking what I had when I saw it. My betrothed was dead; I could have wed Patrick and lived a fine life with him. But I hesitated. I did not tell him of his son, I did not tell him of my love, until it was too late. I'd none but Siobhan to share the secret of it, and even now I would still love him."

Connal bowed his head and felt her hand graze his hair.

"You love Sinead."

He looked up. "Aye, I do."

She squeezed his hand. "And your gift of the senses has grown, I see." Her smile was as weak as her heart. " 'Tis the boon I have had, too; we all have a bit of it. I know the heart of thoughts. Tell her the truth afore 'tis too late, Connal. Confess afore you make the mistakes I did and lose all you hold dear. For living without love is only a slow death."

Connal looked at the fire, thinking on her words, knowing Sinead deserved it. But to destroy what he'd only just tasted. To ruin her love and mayhaps lose her forever by confessing that they were already wed against her wishes?

"Can you forgive me, Connal?"

He met her gaze. Hours ago, he would not have. Even in love, one made mistakes, he thought, and in the hope that Sinead would forgive him for his deception, he nodded.

Rhiannon sighed, quiet tears falling, and she smiled for the first time in years. Then, leaning her head back against the chair and closing her eyes, she welcomed her death. It came on swift wings and Connal waited, her fragile hand in his, as Rhiannon ban Murrough found peace in the arms of angels.

* * *

Sinead was in the outer courtyard when he came out of the stone abbey. She'd seen a novitiate rush past earlier to return with the abbess, both looking bleak.

Connal approached her, stone crunching beneath his feet. He stopped a breath from her and said naught, then simply took her into his arms and held her tightly.

"She is at peace."

"And so am I," he said, looking down at her. "Thank you for showing me the way, love." He pressed his lips to her forehead. Connal released a long sigh, then urged her toward the gates.

"To Dublin?" she asked as he mounted the steed behind her.

He took up the reins, giving the abbey one last glance afore turning south. "Aye, then to England. And to Richard."

Sinead's smile was weak, and he knew, as she did, that getting to England would not be as difficult as crossing the land to meet with the king.

"This land is far too cold."

"England will be little better, Najar."

The Moor, wrapped in more fur than Connal had seen in years, stood beside him as he unfastened his packs from his horse. Like a wash over a painting, the scent of the sea glistened on the mist. Square-rigged ships rocked in their berths as deckhands scrambled up planks and rigging, preparing to sail. Connal's gaze slipped over the activity. Carts and wagons passed by the docks in rapid pace; people moved like ants over rotted food, hawking wares, begging for food, and sleeping off a drunk in an alleyway. His troops were about, with orders to assemble on the docks at dawn, lest they be left behind. The two ships he'd purchased in Syria floated in the harbor, the rough icy sea giving no mercy as it slapped against Ireland's shore. The Persian-made crafts were larger than the others, their hulls deep and wide enough to take on more cargo and horses. And garner a great deal of attention.

One of his ships was already under sail and filled with equipment; the second, though, had a lighter load and only two small cabins. One was occupied by the captain and a few of his mates, and the other would keep Sinead from the eyes of the crew and soldiers.

His gaze fell on Sinead where she talked with Galeron, Branor at her back and studying the crowds for danger. The half-Scot knight rested his rear on a keg, his arms folded as he flirted with her. Connal suppressed the surge of jealousy and handed the packs to Ansel, his squire.

"Have you taken Lady Sinead's things aboard as well?"

Ansel nodded. "She did not have much, my lord."

He would change that once they arrived in England. The less they carried now, the swifter they could travel.

"I saw the cabin cleaned." Ansel shrugged. "As best it could be. And she sent her horse home." The lad frowned. "How's a blind horse supposed to find 'er way home, my lord?"

"Instinct, lad." Something Connal had learned to trust, he thought, leading Ronan onto the plank.

"My lord?"

Connal half turned to look back at him.

"Thank your lady for the powders for me wound."

"Why not thank her yourself, Ansel? She is—will be my wife; you might as well grow accustomed to her."

Ansel glanced warily at Sinead, and she looked up, smiling at the boy before her gaze dropped to where he'd taken the arrow in the thigh. "I will, sir. I will."

As the boy raced on ahead aboard ship, her gaze shifted to Connal. He grinned, winking at her, and she smiled.

Nahjar looked between the pair. "You have made her yours, Sajin?"

"She's mine regardless of what is said and done." Connal took a step back onto the gangplank.

"You have the gift of love, Sajin; do not toy with it unwisely."

He paused, frowning at Nahjar. "You're full of wisdom this morning. And I am too tired to reason with it." He'd gained little sleep last night, half from sensing they were about to be betrayed.

"She knows of the message from her castle, then?"

Connal's gaze snapped to the Moor's. "What do you know of that?"

"Monroe saw the messenger at DeCourcy's castle and wondered why his own vassal did not come to him and simply rode off."

Inwardly, Connal groaned. His time was running out. Sinead would soon learn of the contracts, and he wanted her to hear it from him. He'd tell her this night, he thought, and suspected the voyage to England would be a rough one.

Connal back-stepped up the ramp, pulling Ronan. He spoke soothingly to the great war horse, leading him down below into the hull and securing him. Men were already aboard and Connal wanted to be underway. He returned topside, coming to Sinead's side.

He smiled down at her, absorbing her presence and hiding his regret. This close to her, what he sensed and what he felt became entangled till all he knew was the beat of her heart. And how it drew him closer to her, wanting her more. And now he was trapped in a game of his own making. How was he to tell her of the contract? That her father had taken away the choice she valued so greatly? For Sinead, 'twas her only leverage, and now it was gone. She was his wife in the eyes of the king. His bride.

God above, she was going to be furious, and he held little hope that this would fall on her father's shoulders.

"Connal?"

He focused on her, leaning down to kiss her. Her response was eager with freedom and Connal wanted to get her alone to taste more of it.

"We leave now?"

"Aye, the tide is high enough." He signaled the captain, and the men rushed to prepare for sail. He took her arm, leading her to the vessel.

"So ... when is the wedding?" Galeron spoke up from behind.

Branor snapped a look at them, his gaze jerking between and settling on Connal. "So you've convinced her, then."

"Thank God," Monroe said on a sigh.

Connal's gaze was on Sinead, his breath held.

"As soon as 'tis wise and possible," she said. "Aye?"

Connal choked. "I've been damn near begging and you think now I would back away?"

She cocked her head. "You demanded for the king, Connal. Not once did you beseech *me.*"

He adjusted the cloak around her neck, pulling up the hood. The wind licked at the white fur, dancing the edges across her cheek. He'd never known such fortune and was fain to lose it. "I love you, Sinead," he said for all to hear. "Will you marry me?"

"Aye," she chirped and threw her arms around his neck, kissing him. A cheer rose from the men and, as she leaned back, a blush stole over her cheeks. Connal laughed and, taking her arm, led her to the ship. He set foot on the deck and stilled, turning sharply, scowling at the crowds melting down the avenue.

" 'Tis the same you felt afore?" she whispered.

"Aye. Rage, a strange kinship."

"Think you mayhaps this killer is Irish, Connal?"

"Mayhaps." He studied the faces. "Though De-Courcy said that Walter DeLacy had seen Richard's banner in a fallen trunk."

"But some of your men have been here a while. Could it not have been one of them and the banner one from your collection?"

"Aye, it could have." But Connal had given no orders to seclude themselves. His plans here in Ireland had never been a grand secret and he suspected that Prince John's justiciar, Pipard, was up to no good. He motioned to Branor.

"We cast off. Now."

"Aye, my lord." Sir Branor glanced at the streets, then immediately shouted orders, and men raced aboard.

Connal left Sinead at the bow and went to help. The sail unfurled, filling with air. Then, just as quickly, the lines snapped, the sail falling to the deck. A heartbeat passed afore a hail of arrows sliced the air, showering the vessel.

Chapter Eighteen

Arrows thunked into flesh and wood. Screams of pain and shouts of command crossed like racing steeds. Connal shouted to arms and his troop returned fire as plainly dressed men raced from the alleyways and toward the vessel. When a few tried to overtake the gangplank, Connal heaved it into the sea. Some men fell into the icy water; others were killed with PenDragon arrows.

Yet the rain of firepower kept coming.

And without sail, they could not move.

Then a flame-tipped arrow plunged into the deck and fire erupted.

Connal spun about and looked to Sinead. Instantly she lowered her hand and the fire extinguished; then she stood at the bow, facing the mast, and Connal knew he'd see her riddled with arrows.

Yet she shouted to the wind and water, raising her arms to the sky. The sail lifted from the deck, filling with air. The sea churned and in a great shove pushed the ship away.

On shore, like an avalanche of men and horses, DeCourcy's vassals swarmed down the streets and beset their attackers. Connal was grateful that DeCourcy had acted on his suspicions, yet not afore more flaming arrows hit the deck. Men scrambled to douse the flames as they broke away from the wharf, lurching deeply. Still the arrows came, and Connal climbed over ropes and kegs to get to Sinead. Out of the corner of his eye, and amid the fighting on shore, he saw a man running toward the ship, a javelin poised on his shoulder.

Connal shouted, "Get down!" a moment afore the staff flew through the air. It pierced the deck at Sinead's feet, vibrating with the impact. Sinead's eyes widened at the sight of it, yet she concentrated on keeping the sails filled with air. She chanted, willing the wind to knock their attackers into the sea. The dock broke under their feet, men and carts tumbling into the cold, dark water.

The crew and soldiers cheered.

Connal bellowed orders to the sailors, and like monkeys he'd seen in the east, they scrambled up rope lines to make repairs. When the ship was too far away for an arrow's range, Connal came to Sinead. Her lips moved silently as the lads tied off new ropes.

" 'Tis done," he said, and she fell back against him. "My thanks, love."

She looked up at him. " 'Tis an Irish weapon, Connal," she said, pointing to the javelin. Connal jerked it out of the wood deck, his gaze shifting from the weapon to the men still on shore.

"They wanted to stop us from reaching England. That means that Prince John is near completing his quest for the throne." He looked at her. "Can you help us get to England faster?"

"Aye."

He was staring at the shore, at the attackers, and thought he recognized one of them but couldn't be certain. He snapped the javelin across his knee and threw the pieces into the ocean. He should have had the ship sail farther up the coast and meet them in the north, he thought, but the coves were not deep enough to accommodate the Syrian vessel.

"Go to the cabin." He pointed. "Lock yourself in."

"Connal?"

"Go, Sinead. Do not let anyone but me inside. And do what you can to speed our journey."

For once she obeyed, hurrying to the small door and ducking inside.

Magic called to the wind and sea, sending the pair of vessels across the ocean in half the time and enabling them to land on the shores of England without incident. Connal considered it more magic than a stroke of luck that they were not met by Prince John's army, and yet his reservations grew when Richard was not at the rendezvous. Had he not gained his ransom? Was the king traveling still? There was no way of knowing either, yet he left behind two squads and, with Sinead, crossed the land to his manor.

When they arrived, it was Sinead's expression that made him laugh.

"This is yours?"

"Aye." He rubbed his mouth to hide a smile.

"And you thought it best to not tell me?"

"I simply forgot."

She sent him an impatient glance, then let her gaze move over the manor. 'Twas massive, elegant, towering over a small courtyard and bailey and, being Connal's, 'twas fortified with a wall twelve feet thick.

"And so why were you needin' my lands and castle, PenDragon?"

Connal winced. " 'Twas the location that made the difference, Sinead," he said, escorting her over the threshold. "And now you."

Pausing, she met his gaze, her smile filled with tender love as she touched the side of his face and kissed him. His arm tightened around her and he whispered his love, then led her inside.

She inhaled at the opulent decor, the walls draped in silks and wools to keep back the cold. The entrance so unlike the castles she'd seen, but more like a room, a chamber.

Connal watched her expression, adoring her wonder, and when she rushed to a chair and sat, testing its cushion, he smothered a laugh.

" 'Tis beautiful, so fine." Her gaze shot to him as she stood. "You do not let knights in armor and mud in here, do you?"

"Nay, lassie, not if I have any say," another voice spoke up.

"And you say a great deal," Connal shot back, tossing his cloak to a waiting servant.

Sinead whipped around as a round little woman hustled from somewhere in the back of the house, rubbing her hands on the apron tied about her middle.

"Ooo, my lord, you've brought her to us."

Sinead looked at Connal, then the woman, as she rushed her and gave her a warm hug. Sinead laughed and returned it.

Connal came near, taking Sinead's cloak. "This is the Lady Sinead O'Donnel DeClare. Sinead, my, ah, steward, Mistress Murphy."

Murphy grinned, her face rosy like a ripe apple in the sun. "Ah, the Princess of the Nine Gleanns," Murphy said reverently. "Oh, Goddess be blessed."

Sinead smiled and nodded. "What is that you do here, mistress?"

"Oh, call me Murphy, never was one for the formal titles."

"Murphy feels 'tis her duty to peck me to death, make me wash behind my ears, and eat green food." He shivered.

Sinead burst with laughter, looking at Connal through new eyes.

"Oh, he goes on like that, but he needs looking after, you know."

Sinead only glanced up and down at Connal.

"And he's never here, oh land, he be staying a bit now."

Connal did not want to disappoint the woman by revealing that their time here would be short. He already missed Ireland. "Is everything prepared, Murphy?"

"Aye, my lord, all is right and well."

"Show the Lady Sinead to her chamber then."

Murphy nodded and gestured, but Sinead turned to Connal, her hands on her hips. "What are you about, PenDragon? I can tell by that look."

"What look?"

"The one that says you've secrets to keep."

His expression softened and he grasped her shoulders and confessed, "I've sent for a priest."

"Oh."

"That's it, oh?"

She smiled slyly, running her hand over the fine brown velvet of his tunic, and said, "We do not need a ceremony, Connal; we exchanged binding words in the forest and all of nature witnessed our joining. 'Tis done. For eternity."

He grinned widely, ignoring Murphy's overloud tisking. "I want this marriage binding by law."

She shrugged. "Fine."

"Fine?"

"A priest's words mean naught to me, but call him, if 'tis your desire."

He bent close and whispered, "My desire right now is to have you in my bed, naked and panting."

They'd shared a bed but not each other on the ship. Mostly because Connal suspected they'd brought a traitor on board and he manned a watch. But during the trip, with her near him, undressing in front of him, kissing him like tomorrow would not come, his little witch left him walking about with an uncomfortable heaviness in his groin. The thought of satisfying her made him harder.

"Ah, you are just in a rutting mood, then."

He choked.

"Well, then," she said, slipping out of his arms, "mayhaps we should remain apart till your priest arrives."

He scowled. Her look was too dammed innocent just then. "Not bloody likely."

"A fine notion, aye," Murphy put in, her head bobbing, though no one had asked her opinion.

Sinead headed to the stairs, then paused to cock a look back over her shoulder. Her eyes teased with mischief. "I shall see you when he has arrived."

With a look of dark promise, Connal headed after her, and she shrieked and ran up the stairs, her skirt hiked. Murphy stood at the base, watching them, smiling when her lord caught his lady and swept her into his arms and headed toward his chamber.

"Was that the new lady?" Peg, a young woman asked, fixing her cap.

"Aye, 'twas her, the princess, the witch."

Peg gasped.

"And she's brought love into this house. And to our Connal." Murphy could not be more pleased.

Peg smiled, her gaze shifting toward the door.

With a scream that made Murphy wince, the other woman called out to Galeron and ran. He scooped her up in his arms and kissed her soundly.

"Ah!" Murphy crowed. "Put that child down and behave, Sir Galeron. Or I'll be tossing you into the pigsty again."

"Aye lady Murphy." He kissed Peg anyway, cupping her soft behind.

"Oh tish tosh," Murphy fussed and headed for the kitchen.

At the news, Prince John threw the goblet, yet took no satisfaction as the costly mirror shattered and fell to the carpet.

The room went silent, a man backing away.

He whirled and pointed. "Stay!"

The Irishman froze.

"The rest of you, get out!" The chamber emptied, and the two men stood alone. John walked up to him, his stare unwavering. "One man, and you could not kill him."

"I couldn't get close enough t—"

The look on the prince's face froze the words in his throat.

"Bring me the witch, and he will come."

The man nodded.

The prince took a step away, then turned back. "This is your last chance, then the task is mine."

The Irishman nodded. John flicked a hand toward them, and as the man left, he turned toward the window.

He stared at naught, his mind racing.

He heard someone enter.

"I will arrive in a day's time," he said, still looking out the window, his hands folded at the small of his back. "I expect things to be handled well."

"Aye, your highness. If I have to kill him myself."

John cocked a look at the dark-haired man. "Why? He's done naught to you."

The sheriff shrugged. "Interesting prospect, killing the king's first knight."

John held his gaze a moment longer, then smiled. "Take who and what you need and follow the Irishman. I do not trust him. PenDragon has gathered strange loyalties in Ireland. And I would not count that Richard is far behind."

"Then we must act quickly, sire."

"Then, my dear sheriff, what are you still doing here?"

Abovestairs, in the biggest bed Sinead had ever seen, Connal plunged into her, his mouth a heated brand on hers. Their bodies slick with sweat, they moved like the sea, in perfect rhythm, as he claimed her again. Each long, measured thrust built the fire atween them. Sinead locked her legs around his waist, pulling him back harder, and 'twas a nuance of hers Connal was beginning to understand. He shoved harder and she moaned deeply, her fingers digging into his arms.

She was exquisite in the arms of desire, free with her love and her body, and Connal watched her pleasure erupt in a sweet rippling wave that pulled him into her. He scooped her up off the bed, driving deeper, clinging to her as his world shattered and came together in one moment of pleasure.

"Ah, Connal," she said against his mouth as the last shudders twisted through her. He felt each tremor, the pulse of her erotically tight. Around them, the vines receded, the bed reshaped from the tree limbs to the carved frame. The fire settled in the hearth. He was growing accustomed to the changes in their surroundings, and yet each time it left him in awe.

He looked down at her, pushing damp curls from her face.

"I do not think I could have waited for your priest," she said, her eyes sparkling.

He laughed quietly. "Nor I."

They fell down onto the bed, and Connal kissed her gently, his hand moving down her spine and cupping her buttocks. "My want of you beneath my hands is a constant madness."

She smiled. "You used more than hands," she said boldly, her eyes sparkling. "Clever man."

He laughed and rolled to his back, taking her with him. Sinead gazed into his green eyes, sighing with contentment. Physical love was new to her, exciting, and the passion bottled up inside her was only just beginning to open. She wanted him, right now, she thought with a bit of surprise. For he understood her needs as she did his, each touch and kiss speaking of boundless love, and once hidden, the uncapping of it showered on her.

She smiled at him.

"What?"

"I'm wishing your priest has been and gone and I was your wife."

"You already are," he said without thinking, and cursed himself ten times the fool.

Her eyes flew wide and she sat up. "What say you, Connal?"

He hedged for a moment. "Your father signed the contracts and sent them in secret by messenger to me at DeCourcy's."

"Afore the forest." Her voice sounded lifeless and his guilt spread to shame.

"I could not tell you. 'Twas what you prided so well, love."

"All that was said was a lie?" Tears wet her eyes and slashed his heart.

"Nay, dammit, nay! You know I speak the truth." When she made to leave the bed, he grabbed her arms and held her there. "I love you. The papers mean little."

"To you, mayhaps. But men control a woman's world, Connal, and that was *my* choice that father gave to you."

"Then be mad at him, not me."

"You wanted it all along and yet you kept it from me."

"Aye, and still, at this hour, this day, I would have, for I wanted your love, I wanted you to come to me for love! And not because of a signature on a paper!"

When she simply stared, looking wounded and fragile, he thrust from the bed, and naked, he searched his packs for the missives and handed them to her. "Read your father's letter. He feared for your life still and thought it best."

She studied her father's writing, then lifted her gaze.

"Without these, I could not challenge anyone for you," he said, pulling on his chausses. "You know this. In the eyes of the king we are husband and wife, but"— the sharpness suddenly left his voice—" 'tis only the view from your eyes that matters to me."

He faced her and stood rock still, his expression open with regret.

The single tear falling down her cheek cut him deeper than an enemy's blade. "Say something, Sinead, shout, create a storm! Be angry, for your silence is killing me." Connal saw his world falling apart, all he'd gained chipping away like a caving mountain.

"Why did you not tell me this afore?"

His throat worked. "I—I was afraid."

"You?"

"Aye. I was terrified of losing what we'd made atween us. I could not destroy the only power you had left."

She looked away briefly. "What is between us now and will be does not come from paper or your king, Connal. For I could not have shared myself with you if we did not love."

He frowned.

"To mate with a man not of true heart . . . I would have died then and there."

The impact of her words hit him like a blow from a mace. "You risked death?"

She nodded. "I had to be certain of your love. This"—she tossed the paper aside—"was the only way to keep the hand of men from forcing me to make another mistake. I was not sure if what I was feeling for you was that of a girl, or of a woman, new or old." She wrapped the sheet around herself, tucking it in. But Connal saw her hands shake.

He moved closer to the bed, his body rigid. "I love you, Sinead—God knows I do, but I had to do what my king required of me."

"Aye, I understand what duty means to you."

The quiet in her tone made his breath catch.

"It means naught if I lose you."

"But you did not trust me with this."

"Aye. Aye!" He plowed his fingers through his hair. "I felt trapped by the king's orders and my love for you. But . . ." He went quiet for a moment, a terrible decision coming to him. "If you wish it, I will beg his favor and ask him to release you from this contract."

Sinead inhaled, her heart dropping to her stomach. "You want that?"

"Nay, I do *not!* But I will not have you thinking I spoke words of love just to get your lands and get you into my bed!"

"You'd always wanted the holdings, Connal; that you never made secret. If you'd spoken of love firstly, I would never have trusted a thing you said."

"And now?"

"What do you think?"

"God above, I never know the twist of your mind."

"Oh, Connal," she said softly and, gathering hope in the look on her face, he bent a knee to the bed. "You have punished yourself for Patrick and Rhiannon's crime, do not punish yourself for my father's." Scarred and seasoned, he stood afore her, his heart exposed, waiting. Sinead understood how much he loved her, for to defy Richard to please her would cost him more than his knighthood. It would cost him who he was.

"I have lied to you," he said dully.

On her knees on the bed, she met his gaze. "My father has, and he let the responsibility fall on you." She laughed gently, sympathetically. "For which he will answer. But I have wanted you for all time, Connal. I have already willingly given my consent. What matters now with that?" She flicked a hand at the documents. "You can forgive me?"

She reached for him and he wrapped his arms around her. "Aye. You are the man I love, have *always* loved."

"God," he groaned, squeezing her.

"You are sworn to Richard, but a knight for Ireland."

He smiled, his throat thick.

"I trust you, Connal." He leaned back to meet her gaze. "With my heart, and now my lands, and the care of my people." A faint yellow light glowed from around her.

"Sinead?" He sat back on his haunches as she closed her eyes, extending her arms out just above her bare waist, palms up, as if to catch something in her hands. "Sinead?"

"Hush, my love."

A serenity swept her expression, a calm he felt in his soul.

"*Tuatha De Dannon,* Warrior creed. Strength is born, in silver seed."

The air above her hands shifted like lustrous water. Thickening, luminescent.

"From the earth and forged by fire. Grant my knight, his right of power."

. A breath later, his sword, the one he'd cast aside so long ago in a fit of rage, lay upon her palms.

Slowly her eyes opened. "What is mine, I share with you, Connal."

She held out the sword. He did not touch it.

An incredible sense of humility engulfed him, and Connal swallowed. "Sinead, I—I—" His gaze swept up and down the steel hammered and polished to a fine silver. Did she know what this meant to him? To have this sword in his grasp? To have her return it to him? When she'd first produced it in the solar of *Croi an Banrion,* he'd felt his entire body call to it. His heart screamed for him to return to the man he was before he'd thrown it at his father's feet. And now she offered it back.

" 'Tis no ordinary sword, Connal." She studied briefly the Celtic knots carved into the shaft, the hilt, and blending onto the blade in never-ending curls. "My father and mother gave it to you when you were knighted, aye, yet 'twas forged on Rathlin Island, by Cathal."

His gaze flashed to her. Cathal. The Druid prince and her grandfather, lover to Queen Egrain. Fionna's parents.

"The metal is from beyond the mark of time, and it shines because of Egrain's touch." Still he did not take it. "They knew then, what was to be."

"You said you kept it because the prince was no longer."

"You are not a prince, aye." She laid the sword across his hands, her gaze locked tight with his as she said, "But you are the laird of the Nine Gleanns, my love."

Connal held the sword reverently for a moment; then the warrior in him turned it to test the balance. The grip molded to the shape of his hand, hummed with strength and power.

Sinead smiled, swiping at a tear. He cupped the back of her head and drew her down for a soul-stripping kiss. "Thank you, my heart." His voice fractured. "You have no notion how much this means to me."

"Aye, I do."

He met her gaze and knew she was right. Laying the sword on the side of the bed, he pulled her into his arms and drew her down onto the bedding.

"I am a fortunate man," he whispered against her temple.

"Aye, that you are, and I shall be remindin' you of it nightly, my lord."

He laughed and rolled on top of her, and Connal PenDragon decided then that the luck of the Irish held little in comparison to the fortune of loving a red-haired, fast-tempered Irish witch. Aye, he thought. He'd won the heart of the Queen of the Gleanns. And with it came deliverance.

The ceremony was held outside, at midnight. The witching hour.

Connal though it rather appropriate; Sinead said 'twas simply the thinnest time atween two worlds and she wanted the spirits of Cathal and Egrain to witness this moment they predicted before she and Connal were even born.

Yet as he stood a couple of feet from her in the courtyard, his gaze moving over her face and the deep green garments she'd worn that first day on the beach, Connal knew now that he was helpless but to love her and only her.

He murmured the words, and as Sinead stumbled over a few, they noticed little around them. Not the friar shaking in his leather shoes. Nor the smiling crowd of knights and soldiers perched like elves about the barren stone walls. Nor the firelight of faeries whipping to and fro.

They only saw each other. Her hands in his grasp, Connal decided she was highly amused by all this and found it unnecessary in her eyes. To her the first time they'd made love was enough to seal them forever. That she did this to please him, to please the masses, made him love her more for it.

The friar cleared his throat. "Ah ... my lord, 'tis done."

Sinead smiled and stepped into Connal's open arms, kissing him deeply. Above them the black sky lit with lightning, shimmered with blue and yellow stars.

The bonfire rose and kissed the clouds.

Connal drew back and looked heavenward. Then he laughed and kissed her again.

"I love you," he said against her mouth.

"That, my knight, I know."

A moment later she was yanked from him and kissed by Galeron. The eagerness of it told Connal the man had wanted to do such for a while. Connal shoved his shoulder, breaking them apart, then glared at the man. Galeron simply smacked his lips and wiggled his brows. While Branor only brushed a quick kiss to her cheek. Nahjar, who grinned through the entire process, stood with his arms folded over his chest, his gaze moving from one to the other.

"Nary a bit of wisdom to impart, Nahjar?" Connal asked as everyone around them proceeded to get drunk.

"Keep his bed warm," he said to Sinead. "And her heart happy," he said to Connal. "For a man with an unhappy wife leads a miserable life."

"Speaking from experience are you now, Nahjar?" Sinead said.

"Yes, Sajin's lady."

Connal looked down at his wife. "Well then, think you should get started on that?"

"My task is easy; what about yours?" She arched a red brow.

"I endeavor to please thee."

"Then pay the priest. If he crosses himself once more I fear he'll bore a hole in his forehead."

Laughing to himself, Connal did just that, offering food and drink to the stout friar. The man, amazed and awed by what he'd witnessed during the ceremony, refused, crossed himself, and ran to his pony.

Murphy stood off to the side, sobbing into her apron. Connal hugged her, patting her back, and the woman wailed loudly, clutching him to her. When she was calm, he kissed her plump cheek. She blushed rosily and said, "Now give me some babies to care for."

Connal grinned and winked at her, moving to his wife and scooping her up in his arms. He carried her through their home, to his bed. In the darkness of his chamber, surrounded by vines and trees, the scent of moss and flowers lingering, Connal made slow, patient love to his bride. And never in his life knew such happiness. And was completely unaware that their loving world was about to come tumbling down around them, and his faith in her magic would be tested.

Chapter Nineteen

Hidden in the woods, a mile from PenDragon's manor, Angus O'Brien squatted by a small fire. Across from him sat two other men, his brother's vassals. Both were near asleep where they sat.

Angus chewed on a piece of smoked meat, not meeting their gazes, but their gaunt faces and beggarly garments were a testimony to all they'd lost. The men had lost rights and pride. Angus had lost people. The impact of it was startling in the quiet darkness. He should be accustomed to this, he thought, rubbing his forehead, and missing his brothers. His home. Christ, he hated England.

Aye, he thought, he just plain hated. PenDragon, Richard, the witch. Naught that all he'd lost could be returned to him, and he knew Prince John would not pay him more, nor would he be rewarded for killing the knight and his witch.

Angus never expected reward from Prince John.

For that, he'd had to be of some great benefit to the prince. And Angus was neither a landholder nor a man with connections and power. He'd naught left to lose, and all Prince John held over him was his life.

He no longer cared, and that made him dangerous, he thought.

This was satisfaction of honor. Those who committed the crimes needed to be held accountable. PenDragon would pay for taking Angus's little brother to war and getting the lad killed. Angus chose not to see that his brother had gone willingly. That Keith had been awestruck when he'd first seen PenDragon astride his dark silver mount and fully armored. Naught could convince the youth that death came to those who followed PenDragon and King Richard.

The Lion Hearted would come back to naught, he thought with a smirk. And he deserved to lose his throne. Not that Prince John was any better at leading. But 'twas Richard who'd stripped his sect of the O'Briens of their lands and holdings.

Because of Markus. For DeClare. For the witch.

A part of him still wrapped in decency cursed Markus for his behavior. Angus had warned him that marrying Sinead was wrong, and keeping her for her power would come back to him threefold. And it had. Angus rubbed his face with both hands, the memory of DeClare taking his brother's head in one swipe repeating in his mind. The blood had splashed him, wet his boots.

And he'd pissed in his chausses.

Markus had never understood that the witch's power came from her Druid blood and a pure heart. No one could take it, nor force her to use it.

But Angus knew how to stop her. He'd already managed to get an arrow in her, and 'twas good for him that he'd had another man in the trees. He'd slipped away without notice whilst the archers had turned Michael into a quilled hedgehog. Taking another bite of the dried meat, he used his foot to nudge a log farther into the flames.

"How we gonna get to him, Angus? He's inside the walls."

"I'm thinking." Angus hadn't counted on Prince John wanting the witch. God, he was just like Markus. But if Angus didn't bring the witch out and to the prince, then he'd find his own head on a pike in London. Though he'd bet his last coin that Prince John was already heading this way. He enjoyed amusement too much. Enjoyed wielding his power and cutting lives out of existence.

Angus did not care if he died, only that PenDragon and the witch died with him.

"Angus?"

"Shut up, I'm thinking, I say."

"A strain, I'm sure."

Angus looked up, his features tightening as a tall slender figure moved into the light. He went for his sword and felt the impact of a boot to his head an instant later.

"Do *not* ever draw on me."

Angus shook his head, a heavy buzzing atween his ears. There were two other knights behind him. "He said I had one more chance to kill him."

"A misconception. But then, you haven't been awarded his holdings, have you?"

Angus smirked to himself, touching the bloody spot on the back of his head and rubbing the stain between his fingers. "You think to get the witch's lands by killing

him. They do not belong to him. Only yon manor."
Angus enjoyed the sheriff's surprise, and his doubt.
"Aye, she is the ruler, and even if you did kill him
and claim them, the earls will not stand for that, for
PenDragon has done naught to you. Or the prince.
There is only so much thievery a royal . . . or a sheriff
can do afore the whole of England demands justice."

The sheriff inspected a tassel hanging from his cloak.
"Yet you planned to kill them."

"I've me own reasons. I want only their death and
I've naught to lose."

The sheriff whipped his blade to stop just under
Angus's throat. "Your life?"

Angus met his gaze steadily. "Fine, take it. But I know
much about the witch and PenDragon. All you know is
hearsay."

The sheriff considered that for a moment, then lowered the blade. "Tell me what she can do."

Angus laughed, an ugly tortured sound.

The dream woke her. She flinched against Connal
and he stirred. "Sinead, what is the matter?" His speech
was slurred with sleep.

"Shh," she hushed quietly. "Return to sleep, love."

She eased out of his embrace, and Connal caught her
hand, his lids lifting slowly. " 'Twas the dream?"

"Aye." She leaned to kiss him and whispered, "Sleep.
I only need a bit of air."

"Stay inside and be careful."

"I will." She smiled against his mouth. "Dream of
me loving you."

He gave her a sleepy grin. "Always, my witch." She
covered him against the cold and slipped from the bed,

donning her velvet robe as she moved to the door. She stopped suddenly and shrugged to herself; then, concentrating on where she wanted to be, she turned slowly, whispering the words of change. An instant later she was in the cook house.

She was starving and foraged in the cupboards and peeked under limp cloths. Finding bread and cheese and a bit of roasted meat, she sliced off a portion of each, thinking that she should bring some back to the chamber for Connal. She nibbled, looking around. The stone-walled room was immaculate, the floor swept of debris and crumbs, and she noticed a scrap pot near the door, likely for the pigs or dogs, though she'd seen neither when she arrived.

"M'lady?" came in a whisper, and Sinead spun about, looking guilty with a crust of bread hanging out of her mouth. She snatched it.

"Forgive me, Murphy."

"Tish tosh, you're hungry, and if I may say, lass, 'tis good to see you about." The older woman righted her cap as she trotted over to the worktable. "We was all wonderin' if the master was going to let you out of his sight."

Sinead blushed, knowing they'd spent a day and a night in their chambers and had not shown themselves belowstairs for meals. She could only imagine the talk when Connal had bellowed for food and wine, then shut the door again.

Murphy pulled back several cloths tucked over bowls and platters.

"Oh, nay, this is plenty." She gestured to the bread and cheese. "Will you join me, though?"

"I was plannin' on it." Murphy inspected the treats, then spooned up a concoction that was thick with cream, apples, and—aye, Sinead smelled cinnamon. Connal had brought some home, and 'twas a divine scent.

They shared the food, talking softly. Sinead was fascinated by the stories the woman told of Connal's return. When he had not been off fighting for Richard, mostly in the west, he was here in this house. Brooding and stomping about, as Murphy was like to say.

"I've a treat, lovey," Murphy said and slid off her stool. "We've got us some fresh milk out back, and with that spice my lord brought back from the Holy Land, well, you've never had such so good." She was nearly to the rear door when she paused and said, "Did he show you his treasures?"

Sinead shook her head.

"He brought gold and fabrics and spices of all kinds, sacks of them, and fruits and berries, and this odd little bean that you cannot eat."

"Then what do you do with it?"

"That's the thing, lassie. We roast it slowly and crush it, then put it in boilin' water for a bit. Turns the water muddy as a moat, and after straining, my lord drinks it."

"Sounds very unappealing."

"Aye, 'tis bitter, and needs quite a bit of sweetening, if you ask me. I'll give you a taste of it in the morn, for once drunk, you willna be sleepin' for a while." She moved to the rear door again, pushing it open and staring out into the darkness. The sun was just turning the sky purple. "Now, where is that blasted thing? I swear, if Galeron snatched it again, that brute of a man . . ." she groused. Her voice grew distant as she moved farther from the door.

"Murphy, do come back in," she called. " 'Tis too cold out for you to be traipsing in naught but a robe and slippers." Sinead took a step, pushing the door and calling again. She heard heavy footsteps, the crunch of stone, and Galeron appeared in the door.

He smiled. "Ah, Lady Sinead, so he's finally released you."

"I was not a prisoner, and guard what you say, Galeron, or a toad will be wearing your armor." She rapped on his breastplate and he simply grinned. "Find Murphy; she stepped out and has not returned."

Galeron was turning away when he caught something in his line of vision. A flick of a shadow. Pushing Sinead behind him, he stepped into the kitchen, his sword out.

The instant he passed the door, he relaxed his guard and frowned. "What are you doing in here at this hour?" he said before something struck the back of his head with a sickening crunch. As Galeron folded to the floor, Sinead turned to run, raising her arms to summon the powers. Someone snatched her wrist, jerking her off her feet and back against his chest. She winced and looked up as a ragged, bushy-faced man wrenched her arm behind her.

"I've got the little witch," he shouted.

One hand free, Sinead snapped her fingers, creating fire in her palm and tossing it in his face. He howled in agony, his hair and shirt catching, and he released her. She ran hard, her concentration failing her as she called for Connal.

A man leaped out of the darkness, latching onto her legs and toppling her to the ground. He fell on her, her breath forced out of her with his weight.

"I've got the witch!" he shouted. "Gimme that," he said to someone else, and she felt her hands being bound.

She tipped her head down and whispered, "Tuatha, Tuath—"

"Damn, she's chanting."

"Well, stop her!"

The man was off her and flipping her onto her back. He raised his arm to strike her. "Cease, woman, or I'll do it for ye."

"Gabh sidhe fae. Gabh de Dannon—" Come faery folk, Come warriors.

He struck her, her head whipping to the side. Sinead worked her jaw, lifting her gaze to him. Her eyes narrowed. "I know you. You are O'Brien's kin."

"I haven't kin, witch, because of you and that ... knight," he said with disgust.

"And you will be the last of your line, for Connal will not let you live."

"He'll be snoring in his bed afore he learns of this."

"Do not wager that."

Connal, she chanted in her mind.

Connal slid along the wall outside the kitchens, gesturing silently to Nahjar to use the opposite entrance, that led from the front of the manor. He'd sensed the danger only moments ago, and then heard Sinead's call for help.

His urge to move quickly was tamped down by caution, her warning of the dream she continued to have each night. Gingerly he eased into the kitchen, and one glance took in the candles overturned, yet still burning on the worktable. It shadowed the figure sprawled on the floor in a pool of blood.

A stab of grief lanced through him. 'Twas no doubt that Galeron was dead. Half his skull was missing. He crossed the kitchen, stepping outside and moving along the outer wall. Nahjar moved up behind him.

"Sajin, there are no guards."

"They are dead or we have been betrayed."

"Dead." Nahjar pointed to the body slung over the wall.

Connal looked, fear sweeping through him. To attack his manor was a grave offense, for by right and law he'd done naught to warrant it.

Connal, he heard in his head. *Careful.*

He moved toward the courtyard, wondering why Sinead hadn't used her magic, but when he met the edge, he saw why. She was on the ground, her hands bound behind her back, and a man straddling her hips. He was forcing her to drink something. And God love her, she refused.

A man leaned down in her face and said something to her. Her neck stretched as she looked around at the walls, at the men slumped over the stone parapets. She opened her mouth to drink the potion.

Do not, he called to her in his mind. *Do not drink!*

She stilled and clamped her lips shut. Angry, the man hauled her to her knees, glancing around. He muttered something to a giant man standing to his right.

Connal stood back in the shadows, surveying the small bailey. The gate was open, the guards dead, and though he'd men positioned in the upper floors, where was Branor and Monroe, and his squire, Ansel? His gaze snapped to the stable. Shadows moved slowly within the faint light.

"Come out, PenDragon, I know you're there," Sinead's captor called out.

Connal remained still and silent, ignoring the fear pounding in his heart, waiting for the opportunity to take his wife back. He looked about for a diversion, then took a risk and whistled for his mount. Ronan's hooves smashed at the walls of the stable, the wood splintering and the horse's neigh screeching in the night. Several turned toward it, and Connal counted only a half dozen men. But that did not mean there weren't more.

Taking advantage of the distraction, Connal rushed her captor, knocking him to the ground.

Behind him, Nahjar swung his curved sword. A half dozen more of his men raced into the bailey, yet Connal saw only Sinead.

Her eyes widened. "Behind you!"

He turned as someone struck him on the side of the head. He stumbled, and sheer will kept him on his feet, his sword in his fist. Yet 'twas time enough for another foe to grab his wife and put a knife to her throat.

"Do not move!" Connal shouted to his men.

The slightest touch and Sinead would be bleeding to death at his feet.

Silence pulled at him, and he forced his gaze from her when a man stepped from the darkness, his gate loose-limbed and almost vulgar. A sword swung at his side, but he did not touch it.

"Well, well, PenDragon." The man pushed his black gloves deeper between his fingers.

"Release her or die."

The man flicked a hand and his comrade lifted Sinead by the hair as another man put a cup to her mouth.

"Nay! Sinead, do not!"

" 'Tis a drug, not a poison," she whispered, and 'twas like a shout in his head. "You will find me. Let them go, so you can find me."

He shook his head.

"I think we need some . . . inspiration here," the dark-haired man said.

The bearded man pricked her throat.

Connal saw no fear in her eyes, only her trust in him.

Sinead swallowed hard, despite the blade at her throat. "You must; the troops are drugged, not dead, Connal. But he will kill them."

"Nay, fair lady witch, not when I will earn them as my own soon," the man, dark-haired and slender, said with a glance over his shoulder at her. "But I will kill *him.*" He withdrew his sword.

"Nay!" Sinead shouted, and the man holding the cup poured the liquid into her mouth. He clamped a hand over her nose and mouth, forcing her to swallow or choke. Sinead's eyes narrowed, speaking of retribution, then they closed in a drugged sleep. They let her fall helplessly to the ground.

Connal's heart thundered with anger. "Who are you?" he demanded, his sword aready.

"A messenger from Prince John."

Nahjar stood at his back as men circled them. "We are outnumbered, Sajin."

"Kill as many as you can."

Nahjar nodded and sliced out, cutting a man's arm off cleanly at the shoulder. He fell, screaming, and Nahjar muttered, "You will live," then attacked a second.

Monroe, Sir Kerry, and three more joined him, and Connal and his men positioned themselves in a circle of power, protecting each other's backs as they fought. Years of service, the Crusades, and internal patience made them strike with precision and leathal intensity. Swords hummed through the air, cutting through tender flesh and bone, each man knowing the weakness of armor.

Their opponents dropped to the ground like unwanted baggage and they widened the circle, protecting his people, his home. He edged toward Sinead, lying on the ground, motionless.

Then the invaders threw a torch to the ground, the winter-dry earth igniting quickly as Connal swung at the leader. Swords clashed, the sound ringing in the burning bailey. Servants rushed to put out the fire as men fought and died. Out of the corner of his vision he saw men carry Sinead to a horse, and panic filled him.

"I consider this an honor," his opponent said, slashing hard at Connal.

He blocked and paried, his blade catching his cloak and slicing off a chunk of it. "Really."

"You're a bit of a legend, PenDragon. Something like your lady there."

"She is my wife."

"Delightful," he said without a shred of pleasure. "When you die, I'll marry her and get your lands."

Fury boiled in Connal's blood, clearing his mind. "You will never have Sinead. Never."

"Oh?"

They struck blades, Connal's hilt locking with his opponents and bringing them face-to-face. "You will never have even a fistful of Ireland. And if I were you I'd be very careful what you did to my wife. She has a mean temper."

The man paled. Connal shoved him back, fury unleashing as he pounded the man, slash for slash. His home invaded, his friend killed, his wife taken. This man would not live.

The man back-stepped, his cloak falling to the ground in shreds, and knew PenDragon was playing with him.

Connal swiped with precision, and his opponent's sword belt tangled at his feet, the cut leaving behind a bleeding slice in his belly. He could hear the man's harsh breathing, and he stumbled backwards.

"You're out of practice, aye?" Connal said, wanting to be done with this. "I, sir, am not."

Connal advanced, merciless with his silver blade, and the man glanced around in panic at his fallen men, then at one coming toward him. "Take her away," the intruder ordered one of his men.

"But Sheriff—" O'Brien said.

"Take her now!"

"You will die for this, O'Brien, like your brother," Connal swore, his eyes speaking of retribution. As they dragged Sinead across the ground, Connal rushed the sheriff, the serration of his sword tearing through fabric and flesh and leaving a bloody sheen on his blade. "I *will* kill you."

The sheriff rushed backwards, then suddenly the sheriff stopped, pressed his sword into the ground, and folded his hands over it. "Nay, you will not." The sheriff nodded.

Connal turned sharply and faced Branor. His gaze dropped to the thin blade his knight held. An instant later, Branor stabbed out, the sharp steel singing deeply into Connal's flesh and coming out the other side. Pain burned through him, spilling in his groan. He blinked, stunned.

"Why?" he managed, folding his fingers over the bare blade. It cut into his hand as he tried yanking out the sword.

"You follow King Richard's pet for years without rewards and ask that?" was all Branor said.

"I would have given you aught you wanted . . .

friend," Connal choked, falling to his knees with a jolt. His breathing rapid, he yanked on the blade, growling as he tossed it aside. "Damn you!"

A moment later, Nahjar let out a harsh battle cry. Branor turned. Nahjar swung, his scimitar cutting through Branor's neck and severing his head so quickly, his body remained upright for several seconds. Till Monroe kicked it to the ground.

Connal clutched his side and staggered to where Sinead was bent over a horse's withers, her hair touching the ground. Three men set fire to the hay behind him, the winter-dead grasses instantly going up in flames. He lifted his hand to her, calling her name. The edges of his vision blurred, and he dropped to the ground, his gaze struggling to remain on her. Blood flowed over his fingers, soaking the ground, and Connal knew her prophecy had come true.

"Sinead!" he coughed. The sheriff rode out the gates with his wife, her hair a flying red banner across the horse's black coat. 'Twas the last thing he saw.

Chapter Twenty

The sheriff sanded his hands together more for warmth than glee as he moved to the table laden with food. Prince John would be terrible pleased, he thought, sampling bread and dipping it in a pot of clotted cream. Several of his men, including his cousin, lounged about, eating. Their numbers were fewer, yet anyone who'd failed him at PenDragon's manor was dead anyway.

"Where did you put her, cousin?"

"In the tower." Guy sucked grease from his fingers.

"Ah, well. Bound and gagged as well?"

"Aye. She cannot get free."

The sheriff's gaze snapped up. "You are quite certain of this? For if she is missing when Prince John arrives, you are dead. Make no mistake of that."

Guy stood, giving him a sour look as he tossed the turkey leg to the dogs and trudged off toward the captive.

"Out, all of you," the sheriff said, settling into a still warm chair and pulling his cloak about him. He gestured to a servant to stoke the fire.

PenDragon was dead. His betrayer dead. Now, if the thieves would cease praying on his people and the barons would arrive, he'd be in a much better mood.

A howl came from abovestairs and he paused in biting into a piece of meat and sighed. "I am surrounded by inept people," he muttered, biting into the food. A second cry came, and he cursed and left the chamber.

As he climbed the stairs he tested his arm, the cut PenDragon had given him clean but deep. He hated scars, he thought, and stopped outside the tower chamber. He pushed open the door and found Guy strung against the wall like a crow for the fields.

His gaze snapped to the witch and he took a step back.

Sinead's call to the faery folk had been incomplete, yet they'd heard her pleas. And now Kiarae, Galwyn, Brigit, and Sairah hovered over her husband.

Connal lay between life and death, the veil thin. Galwyn looked at his lover, his expression grave. "I fear he will not live."

Kiarae flew down to stand near Connal's head. "He must or she dies, too." She touched his forehead, hot with fever.

Monroe slipped into the room and the faeries remained, looking up at him defiantly. He sighed, not truly startled to see them again, and brought the tray he carried to the side of the bed. He sat in a chair, then pulled gently at the bandages stained dark red.

Nahjar entered after him. "Most are alive, Monroe."

"Good. Galeron?"

"I have buried him on the hillside."

Monroe's features tightened. He'd grown fond of the man, and his death was useless. "Why would Branor betray them? Us? He was treated like a brother."

"Ah, but not as favored. Some men are greedy for things they cannot have and believe owed to them."

"How long have you known him?"

Nahjar thought on that as he motioned Monroe aside and tended to Connal's wound. Tugging the ties of a leather case, he rolled out his tools and, after cleansing the wound, began to stitch. "Branor was always secretive." Nahjar shrugged, his thick arms and big hands moving with a delicacy that belied their size. "I knew him years and did not suspect his discontent. It no longer matters." The faeries perched themselves on the pillow above Connal's head. Nahjar glared at them. "You are a genie?"

Galwyn tipped his chin and shook his head.

Nahjar took another stitch. "Can you not heal him?"

Kiarae glanced up sullenly. "Nay. Her mother mayhap, but she is too far to come."

Nahjar worked over him, pushing Connal on his side to repair the torn skin near his waist. The faeries buzzed close, blocking his view.

"You, go!" he barked, and they flew high. "Find a plant for healing. And one to purge."

"He will live?"

"Sajin PenDragon has endured worse." Laying him on his back, Nahjar pointed to the scar on his opposite side below his ribs. "Go," he growled. The faeries looked at him with wide eyes, then blinked out of existence. "The men are rousing," Nahjar said. "But 'tis taking a while. Each is spewing up his last meal."

Monroe rubbed his face, exhausted, and angry they'd been fooled by Branor and taken so easily by a handful of men. "Damn him, Branor! He must have put something in the water. Anyone who drank it was asleep during the assault. At least they are not dead, thank God. Oh, a goodly portion of the horses were released, too."

"A careful plan." A tinge of admiration colored Nahjar's voice.

"Aye. One we should have expected."

"You are not at fault, Monroe. Neither am I. We thought the threat came in Ireland, as it had in O'Brien's brother. Branor fooled us all well, including his friend." He gesture to Connal, then wrapped the wound. "We could not know the threat was in this household."

" 'Tis damn good he's dead," Monroe snapped, then sighed and said softly, "I will go find Mistress Murphy. She must be beside herself with worry."

"Tell her to prepare food stores for a trip."

"What?"

"We will leave. When he wakes. He will not be contained."

Monroe nodded, crushing back his own worry for Sinead. Married or nay, she was his charge to guard.

"Go, brother," Nahjar said softly and tipped his head toward the man. "And learn who that black-haired bastard was."

"Oh, I know," a voice said from the doorway.

They looked and found Peg, her pretty face creased with worry and showing the signs of a good cry. " 'Twas the sheriff."

Monroe frowned. "The sheriff of what? Who would give that arrogant pisspot such a position of power?"

"Prince John. That man, he's got the prince's confidence, and he's helpin' him rally the barons and paying them for their oath to John."

" 'Tis the only way they will gain a path to that weasel." Monroe's anger grew.

Nahjar stood, stroking the wicked blade sheathed in the wide waistband. "So where do we find this sheriff, little one?"

"In the west, Derbyshire, m'lord. The shire of Nottingham."

"Good God, how did you get like that?" the sheriff, Eustance, demanded.

Guy nudged the air with his chin.

The lady stood by the bed, her hands free of the shackles, and if he had to guess, her temper high.

"My, you are lovely," he said, walking closer, his gaze moving over the gown he'd provided for her. "That color suits you."

Sinead put up her hands and the sheriff went flying backwards, smacking against the wall. "Do not make me angry, Sheriff."

Eustance shook his head and climbed to his feet.

"I would not do that again if I were you, and release him. That looks ridiculous."

Sinead folded her arms and refused. Sir Guy had already tried to climb beneath her skirts, thinking she was still drugged and helpless. He deserved worse and her look said as much. She turned her gaze on the sheriff, a slender man with midnight black hair and a tiny scrap of a beard dappling below his lip and chin. It made his face look pointy.

"You are being uncooperative, I see," Eustance said,

sighing dramatically, then striding to the door. He called for a guard.

Sinead kept her gaze on him as he whispered to the guard, and then the ugly little man with the pockmarked face left.

The sheriff looked at her, folding his arms and leaning back against the wall. "I will ask politely, free him."

Sinead glared. "Where is my husband? What have you done?"

"Your husband is dead."

Sinead did not pale, did not wince. "Do not think to tell me what I know to be a lie. He lives and you, sir, will pay for this crime."

"Will I? I think I hold all the pieces, my lady." He strolled closer. With the flick of her hand, Sinead sent him stumbling back.

"Keep your distance sir, or you will end up like him."

Eustance glanced at Guy, noticing the redness of his face, yet naught shackled him to the wall. "Fight it!" the sheriff demanded.

"I am!"

"Be stronger. She cannot fight free will."

Sinead's features stretch taut. O'Brien must have told him that. "Bring O'Brien to me."

"Demanding little witch, aren't you? Nay, I think not. But you will obey me and behave or I shall drug you again."

The guard returned, pulling someone along, and Sinead's eyes widened when she saw Murphy. "Oh, Goddess bless," she said. "I though they'd killed you."

Murphy yanked her hand from the guard's and sniffed, righting her clothing. "The creatures tossed me over a horse and took me out of the castle afore the fightin' started. I saw it from the hill."

Sinead swung on the sheriff. "What point was taking her?" Then she knew.

"Ah, good. You do see my purpose." His smile was thin and oily. "You behave and she lives. Now release him."

She looked at Guy, who managed to get one hand free. She waved and he fell to the floor. Sinead went to Murphy, wrapping her arm around her. "She stays with me."

"Oh, nay, nay, and have you put a spell on her or something? Nay." He called for the guard. And they took Murphy away. Sinead's heart broke at the fear she tried to hide.

"I will behave as well as I can."

Eustance eyed her, then nodded. "Someone will be up to feed you."

"You drug me and expect me to eat your food? Nay, I want naught more of yours."

"Then fine, you won't get any. Atall." The sheriff left, closing the thick door.

Sinead let out a breath and said to the darkness, "And I find, dear sheriff, that I cannot behave atall." With a quick spin, she vanished.

Murphy lurched back when Sinead appeared. "Land—!" Sinead covered her mouth, looking to the door. Murphy's chamber had a small window in it and she hustled the woman over into a corner and hoped they could not be seen.

"Connal—did you see him?"

Murphy's expression turned grave. "He was fighting the sheriff, and Branor stabbed him."

Sinead inhaled. The dream. Oh, Goddess nay, the dream. Branor was what she could not see. "Why?" she whispered, her hands trembling.

Murphy shrugged. "Connal was not expecting it, that I can tell you. Land, when I think on the times I fed that man, washed his clothes . . . welcomed him like a brother."

Sinead thought back, at Branor's disapproval of her, and even after all this time he was one man she'd not won over. He'd known their plans and was likely relaying news to Prince John's conspirators through their entire trip. He was the one off to "find" the attackers and came back with no one. He was the one left guarding the archer in the cell at Rory's castle. Had he been working his own plan or someone else's?

"I saw Nahjar kill him," Murphy was saying and was about to say more when a thin voice called to them. Sinead frowned and moved to the door, peering out. There were no guards, and she realized that the sheriff did not consider the woman a threat.

"Who is there?"

A female, Sinead decided. "I am Sinead, wife to Pen-Dragon."

The woman gasped, the sound like wind through the trees. "PenDragon! Then Richard comes home?"

"My husband precedes him. Who are you?"

"I am Marian, the king's cousin."

Sinead glanced back at Murphy.

Murphy shrugged. "I don't know the royals, lass."

"Why are you here?" Sinead asked in barely a whisper.

"The sheriff uses me as bait. Can you release me?" Marian called. "Please I must get out, now." She rattled the door, and Sinead glimpsed a face pressed to the small cut in the wood.

"Shhh. Will you believe me if I say you are safer there?"

"Nay, I will not!"

"I did not think so," Sinead said on a sigh. "I cannot release you. I am trapped as well."

'Twas not a lie, for she was. If she left, not only would Nottingham take it out on Murphy, she would not be able to know what these men were about. They posed a great threat to King Richard, and though Sinead had no fondness for either brother, she knew Connal would not follow a bad king so loyally.

Sinead stepped away from the door and looked at Murphy. "They will use you to keep me from leaving here, my friend. I fear they will do you grave harm regardless."

"Can you not—?" Murphy waved her hands wildly. "To protect us?"

Sinead grinned. "You must ask."

"Please, little one. Protect me and go to Connal. Do your best and Goddess be praised."

Sinead stood, her arms raised to the ceiling as she invoked the Goddess and asked her for help. "Lord and Lady, all about, guard her day and night throughout. Guide her through each passing hour and grant Murphy your protective power. From head to toe, from sky to ground, keep her safe and well and sound. Pure of heart and words of old, to those who harm, turn back threefold. So I say, so mote it be!"

Murphy smiled, her body warm, her skin pricking as a sheet of pale lavender mist hovered above, then fell, draping her in cool peace.

Sinead lowered her hand, hugging the woman, whispering, "I must return to my cell afore he notices," then turned and vanished.

"Hello," the woman called out .

Murphy walked to the door, peering out. "Hush.

You'll be bringing the guards and trouble, lass. King's kin or nay, I'll tell you to shut yer yap.''

"I beg your pardon."

"Lady Sinead will help us. Trust in that."

There was a sound of frustration from the other cell, and Murphy smiled. "Takes a bit of getting used to, I know."

Her smile fell as she thought of Connal, and she prayed he survived Branor's wound and found his bride—and gave that skinny English sheriff his due.

Connal was dressed when Monroe entered the chamber, and he did not cease stuffing his packs.

"Aw, my lord, give it a day, I beg you."

Only Connal's gaze shifted. "Would you?"

"Nay, but your injury . . ."

" 'Tis not so bad; sore, aye, but I will live." If only to kill Nottingham.

"Then eat first."

Connal agreed, taking bread and meat, folding it over and chomping into it afore he left the chamber. He called to Nahjar and Sir Kerry.

"Sajin, we ride?"

"Aye, and think on a plan as we do, my friend, for if she is drugged and shackled, she is helpless."

"When have you ever known Sinead to be helpless, my lord?"

Connal met his gaze, a smile tugging at his mouth. "Aye."

"Pity the sheriff and Prince John," Monroe said, "but not her."

Connal only nodded, yet the memory of her dying,

of her spirit slipping from him, reminded him that enchanted though she was, she was still a fragile human.

They covered the distance into Derbyshire, then to Nottingham in less than a day. The sound of the army, the hooves, came like thunder, drawing folk from their homes and into the roads. Connal recognized the conditions much like those in Ireland, the people hungry and beggarly.

Some threw stones and sticks as they passed, and a friar warned them to avoid the forest. Connal did not; 'twas the quickest path to the castle, and on the edge of the woods he found a lock of Sinead's hair clinging to a bush, torn free in the ride. He stuffed it inside his surcoat and rode into the mist-filled woods.

Nahjar glanced about, scowling at the trees. "The forest has eyes, Sajin."

"And feet and hands and weapons." Connal looked to the treetops, reining back. "Show yourselves," he said, "or we shoot."

Behind him, his archers readied bows and shafts.

"And if we shoot first?" A man dropped from the trees directly in front of him.

Connal's gaze swiped over the man, noticing his mismatch of clothes and the multitude of weapons he wore. "Then we have a war that is unnecessary. I've no quarrel with you."

"And who would your fight be with, sir?"

Connal frowned, and though he did not sense a threat, something nagged at his memory. " 'Tis my business."

The sword whispered out of its sheath and pointed at the chest of Connal's mount. Still, he did not draw his own sword. "I'd be very upset if you killed my horse."

"I'd hate to do that, since he was ever faithful to you that day in Syria."

Connal blinked and leaned forward, trying to see the man's features in the dappled light. "Locksley?"

The man grinned. "Welcome to Sherwood, Pen-Dragon."

Connal smiled. "Sweet mother, I thought you dead!"

"The same of you, too."

Locksley sheathed his sword and whistled. Nearly fifty men emerged from behind trees or dropped from branches. Connal ordered his men to shoulder arms and slid from the saddle. He winced, grabbing his side, and was thankful that Branor's aim was off and the blade too narrow to do much damage. But God above, it hurt like hell. He looked at Locksley, then pushed away from his mount. The two men stared for a bit, then shook hands, the greeting ending in a back-slapping hug.

"Why on earth are you here?"

Sir Robert gestured to the land. " 'Tis my home and these are my friends," he said, enjoying PenDragon's surprise. "Come, we can share what little we have and I'll tell you a story."

An hour later Connal sat near a fire, Locksley at his side. "My sympathy for your family, Robert. And that the sheriff has made you an outlaw."

Robert leaned back against a rock, idly tossing pebbles into the blaze. Around them children played, women worked, and men prepared for attack. "I learned in the Holy Lands that none could know what the next day brings. And war must have a greater purpose than one man's belief in religion."

Connal glanced at Robert, understanding the man's feeling more than he let on. Though they followed

Richard, neither could forgive him for ordering thousands of Muslims executed.

"So, who is this lady of yours?"

"Marian. I've known her since I was a boy. She always hated me." Robert smirked to himself. "But not now."

Connal snickered a laugh. "I understand that. I have known my wife since she was four. She declared her heart to me, and I broke it several times. 'Tis been a long road to regain what I thought I did not need." Or could not have.

Robert grinned. "Your men speak highly of her, Irishman."

Pride swelled in Connal. "One cannot help but adore her."

"Then how do we get them back?"

"I'd hoped you had a plan to get inside the castle."

"I've not enough men to lay siege, and that could bring harm to both women."

"Three women; they have my steward, too." At least he hoped so, for there was no sign of Murphy anywhere, and during the battle only Peg had said she'd seen a single rider on the hillside

"You do not fear for her safety? For I know the sheriff would not hesitate to abuse Marian if he thought it would make me fight him."

Silent and still, Connal concentrated, his brows working for a moment. Then a grin stretched his features. "Nay, she is well enough."

Robert scowled at him. "How the bloody hell do you know that?"

"I can feel her heart beat."

" 'Tis twisted, that," Robert said.

Connal could not reveal his gift, not now, nor that his wife was a powerful witch. These people did not need to be more frightened than they were already. "Not if you loved her like I do."

Robert looked at him oddly. "Good God, you've gone all softhearted mush, PenDragon." He shook his head sadly. "I never thought to see it."

Connal smiled, his heart relieved that he knew Sinead was alive, yet he could not ease the worry plaguing him. Not till he held her again. He prayed she held her tongue and did not antagonize the sheriff. She was only a woman, he thought, and she bled like any other.

On the shores of Dover, a weathered ship scraped against the sand, and men hopped into the water to pull the small craft farther onto shore. A single figure stood at the bow, his gaze moving over the landscape for a moment before he stepped onto the land.

A cheer rose, and he smiled, then looked up toward the cliffs. A narrow road cut the side of the earth, and riders traveled single file. Well-ordered power, he thought, as they rode down toward the water. King Richard smiled, noticing PenDragon's banner a few yards behind his own. Success, he thought.

Prince John waited impatiently for the witch to appear. Through the door, he amended with a smirk. He'd arrived only an hour earlier, under disguise of course, since he could trust so few right now. He'd already taken the oaths of a dozen barons, and the tithe paid would ensure him a healthy start as king. He glanced around the room, at the Irishman who'd betrayed his people, and wondered what the man would say when he told him the witch would not die, not yet. Not till he was finished with her.

He'd so hoped the man had died some time ago.

The stir of voices and footsteps drew his attention to the entrance, and he waited, his heart pounding a little faster. She stopped on the threshold, her gaze going directly to him.

It hit him like a punch, those pale blue eyes, that rich red hair. He was transfixed. Clad in a fine blue gown richly appointed with silver, she did not cover her hair like Englishwomen. And he was glad of it, for the wild curls spilled riotously over her shoulders to her knees, and in the mass he saw little flecks of silver in the braids peppering the curls.

"You have summoned, so I am here, Prince," she said, and her Irish lilt clipped the words.

"A pleasure to meet you, Lady PenDragon."

"I cannot offer the same," she said, taking purposeful steps toward him.

Sinead enjoyed that he retreated a step. She should not have, for fear was not what she wanted people to have near her, but now 'twas an advantage. And with Murphy in the tower with Lady Marian, she had too few.

She looked him over. He was not overly tall and yet undoubtedly handsome. Boyishly so, she thought, mentally comparing him to her husband. *Oh, Prince John, you haven't true power,* she thought, and the image of the two men facing each other made her smile.

John, thinking she was pleased, smiled back. " 'Twas rather convenient of you to come to England."

"I came for my husband, and for King Richard."

John's features tightened at that. "Richard wallows in a prison."

"One you arranged, I am certain."

"Did your husband tell you that, afore he died?"

She simply arched a tapered brow, refusing to feed their hope that Connal was dead. He was not, Sinead knew without a doubt, and had faith that he would find her and put this bug of a man in his place.

"So, m'lady, prove to me that you are a witch."

Sinead swung her gaze to Angus O'Brien. He stood at the far end of a table, a pearled goblet in his hand, dressed finer than when she'd seen him last. He took a step back, his gaze cracking between her and the prince.

"As much as I would like that, your highness," she said with a glance over O'Brien, "I shall not perform like a trained animal."

"You cannot do aught with magic," the prince scoffed, folding his arms over his chest, his stance speaking of challenge.

"I can do most everything." Sinead's smile was thin. "But I will not need to." She took a step closer, her gaze intense and clear. "Prepare, John Lackland," she said softly. "Ireland has a new champion and your ruin is about to come."

Chapter Twenty-one

Prince John sneered. "I do not think so, my lady."
He looked at the sheriff. "Tell her."

"Aye, I saw him die."

"You saw him fall."

"How can you be so certain that he lives?" the prince
asked, picking up a goblet.

"I simply am." Sinead's smile was brittle as she waved
a hand through the air.

The Prince sipped, then spat the wine on the floor.
He examined the goblet. " 'Tis sour."

The sheriff inclined his head to the woman.

Sinead moved away, her gaze lingering on O'Brien.
He took a step back and muttered, "Harm none."

"Do not think to tell me the rules, O'Brien." She
focused her attention on the prince's back. The man
turned sharply, looking her up and down.

John returned the stare. "I'll have you show me what I have bought."

"Bought?" She laughed, her eyes feline bright. "You cannot rule me, Prince, and dare you toy with magic, 'twill come back to you threefold."

"I bought you, witch. I paid a traitor and here you stand. You haven't proven a thing to me. And for my money, you owe that."

Sinead was furious, and her expression said as much. "Would you like to be afraid then, sire?"

"You do not frighten me."

Sinead snapped her fingers and fire appeared. She looked at the sheriff. "Like this castle, do you, Sheriff?" The man nodded, awed.

John gulped, his gaze riveted to the flames dancing on her palm.

"I'd step back, your highness," O'Brien said from behind, and the prince heeded.

Just as quickly the fire vanished, leaving behind a telling wisp of smoke.

"Continue," Prince John said. "Let us see the trained animal."

Sinead's eyes narrowed, her anger riding up her spine. She took a breath, calming herself, for she knew she could do much damage, and innocents would suffer. Yet not a man in this chamber was innocent. And suddenly she wanted justice. For Galeron, for Dillon and his family, for Ireland. Her temper crested.

She turned sharply, walking away and throwing her hands up. The windows shattered, a great wind stirring the glass. She faced her enemies and lowered her arms, and the room went still.

John stumbled back. "Lock her in chains."

"I've already tried that." The sheriff gawked at the

floor and his expensive glass naught but powder at his feet.

"Then drug her, now!"

"Sire—"

John looked at her, his expression violent. "Drug her, and if she disobeys, use the old woman to keep her in tow."

Sinead took a step closer to the prince. "You wanted proof and now it scares you. Did I not warn you?"

"This power will be mine," he said, with almost giddy finality.

She nodded to O'Brien. "Ask him what happens to those who think they can abuse it. And if you hurt Murphy"—her temper rose, heating the room—"I swear by the Goddess I will break every rule of the craft and bring this castle down upon your ears!"

Men grabbed her arms, flanking her.

Prince John was smug. "So . . . you cannot do a thing now."

"Do not count on that, Prince."

Sinead was tempted to vanish right that moment, but they would only hurt Murphy. And naught could truly stop free will. Not even her.

"Take her away."

Sinead closed her eyes, and the men holding her let go, rubbing their palms. At the prince's scowl, they said, "It burns."

She met Prince John's gaze. "I will go of my own will, sire." Sinead walked past them and out the door.

John brushed fragments of glass from his sleeves and looked at O'Brien. "You said she could walk between worlds."

"She can, and I would bet a bag of gold she's not in the corridor."

"Then how are we to hold this woman?"

"I'll find a way," the sheriff said, marveling at the power he'd just witnessed and, admittedly, afraid of it.

"There must be a way, and if not, we must kill her. For her affection for Richard is clear enough to me." John looked at O'Brien. "How do we kill a witch?"

He shrugged. "She dies like any of us, sire."

"Well, that is not good enough." John approached O'Brien, his expression lethal. "We cannot touch her; she burns us. We anger her, she will destroy the castle and God knows what else. How do I kill her?"

"She survived a poisoned arrow, sire," O'Brien stammered. "I—think . . . mayhap . . ." He let out a breath. "I do not know, sire."

"Then you are of no use to me!"

Prince John pulled the blade from his belt and drove it downward into O'Brien's chest. The man choked, his face full of shock as he crumpled to the floor.

"God, I hate the Irish," John muttered, and strode out of the room, glass crunching beneath his boots.

The instant the guard turned the lock on her door, Sinead whispered into mist, appearing in a cell down the corridor. She cleared her throat, and the woman standing at the window turned sharply.

"Who are you? How did you get in here?" Her gaze shot to the door, then back to the woman.

"That matters not, but—"

"It matters a great deal. If you can get in, then we can get out." Marian rushed to the door, giving it a shake.

Sinead sighed. "Lady Marian, I am Sinead."

Marian turned. "PenDragon's wife? How did you get in here?"

"Magic."

Marian scoffed uneasily. "I beg your pardon?"

"Please do not be frightened."

"I am not afraid."

"Good, then we at least have that."

"I do not believe in magic."

Sinead shrugged. " 'Tis your choice, m'lady. But I've come to tell you to be a bit patient. My husband will get us out."

"If you're so magical, then why do you not go to him as you came in here?" Marian glanced at the door, frowning, trying to understand and truly not wanting to admit the woman was a sorceress.

"I can but will not. My friend is kept prisoner, too, and I know the prince or the sheriff will do her harm if I leave." She'd regretted showing her gift and blamed her temper.

Marian sighed and dropped to the thin bed tucked against the wall. " 'Tis why I am here—to keep me from going to Richard and to force Robert to come to me."

"He won't?"

"Not without a plan, and to be honest, I cannot see him getting all the way up here."

"He will not have to."

Marian looked up, frowning.

"When the time is right and Connal is inside, I will free you."

"Do it now."

"Nay. We will never get out with all the guards. There are four on the stairs alone. The sheriff sleeps only one floor below us. They have to come to us, but I can make it a wee bit easier."

"How?" Sinead opened her mouth, but Marian put a hand up. "I know, magic." She looked thoughtful. "Why do you not just knock out the guards, club the sheriff, and get us out?"

Sinead folded her arms and tapped her foot, disappointed. "I cannot, nor will I, do harm to anyone."

"Ah, but you'd let them harm me."

Sinead glanced her over. "You look fit enough, m'lady, and if you wish me to protect that body, then you must ask."

"Ask for a . . . spell cast on me? You must be mad."

Sinead shrugged. "Fine. 'Tis your choice. Now, who is Robert?"

Marian's expression softened and she smiled. "Robert of Locksley, known now as Robin of the Hood."

Marian explained her situation to Sinead, and in the middle of it, they heard voices in the corridor. Sinead rushed to the door, then looked at Marian. "Someone comes." They bring the potion of sleep, she thought.

"What does Prince John want with you?"

"Like most men of power, they want my magic."

" 'Tis ridiculous."

"I would not doubt that the prince thinks I can move armies and create gold from thin air."

Marian swallowed. "Ca—can you?"

Sinead gave her a sour look. "I have the gift of the elements, Lady Marian, 'tis all."

Sinead turned and melted into red mist.

Lady Marian stared at the empty spot, then swiped the air and watched the mist dissipate. "Well now, 'tis a bit more than elements, that!"

* * *

The hint of dusk brushed the day, pushing it into night, creating shadows and secrets to cover the silent attack. Dressed in common rags, Robert's woodsmen and a few of Connal's vassals strolled into Nottingham's bailey, some hawking wares, some begging for alms. The remainder of Connal's vassals—mostly the Irishmen, for their accents would raise suspicions—were in the forest, prepared to attack under Monroe's command.

Following Robert, he and Connal moved to the west wall and the portal there. "Now we wait."

Connal gritted his teeth in frustration. The men inside were to work their way to the door and unlock it, and he hoped they killed the guards silently. For if they could not get inside, they had no hope. And Connal was rapidly losing his, for he could not sense Sinead clearly. She had not come to him in the forest, not once, and his mind was a terrible creature, rearing up to torture him with images of her.

The door rattled, something falling against it. Connal looked at Robert. The man shrugged and tried the lock. It sprang free but would not move.

"Hold yer arse there, Robin," came from the other side, and the door shifted a fraction. Robert peered around it to see John and Will drag the unconscious guard aside.

They stepped through, hunching low and finding a shield behind the cart.

"I heard talk she's in the tower."

"Both of them?" Connal said.

Little John shook his head. "Lady Marian is, but your wife—"

Connal's impatience showed in his face and Will gestured.

"Good God," Robert said, looking skyward.

Connal looked up to the tower, then higher, and his heart sank like a stone. "I will kill him," he vowed, and Robert grabbed his arm, stopping him from rushing forward.

"Do not be rash, old friend."

Connal jerked from his grasp, glaring up at the tower. On the parapet, a plank hung over the bailey, a rope extending off the edge. And dangling from it was a body. He knew without doubt 'twas Sinead. She was powerful, and only frightened men would be forced to do that to another human. She was wrapped for burial, her body tightly shrouded in white cloth, yet Nottingham had made a point of leaving her hair free to stream down her back. The silver charms were unmistakable.

"Oh Sweet Christ," Connal whispered. "How do I get her down from that?"

"We first must get up there, lads," John Little said and pulled the uniform off the unconscious guard and handed it to Will. "Too small for me," he said, then nodded. "This way, and for the love of Christ, Connal, do not talk."

Connal walked behind them, uncertain of the layout, though it had been described to him countless times during the night. He glanced up at the tower, his heart ripping at the horrible sight. *This is why she has not come to me. Sinead,* he called silently, and kept calling in his mind, praying he'd gain something. All he knew was that her heart still beat.

Their backs to the wall, the four moved quietly to the west entrance, around the cook house and buttery. Connal picked up a bucket and strode easily closer, hunching his shoulder and praying none spoke to him. Robert hefted a sack of seed and followed. John and

Will split off and moved to the next entrance into the castle.

Inside, Connal set the bucket aside and was surprised no one in the kitchen made a bit of noise when they entered. Robert pushed off his hood, and the cook smiled, nudging the girl next to her.

The girl gasped. "Robin Hood," she whispered.

"Where is Lady Marian?"

"The tower, I think."

Robert strode closer, pressing a handful of coins into the girl's hand, then kissing her forehead. Connal eyed them both with an arched brow, and the wench all but swooned as he moved past.

"A sideline, Robert? Charming the lasses," Connal whispered.

"Outlaws are a thrill," he said, then wiggled his brows. "I gave them money we stole from the barons. 'Twas their tithe to John."

Connal smirked, shaking his head. Robert hushed him, and they flattened against the wall. A pair of guards strode down the hall, and Robert inclined his head. Connal stepped out with him, and together they each clubbed one in the back of the head, then caught the men. Dragging them into an alcove, they made quick work of their garments.

"This should help," Robert said, pulling on the mail hood.

They hurried down the corridor, their boot heels echoing. "What are the chambers below the tower?" Connal asked.

Robert frowned. "The sheriff's private rooms."

"That is where I must go to reach Sinead."

Robert frowned, then nodded, and the pair headed

forward. They met the first onslaught outside the chapel.

Robert warned them, "Lay down your weapons. My fight is not with you," but the prince's soldiers came. Robert took the first attack, his sword running cleanly into the man's gullet as Connal knocked another off his feet, then pushed his sword into his opponent's chest. Two more fell, the metal sabers ringing in the darkened corridor, and bringing more. One looked at Connal striding purposely toward them and half retreated, calling to arms. But Connal kept coming, slaying the first man brave enough to remain, the serrated edge of his Celtic sword ripping fabric and flesh.

"Connal," Robert shouted from farther down the hall, and gestured to the staircase. "There are two stairwells; both lead to the chambers above, then the tower."

Connal hesitated, not wanting to leave his friend alone.

"Go. Marian is this way." Robert swung at a soldier, and when the strike sent him to the right, Robert slammed his head into the stone. He was tired of killing, he thought, stepping over the groaning man and mounting the stairs.

At the noise, the sheriff ran from his rooms and down the corridor. The way was clear, with not a guard in sight. He took the landing and several steps down to the next level, only to find himself face to face with Robert of Locksley.

Robert smiled. "You are under siege."

"Impossible!"

"Not really. You did not count on PenDragon throwing in with me."

PenDragon, he thought, withdrawing his sword. "I

should have known that Irish whelp would survive. I should have killed the man myself."

"Where is she?" Robert demanded, his sword at the sheriff's chest. Nottingham batted it away with his own and the battle began.

"She's dead."

"You lie!" Robert swiped at him, the blade cutting his chest.

The sheriff winced and grabbed the spot. "Have I lied about your father? Your holdings that are forfeit to me?" He said the last word with glee, and Robert felt blinding rage engulf him. She could not be dead. Connal swore Sinead would protect her.

Then Marian screamed his name and Robert looked to the staircase, then to the sheriff. Hope flooded him and he smiled, slashing at Nottingham, forcing him back up the staircase. The clash of swords rang loud in the corridor, an echo of death.

"I will see you die this night."

"Oh, really?" Nottingham said, grabbing Robert's tunic and shoving him down the case.

He hit the wall hard, yet when Marian called his name he rushed the sheriff, driving his sword into his chest.

The sheriff stared at him, shocked, and Robert turned, trading places on the staircase, then pushing him back. He held on to his sword, and as Nottingham fell back, it came free. Robert did not waste time watching him fall. As he overtook the landing, Marian appeared.

"I knew you would come," she said tearily, and they fell into each other's arms.

"Marian, thank God," he groaned, breathing in her scent, reveling in her touch.

"Sinead; is she—?" His look stopped her cold.

"Nay, oh nay," Marian cried. "She fullfilled her promises to release me, yet I haven't seen her."

"There is hope, love. Come, I must signal the others now."

Outside the sheriff's chamber, Connal kicked in the door and rushed to the window, pulling it open. "Sinead."

She didn't respond, her body twirling like a ball on a string. Connal eased onto the ledge, trying to reach for her, but she was too far out. He stepped back in the chamber, tearing the room apart for something he could use to catch her and bring her within his grasp. Beyond the walls, he heard the men attack, and knew Monroe had seen Robert's signal. A flaming arrow over the wall; Marian was safe. The thought brought little relief and Connal's frustration mounted. He would have to try the roof. Leaving the chamber, he raced up the staircase, rushing past Robert and Marian and hitting the parapet door, fracturing it off its hinges. He would pare Prince John down to naught fit for pigs if Sinead died.

He hurried to the ledge, the plank held down with massive stones. The effort to get them up there spoke of their fear of her. He leaned over the edge, his heart seizing. She was trapped in the cloth, the rope netted around her torso, threading up behind her to the plank and running its length along the wood. He looked back at the boulders. Both the plank and the rope were secured beneath the stones.

He was alone and time was wasting. She could be dying wrapped in there, smothering. She could turn to mist, he reasoned, but drugged, and without control of her mind, she was helpless. Connal knew no other way than to lift her from the plank. The rope would cut if it scraped along the plank over long, and though she was light in his arms, against the jagged lumber, it would be a saw against a blade.

"Sinead," he called down.

She did not respond, her body twirling. He called again, his voice growing hoarse. Then, cursing, he tested the plank, easing out. In his mind he called to her, shouting his love while his world was focused on one piece of wood, one rope. He swallowed, inching his way to the end, thinking he'd have to pull her up slowly to be certain the rope did not wear.

Connal, he heard in the recess of his mind.

He stilled. "Ah, sweet God, Sinead. I'm here."

Nay, stay back.

"You will fall!" he shouted, and laying flat on the plank, he started pulling on the rope. His muscles strained as he yanked, his wound at his side opening. She swung like a pendulum and he cursed the prince. They never meant her to live through this.

Almost there.

Trust in me, my love.

I do! But you need your hands for your strongest power.

Trust in my magic. Connal, whispered through his mind, *I love you. You are my soul.*

His eyes burned. "I love you," Connal whispered, and prayed 'twas not the last time he spoke the words.

The plank snapped under his weight, fracturing in half and jerking the rope. It slipped through his finger and severed. And as Connal grabbed the rope leading from the stones, the force swung him back against the wall. He smashed hard, watching in horror as Sinead plummeted toward the ground.

"Nay!" he screamed, the sound tortured, savage.

Seconds before she hit, the burial sack fluttered in the air, spinning, light and empty. He blinked, swiping at tears as a dove rose from the folds, climbing toward the sky as the fabric settled softly on the ground. Connal dangled, tipping his head to the sun as the bird climbed.

He looked at the ground again, at the soldiers fighting, at the few standing still to look at the empty sack. Hand over hand, he climbed the rope, and found Robert pulling the end. Connal flung his leg over the edge and fell to the floor, choking on his heart, and then looking up.

"Sweet God, Connal, I'm so sorry."

"Where is the bird?"

Lady Marian frowned.

"Where is it?"

Marian pointed behind the boulder, and Connal shouted for them to stay back as he moved around it. He cried openly, sinking to his knees before the pure white dove. "Sinead?"

The air shimmered around the dove, silver white and blinding. At once the creature's feathers lengthened, blending to slender limbs as the beak receded to form nose and lips, the blue eyes rounding, and the feathered plumes twisting into long red curls. Connal gasped for breath as she tipped her face up.

And smiled.

He gathered her into his arms, clutching her tightly, sighing her name. "Oh God, oh God, Sinead."

She kissed his throat, his chin, then assaulted his mouth, her body bare and lush and warm in his arms. On their knees atop the castle, Sinead sobbed against his mouth, plowing her fingers through his hair.

"I cannot believe you are alive; when you fell I thought—God above."

"I know, I know," she soothed.

"I thought you needed your hands for your strongest magic."

"Apparently, not always," she said between kisses. "Not always."

"Thank God." Later, Sinead thought, as he kissed her again. Later she would tell him of being drugged and powerless, and how the silence of the trappings had freed her mind and revived her control. Aye, she thought, later.

Someone cleared her throat.

Connal dragged his mouth from hers and twisted. Lady Marian held out her cloak and Connal nodded, taking it and wrapping her.

" 'Tis over," Robert said. "And I do believe Richard has arrived."

Sinead stood and rushed to the edge to see, and Connal yanked her back, eyeing her a warning. He looked down, the battle below subdued as King Richard rode into the bailey.

"Now John is in for it."

"Prince John is gone," Sinead said.

"Really?" Robert said.

"Aye. He said if Richard could control me, he could have me."

Connal choked on a laugh.

"Somehow Lady Sinead, I do not think even Connal can do that." Robert looked at Marian. "Come let us greet your cousin."

As Robert led her below, Lady Marian kept glancing back at the pair, still stunned by what she'd witnessed, and touched by the love shining like a sunbeam around the Irish couple. And she decided that, for now, she believed in magic. Very much.

Sinead looked up at her husband and smiled, and Connal threw his head back and laughed to the sky, picking her up, then burying his face in the curve of her throat. He chanted his love for her, how she made him whole and strong and he never wanted to be parted from her. Aye, 'twas a life of surprise when Sinead had rein of her world. He set her on her feet, kissing her, then pressing his forehead to hers.

"I love you, Connal."

He grinned, touching her hair, her face. "Richard will be pleased to meet you."

"Well, then," Sinead said, "I suggest you hotfoot it belowstairs."

Connal's brows furrowed.

"My only gown is on the ground, Connal, unless of course you'd like your king to meet me like this." She opened the cloak, showing him her naked beauty, and Connal grabbed her up, laughing as he pulled her hard against him.

He looked down at her, his expression fierce as he pushed his fingers in her hair, and growled, "I love you, woman, *I love you,*" giving a little shake for emphasis.

She touched his hand. "Ah, Connal, 'tis my strength in that, the center of my soul is you. I love you."

He kissed her, and kissed her, as if trying to bring her into himself, for he'd been warned this day not to waste a moment of life.

"Well, that's a fine thing," Murphy said from somewhere behind, and the pair turned. She held a fresh gown, garnered God knew where. "The king arrives and our lady is bare as a bride. Shame on you, my lord." Murphy tisked, butting between them, and both noticed the tears in her eyes. She helped Sinead into the gown and Connal folded his arms, watching her fuss, his gaze never leaving his wife's. "I tell you, I'm a wee bit tired of England."

"Then we go home," Connal said, and Murphy sobbed as she laced Sinead in.

"Good; then you'll both be givin' me babies to care for soon, aye."

Sinead arched a brow, silent and grinning.

He held out his hand and Sinead came to him, slipping into his arms and tipping her face back. "Aye, let us go home and do that."

Connal kissed his wife, ignoring Murphy's clucking. The shout of Nahjar's accented voice came up from the stairwell. And the bellow of the king.

Naught mattered but the woman in his arms, the happiness spilling in the heated kiss.

The air spun wildly, pushing at their hair, their clothes, and bringing the wet mist of their homeland. Below on the ground, blazes set in anger rose high and straight, startling people and sending tendrils of flame and smoke to tease the heavens. Flowering vines burst from barren stone, rivering across the parapet to climb and envelop them in fragrant flowers, sealing them together.

The moon, new in the sky, shone down on them, silver soft and liquid with rapture.

Sinead and Connal sighed together, the power of their love lighting the stars in the sky.

Earth, wind, fire, and water spoke for them, showing the world what they knew. And against her mouth, Connal smiled.

A life born in betrayal, a heart wounded in bitterness, now healed, not for the power of magic but the love of a hot-tempered woman willing to share her tender soul with him. And he knew, in the center of his world, lay the spirit, the first element, cast centuries afore, a destiny now fulfilled.

Epilogue

Croi an Banrion Castle, Ireland

Connal watched the chaos of people celebrating the return of the Laird of the O'Malleys. Dillon was in the center of it, his expression filled with happiness as he danced with his sister, Moira. And Connal did not know what pleased him more, his holdings returned or that devilish grin of Moira's that was attracting every man in the hall.

"You are looking rather pleased with yourself."

"I had little to do with it, love. 'Twas you who convinced Richard that Ireland would prosper if he left more of it in the hands of those who'd worked the land and ruled for centuries."

"He's not such a bad sort."

His lips twitched. She had fascinated King Richard and yet she was only mildly impressed, insisting that her husband held more power in a single look. 'Twas just as well, for he wanted to be the only man with power over Sinead. "I'm glad you think so."

"You wish to be with him?"

Connal laughed to himself as he looked down at her. "Nay, my love, I do not." His gaze skipped over her with heat and love.

Sinead felt her insides pull tight. "You've a while afore you can truly do aught with that sort of look, PenDragon."

His gaze lowered to her round belly; then his hand swept over it, feeling their child push at him. "She stirs."

"You're certain 'tis a girl, then."

"Aye." He smiled widely. "With red hair and green eyes."

Sinead felt a sharp punch to her middle and folded, reaching for him. He helped her to a chair, waving away Murphy, who was never more than a few feet from her. Nahjar, she noticed, paled a bit.

"There is something I must tell you, love. And I do not know why I have not."

Connal knelt and frowned. "What? Are you ill? 'Tis your time?"

"Aye, 'tis my time." He started to panic. "Nay, wait; she will for a while."

"Ah, so you are certain, too, 'tis a girl."

"Well," Sinead hedged, " 'tis the girl herself that I must tell you about."

Connal touched the side of her face, worry written in every line.

"Speak of it, love; we have no secrets."

"Well, 'tis not a secret but—"

"Sinead," he warned.

"If this child be a girl, Connal, she will be like me."

He grinned. "Aye, I knew that."

"Nay, she will be more powerful than I am."

His eyes flew wide and the color drained from his face. "What!"

She winced. "And every girl child born of this child will grow stronger."

"Oh, God." Connal sank to the floor at her feet. She stroked his hair and he lifted his gaze to her. "Only the girls?"

She shrugged. "I'm not sure. My uncle Quinn is rather talented."

"Sinead!"

"Aye, more than the males," she blurted.

"We are in for it now."

"Nay. Listen. Do you remember when we loved?"

His smile was warm and seductive. And Sinead loved him more for the memory playing in his eyes. "Of course."

"Had I not loved you, I would have died, and so the line would have been broken, the line of women. Should a witch of the druid blood marry for aught but love, so will the line break."

"And then what?"

"And then 'twill take centuries to rebuild the power."

The thought made Connal sad.

"But 'tis nay our worry, love, not now."

Sinead winced, the pain throbbing through her abdomen. "You must be with me when she comes."

Now he paled.

"You must be the first to hold her, Connal. To give your blessing and love. My mother did not have Doyle's love, or Cathal's blessing, and her life was ruined for years." Sinead gripped his hand and whispered, "And we best be doing it now."

* * *

Several hours later, at the stroke of midnight, Connal
saw his child born. He hurt for Sinead, for the pain he
knew she was suffering, but witnessing the miracle left
him naught short of breathless. Murphy handed him the
squalling baby wrapped in a simple cloth, and Connal
listened to his daughter take her first breath, test her
voice. And 'twas loud.

Her face scrunched up and turned red.

"She's got your temper," he said, looking at Sinead,
tears in his eyes. Her hair was damp and twisted atop
her head. Murphy busied herself with cleaning her up,
yet Connal came to her, sitting beside her and kissing
her gently. Sinead touched the child.

"She hasn't a name yet."

" 'Twill come to you," she said.

"Me?"

"Aye."

"Nay, you name her."

Sinead sighed and closed her eyes, refusing to give
on this. Connal shook his head, knowing when to give up
the fight, and rose. He walked to the window, pushing it
open, the warmth of summer drifting on scented wings
into the chamber. The night sky was alight with faeries
dancing on the gleanns. Fires glowed from below, a
celebration of her birth, he knew. He pointed to the
stars above, whispering to his daughter.

The baby snuggled into his chest, and Connal knew
unconditional love and felt it bloom through him.
"We'll call you Etain," he whispered. "Shining one."
Pleased at his choice, he walked back to Sinead, climbing into the bed and handing her their child. She sighed
against him, whispering his name, her love. Connal

wrapped his arms around his family, thinking that the Crusades and kings were a thousand lifetimes ago. He'd returned home with a fortune in his purse and a desperate need for a piece of Ireland of his own and found more than he'd dreamed. In his arms was the proof, a magical feeling to sing through the centuries and touch their descendants. And they will know, he thought, to cherish it, for its fortune lay not in the power of magic one can see and touch, but in the love that flourishes beyond it when two hearts meet and beat as one.

He looked down at his daughter. And please Goddess, don't let her turn any man into a goat.

Author's Note

Thank you for reading *The Irish Knight,* and I hope you've enjoyed the last of the Irish trilogy. Though the story is wholly a product of my imagination, there is some truth to it. In *The History of Medieval Ireland,* a book I've referenced for the most accurate accountings of Ireland's history for the three stories, claims that Prince John, the "count" of Ireland, appointed his own people of authority, over his father's (Henry) choices. While Ireland suffered, John was, at the time of this tale, in England plotting to de-throne his brother with barons and Nottingham while leaving his brother Richard to rot in Leopold's prison. In March he was put down, by Richard himself, as some history records, but legend speculates it was Robin Hood. Hood, I've learned, could have been a number of different men, the most frequent and common reference was Robert, the earl of Huntington, Lord Locksley.

In the choice of a name for the sheriff of Nottingham, my research brought no concrete name associated with Hood, King Richard, and Sherwood Forest. In taking literary license, I chose Eustance of Lowdham, the thirteenth-century sheriff. Besides, he was an ugly man and deserved an unattractive name.

Erin Gòh Braugh!

BOOK YOUR PLACE ON OUR WEBSITE AND MAKE THE READING CONNECTION!

We've created a customized website just for our very special readers, where you can get the inside scoop on everything that's going on with Zebra, Pinnacle and Kensington books.

When you come online, you'll have the exciting opportunity to:

- View covers of upcoming books
- Read sample chapters
- Learn about our future publishing schedule (listed by publication month *and author*)
- Find out when your favorite authors will be visiting a city near you
- Search for and order backlist books from our online catalog
- Check out author bios and background information
- Send e-mail to your favorite authors
- Meet the Kensington staff online
- Join us in weekly chats with authors, readers and other guests
- Get writing guidelines
- AND MUCH MORE!

**Visit our website at
http://www.kensingtonbooks.com**